VENATORS

MAGIC UNLEASHED

BOOK ONE

THE VENATORS SERIES

VENATORS

MAGIC UNLEASHED

DEVRI WALLS

BROWN BOOKS
PUBLISHING GROUP

This is a work of fiction. Any similarity to real persons, living or
dead, is coincidental and not intended by the author.

Venators: Magic Unleashed

Brown Books Publishing Group
16250 Knoll Trail Drive, Suite 205
Dallas, Texas 75248
www.BrownBooks.com
(972) 381-0009

A New Era in Publishing®

Names: Walls, Devri.
Title: Venators : magic unleashed / Devri Walls.
Description: Dallas, Texas : Brown Books Publishing Group,
    [2018] | Series: The Venators series ; book 1
Identifiers: ISBN 9781612549873
Subjects: LCSH: Supernatural--Fiction. | Good and evil--
    Fiction. | Kidnapping--Fiction. | Imaginary places--Fiction.
    | Transgenic organisms--Fiction. | LCGFT: Fantasy fiction.
Classification: LCC PS3623.A4452 V46 2018 | DDC 813/.6--
    dc23

ISBN 978-1-61254-9-873
LCCN 2017964360

Printed in the United States
10 9 8 7 6 5 4 3 2 1

For more information or to contact the author,
please go to www.DevriWalls.com.

For my love, who has turned his life upside down to support me in mine.

.

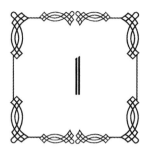

THE OTHER SIDE

Rain dripped from Tate's nose and trickled into his ears. The clouds had threatened this downpour all day but in true form had waited until the temperature plummeted with the setting of the sun.

An unwelcome shiver ran from neck to knee. He scowled and scanned the area. Back and forth, then back again. The branches of heavy pines sloped down like the thick arms of giants dragging against the ground. Even larger, a spattering of mammoth oaks stretched for the sky, dwarfing everything beneath wide umbrellas. And then a break in the forest gave way to a meadow. It spread out in a carpet of green, interspersed by clumps of grass with razor-sharp edges that stood over six feet. They waved back and forth in the wind and seemed to be whispering, but the words were lost in the breeze.

After days of searching for the enemy, he knew how many steps were between each tree and the precise angle of the broken limb on the pine to the east. He knew where the meadow rats burrowed—because he'd almost put a bolt through one that set a patch of dead pine needles wiggling. He knew where a thick pocket of berry bushes had been hiding—they were just empty twigs now; he'd picked the last of the fruit yesterday. The days of extended hypervigilance had taken their toll, chafing his nerves raw and setting them afire.

He was missing something. He knew it. But knowing hadn't done the least bit of good.

It simply wasn't possible that Zio remained unaware of what was about to happen. Arwin had alerted him four days ago to the magical frequency that preceded a portal opening. The vibrations the old wizard had picked up would continue to pulse until the gate actually opened. By now it would've alerted everyone listening . . . and probably those who weren't. He'd been here, in this spot, waiting and watching. Despite his diligence, he hadn't seen a single one of Zio's soldiers. That had ceased to be surprising two days ago. Now, it reeked of suspicion.

Leaning against the trunk of a tree, he pressed his back into the uneven bark and twisted to work out the knots in his muscles. His back began to unwind, but he still needed more relief. He lowered to sitting, grimacing as stiff muscles rippled and stretched.

Better.

But now a branch obscured his view. It twisted in the breeze, dipping beneath water droplets in a joyous dance. He glowered at the leaves, then kicked the branch into the mud, clearing a vantage point.

Something flashed, but then it was gone. Tate peered through the darkness, blinking water from his eyelashes. There it was again! And now gone. He snarled under his breath.

Staring at the same empty space for days must have been driving him mad. The longer he looked, the more the drizzles began to act like strange hallucinations—bending and waving like the start of something magnificent, teasing him with what he desired instead of leaving reality as it was.

The minutes ticked by, turning into hours. A deep heaviness pulled at his eyelids and added weight to his head until it seemed his neck wouldn't be able to hold it. Tate rubbed at bleary eyes.

He couldn't sleep. Not now. The gate could open at any second.

Still, a body was not meant to be awake for so long. His mind fluttered strangely under the exhaustion, peeling open memories he'd rather not relive.

A flash of a sword, the metallic taste of blood, the fear of death permeating every room and every arena like a living, breathing thing. Gladiator. A throat opened, spurting blood, sliced by his sword. And then, mercy—the smile that belonged to his light in the darkness—beautiful hazel eyes looking at him in a way that none ever had before.

He jerked to standing and slammed a fist into the tree. The bark cut his knuckles. The pain served its purpose, offering a passageway back to reality as the rain quickly sluiced away the blood.

That was quite enough memories for the night.

The bad recollections always came sharply, as if he were reliving them, and left a bad taste in the back of his mouth—metallic. The good ones were in the past now and therefore equally painful. It'd been years since he'd seen his wife and son, and thinking of them nearly cleaved his heart in two.

Tate rolled his neck, stretching his sore body. Everything he'd done since leaving was all for them; he had to remember that. There was no place for guilt or grief, two dangerous emotions that only served to cloud the senses. No. Staying alive required a clear head— he couldn't return to his family from the grave.

Offering commentary on his choices, the rain increased to a downpour. The water ran in a stream from the bottom hem of his trench coat down his black pants and seeped into tightly laced boots.

There was a small flash. He wrote it off as another illusion, but it grew brighter, starting as a pinpoint and enlarging to a free-hanging, glowing orb three times as tall and wide as him. It was the largest portal he'd ever seen.

The curse was growing weaker.

He launched forward, but within four steps, Zio's henchmen materialized ahead of him from the center of an oak tree that peeled apart like a beetle splitting its skin. It took only a moment for Tate to realize what he'd missed—the largest oak in the area was really Zio's shifter, sent to hide the goblins. They'd been here from the beginning. One turned as it ran and grinned at him around grotesque tusks.

He swore and raced ahead, leaning into the rain, pumping as hard as he could. His crossbow bounced against his back.

But the goblins held a generous lead. Even running on their short, stubby legs, the greasy beasts made it to the gate before him and leapt through.

Tate dove through the opening, having no idea where the gate would drop him on the other side. But he'd found the Venators once—he could find them again. No matter where he landed.

THE ITCH

Rune stood in the doorway and watched her brother from across the room. He was staring at an advertisement on television. Clenching the arm of the secondhand blue couch with one hand, he crushed the controller with the other. A muscle in his jaw ticked, and his nostrils flared, releasing rapid breaths.

The commercial was for a car dealership that had chosen a werewolf for their mascot, because people would get a *howling* good deal. The wolf-man jumped on the hood of a cherry-red mustang and howled at the moon. The concept was ridiculous, and their costuming even worse. Still, she was drawn to it in a way she couldn't explain . . . in the way Ryker was. Blood pounded in her ears, and her fingers twitched.

Stop it. Now.

Rune tore her eyes from the screen and stared at the matted brown carpet that desperately needed to be vacuumed. Crumbs, dirt, and paper scraps were wrapped in the fingerlike fibers. A tiny flurry of movement caught her attention. It appeared the ants had found the smorgasbord.

College boys and their unsanitary habits. Disgusting.

Her heartbeat gradually returned to normal. Back under control, she cleared her throat. "Hey."

Ryker jerked as if he'd been caught in a crime. Upon seeing his sister he relaxed slightly, fumbling with the remote to shut off the TV. "Stupid commercial," he muttered.

"I know. Who'd pick a werewolf mascot for a car dealership?"

Ryker visibly flinched at the word *werewolf,* and she forced a laugh as if she hadn't noticed.

She pulled a soda out of the small refrigerator near the door, trying not to gag at the unearthly odor that escaped. "You should try cleaning. Maybe you wouldn't lose your appetite when you open the fridge."

"Volunteering?"

"Uh, no." She popped the top and took a swig. "So, where's your roommate?"

"I don't know." He shrugged. "We're going out tonight, though. I'll pick you up around seven."

He didn't ask if she *wanted* to go out. It was just assumed. She clenched the soda can. "Really?"

Ryker glanced over his shoulder. "Too early? I could push it back to eight thirty."

He didn't notice the irritated tone in her voice, but that was normal—boys were so clueless. "No," she said tightly, swallowing her lecture. "Seven's fine." She plopped down on the sofa next to him.

Ryker's eyes, haunted and unseeing, were still glued to the blank TV. She nudged him with an elbow. "Everything all right?"

"Hmm? Oh, yeah. Just tired. I was up late last night studying for my chem test."

"I don't know how you take those classes." She shuddered. Her basic math class had about done her in. She excelled on the field and the court. In school she pulled As, but that was only because of her rigid work ethic—every subject aside from history and English felt like she was forcing her brain to do tasks it wasn't designed for. "How'd you do?"

"Failed it."

She nearly snorted soda out her nose. Coughing, she laughed and wiped her face with the back of her hand. "Mom's going to kill you."

"I know. But all she can do is yell at me over the phone." He grinned and stretched out, draping one arm over the back of the couch. "I don't even have to see the classic 'disappointed in you' face."

"Well, there you go." She lifted her soda in a mock toast. "College is good for something, right?"

He finally seemed to shake the trancelike state he'd been in when she'd arrived, and he turned to look at her. Ryker was built like an ox—broad shoulders, wide chest, heavily wrapped in a thick layer of muscle. That, along with his light-brown hair and hazel eyes, was a combination girls seemed to find irresistible.

It was insanely annoying.

"Are you kidding? College is good for a lot of things! Parties and freedom and—" He winked. "Parties."

There was a gleam in his eye Rune recognized. She moaned. "You're getting drunk tonight, aren't you?"

She hated when Ryker got drunk. He was never happy with a good buzz, always getting completely hammered. That meant too loud, too crass, and too mean. Then he'd pass out and leave her to make sure his sorry ass made it back to the dorm. She'd contemplated leaving him on several occasions. But if her parents ever found out . . . She couldn't bear it. Even from the other end of a phone line.

"Rune, it's Friday. Yeah, I'm getting drunk."

She looked down, fingering the pop tab on her can. "I wish you wouldn't."

He snorted. "I wish *you* would. Come on! We finally have some freedom, and you act like she's still standing over you, approving every move you make."

Rune bit her tongue. She wanted to scream at him: *Every move I make? Every move we make. We're twins—we're supposed to be a team. When Mom lost you to whatever the hell is eating you alive from the inside out, she threw it all on me.*

Every expectation, every hope, had landed on Rune's shoulders. All while her mother expected her to keep her wayward brother out of trouble.

But instead of yelling, Rune bit her tongue like she always did. Because if she were to snap, Ryker would get drunk without her, and how could she keep him from his own stupidity then? She gave a weak smile. "Just . . . don't puke on me this time, OK?"

"I can't make any promises. However, I will point out that if you were drunk, it would be less noticeable if I did."

Rune rolled her eyes. "Ya think?"

There was no response. Ryker had turned to the empty gray screen of the TV. She knew what he saw, because she could see the same thing. The imprint of the "howling good time" running across the screen. Confirmation of her suspicion came as Ryker's hand slowly tightened into a fist.

She reached over and gently touched his leg. "I'm going to go get ready. Pick me up at the library."

He jolted again, cheeks flushing with shame at being caught. "Yeah, um . . . sure."

The computer lab was warmer than the rest of the library by a few degrees. Rows of bright screens poured off heat that the air conditioning system had not been built to handle. Sweat trickled down the back of Rune's neck. She fished an elastic from her pocket and pulled her hair into a ponytail, waiting for the lagging hard drive to pull the file from Dropbox.

The lab was almost empty, as it usually was Friday nights. She glanced up at the clock: 6:45. Only fifteen minutes until the paper was due.

"Cutting it a little close, Jenkins," she muttered.

Clicking on her homework assignment, she attached it to the email. It wasn't her best work. She'd been so distracted lately—worse than normal. But hopefully it would pull a B. Her other grades were high enough to absorb the lower score. The email flew off to her professor. On the way out she walked by a kid with unruly hair and thick glasses, frantically clicking through files while whispering, "No, no, no!"

She offered a look of pity. He was too frenzied to notice.

As she turned the corner out of the lab, a familiar silhouette appeared in her peripheral vision, and her steps slowed.

A tall figure wearing a trench coat sat at a round table, hunched over a wide spread of textbooks. Chin-length black hair fell forward, hiding his features. Although he appeared to be a walking stereo-type, the ones who only play at being outcasts for attention, Rune knew better.

Grey really didn't want to be noticed by anyone.

She didn't understand it, but that was Grey. She didn't under-stand that coat either, but that was also Grey.

They'd been in the same classes since junior high, worked on the occasional project together, and somehow landed at the same college, and in all that time, that trench coat had been a permanent accessory. No matter the weather, no matter the jokes and taunting, that coat did not leave his body.

She smiled, looking at him now, remembering him sitting at a desk with his new coat—the shoulder seams nearly to his elbow, the bottom pooling around his ratty shoes, and the sleeves rolled up so many times it looked like he had a doughnut around each wrist.

Year by year he'd grown into it. The color faded from dark black to almost gray, and the telltale signs of poorly done repairs and fraying threads became evident. But whenever she'd asked about his unnatural attachment to it, Grey would just shrug and duck his head.

Despite his quirks, there was something about him that gave her a certain feeling of affection. She considered swinging over to say hi. It had been a little while since they'd talked . . . and she *still* felt bad about the monstrous prank Ryker had pulled on him—although not as bad as she did about the fact that he'd then uploaded it to the internet—but Grey looked to be knee deep in whatever he was working on.

She glanced again at the clock—her brother was probably wait-ing in the parking lot by now—and turned toward the elevator. On her way out, an advertisement for the university's next production of *Dracula* caught her eye, and she froze.

She'd been able to control herself at Ryker's, but now the pointed canines and red eyes triggered an internal reaction that immediately spiraled out of control. A roar built behind her eardrums, while a painful tightness lodged in her heart, stuttering the beats in an odd syncopation. A snarl tugged at the outer corner of her lip, animalistic in its illogical hatred. She wanted to rip the thing from the wall and tear it into a hundred pieces.

This is crazy, insane. It's just a picture. It's paper! She forced the thoughts that usually stopped the reactions. *Stop it, Rune. Let it go. Look away.*

It wasn't working. The inability to avert her eyes was maddening. Her arms shook, and she wanted to bawl and scream and punch something all at the same time . . . after she destroyed the poster.

Stop it! Stop it. Look at the floor, the ceiling, anything!

It wasn't just Ryker that went into this . . . fury. The severity of the attacks varied, but they happened anytime something supernatural came into view. It was like a pull deep inside that she couldn't understand, let alone articulate. It rose from her gut and trickled out to the tips of her fingers and the soles of her feet. A burning desire to do *something.*

But what that "something" was . . . she had no idea. All she knew was that denying it made her feel like a drug addict who couldn't get a fix.

But there was never a fix—not anymore.

She stared at the red, photoshopped eyes. *Stop it.* The alabaster pallor of his skin. *Stop it.* The canines. She'd like to rip them out. *No!*

It's just a picture, it's not real.

Her nails cut into her palms.

I just need to talk to someone. Maybe if I wait until Ryker is drunk, he won't get so angry when I bring it up. Maybe . . .

Grey! The name burst to the surface. The answer to her problems. Grey was obsessed with the supernatural, and she'd used him before, when things got really bad, when her body craved an outlet. Inexplicably, just talking to him lessened the itch. *Talk to Grey.*

Red eyes.

Blood.

Pointed teeth.

Danger.

Talk to Grey! she shouted at herself.

Rune ripped her attention from the poster and whirled to the side, gasping. This had to stop. But it was only getting worse, and she didn't understand why.

❖◈✷◈❖

Grey breathed in the smell of books, old and new. It smelled like knowledge . . . and security. Books didn't expect you to answer back. And they didn't laugh when your response was socially unacceptable. They were perfect.

He'd finished his schoolwork hours ago and was now working on his own personal research project—one he'd been working on for years. College had opened up shelves upon shelves of books he'd never seen. Information on every topic and era, anything he could possibly wish for, was encased in this four-story box of knowledge.

He flipped a page, coming across a drawing of an ancient medieval torture practice. This particular one involved the insertion of a gruesome device called the pear of agony into the victim's mouth.

What he found interesting about this image was how the victim's face was drawn in a way that was more canine than human. He scribbled a note of the time period, 1125 AD, and a small note with a question mark: *Werewolf?*

He looked up from the book and rubbed his eyes. He'd been reading since his last class got out at two, with the exception of a quick break he'd taken to grab some dinner at the cafeteria. Looking up, he saw Rune standing next to the computer lab entrance. Her shoulders were tense, her hands hanging at her sides in tight fists.

He tried not to stare—it was rude—despite the fact that he found it almost impossible not to. But more worrisome than his lack of manners was Rune's brother, who'd caught him staring on several occasions. Ryker Jenkins was a bully and an absolute ass. Grey couldn't help but take a quick look around to see if he was in the vicinity.

Rune spun hard to the side, as if she were tearing herself away from an invisible assailant. She looked directly at him, her eyes wide and her chest rising and falling like she'd only narrowly escaped disaster.

Rune faced down life with all the reserve of an attacking polar bear. The only times he'd seen fear on her face were times like this—where nothing seemed to have triggered the response. Which left him questioning whether he'd seen anything at all.

As if hearing his thoughts, Rune's breaths slowed, and her shoulders began to relax. She caught his eye, smiled, and waved.

He knew her face so well he could've drawn it from memory. The thing he loved most was that she wasn't one of those girls who looked like she'd stepped off a magazine cover. Rune had an athletic body and natural hair that had been the same chestnut color since elementary school. Her eyes were a deep brown, and a light spray of freckles kissed her nose and cheeks. She tilted her head to the side at his lack of response and waved again.

Grey gingerly lifted his hand off the table to acknowledge the gesture and tried to keep his expression neutral. His stomach rolled in nervous anticipation.

Rune was one of the very few that were genuinely nice to him—always had been, although he couldn't figure out why. She was smart, pretty, athletic, and came from a family that . . . well, produced one asshat of a brother.

She crossed the library. The tenseness of her body language continued to ease with each step. By the time she plopped down across from him, she looked totally relaxed. "Hey, Grey. I'm sorry . . . again. About Ryker."

His ears burned at the reminder.

Sorry was what you said when you bumped into someone or when their goldfish died. In this situation, sorry didn't really cut it. "Did you see it went viral?"

She looked down. "Yeah."

"How many times have *you* watched it?" Bitterness iced his question.

"I haven't, actually." Rune took in a deep breath, then let it all out in a huff. "Didn't want to see it."

That made one person on the campus. He supposed he should be grateful.

College was supposed to have been a fresh start. As far away from his mom and drunken, abusive stepfather as in-state tuition would allow. Away from all the kids who knew him. Away from everything.

Imagine his surprise when a familiar nemesis had walked past his new dorm room carrying boxes.

Ryker had immediately taken up his former roll of informing anyone and everyone of Grey's interest in all things paranormal, strange—in other words, ridiculous. It might have been ignored, but Ryker and a few of his friends had snuck into Grey's room with a video camera. They'd hid in the closet, and Ryker had made a noise Grey had heard only once—how Ryker could possibly have known it or its significance, Grey had no idea. But his blood had run cold, and he'd grabbed his two Japanese sai on instinct, rushing the closet.

Ryker was lucky Grey hadn't stabbed him through the neck.

After the video released, Grey almost wished he had.

He opened his mouth, anxious to move away from his least favorite topic, when two girls emerged from the library stacks to their right. They recognized Grey immediately and broke into giggles.

He pulled his shoulders up, like a turtle with a too-small black shell.

"Shut up!" Rune snapped at the girls, glaring. "Leave him alone."

They rolled their eyes but moved on, heading toward the elevator.

When the doors slid shut, Rune turned back to Grey and offered another smile, this one an apology—eyebrows raised, lips tighter and pulled a little to the left side.

"Thanks," he muttered.

"Don't thank me." She tucked a stray piece of hair behind her ear. "So, what are you working on?"

The change of subject was appreciated.

Torn between hurt, embarrassment that she felt the need to rescue him, and the ever-present lovesick flutter in his stomach, he cleared his throat—worried his voice would betray him with a pubescent squeak. "Just some research for a mythology project. What are you doing here on a Friday night?"

"Turning in some last-minute homework."

She leaned in on one elbow and peeked over the top of his book. "Oh, wow. That looks brutal."

Realizing his notes were in clear view, Grey flipped the book shut and scooted it over to cover the notebook. "I'm sure it was."

"I wish I could major in mythology. That would be *so* cool."

"My major is history, actually." Grey leaned back, evaluating her. "But if you want to major in something different, why don't you?"

She snorted. "Right. When I was a sophomore in high school, my parents sat down with me, a guidance counselor, and a course book to ensure I picked something 'practical and responsible.' If I'd told them I wanted to major in"—she waved her hand over the books he had spread out across the table—"mythology—"

"History."

"Whatever. They would've told me to pay for college myself."

He smiled. "They sat you down as a sophomore?"

"Yep. It was the responsible thing to do." She made air quotes. "My mother believes that perfection is not only achievable but expected."

His smile fled, swallowed by a sorrow that had nestled in his heart for years.

There were advantages to being the invisible kid. Sometimes while not being seen, you *see*. He distinctly remembered sitting beneath the gym bleachers in eighth grade—with the candy wrappers and dust bunnies and other discarded things—not wanting to go home. That night Rune had single-handedly secured a win for the basketball team. On the way to the locker room, just feet from where Grey sat, Rune's mother had grabbed her arm and lectured her about the one free-throw shot she'd missed.

Tears had swum in Rune's eyes as she tore away, and Grey had felt his first round of pity for the girl who appeared to have it all.

"What?" Rune asked.

"I just . . . Who decides what's perfect?"

Rune's eyes widened, blinking furiously. Grey thought she'd say something, but she looked away instead, nervously brushing that same piece of hair behind her ear.

He shifted uncomfortably in his seat, then tried to nudge the conversation back to where it had been before he'd derailed it. "Well, since I'm paying for college myself, looks like I get to pick." He tried to push the long black hair out of his face, but it fell forward again, which was usually where he liked it. But Rune gave him the tiniest desire to not hide from the world . . . or at least not from her.

She leaned back, already having shaken off the emotion she'd let slip. Her brown eyes glittered in the way they always did when she was about to dive into her favorite topic—anything supernatural. "What do you think about zombies?"

Here we go. His favorite topic also made him the most uncomfortable to talk about. People's reactions were very predictable—mock interest followed by genuine mocking. He shrugged. "What do *you* think about zombies?"

"Don't throw this back on me. I'm here to ask the expert."

He grabbed the pen from the table, suddenly very interested in straightening the cap.

"Come on, Grey. Spill it!"

"You . . ." He shrugged. "You know what I think."

"Yeah, yeah—all stories exist for a reason."

"Exactly." The art of deflection was a skill learned of necessity and one he wielded expertly. "You know what my answer is. So the real question is—why are you so interested?"

She laughed, but it sounded stiff and forced. "Funny question coming from you."

"I'm serious, Rune. I can't be good for your reputation. Why do you spend so much time talking to me about this?"

She jerked back. "My *reputation?*" Hurt radiated from her eyes, pouring over him in unspoken accusation. She pushed up to leave.

"No, no. I'm sorry, that's not what I meant."

It was exactly what he'd meant. He just hadn't expected her to react so severely.

"Rune, no. I just—" He tossed the pen back on the table and ran his fingers through his hair, clutching his head in frustration. "I'm sorry."

She hesitated, halfway between standing and sitting.

"Please, don't go. Please. I really am sorry."

Her arms and hands trembled as she dropped back into the chair, which was strange. Rune never looked nervous. He'd seen her play in the state volleyball championship, and the girl had never flinched under pressure.

Although he'd avoided most activities in high school, he'd snuck in to watch her play more than once.

"Hey." He sounded hesitant and unsure. Damn it, why couldn't he just talk as if he deserved to be talking to her? They'd known each other for years! "Are you all right?" She didn't seem to hear him. He wanted to reach out and grab her hand but couldn't make himself. "Rune?"

"All this stuff," she blurted, as if she'd been screwing up courage the whole time. "The paranormal. Fairies, vampires, everything. Why are you so interested in it? I mean . . . Oh, that's not what I meant. What I mean is . . ." Her head dropped forward like a puppet who'd lost its master. "You're going to think I'm crazy."

"Oh, I doubt it."

"When you're doing all your research, how does it make you *feel*?"

The breath burst out of him like a popped balloon. "What?"

She shook her head. "Never mind. I'm sorry I bothered you. It's stupid."

"No. It's fine. I . . . uh . . ." How did it make him *feel*? He'd never really tried to explain his obsession to anyone. In order to maintain a measure of mental sanity, he'd chosen to fully embrace life as a freak amongst his peers.

It had worked out for the best anyway. Friends expected you to tell them your secrets. But his were dark and deep and buried where they belonged—some kept hidden by choice, others out of necessity.

But her question was pointed in a way that made him feel like she'd seen through the walls and the lies and sensed a semblance of truth. This was both horrifying and a tremendous relief. The two opposing emotions ripped in different directions. His chest ached, and he was seized with the insane desire to connect with someone in a way he'd deemed impossible.

"It's like a pull," he began slowly. The words felt like molasses in his mouth. "An obsession I can't turn off. Believe me, I've tried."

She nodded rapidly, like she understood. Excitement lit her face. "What else? What do you *feel*?"

"Rune—"

"Please!" She leaned forward and grasped his hands, squeezing desperately. "*Please*, tell me."

Grey looked at her hands, curving over his own. Her skin was soft, and to his utter surprise he didn't have the urge to flinch away from her touch. He couldn't remember the last time that had happened. The pleasant intimacy birthed hope, and his heart screamed at him, *Just tell her!*

He opened his mouth, ready to share what he'd never told anyone—just a small piece of the secret, of course, to test the waters. He could always stop before irreparable damage was done. He gave a quick glance around, wanting to ensure they were alone.

But they weren't. Coming out of the elevator was his least favorite person.

Grey's mouth went bone dry. He jerked his hands free of Rune's and shoved them under the table. She looked confused and hurt. Her lips parted with what could've been an objection or a plea. But Ryker had located them immediately and made a beeline, placing his hand protectively on his sister's shoulder.

He scowled at the books on the table. "What are you working on today, Grey?" he sneered. "How to kill vampires? Werewolves? How to get a date with Edward Cullen?"

"Knock it off, Ryker," Rune said.

"Lighten up." He looked down at his sister with a grin reserved just for her. "Grey knows I'm just teasing. Don't you?"

"Sure," Grey muttered, shaking his hair forward again.

"Come on, we're late." Ryker grabbed her arm and half pulled Rune out of the chair. "Everyone's waiting for us."

Grey clenched his jaw, grinding his teeth together so hard he heard the enamel scraping. He hated when Ryker acted like he owned her.

Rune jerked her arm free. "I can walk without your help."

"Sorry." He held his hands up. There was that grin again. He playfully jerked his head. "Let's go."

Rune gave a backward glance, mouthing, *I'm sorry*.

Grey's heart sank as he watched them leave, set aflame with thick, burning rage. He hated Ryker with an intensity rivaled only by his hate for his stepfather.

He gathered up the books and put them on the cart to be reshelved. He tipped his head down, letting his hair fall forward, and popped the collar of the trench coat up to his chin, creating a wall of hair and fabric that rendered his face invisible.

Although he'd grown accustomed to the security of invisibility, it wasn't what he wanted. Sometimes, when he lay in bed at night, it felt like he'd taken who he was supposed to be, shoved it into a box, locked the key, and hid it under his long black coat.

Deep within, something whispered that invisible was not what he'd been born to be.

But . . . then again, maybe it was better this way.

"Ryker!" Rune shoved him the moment the elevator doors closed. "Why do you always have to be such a jerk?"

She still wasn't exactly sure what had happened, but the first day Grey showed up in that trench coat, a switch had flipped in Ryker. Her brother had attacked and never backed down.

"I'm not *always* a jerk." He punched the button for the ground floor.

She put her hands on her hips and quirked an eyebrow, daring him to continue on in that line of argument.

He glanced at her, then leaned against the side of the elevator, crossing his arms. "Come on, he's a total freak. We've been through this a thousand times. I don't know why you waste your time talking to him."

"Just because he wears dark clothes and keeps to himself doesn't make him a freak."

"No." He snorted. "The silver powder he carries in his pocket does. And the sai. And the—"

"Just . . . *stop it.*" The elevator dinged, and Rune marched ahead of him.

"What?" he called after her, jogging to keep up. "I swear, Rune, you protect him like he's a pet or something."

"He's not a pet. He's a person!" she snapped, sliding into the passenger seat of the blue Honda their parents had sent them to school in. "It's been almost six years now—maybe you could just lay off. Doesn't the guy deserve a fresh start? You ruined that for him. You and that stupid video. It went viral!"

Ryker got into the driver's seat, grinning.

"It's not funny."

He burst into laughter. "It *is*. You should've seen his face. You would've thought the damn *apocalypse* was going down in his dorm room." He broke into an announcer voice. "Folks, the beginning of the end started tonight in the boys' dormitory—"

Rune slugged him in the arm. "I *did* see his face. Me and half the planet."

"Did you? Last I heard you were refusing to watch it. Finally come down off your moral high horse?"

"Yeah, well, it's hard not to watch when people are playing it on their phones in every class."

"*Every* class? Awesome."

"Why do you have to pick on him? Does it make you feel better about yourself?"

He scoffed. "Yeah, loads better. My precious self-esteem depends on Grey Malteer."

"Well, you sure as hell act like you get something out of making his life miserable."

Ryker turned the key in the ignition, and the radio blared to life. The smile slid from his face. "Maybe you should just stay away from him."

"Why? Because you said so?"

"I've seen the way he looks at you, Ru." He made a disgusted sound in his throat. "Like you're some sort of savior. It's just weird."

"Maybe it's because I'm nice to him."

He rolled his head to look at her, opening his eyes wide and batting his lashes. "Or maybe it's because he thinks you're the most *bootiful* girl he's ever seen," he finished in a singsong cartoon voice.

Rune rolled her eyes. "Shut up."

He laughed again and threw the car into drive. "Come on, I'm just looking out for my baby sister."

"Ten minutes does not make me your baby sister."

Reaching over, he ruffled her hair before pulling out onto the street. "Yes, it does."

CONTROLLED

The night went as expected, with Ryker so drunk he could barely walk. Rune struggled to get him into the car and back to the dorm. Halfway up the stairs, she stopped, leaning against the wall to catch her breath. She was so sick of this cycle, so *sick* of standing between Ryker and his own stupidity. She jerked his arm around her shoulder and tried to muscle him up the last few steps.

"Come on, Ryker," she grunted. "I can't carry you."

Her brother wasn't exceptionally tall, but he was thick. He liked the gym, and he loved football. They both had naturally athletic frames, thank heavens, or he would've already crushed her. The yin-and-yang necklace he always wore had come out from beneath his shirt and was digging into her arm.

Instead of offering any assistance, like using his own two feet, he rolled his head onto her shoulder and stared. "I love you, Rune," he slurred.

Damn it. "Yeah," she sighed. "I love you too. I'll love you more when you're in the bed."

"You really should try this." He stumbled forward. "It's so great." He exhaled heavily, bathing her in the stench of alcohol fumes.

"Yep." She kicked the stairwell door open. "Looks like a blast."

"Mom would be so . . . pissed." He giggled.

Rune rolled her eyes. He was giggling. Great. There were only a few steps between that and vomit on her new shoes. "You know, you don't have to do things just to piss Mom off."

His face twisted into some drunken contortion of thought. "Yes, I do."

Mom was controlling. Rune had rolled with it. Ryker had kicked back—and paid for it. She leaned against his dorm door and fumbled with one hand for the knob. The latch gave way, and she stumbled backward, Ryker's weight almost pushing her to the floor.

"Ryker!"

He just hung there, laughing.

She got one foot steady and then the other, readjusting her grip. Her muscles strained as she struggled to pull him across the room to the bed and get him turned around. With his calves pressed against the edge, she dropped him unceremoniously onto the mattress. He exerted the tiniest bit of effort to get situated, but one leg hung off the side at an angle that would hurt in the morning. She decided she didn't care. Consequences suck.

Her back ached, and her shoulder was throbbing. She hobbled over to the desk like a wounded duck, trying to stretch out the knots on the way. She hadn't even managed to get her butt in the chair before Ryker started to snore.

Rune dropped into the seat and leaned her elbows against the desk, chin in hand.

How had they gotten here? One day, life was good, and she'd had a best friend who told her everything. Then, overnight, Ryker had just . . . changed. She'd asked and pushed but had accomplished nothing besides damaging their relationship. Finally, she had learned to keep her mouth shut, just like she did with Mom.

But it hurt more with Ryker.

⊰⊱⊰⊱

Grey got behind the wheel of his Jeep Cherokee and headed up to the foothills that surrounded campus. The floorboards of the car were nearly rusted through, and the fabric had been torn from the ceiling, leaving nothing to camouflage the fact that he was driving a metal can. It didn't matter. He loved this Jeep and the freedom it afforded. It had taken three years of cleaning the karate studio he studied at to save enough money.

The road started to slope upward. The headlights illuminated the end of the asphalt and the beginning of the dirt road that would wind all the way to the top.

He spent a lot of time in these foothills, running, which always lessened the strange internal itch. But it was also his preferred escape when he was really upset about anything . . . like what had just happened with Rune.

What was all that about, anyway? Her insistence on knowing what he felt, almost begging, only to act like nothing had happened as soon as Ryker showed up. She could've at least said something in Grey's defense. But she hadn't, and he'd almost revealed things he'd vowed not to tell anyone.

Such an idiot.

Friday night in the foothills meant parties, and he slowed to carefully pass the host of parked vehicles that were lined up on the side of the dirt road like Matchbox cars haphazardly placed by a four-year-old.

Despite the traffic, he loved coming up here on the weekends. It kept him out of the dorm and away from drunken Ryker, who was infinitely worse than sober Ryker. Grey drove past where the last car was parked and moved another half mile into the hills before pulling over to the side. To do what he was here for, he would need to hike in deep, where the steep hills and valleys would hide him from the road and detour the kegger parties that were in the more accessible parts of the hills.

He got out of the Jeep, breathing in the distinctive smell of sage and dirt that he'd learned to love. They were in a high desert, and although the campus itself was landscaped with a variety of trees and bushes, none were native. The foothills that arched around most of the college were parched and covered in a fragrant mix of sagebrush and dry grasses. The trail that cut between the hills was peppered with volcanic rocks, large and small, and hugged by a rugged beauty that was hard to see at first glance.

Already anticipating what was to come, little pins and needles prickled his extremities. His heart pounded. A smile tugged at his lips, and the farther in he went, the taller he walked. With every step he shed a piece of Grey the nobody and became Grey Malteer—the somebody. Alone, he was free from the confines of his persona and antsy to embrace the warrior.

Shrugging out of the trench coat, he let it fall to the ground. The gentle breeze picked up a strand of hair, and it tickled his nose.

Grey sneezed, then rolled his shoulders and stretched his legs to one side and then the other, loosening up his muscles.

The hill to his right was nearly eighty feet high and a perfect plateau. In a feature unique to this area, the tabletop was rimmed with an eight-foot section of black volcanic tube rock. It was perfectly edged, like human hands had created it. In the dark, he could barely make out the shadow where the sheer rock face began. He'd have to jump to get to the top.

Grey ran.

The speed kicked in immediately, and he went straight up and came down even faster. The wind blew his hair back, and his body howled in glorious approval.

He'd tried to clock himself a year ago, the calculations coming in at nearly sixty miles an hour. Although the thought boggled his mind, he was reasonably sure he could go faster. Leaping over a dried-up streambed in the valley, he pumped up the incline on the opposite side. Once at the top, he pushed into open air, arching outward as the hill vanished below, landing and leaping again, coming down in several bounds. The itch that had been building dissipated immediately, and he felt amazing. It was always like this—like somehow he'd outrun all his cares and worries.

But when his legs stopped moving, and his heart rate dipped to normal, he became Grey—the less-than-average boy in the trench coat. And the baggage was always waiting.

He slid to a stop at the top of the second plateau and looked over the valley. Lights twinkled from houses and supermarkets and movie theaters. It looked peaceful, like a Disney storybook. But it wasn't—at least not for him. Down amongst the pretty lights waited a life where he didn't fit in.

He'd discovered his abilities six years ago, the same time he'd discovered that everything supernatural was as real as he was. Unfortunately, the only time he could enjoy his gifts was while hidden somewhere—unable, even, to use them to stop the hell at home. Grey was utterly paralyzed by the fear that he would be found out.

This wasn't natural, what he could do. And being discovered would probably end up with him in a lab or scrutinized under media frenzy. The nightmares leapt back and forth between the leering faces of his stepfather and a scientist peeking through a glass pane on the door in a white room.

He shuddered.

To be capable of stopping the abuse but so paralyzed by the fear of being exposed that he didn't left a trail of guilt and self-loathing that ran clear through his soul.

Thinking about home gave him the undeniable urge to keep running. He dropped down the hill and kept going. Up, over, up, over. He'd determined long ago that the moment he stepped out of the house for college, that would be it. He was never going back.

But he couldn't outrun it—the pain, the fear . . . the shame. It never left. The wind shifted, and a scent entered his nostrils that stopped him dead in his tracks and turned his bowels to water. It was death and garbage and wet dog rolled into one memory-inducing aroma. A vivid rush of sights and sounds hijacked his nervous system. He leaned over his knees and vomited.

The wind turned as quickly as it had come, and the smell was wiped clean, leaving only the odor of vomit and a bitter, fearful wondering of whether he'd only imagined it.

Straightening, he scanned the area in a slow turn, trying to keep the panic at bay. There was nothing out of the ordinary. But it was dark, and the hill was full of lurking shadows cast by sagebrush and boulders. How could he possibly know if one of the shapes wasn't inanimate, but a hulking, breathing thing?

A sense of foreboding rippled through him.

It couldn't be.

Despite the disbelief, Grey was yanked back to when he was thirteen. The night he'd been attacked by creatures he'd never seen before, never even read about. They were a nightmarish mix between trolls, eels, and pigs—with beady eyes, sallow skin, greasy black hair, and thick lips that were parted with a set of yellowing tusks.

The smell hit him again, and his mind reeled under a panic-induced adrenaline overdose.

Under its effects, the boulders and sagebrush started to take on different shapes, as if brought to life by an artist pushing play on a stop-motion film. The branches became arms and legs, the centers rotund bellies. Threats and death and the past loomed in every shadow. But between one blink and the next, reality returned, and Grey was alone—the objects just objects once more.

Six years ago it had been an alley that he'd foolishly chosen as a short cut. Those monstrous creatures had stepped out from behind a large trash bin in the alley, and when he'd turned to run, there had been more behind him. The goblins had advanced, bloodlust gleaming in their eyes. Light from the fluorescent bulbs on the store across the street had glinted off the steel of their swords. With nowhere to go, he'd thought he was dead. In fact, he'd been certain of it.

He vaguely remembered screaming.

Grey's throat tightened now in response to the memory, those childhood cries for help trying to burst up all over again.

No!

He forced himself to pull in a deep breath, looking for sanity, and was rewarded with the familiar scent of sage. No wet dog, no smell of rotting flesh. No threat unseen.

See? Nothing.

"Your imagination is getting the best of you. Pull it together." Grey hoped the sound of his own voice would break the spell. But what he was experiencing wasn't really an overactive imagination. These were memoires come back to haunt him.

He was still rattled by the sound Ryker had made and the subsequent video. It had been six years since that night, since the monsters had emerged from the shadows making *that sound*—he'd only just stopped looking around every corner and carrying a flashlight in his pocket.

How had the bastard known it?

Grey kicked a rock in frustration. It hopped and jumped a few feet forward. He kicked another. How could Ryker have possibly *guessed* that mouth breathing, clacking of teeth, and a high-pitched giggle— in that exact order—was the recipe to scare the hell out of him?

There was a rustle somewhere to his left. Then . . . clacking teeth. Faint. But there.

Grey snapped. "Damn it, Ryker!" he yelled into the darkness. "Enough! If you think . . ." He trailed off as logic kicked in.

Even if Ryker *had* left the party he and Rune had been headed too, and if he'd just *happened* to see Grey head this way, and even *if* he'd followed him—Grey had been running at nearly sixty miles an hour, up and over hills that weren't accessible by car.

It was quite literally impossible that he'd been followed. His heart pounded faster, and he took a step back, pivoting on the balls of his feet to go back the way he'd come.

More rustling. Closer this time. Grey whirled back around to face the threat. There, up on the hill in front of him, a shadow moved between one bush and another. It was short. Far too short to be Ryker, or a human for that matter, but moving on two legs.

Tate crouched on the top of a plateau. His trench coat resisted the force of the breeze, weighed down with numerous weapons that hung inside and the crossbow strapped to his back.

It had taken months to finally find Grey, and as he prepared to approach the boy—no, the *man*—Grey had gotten into a car and driven away.

For a world without magic, the things these humans managed to create were remarkable.

He watched Grey moving up and down the hills, and his mouth twisted in a smile. The boy had been learning. Tate suspected he was nearing the speeds he would eventually be capable of. That was good. Once word got out that the Venators had come home, there would be little time for training before their skills were put to the test. And Tate needed them to survive.

He'd volunteered for this mission to circumvent the council— they would've found their Venators with or without him. But by coming here and handpicking the candidates, he'd increased the chances of this plan succeeding exponentially.

Out of the few Venators he'd been able to locate, he'd chosen these two for their hearts. Everything hinged on that. The goal was to turn their hearts before the council could indoctrinate and corrupt them in the ways of his world. He needed these two to see the *truth*, not the lies the council would spin. There was no certainty his plan would work, and measures were in place in case Grey and Rune proved that their species' nature was too much to temper.

If the council discovered his true intentions, he was dead. But not before they destroyed everything and everyone he cared about.

Grey disappeared for a moment in the deeper shadows where two hills met. This world's moon and stars weren't as bright as the ones from home, and that dulled things. It had grated on his nerves since crossing through.

The boy came back into view, slid to a stop, and vomited.

Tate frowned. The exertion should not have been too much for a Venator's body to handle. Weakness would not be tolerated by the council. It made him uneasy.

But danger was closing in. With the boy finally standing still, it was time to make the reintroduction. He wasn't sure how Grey would react. He started to stand.

Something caught Grey's attention, and his head snapped to the side, body tense.

Tate's life had taught him to be cautious and overlook nothing. He slowly lowered back into a crouch. He couldn't see anything out of the ordinary, but that meant nothing. The night was dark, and there were ample hiding spots. He'd lost Zio's goblins several times since crossing, but all that really meant was that *they* had found *him* several times. The beasts were getting much, much better under Zio's direction.

Tate's eyes flicked back to Grey. During the boy's first encounter with Zio's henchman, he had been too young to be affected physically. But he was a man now. Grey's markings hadn't activated yet, which was good. But if the goblins got close enough to flip the switch on his Venator side, the odds of getting Grey out alive decreased substantially.

Grey stood motionless, still turned in the direction of whatever had startled him.

Something was definitely out there. Tate placed a hand on the ground and leaned forward, squinting.

Nothing moved . . . until Grey turned to go. With the Venator's back offered, two shadows emerged from behind a boulder halfway up the hill. They were short and wide and clutching battle-axes in their meaty hands. Goblins liked to kill up close. It wasn't enough to bring death—they wanted to feel it.

Tate swore under his breath. How many more were here?

Hearing the attack, Grey turned again. The goblins cut back into the shadows. Although hidden from Grey, they were not hidden from Tate. The weary light of the moon offered just enough to add an odd gleam off the metal of their axes.

He stood, swiped his coat to the side, and pulled at the leather strap that crossed his chest, swinging the crossbow to the front. He grabbed a bolt, loosed, reloaded, then loosed again.

The first goblin fell, followed by the second. Tate waited. Neither moved again.

Talking to the boy would have to wait a little longer. Grey needed to get out alive, and right now Tate held the perfect vantage point to take out any other threats.

He crouched back down, crossbow at the ready, and waited.

Grey scrubbed a hand over his face. There was a grunt, followed by a thud. His head popped up. The sounds came again: a grunt and a thud. But as hard as he scanned, he could find no sign of movement.

He took a step back and another one. A breeze picked up again, and it seemed to whisper as it brushed through the grasses, *Venator.*

That's what the creatures had called him, in the alley. One had hissed it—*Venator.* The word had barely escaped its mouth when a large man in a floor-length trench coat came bursting into the alleyway, swords flying.

Grey took a ragged breath and looked around one more time, unable to shake the sense of foreboding that crawled up his spine like a host of thin-legged spiders. It was time to go. He turned for the car, fears and memories still jabbing at him, but determined to walk at least part of the way to prove he wasn't a scared thirteen-year-old boy anymore. But he hadn't taken more than a few steps before his fight-or-flight response overwhelmed him.

Grey ran.

It was nearly 3:00 a.m. by the time he reached the car, drenched in sweat and heart pounding from fear instead of exertion. Still running from nightmares, even a thousand miles from home. He gave a bitter chuckle.

Throwing the trench coat in the passenger seat, he climbed in and slid the key into the ignition. The lock on the door loomed in his peripheral vision; he reached over and pushed it down.

Grey groaned and dropped his head against the steering wheel.

That night had changed everything for him. Time was divided into a distinct before . . . and after.

Feeling safer in the locked confines of his Jeep and exhausted of trying to fight the memories, he closed his eyes and gave himself over. The pictures flowed behind his eyelids, fast and furious. The swords of his rescuer had slashed and cut for what seemed like forever. Blood had streamed over the pavement, turning the white trim of his shoes pink. He hadn't been able to look away as the blood licked at his feet, flowing with a thicker viscosity than water.

The violence and gore fed into thousands of his dreams in one form or another.

When the attack was finally over, he and his rescuer had stood facing each other, surrounded by mangled creatures. The man had grabbed him by the shoulders and given him a slight shake, asking if he was all right. The world had been a blur. He'd blinked. When the man's face had finally come into focus, Grey had discovered that his skin wasn't actually black, as he'd thought, but a deep hue of blue.

His mouth had hung open. But then he'd stopped thinking about the creatures or the savior with blue skin. Instead, he'd thought of a different nightmare—of his own personal hell that was far from over. At thirteen, a horrible truth had rocked through him. He'd just been saved from death . . . and wished he hadn't been.

In the Jeep, a shudder ran up Grey's spine, and he blinked back tears.

He'd been a child, and the thought had sunk in like a great weight. Grey had closed his mouth, licked his lips, and screwed up the courage to reveal his biggest secret to a complete stranger. He'd been ready to ask for a different kind of saving when another scream tore through the night.

The man had whirled, one finger on his lips. His head had turned as he listened. Then he'd pulled a black orb from his pocket and shoved it into Grey's hand. "Keep this with you," he'd said. "Always."

Grey's hand slid off his leg and reached across the seat to pat the pocket of his coat, feeling for the orb. The lump, always in his right side pocket, was both comforting and the equivalent of a pebble in his shoe.

The man with the blue skin had run out of the alley, disappearing as quickly as he'd come.

After that, the evenings had been filled with nightmares—blood and demons and death. The waking hours had been filled with daydreams, frequent and vivid, always about the man who'd rescued him six years ago finally returning to take him away from his hell. To where? He didn't care.

But the man had never come back.

The threat on Grey's life was temporarily abated, but this was a problem. If Zio's beasts were here, they'd found where Grey lived and followed the boy, just as Tate had. There was no telling where the rest of the goblins were or how many had actually gotten through the gate, but they were near, and they'd identified the Venator.

Tate had to get Grey through the gate, tonight. But he couldn't just leave the bodies of two creatures that didn't exist in this world dead in the desert. He would have to clean up the mess first.

Tate leapt from the ledge of the plateau and sped toward the carcasses.

GOBLINS

Ryker's snoring had grown to a delightful combination of a gravel truck and a freight train. The internal resentment Rune always felt was growing, and the irritating sound fed everything that bothered her—like an infection spreading from one cell to the next. It had been building for years, but tonight it finally hit critical mass.

She jerked to her feet, driven by a need to do something, and moved to the window.

She loved her brother, but damn it, she hated him too. What could possibly have been so horrible that it was worth sacrificing not only his life but hers too? Surely he knew that's what he'd done. How could he not see that she'd given up everything because of him?

Her life consisted of two things: chasing after Ryker to make sure he didn't kill himself and making sure she pulled the grades and sunk the shots to make Mom proud. A Herculean effort. And futile.

What about what *she* wanted? Didn't that matter to anyone?

A sob escaped, and she wrapped her arms around herself. Did *she* even know what she wanted? There had been a time when she'd enjoyed drawing. Creating images of vampires and demons had made the itch stop after her and Ryker's games ceased. But the pictures had turned so dark they'd scared her mother, so Rune had let it go.

She also loved to teach and had thought about being a coach. According to her parents, "teachers didn't make enough money," so teaching was therefore unacceptable. Because nothing made you so happy as a house full of expensive items you didn't need.

Fury and resentment smoldered behind her ribs, directed at both her parents and her drunken idiot of a brother. Past history and overflowing stores of anger provided plenty of dry tinder, and her emotions rose violently, flaming to an unbearably hot inferno. She shook with sobs that her unconscious brother wouldn't hear. Years of self-sacrifice ran down her cheeks in liquid streams, and then . . . something snapped inside.

An odd calm wrapped her in its embrace, followed by a clear knowledge of what would stop the pain. She let out a slow breath and straightened, wiping the tears from her cheeks.

She was done.

Screw Ryker. Screw her parents. They could figure out life without controlling hers.

It was nearly 4:00 a.m. by the time Grey's eyelids were too heavy to keep open. He headed back to campus, wincing in the oncoming traffic lights.

He parked the Jeep in the farthest corner of the lot and trudged toward the building. The usual sound of parties had died to a dull throb with the occasional burst of laughter. He made it up four flights without seeing another person, but when he jerked open the door from the stairwell, Rune was there, closing the door to Ryker's room. Her eye makeup was smeared on one side, and her nose was red around the edges.

Ryker's room was only three down from his, and he hurried toward his door, trying to avoid a conversation. His hand was on the knob when she turned around.

"Oh, hey." Rune ducked her head and tucked a piece of hair behind her ear.

She looked embarrassed—Ryker must've been on a bender tonight.

Part of him wanted to ignore her and go to bed, to make it abundantly clear that he was mad. But he just couldn't do it. "You all right? You've got something." He motioned.

"Yeah, fine." Rune swiped a finger under each eye, wiping away the smeared mascara. "Just getting Ryker into bed," she said, obviously sober.

"Oh." Before he could stop himself, he blurted out the question he'd wondered about for some time. "Why don't you ever drink with him?"

"I don't like losing control. Besides," her voice was suddenly laced with venom, "if I did, who would get him home?"

The anger made him uncomfortable, despite who it was directed at, and he turned his attention to his pocket, fumbling for keys.

Rune leaned against the wall, watching. "I need to talk to you."

He froze with the key half in the lock. "Uh, right now?"

She cocked her head to the side, looking at him like it was the stupidest question ever. "Yeah, now. While Ryker is in a drunken stupor and can't harass you for talking to me."

He evaluated her, taking in her posture, her eyes. He should've been thrilled with the request, but the emotion was overridden both by the incident at the library and by habit—he always took time to determine someone's motivation. Some might call it paranoia, but he called it self-preservation.

Rune looked sincere enough, and her eyes didn't glitter with ill intent. She just looked tired . . . and sad.

"Yeah," he mumbled. "I know." Grey shoved the key into the lock and pushed the door open. "Come in."

He stepped through first and was met with a gust of night air. He froze, staring at the fluttering curtain.

Rune ran straight into his back. "Hey! I—"

"My window is open."

"So?"

"I don't leave my window open." Walking over, he leaned his head out and looked around the deserted quad. Given what had happened at the beginning of the year, normally he would assume it was someone trying to play another prank. But his skin prickled with a specific nervousness for the second time today—a sickening nudge that something wasn't right.

Not now, please, not now. Not with her here.

He straightened and subtly patted his pocket to make sure the orb was there, just in case. He felt the round black device and relaxed slightly, even though he had no idea what the thing did.

There was that smell again, though it was faint. Was he losing his mind?

He looked around with a frown, but nothing seemed out of place. "I'm sorry, it's just—"

"Grey?" Rune whispered. She pointed across the room with a shaking hand.

Something glinted in his closet.

A strange burning sensation started along his spine and ran up. It spanned his neck, flowed down his shoulders, then spilled across his forearms like a blast of hot steam. He gasped. Eerie patterns began to glow under his skin, flickering red and green. They looked tribal—smooth, wide swirls and geometric angles mixed with jagged points.

"Rune, get out of here!"

But despite the panic in his voice, she didn't move. She just stood there, holding out her arms and staring at the swirling patterns that washed across her own forearms and disappeared under white cap sleeves. The markings weren't as thick as Grey's, but they too were flickering red and green around the edges.

She shook her arms as if the motion could somehow dislodge the patterns from her body. "What is this?" she stammered. "What's going on?"

The closet door swung open and banged against the wall, revealing two dark shapes. Rune yelped, strange markings forgotten.

The world drifted out from beneath Grey's feet. His vision tunneled. He remembered those silhouettes clearly and felt like a child again, his mind unraveling into panic. *No.* The thought came in a self-reprimanding, vicious lash. *You have to stay calm.* He'd prepared for this.

"Rune." He forced the note of fear from his voice. "I need you to go, right now—"

The creatures stepped into the light. Their skin was a blackish gray and wrinkled. The majorities of their faces were occupied with noses that pulled up at the tip—like swine. Greasy black hair lay in thin, plastered strings around their bulbous heads.

The monsters grinned around large tusks, like those of a warthog, as they pulled two silver sabers from their waists. The blades were mottled with swirling designs.

Grey subtly moved one foot back and centered his weight as he'd been taught. But he needed his weapons. Which were, of course, in the closet. One of the creatures saw his eyes flicker to the pair of sai, their thin blades as long as his forearm. It reached back to grab one, gripping right below the curved side guards, and waved it with a mocking grin.

Years of training in case the beasts came back, and this was how it was going down.

He yelled and snatched the first thing he saw, the library's copy of *Great Expectations*, and chucked the sad excuse for a weapon at the monsters. The second creature spun his sword upward and cut through the book like it was butter. At the sight of pages fluttering to the ground, the other made a sound of complete joy that ended in a gleeful snarl as he tossed Grey's sword back to the closet floor.

"Grey." Rune stumbled backward.

"Ssstop talking," one of the creatures hissed. "Ssstupid Venators."

"Very stupid." The other raised his sword. "Sssee how they ssstand for the ssslaughter."

"They know nothing," the first one agreed with a sneer.

"Get down." A voice came from behind. It wasn't overly loud, but it was a command.

Grey glanced back and saw *him*. The same man who'd come to his rescue the first time. He dropped, pulling Rune with him.

There was a loud *twang*, and the first creature was caught in the chest by a bolt whose shaft was as thick as a broom handle. The creature snarled and fell back, twitching violently on the floor.

The other screeched and turned to face the attacker. "Venshii." It spat. "How dare you?"

"You can't have them," the man said calmly.

He was dressed in black from head to toe and wore the same long trench coat, which opened to reveal an arsenal of weapons wrapped around his waist and shoulders. His skin was a dark, rich blue. Raised white marks ran down the side of his neck and disappeared under the coat collar. His head was shaved, emphasizing a perfectly manicured black goatee.

Instead of charging, the creature moved with lightning speed. It pulled one arm back and threw the sword. It flew end over end toward their protector, whistling through the air. The man ducked a moment before it thudded into the wall behind him.

Grey questioned the stupidity of throwing your weapon away, but the creature quickly grabbed the sword from his fallen comrade and leapt forward. The man pulled his own sword in one fluid movement as he stood, meeting the attacker's blade.

Rune moved to get up, but Grey grabbed her arm, pulling her flat to the floor. "What are you doing?" he hissed.

"We have to help!"

"No. Experience in basketball won't do much good, Rune. Stay down. I'll go." There was a clear path to the closet, and Grey scrambled to his feet, sprinting across the dorm room. The creature saw the movement from the corner of his eye and snarled, turning to deal with Grey, but the man sliced downward, and the creature was forced to return his attention to the fight.

The sound of metal against metal rang through the room. The monster dodged a blow, then, using the close proximity, reached up and slammed the hilt against the man's head. He stumbled to the side from the impact.

Grey grabbed a sai and turned to help, but the monster moved fast. It leapt through the air, leaving him no time to do anything except raise his weapon in defense.

A second *thwack* sounded from the man's crossbow, and a bolt punched through the monster's back. Its arms and legs splayed in midair, continuing in forward motion. The grotesque body landed—completely impaled—onto Grey's thin blade. He and the creature crashed to the ground. A wet warmth ran down Grey's hand and spread over his chest. He didn't know if it was the bolt or the sai that had killed it, but the dead weight pressing down on him made his stomach clench. He struggled to push the creature off, but it was so heavy it crushed his arms against his sides. Swallowing, he rammed one shoulder blade into the floor, leveraging his body and twisting at an angle. The body finally rolled, its head thudding sickly against the floor. Grey scrambled to his feet, breathing hard.

"Are you OK?" Rune called.

He nodded numbly.

Rune stood, her eyes slowly roaming the room.

"Good to see you again," the man said, looking over Grey. "You've grown."

"It's been a while," he replied tightly. "Kids do that."

TURNING POINT

The man came over and poked the body of the dead creature with the toe of his boot.

Rune stared. His features were strong—a chiseled nose and square jaw, with deep-set eyes that were nearly black. The marks that ran down his neck looked like a brand, raised and slightly puckered but bright white against his skin.

"You're blue," she blurted.

He threw her a sidelong glance. "Yes. I've been told it's a nice shade." Once he was convinced the creature was dead, he turned. "Rune, I'm sorry we had our first meeting under these circumstances. It was my intent to reach you before they did. But unless you want to meet more . . ." He slipped the leather strap that was attached to the butt of the crossbow over his shoulder and twisted it like a rifle strap until the bow rested against his back. "We need to go."

She should've said no. She should've asked who he was or what dream she'd jumped into. She *should've* asked how he knew her name. But that strange calm she'd felt when she snipped the cord of responsibility for Ryker was still wrapped around her, and she wasn't willing to let it go.

Even stranger, the constant inner itch had all but disappeared, which only added to the ease of what she said next. "All right."

Grey jolted in surprise. "All *right*?"

"Yes." She threw her shoulders back and leveled a defiant stare at him. "Are you coming or what?"

The man's mouth quirked at the exchange.

Grey nodded dumbly, speechless.

"Excellent," the man said. "Grey, I trust you have what I left with you last time?"

His lips thinned, tightening at the edges. "It's been six *years*."

Six years? Rune stared at the two, sensing pieces to her biggest mystery. Six years ago was exactly when Ryker had shut her out and when he'd turned on Grey. Six years ago was when Grey had taken up wearing his signature trench coat, which bore an eerie similarity to the coat the man wore. She remembered the day Grey had started wearing it, because the temperature had been over ninety, and she couldn't believe he'd kept the stupid, ill-fitting thing on all day.

"You have it?" the man repeated.

"Yes."

"Good. We just need to dispose of these bodies before—" Something scratched at the window. "We're out of time." The man grabbed her and Grey by the arms, jerking them into the hall. "More goblins got through. Go!"

"Goblins!" Rune wrenched her arm away from his overly tight grip. "Got through what?" She stayed at his side, jogging to keep up.

The man glanced at her in exasperation. "We're being hunted. Questions later."

They were halfway to the stairs when a window broke behind them. The man yanked open the stairwell door, then snarled. Squatty, heavily armed shadows loomed up the walls. He slammed it shut again.

Another window shattered somewhere in the building, and he turned, holding out his hand. "Grey, I need it."

"You never even told me your name." Grey fished a black orb from his pocket and handed it over.

"Tate."

"How do you two know each other?" Rune asked, looking back over her shoulder.

"Pinned in a box and stuck with two untrained Venators," Tate grumbled to himself. "Both worlds are going to hell in a handbasket." He threw the ball at the wall. It flashed, and the hard plane evaporated, leaving a doorway that opened to a grassy area and a sidewalk. The edges shimmered, beckoning them forward.

"This is going to hurt a little." Tate gestured toward the newly made door. "After you."

More of the creatures spilled out into the hall from Grey's room just as the stairwell door flew open. The goblin at the front of the line grinned, its lips stretching around two tusks.

Maybe it was the stench that flowed down the hall and twisted its fist in her nostrils. Or maybe it was the sight of an entire host of the ugly beasts. Or maybe it had been the shattering glass, knowing the window could've been the one in Ryker's room. Whatever it was, reality finally hit.

"Wait!" Rune cried, digging her heels in. Ryker was two doors down, completely incapacitated. "We have to get Ryker."

An ax thudded into the wall inches from Grey's nose, and his eyes widened to the size of saucers, staring at the gleaming silver blade.

Tate grabbed Grey and threw him through the shimmering doorway. He disappeared immediately.

That was impossible. All of this was impossible. Rune's mouth went dry, and her spirit shriveled up, screaming. The calm was definitely gone.

The strange doorway was shrinking, and Tate's enormous hand pressed against Rune's back. "No!"

And then she was flying into the light.

Grey was being wrenched forward and driven back all at the same time. An inescapable weight crushed his ribs, threatening to break the thin bones and punish the organs beneath. He gaped like a fish, trying to fill lungs that refused to be inflated.

Finally the pressure abated, and he stumbled out onto a dimly lit sidewalk. Leaning over his knees, Grey gasped for breath. But the air was thick with a foreign humidity, and it flowed through his aching chest like water instead of oxygen.

Over the sound of his own gasping, the sound of heavy traffic filled the air, strange and out of place. He slowly looked up, peering through strands of hair. What he saw left him frozen and utterly perplexed.

Rune pitched out of the doorway, taking several quick steps to keep her feet under her. Tate stepped out easily, as if he'd done it a thousand times.

On their left was a historic courthouse. It sat at the top of a tall flight of stairs, looking down like an old magistrate passing judgment on the city.

"Whoa." Rune stared in wonder. "Where are we?"

"St. Louis." Grey straightened and pointed to the right, across a busy four-lane street. There, on top of a grassy hill, was a massive, three-sided steel arch that framed a perfectly full moon.

"St. Louis." Rune still looked like her mind couldn't wrap itself around what had just happened. "What—?"

"That orb was designed to take us to a gate." Tate motioned to the arch. "That is one of many doorways to my world."

"*Your* world," Grey repeated. "You mean . . ." He trailed off as he stared at the arch. The implications were enormous.

"I wasn't able to explain the last time I was here—"

The portal they'd come through faded to nothing and uttered a single sigh before it *snicked* away.

That broke Rune from her stunned silence.

"No!" She ran, swiping at the last wisps. "No!" She turned one way and then the other, frantically looking for something that didn't exist. "I have to go back."

"You can't. The door is one way," Tate said. "I'm sorry. It's too late."

Rune looked incredulous. "Too late? What . . . but . . . too late for what?"

"For Ryker. I'm sure they already have him."

There was a moment of stunned silence before the next word burst out in a pain-filled cry. "Why?" Tears pooled in her eyes. "Is he . . . ?"

Tate sighed, and tenderness softened his expression. "No, he's not dead." He took her by the shoulders like a father would take a child—gentle, comforting.

Rune shrugged out of his grasp. "Don't touch me!"

Grey winced, feeling Rune's rejection as if it had been directed at him. But Tate didn't seem to notice. His cool, indifferent nature returned like a piece of clothing he could put on at will. "We need to go."

Rune's eyes flashed, and she set her heels. "I'm not going another step with you until you tell me what's going on."

"Fine." Tate was distracted, his eyes bouncing off every building, bush, and car near them. "Those creatures work for a woman named Zio. She's looking for the same thing I was: you." He jerked his head toward Grey. "And him."

"Zio?" Grey repeated, if for no other reason than to wrap his tongue around the name of the enemy.

"But you didn't need Ryker," Rune said, bitterness making her words sharp. "So you just left him there."

Tate paused in his perimeter check and evaluated her carefully. "Ryker was never supposed to be part of the equation. It's unfortunate that—"

"Unfortunate!"

"The stakes are too high. Maybe someday you'll understand why I couldn't involve your brother."

"Well, he's involved now, isn't he?" Grey would've given almost anything to be free of Ryker, but life once again had seen fit to interweave their fates. He scrubbed his hands over his face. "Where will they take him?"

Tate pointed to the arch. "Our side."

Fear flickered behind Rune's eyes as she stared at the imposing steel structure, but then it was gone. She rolled her shoulders and neck, moving from one foot to the other as if psyching herself up for the big game. "OK, then. That's where we're going."

Grey had spent six years coming to terms with the super-natural. Still, the idea that there was another *world* was difficult for him to comprehend. Rune had had about five minutes and was acting as if everything was normal, including their new blue-skinned friend. "Rune, are you sure? We don't even know where—"

"I don't care where it is. I shouldn't have left Ryker—I never should've left him. Now it's up to me to find him. I'm not going to stand here while my twin brother is—"

A cackle floated over the roar of traffic, and Tate held out a hand for silence. He turned slowly, pulling a sword from his hip in one smooth motion. "They're here."

A bush rustled near the base of the steps. One of the immense wooden doors, carved and probably original to the courthouse, inched open.

"It's a trap," Tate said under his breath, backing up. "Get to the arch, now. Grey, you'll need to help Rune if we're going to survive. I've seen you practicing. You can do this."

"You've seen—" Grey stopped himself. Questions later. He grabbed Rune by both arms and swung her around to face him. "Listen to me—you have to trust everything I say."

She nodded. "I trust you."

Her immediate trust didn't discourage the thought trickling through his brain like an infectious disease: *We're dead. So dead.*

The double doors to the courthouse swung all the way open, and dozens of the gray goblins poured down the steps.

"Run!" Tate yelled.

Two wolves jumped from the bushes, double the size Grey had ever imagined them to be. Their eyes, nestled above long snouts and ragged fur, flashed back the lights of traffic. Drool slid over their lips.

Their eyes roved hungrily, as if anticipating burying their muzzles in Grey's gut. Tearing flesh and innards, tasting blood.

Bile crawled up the back of his throat.

Rune screamed—her first real one of the evening.

Behind them was a narrow set of five steps that led down to a large, grassy area separating the old-world building from the modern black pavement of a multilane road.

"Move, now!" Grey took the stairs in one leap. Rune raced down but tripped on the last one and fell forward.

Seeing opportunity, one of the wolves leapt off the upper edge. Grey grabbed under Rune's arms, pulling her to her feet a moment before the wolf landed. It stretched toward them with open jaws, going for Rune's ankle.

Just before its mouth snapped shut, a bolt thudded into the wolf's spine. It yelped. The beast's teeth scraped against the heel of Rune's shoe as it fell, flopping flat against the walk, still snarling.

Tate jumped from above, the bottom half of his trench flapping like vulture wings. "You aren't running," he yelled, sinking another bolt into the animal's head.

He landed hard, dropping into a deep crouch and then spinning on the balls of his feet as he stood. He loaded and raised the bow for a shot at the remaining wolf running toward them.

"Rune, I know this is new, but if we don't move, we'll die!" Grey grabbed hold of her hand and took off at the fastest sprint he could go without ripping her arm from its socket.

Tall corporate buildings and hotels towered to their right and left, in odd juxtaposition to the old courthouse and the well-manicured grassy expanse that faced the elegant St. Louis Arch.

He dragged her along, dodging flowering bushes that dotted their escape path. "Faster!" he shouted. "You can do more. Let go, and trust me." Finally, he felt her start to match his speed. "That's it, just let it happen."

They were nearing the street. The four lanes of traffic were already thick with cars.

He knew what he had to do but worried about Rune. There was no time to explain. "Don't think. Just jump!"

Grey pushed off—Rune did the same. Lifting into the air, he held on tightly to her arm. But as he'd feared, Rune didn't have faith in her abilities yet, and he was jerked painfully back, her weight pulling him down. They slammed onto the hood of a passing car. Grey's shoulder was wrenched at an odd angle, and he groaned.

A millisecond later, before the driver of the vehicle could react, one of the goblins landed on the roof, its sallow skin looking even sicker in the early light of dawn.

"Hold on!" Grey gripped the lip between the windshield and the hood. Rune understood immediately and twisted, grabbing the edge and burying her head in her shoulder.

The horrified driver slammed on his brakes.

The creature on the roof flew forward and crashed into the trunk of a red Prius.

Grey thought the skin on his fingertips might peel off, but he and Rune managed to stay on the hood. When the vehicle jerked to a stop, he scrambled to get his feet underneath him.

The squeal of brakes sounded everywhere, followed by metallic crunching. Grey looked over his shoulder to see the horrid creatures landing on hoods and roofs, using them like stepping stones to cross the road.

"Jump!" Grey shouted.

Rune gave it more effort this time. They landed on the other side of the road with nothing between them and the arch but the seemingly innocuous grassy hill.

Rune was in awe of her feat. "Did you see—?"

"Yes, run!"

Tate raced toward them with one gray monstrosity clinging to him, hacking at his shoulders with its claws. Tate swung his sword, stabbing the thing in the armpit. He tore it from his back and tossed its lifeless body to the side.

"Come on!"

Rune's speed was increasing as they ran up the hill, the creatures falling behind. A fleeting hope buzzed through Grey. They could make it. But when they crested the top, the base of the arch came into view. The hill had obscured a deadly problem.

Rune and Grey slid to a stop, clinging to each other to keep upright. The visitors' area below was innocent enough, crossed with stone paths and dotted with benches. But waiting under the arch were two more wolves—even larger than the previous ones. They stood chest high with muscled shoulders, far thicker than any natural animal. Adding to the terror of their appearance was the intelligence that wrapped around them like a second skin. They snarled and stalked forward, their eyes focused on him and Rune.

The tattoos on Grey's arms flared cherry red.

"What do we do?" Rune yelled, looking behind at the rapidly approaching goblin horde. "They've got us trapped."

Grey had no idea. He had no weapons and was nearly positive what stood in front of them: werewolves. The intelligence of a man, the power of a beast. Ryker had always teased that Grey carried silver powder in his pockets. Right now, he wished he actually did.

Tate blew by them, turning as he went. He tossed Grey a dagger. "Stay right behind me!"

Grey snatched the blade midair.

The first wolf jumped, and Tate dropped into a roll with one arm out, holding his crossbow. He landed flat on his back, raising the weapon and loosing a bolt as the animal soared over. The three-sided tip cut through its belly, but the wound was superficial. The wolf landed and spun for a second attack.

The other wolf used Tate's distraction to move for Grey.

Being stalked by the most terrifying thing he'd ever seen, Grey realized a glaring fault in his romanticized dreams—the ones where Tate returned to rescue him. This wasn't a dream . . . It was a nightmare.

"Rune, stay back." Grey gripped the dagger—it gave him all the confidence of trying to take down a polar bear with a toothpick.

The wolf was so close now. All he could see was a giant, snarling mouth, glittering brown eyes, and the deliberate movement of the shoulders as it stalked its prey.

The thing leapt, and dinner-plate-sized paws punched into his chest like sledgehammers, knocking him flat on his back and pinning his arms to the ground. Grey struggled, trying to defend himself, but a few hundred pounds of wolf kept him immobilized.

A deep rumble rolled through the werewolf's chest—a very humanlike chuckle. There was a devious glint in its eyes, and it leaned closer, jaw opening wide. The stench of its breath was overwhelmingly foul but played second fiddle to the palatable flavor of death that overrode Grey's senses.

He turned his head away. It was the only defense left. Either look away, or watch his own demise.

There was a blur of legs and shoes, and then Rune barreled into the side of the beast, shoving her shoulder into its ribs like a linebacker, knocking it sideways and clear of Grey. The werewolf snarled, rolling immediately to its feet. Rune scrambled backward onto her heels and the palms of her hands, looking around for anything she could use to defend herself—there was nothing but grass.

Grey struggled up and ran, leaping in front of Rune and brandishing the dagger with feigned confidence. The façade was critical—he'd learned that through many combat classes. Fear was the enemy, and you kept that terror hidden deep. Where it couldn't be read and used against you.

The werewolf's focus broke for a moment, and it looked behind its prey, snarling and giving a stiff shake of the head. Its message was clear: *These two are mine; stay back.*

The small army of goblins stopped a short distance away, but many of the greasy-haired beasts moved anxiously from one foot to the other, itching to continue the attack.

Tate shouted foreign words, and the stainless steel of the arch began to shimmer—first white, then taking on a yellow hue. The change distracted the wolf, and it glanced to the side just as Tate charged toward them. He leapt and wrapped his arms around its thick neck. Swinging over the top, Tate's knees smashed down on the other side, the momentum throwing the furry beast into a flip and effectively clearing the path to the arch.

"Hold hands. No matter what happens, don't let go!" Tate stood and grabbed Grey's left hand. Grey took Rune's hand with his right.

The werewolf tried to get back on its feet but wobbled and collapsed. The goblins bellowed in unison and charged.

Tate pulled a vial from his coat pocket as they ran. The arch flashed and was then filled with a curtain of green light.

"I don't know how bad it'll be on the other side," Tate yelled. "Be prepared."

"On the other side of what?" Rune shouted back.

No answer. They passed through the green, and Tate turned, throwing the vial. It exploded in a brilliant shower of red. Then they were falling.

THROUGH THE ARCH

His face was being ripped off. Little fingers of wind-sharpened air jabbed around his jaw, lips, and eye sockets, pulling and yanking until Grey was sure he was being flayed. The first door had been bad—this one was so much worse.

His heart stuttered awkwardly in his chest. Pain seeped up his throat, into his shoulder, and down one arm, transmitting threats that his heart was about to stop beating all together. His mouth gaped, not for air this time but in a fruitless effort to release the scream bunched in his esophagus like an oil-filled rag. He could see nothing but yellow—bright, pupil-searing yellow. The bones in his right hand were folding over each other as Rune squeezed it as hard as she could.

The pain in his chest intensified. Surely it couldn't get any worse. But it did.

He'd escaped his stepfather, death by goblins three times, and death by werewolves twice only to die by the hands of an invisible assailant in an endless sea of yellow. The injustice of it was nearly comical.

Then, just like that, the pain was gone. Air inflated his lungs. There was blue above—blessed sky blue. He closed his eyes, grateful to be alive.

Then he hit the ground.

Unprepared, Grey smashed onto his back. Hips and spine took the brunt of the force until his neck whiplashed and he heard, as much as felt, his skull crack against hard earth. The freshly acquired air burst out with a wheezing sound while bells went off in his ears and spots swam through his vision like tiny black fish.

Rune fell on top of him. He folded in at the middle as an elbow punched into his stomach, what felt like a knee ground against his sternum, and Rune's extra weight hammered his already bruised spine into a rock.

She groaned weakly and went to roll off, driving her elbow into his gut for leverage.

He gasped and wheezed, sounding like a ninety-year-old man. "Rune!"

She flopped flat, staring up at the sky, while her chest rose and fell with heavy breaths.

"Grey," she said, with an edge of trepidation. "Where are we?"

No idea. He rolled his head to the side, trying not to wince, and looked around. They were on a hill. Long, gray-green grasses rasped against each other and framed a host of wildflowers that waved and nodded their purple-and-blue heads in the breeze. The smell on the air was new, sweet with a hint of cinnamon and musk. He propped up on his elbows.

Tate stood to the side of the glowing opening they'd just exited from. It hung in midair and then started to shrink, pulling in on itself until it sealed and vanished. Tate's hand was under his trench on the hilt of a sword. His eyes darted in every direction, assessing. Then his mouth twisted to the side. "Oh, crap."

Rune bolted straight up. "'Oh, crap'! What do you mean, 'Oh, crap'?" She scrambled to her feet. "Where . . . ?" She trailed off, the words forgotten as a moth the size of her head came fluttering by. Its wings were a brilliant blue, decorated with spots and stripes in cotton candy pinks and greens. The moth swooped down with perfect accuracy and landed on the tip of her nose.

"Hey!" Tate ran toward her, swiping at the bug. "Get out of here."

The moth giggled, the pitch high and sweet like a child's, then swooped away.

Rune held up a shaking finger. "What . . . was that?"

"A faery. Well," Tate shrugged, "it used to be a faery. It's been exiled."

Grey stood and turned in a slow circle, taking in everything, not wanting to forget a single detail. A few trees and bushes were nestled at the base of the hill, waving in the breeze and sporting much brighter hues than Grey was accustomed to despite their familiar shapes. He could see pines and oaks and aspens, but their greens were richer and deeper. His gaze traveled up. The sky was so clear and bright—it had to be free of the contaminants that hovered in their atmosphere. He'd never known it could be so lovely.

The moth that Tate had shooed away returned, made a loop around Grey's head, still giggling, and then paused to hover in front of Grey. Where the moth's head should've been was a tiny humanlike head with antennae that protruded through the short, spiky brown hair. She winked at him with glittering blue eyes and made tiny kissing sounds before zipping off. Above them, something soared through the sky, the wingspan reminding him of a pterodactyl.

His grin spread until he couldn't contain it anymore, and a laugh of utter joy burst out. "It's all real, Rune. All of it!" Satisfaction settled around him like a blanket.

Rune closed her eyes as if mentally counting to ten, then turned away from him. "All right, Tate, what's wrong with my arms?"

Tate strolled past them and headed down the hill. "Nothing's wrong with your arms."

"Really?" Rune shouted, jogging to catch up. "Because I've never had glowing tattoos before."

As they walked, Grey looked down at the red, green, and pink that shimmered through his own markings. It was mesmerizing.

"Of course you have; they just weren't activated. That is the mark of a Venator."

"Latin for 'hunter,'" Grey interjected.

Rune rolled her head to look at him with as much annoyance as she could muster. "You just *happen* to know Latin?"

The tone of her voice and the *you're a moron* look ticked him off. "I *happen* to know a lot of things."

"Yeah, but . . . Latin?"

"I do a lot of research. Many of the old texts are in Latin. Some of the translations are missing things, especially any translated by the Catholic priests. They altered the texts to exclude anything they considered demonic—namely, the supernatural. So I worked with the original documents as much as I could."

She'd come to a stop and was looking at him like he'd just informed her he planned to marry a horse.

"What?" he snapped.

"Latin?"

"Keep up," Tate called.

Rune, not wanting to be left behind, hurried forward.

Grey hadn't realized how tall Tate was until he watched Rune walking next to him. She didn't even come up to his shoulder. As she walked, she scratched at her arms and scowled at the markings as if she could will them away.

"What in the hell 'activated' these stupid things?"

"Your contact with my world. Once one of us gets close enough to one of you, it triggers the markings."

"That can't be right," Grey said. "I saw you years ago."

"You were a child," Tate said shortly, as if it should've been the most obvious thing in the world. "A Venator doesn't get their markings until they become a man." He nodded to Rune. "Or a woman."

"You're trying to tell me that we have to hit puberty for these stupid glowing markings to . . ." She held up a hand, her lips pressed flat. "You know what, never mind. We're here, wherever here is. Now where did they take my brother?"

"I don't know."

"What? But you said Zio had him. You said—"

Tate whirled on her so fast she stumbled back. "Look, I don't have the answers you want." His tone was sharp, but it was the intensity in his gaze that made Rune shrink. "I have no idea where Zio is or what she'll do with your brother. There's a lot I can tell you, and I'm sure the farther we walk, the more questions you'll have. But right now my number-one priority is getting us all out of here before nightfall. We exited the gate in some very nasty fae territory, the kind that like to come out at night and the kind that will be most displeased that I managed to get you two over to this side. They are *very* creative in matters of death and torture, and if the wrong one finds us, you'll be wishing we'd kept moving and left your questions for later."

Rune swallowed and nodded.

"Glad we have an understanding."

The terrain started easily enough, with gentle, rolling hills dotted at the tops with shrubs and masses of wildflowers then ringed at the base with a wide variety of trees. But the soothing, up-down rhythm of the hills soon gave way to a flat expanse that was abruptly broken by a straight line of trees stretching for miles in each direction. One moment there was grass; the next, a wall of trees reaching into the sky like dark sentinels.

Tate strode in.

Grey and Rune both hesitated at the edge, looking down the row of trees, understanding each other's thoughts without saying a word. Something wasn't right about this place . . . but what else could they do but follow Tate?

They stepped past the tree line. Within a few steps, the forest grew inexplicably dark despite the sun blazing overhead. Grey peered up through the branches, not understanding. It was like an invisible sponge over the canopy was sucking in the light.

A shiver ran down his spine.

"Do you hear that?" Rune whispered.

Over the rustle of branches and the chirps and titters of insects and birds, the faint lilt of foreign music tickled his ears. It was intoxicating, even at such a low decibel. It seemed to move and coalesce inside him, calling him toward the source. He knew enough about fae music to be grateful it was faint. The desire was there but manageable—he had no wish to dance until his feet were nubs and he'd lost the will to live.

The deeper they moved into the forest, the stranger things became. Rocks rolled into their path of their own accord. The wildlife became strange and malformed—like a band of children's toys torn apart and reassembled. Birds with the legs of monkeys, woodpeckers with saws for beaks, an owl with glowing red eyes like two marbles. Branches seemed to purposefully rip at his clothes. He finally took his trench coat off after it had caught on every bush and tree he passed.

A small man the size of a garden gnome statue with a receding hairline and a rotund belly darted across the path, hissing at them. Tate pulled a knife and hissed back. The little man scuttled away, disappearing as fast as he'd appeared.

Soon after that, the trees began a gradual change. The bark morphed from varying shades of brown to ebony black. Next the leaves and pine needles faded—green, yellow, and then white. It had looked, for a moment, like a black-and-white checkered game board, the white leaves waving like flags on blackened posts. But then rich crimson saturated through the delicate veins as if pumping blood. Grey stared in fascination as they walked.

Dots of deep maroon appeared at the tips of the leaves, eventually flowing to the bases, moving and twisting like watercolors in a glass. Beautiful, flowing randomness transformed the white leaves to burgundy and the scene to a sinister backdrop. But the architect of this nightmare went a step further. As the leaves fell they changed colors again, from maroon to brilliant red. The now crimson leaves sat in spongy layers on the ground that gave way beneath their feet like dead flesh, coating the dark forest in a bloody warning.

The forest was rubbing his nerves raw. The strange animals, the unnaturalness of the trees, the queasy feeling from stepping on what looked and felt like bloodied flesh, combined with the ever-calling strains of faery music. A black bird with two oversized toes cawed at them from one of the branches before snapping up a large brown moth. Grey wondered whether it had been a moth or a faery.

The madness went on and on. Just when he thought he would unravel, give in, and run for the music—because surely it was better than this—the trees cleared, exposing a river of mud that stretched as far as he could see in both directions.

On the other side of the bank stood a wonderful sight. Trees, normal trees, with brown trunks and green leaves that were gleaming like stained glass as the setting sun shone through them.

Tate sat down and took off his boots.

Grey eyed the thick river. "Are we going through that?"

"Unless you see a way around. The sun is almost down."

Rune sighed and knelt down to take off her shoes. "I would take a bath in mud right now if it meant I didn't have to go back in there." She shuddered. "That was horrible."

"It's not over yet." Tate took off the many weapons that were strapped around his waist and legs, then wrapped them up in the trench coat. "If you feel anything while you're walking, just keep moving. Don't stop under any circumstances."

"Feel anything?" Rune eyed the mud. "What kind of thing?"

Tate waded in, holding the bundle above his head. The mud was deep, and he sunk up to his waist. "Anything they think might make you stop."

Grey tied the shoestrings of his boots together and draped them around his neck. He was going to hold his coat above his head, like Tate, but worried about what was lurking below the mud. He decided he might need his arms for balance and secured the coat around his waist instead. He didn't want it dragging behind and weighing him down.

Rune stood on the bank, alternating glances between the forest behind them and the river of mud in front.

"Coming?" Grey asked.

"Oh, after you," she said wryly. "I insist."

"I thought you were ready to bathe in it?"

"Yeah, not anymore."

He waded in, glancing back to make sure she followed. It wasn't long before he felt bony fingers wrap around his ankles. Grimacing, he jerked his leg free.

Rune shrieked.

"Keep moving!" Tate shouted back. "If you stop, they'll pull you under."

Fingers continued to grab at him, and then something pinched. The abuse grew more violent the closer they got to the other side. Something kicked the back of his knee so hard his leg buckled, and he was grateful he'd left his arms free for balance. A hand with long, pointed nails scraped down his leg, deterred only by the thick fabric of his jeans. Then something—or someone—tore the coat from his waist, and his most prized possession vanished beneath the muck. He swore under his breath as he twisted away from another attack.

Rune stumbled, waving her arms for balance.

"Are you all right?" Grey asked, turning around to go to her.

"Fine." She yelped and glared down. "That hurts, you little—"

"Don't call them names," Tate interrupted. "It just makes it worse."

Rune gritted her teeth, glaring daggers.

On the fae side of the muddy river, a shape appeared out of the shadows, standing in the spot they'd just been. He was Grey's height and wore nothing but a thin strip of fabric around his waist. Flaming-red hair stood out in all directions. His body was thin and chiseled, with hard, lean muscles that were far more defined than humanly possible. The boy faery grinned, exposing wicked, sharp teeth. This smile was not amused or friendly, but wound with danger.

"Um, Tate," Grey called.

"Keep moving," came the brusque reply.

Grey turned his back to the fae creature, his shoulders tense—uncomfortable with the vulnerable position—and fought against the suction of the mud as he made a push for the opposite bank. The river made a thick, sucking sound as Grey finally jerked his feet free. Once out, he offered a hand to Rune, pulling her up onto the bank just as the last rays of the setting sun vanished.

Tate stared at the redheaded faery and muttered, "That was too close."

"Why don't they follow us?" Rune asked.

"There are a few rules by which they actually abide," Tate said. "They will only attack those inside their borders after nightfall. Otherwise, they risk the wrath of the council."

On the fae side of the river, glowing eyes appeared one after the other—on the ground, in trees, inside bushes. The redheaded faery raised one hand and made a threatening gesture Grey had never seen before, then disappeared back into the shadows.

REVELATIONS

They pushed on, obediently following Tate through the trees. The mud from the river had dried to a thick shell on their feet and legs. In the extra folds of Grey's jeans, it had hardened to something that resembled cement, restricting his movements. Rune wasn't faring much better. Tate, on the other hand, was walking normally, and Grey couldn't figure out how he was doing it.

The air was filled with a heady, musk-like scent, rich with decomposing plant matter. He'd frequently wondered during his research how different the world had looked through the eras of time before the rise of machines and technology. Now he felt like he knew the answer.

With the sun down, the forest was filled with shadows and strange noises, but this darkness was natural—the light from the stars and moon penetrated it. The branches no longer reached for him, and the overall feeling of evil that had permeated everything in the black forest was gone.

Grey peeked up through the branches whenever he found a gap.

Without artificial light to dilute the natural brilliance above, the beauty of the night sky was a show he'd only read about.

When he came across a hole in the canopy, Grey pointed. "Rune, look."

The light shone through in a pillar, illuminating a perfect circle on the ground.

She offered her first real smile since crossing over. "It's beautiful."

Tate finally slowed to a stop as they came into a clearing that had obviously been used as a campsite before. A hollowed-out fire ring was surrounded by several fallen logs for seating.

"There are a few hot springs that way. You two get cleaned up, and I'll get a fire started."

Rune warily looked to where Tate had pointed. "There aren't any strange things out there, right?"

"Strange is in the eye of the beholder." Tate stomped his feet, dislodging a sheet of dried mud from his legs that smashed to pieces when it hit the ground. "You'll be safe, if that's what you're asking."

Maybe it was the way Rune had wrapped her arms around herself, or the violent shiver that ran through her whole body, or the fear in her eyes. Whatever it was, Grey was struck with how *small* she looked.

"Come on." He offered a smile that he hoped was reassuring and led the way.

As they walked, Grey had to grip his waistband to keep the weight of the mud from pulling his pants down around his ankles. He bought clothes so big that his belt already struggled to keep them up—without the extra pounds.

He shouldered and pushed branches out of the way, holding them long enough that they didn't slap Rune in the face.

"So," she said. "Tate's blue."

He burst out laughing. "Yeah, I noticed."

"Do you think that's normal over here?"

"Probably. Most likely it's just different skin pigmentation. We have variations on our side too," he felt the need to point out. "Just not . . . blue." Grey almost tripped over a partially obscured fallen branch. "Watch your step."

"You still haven't explained how you know him."

Grey hesitated, but he couldn't see sense in keeping the story to himself any longer. "I was attacked on my way home from the library." A lump formed in his throat. Somehow he'd thought it would be easier to tell this story, given the circumstances.

"Attacked by who?" Rune asked. "Tate?"

"What? No. The same things that came after us tonight. The goblins, at least, not the werewolves by the gate—I don't think I would've survived them long enough for Tate to show up. He appeared out of nowhere, swords flying—a lot like tonight. Without Tate . . . I'd be dead."

"How long ago was that?"

"Six years."

"Wait, *six* years . . . Are you sure?"

"I'm pretty sure," he said with thick sarcasm. When met with nothing but silence, Grey glanced back.

Rune's eyes were cast down, her brows pulled together as she worked to puzzle something out.

"What?" he asked.

She still didn't respond.

Distracted, Grey's grip loosened, and his pants slipped over his hipbone. He hurriedly let go of the branch to grab them.

"Ow!" Rune yelped.

"Sorry!"

She scowled and rubbed at a bright-red welt across her cheek. "How about I take the lead since you're busy trying to keep those pants up?" Grey blushed as she shouldered past him. "How did you manage to hold off those goblins until Tate arrived?"

Grey snorted. "I didn't hold them off. I was thirteen. It was . . ." He nearly said *the most horrible moment of his life*, but that would be a lie. ". . . terrifying. I thought I was going to die."

He stepped on a thick branch, and it snapped. His heart jumped, and Rune gave a little gasp, whirling. Seeing the stick under his foot, she glared.

"Whoops."

She exhaled tightly through her teeth and turned to push forward, her hair flipping hard to the back. "But you'd never seen Tate before that?"

"No." Grey ducked under the spiky reach of an overgrown bush. "You remember how fast he moved today. He seemed even faster then." The mental image of blood on the white trim of his sneakers flashed in front of him. "After Tate killed the goblins, he gave me the orb, said to always keep it with me, and promised that someday he'd be back."

"So you knew about all of this." She motioned to their surroundings.

"Not . . . exactly."

Rune scoffed under her breath. Next thing he knew, a branch came flying for his face. He ducked.

"Oops."

The *oops* sounded less than genuine.

Grey straightened, scowling at Rune's back. "I think Tate meant to explain it to me—at least, he looked like he was about to say something—but there was a scream, and he ran off." That memory still stung a bit. He'd felt abandoned, left in an alley full of blood, dead alien bodies, questions, and his own personal grief. "That was the last time I saw him."

"Where were you when it happened?"

He cleared his throat, trying to lighten his tone to something approximating nonchalance. "The alley near Elm and Pine. I'm sure you know it." It wasn't even a block from Rune's house.

There was a stutter in her step. "Yeah . . . I know it. The scream you heard—was it human? Like from a little boy, maybe?"

Grey thought. "Maybe. It was a long time ago."

"And it was right after that when you started wearing that trench coat of yours, wasn't it?"

"Lay off the coat! I like it." *At least, I did.* He'd worn it for so many years that the feel of air and leaves brushing against his skin was foreign and uncomfortable.

They came around a bend, and Rune jerked to a stop so fast he ran into her back. "Whoa."

Stretched out in front them was something from a dream.

Hot springs dotted the ground, nestled in smooth stone hollows that ranged in size from bathtub to swimming pool. Wisps of steam rose from each basin, slipping through the air and melding together to cover the area with a glistening fog. Within the mist, small purple lights appeared and disappeared like brilliant fireflies, painting everything in a pinkish hue.

Rune's shoulders relaxed, and she let out a deep sigh of pure wonder, walking from one pool to the next. She peeked around a bend where a piece of smooth gray stone taller than she was poked out from the trees. "There are more over here. I'm going to bathe where I can have a little privacy."

Grey didn't love that idea, and she must've seen the worry on his face.

"I'm filthy, Grey. I'm taking a bath." She cocked an eyebrow. "In *private*."

This world obviously held more dangers than the one they'd left, but he didn't see how he could successfully argue that they should bathe together for safety. "Just . . . be careful."

She turned, a familiar coy look on her face through the mist. "If I scream, come running." But that look quickly fell away. "No, really. Come if I scream."

He laughed. "OK."

Looking reassured, she disappeared around the corner.

The mist clung to Grey as he walked, wetting his skin and eyelashes with a fine dew. He sat down on the edge of a pool. The markings on his arms swirled with the same pink and purple as the lights above, and he couldn't help but smile at the irony. In an instant he'd gone from refusing to wear color to being a walking kaleidoscope. The new tattoo-like patterns were incredible, and he felt stronger just looking at them.

No way could he get out of these clothes as caked as they were, so he slid into the water fully dressed, boots and all. He yanked at the gritty laces through the water, then dumped the muddy sludge out of his boots and placed them on the side of the pool. He washed out his shirt and jeans, rinsing them thoroughly before laying them flat on the stones.

The water was now as brown as the river they'd walked through, so he left it for a different pool.

Picking up one leg, he examined the wicked bruises where the fae had pinched and grabbed. But there were fewer than he'd expected, and—even stranger—they seemed to be fading before his eyes. Maybe it was the mist. Squinting, he looked closer. They were definitely lighter than they'd been a moment before.

That was . . . interesting.

From the waist down, the heat of the water started to soothe the aches from the day. He lowered in, leaning his head back on the smooth stone edge to watch the lights dance. The logical side of his brain niggled, desperately sending reminders of what he'd seen in the last twenty-four hours, prompting the remembrance that he should be terrified. But he wasn't. He was happy, giddy even. The truth was . . . he felt like he'd finally come home.

❦❦❦

As soon as she was around the corner, Rune's shoulders sagged with exhaustion. She didn't know how many hours it had been since she'd slept, but it felt like weeks. Adding to the fatigue, her feelings were currently tangled up in a horribly intertwined ball of contradictions.

She wanted to believe this was all just a nightmare—they were still at the dorms, and Ryker had not been kidnapped by some hideous creatures—but she couldn't. Everything was too real and fully fleshed out—sights, smells, sounds—including the nasty, jagged piece of fingernail left by a malicious fae. She jerked it from her jeans and flicked the yellowed nail to the side. *Disgusting.*

The blissful heat of the pool dissipated her thoughts the moment she stepped in.

Wrapped in a brief moment of contentment, she leaned back against the edge and stretched out. The lights flitted and danced through the mist, causing the markings on her arms to flare purple and pink. She pulled one arm out of the water and slowly turned it over, eying the strange patterns that danced across her skin.

Rune had always found the concept of tattoos ridiculous. These were pretty enough, a gently vining pattern . . . but still. She just couldn't imagine liking something enough to keep it her entire life. She didn't even like her clothes a few months after she'd bought them. She always wanted something new and different.

Dunking under the water, she scrubbed her face and hair before coming up. The itch that had plagued her entire life was numbed to as dull a roar as she could remember—peace was a blessing long forgotten. It was exciting and a relief. She'd been exhausted from fighting so hard just to feel . . . normal.

Her inner disciplinarian snapped a ruler across the back of her knuckles. No! This was all wrong. Neither excitement *nor* relief should be in her emotional repertoire right now. Although she'd *finally* done what should've been done years ago—walked away from her brother's needs to worry about her own—she was unable to enjoy the new liberation, nagged instead with the knowledge that, in the end, their mother had been right: she hadn't been there when Ryker needed her.

She'd jumped through that gate willingly enough, ready to race to the rescue like a delusional hero in an action film, virtual guns blazing. But now that she was here, it was terrifying. Her brother was on this side, with those things, and instead of wanting to find him, deep down a scared little girl pounded at the walls, wanting to run screaming back through that gate as fast as she'd arrived. What kind of heartless monster was she?

But would Ryker have come for you?

The question was whispered and nasty, yet she had no one to blame for the cruelty of it but herself. The uncertainty stung because she really didn't know. Maybe? But it didn't matter. She shouldn't have left him. There were things she could've done—insisted Tate go back for him, asked Grey for help, grabbed one of the swords in Grey's room, yelled a warning, *something.*

She sank farther down in the pool. The water slid over her lips and lapped just beneath the bottom of her nose. Remorse and shame, no matter how illogical, fed on empty minds and quiet hands—the longer she sat there, the worse she felt. The guilt sank down like a physical presence, and its unrelenting pressure spurred an early exit from her temporary sanctuary.

Without dry clothes to change into, she wrung out her shirt and pants, then stepped out onto a rock to wiggle back into them. The night air was chilly, and being wet from head to toe rapidly dropped her temperature. Shivering, Rune shoved back the mass of tangled brown hair that hung in her face and began combing through it with her fingers. Anxious to get to a campfire and dry off, she braided her hair while walking, turning her thoughts to the story Grey had told about the time he'd met Tate. But once around the corner, all thoughts vanished, and she pulled up short.

Grey stood shirtless in the middle of the pool, his back to her with his fingers clasped behind his head, staring up at the dancing lights. His tattoos—tribal and powerful—started somewhere below the waterline and flowed up his spine. They flared over his shoulders and down his arms, flickering deep pink and rich purple like dying embers.

But what had stopped her in her tracks was not his markings, but him. Without his baggy clothes, she could see what had been hidden underneath. He'd been working out for years—that was clear. His back muscles were perfectly toned, his shoulders tapering down to his waist like an inverted triangle. There was no part of his body he'd neglected. As an athlete herself, she knew exactly what kind of dedication went into that physique.

"What the *hell?*" The words were out of her mouth before she could stop them.

Startled, he turned around, and she nearly fell over. The back was nice—the front was better.

"Rune!" He looked around like he wanted to duck beneath the water but instead awkwardly folded his arms.

Cheeks flaring, she tried to form sentences, but all that came out was an incoherent string of babble. "What . . . I mean, why . . . I . . . you—" She snapped her mouth shut and looked at him with utter perplexity.

He was gorgeous, especially with his wet hair pushed off his face. She'd seen the hints of his facial structure, but only when looking through and around the hair he always hid behind. She'd never suspected how truly handsome he was. Now she could see what she'd never noticed before—a strong jaw, deep-set eyes, and chiseled cheekbones.

"I don't understand," she managed to say.

He looked away from her and shrugged.

The only explanation that made sense came tumbling out. "Did the water do something to you? Have you seen yourself?"

Grey scowled, his fists clenched at his sides. "I don't look any different than I did an hour ago."

She opened her mouth to apologize, but he interrupted.

"Are you just going to stand there? I need to get my clothes." He jerked his head toward the shirt and pants on the side of the pool.

"Of course, sorry." Her eyes wandered down his abs to the water at his waist. Blinking, she shook her head and hurried toward Tate and the campfire.

Rune pushed at the encroaching branches, stumbling as her mind raced. She was stuck in a strange place, surrounded by creatures that weren't supposed to exist and a man who had *let* her brother be taken. The only person she knew was Grey—he'd offered familiarity and a little security. But with every step and every question, she realized she didn't know him at all—not even a little bit.

HISTORY PAST

Grey pulled his pants on and cinched the belt as tight as it would go. It promptly slipped over the band and dug into his stomach. It was insanely uncomfortable but the only thing that would hold up his soaking-wet jeans. To make matters worse, the shirt didn't billow around him like it usually did, hiding his body, but instead stuck tightly to his skin.

The heat of Rune's gaze still burned, the way those brown eyes had roved over him. Part of him had liked it. A lot. But the other part had flared in anger. He'd always wanted her to look at him like he was something other than a science project, but no matter how much they'd talked, she'd never looked at him like *that*.

He wasn't any different than an hour ago, inside or out.

Grey stomped through the thick undergrowth on the way back, taking his frustration out on every bush and flower. He roughly pushed a branch aside to see a crackling campfire with two small, piglike things roasting on a spit. They were only slightly larger than guinea pigs, with green skin, and all in all, they looked rather unappetizing. Even still, his stomach growled.

Rune sat opposite the flames, facing him. The shadows from the fire danced across her face, painting on a jagged mask. She wouldn't look at him. She'd locked her eyes on the crackling logs, lips set in a tight, thin line.

Grey was a little confused. If anyone had a right to be angry, it was him. Sitting across from her, he scooted closer to the fire, hoping to dry out his clothes. "Where's Tate?"

"Looking for more food." She reached out and gave the roasting sticks a turn, curling up her nose at the two pigs. "He said to go ahead and eat these if they were finished before he got back, but they keep staring at me." Rune looked up, and her rich brown eyes hesitated around his midriff.

Grey glanced down. The wet T-shirt had defined everything. He jerked at the extra fabric, pulling it away while arching his shoulders forward to further camouflage his abs. She frowned in confusion.

Desperate to talk about anything other than the question Grey knew she was dying to ask, he cleared his throat. "So, how are you doing?"

"I'm sitting on the outskirts of a black faery forest that's filled with little demons. I'm great. Thank you for asking."

The sarcasm bit, and Grey had the urge to pull his hair down and hide the way he always did. But it was still slicked back and useless. "Sorry."

"No, I'm sorry." She sighed and dropped her head into her hands. "I feel like I'm losing my mind." She finally looked straight into his eyes.

For a moment, he felt like she was really seeing him—not his interests or his body, but him.

"Everything that's happened is unbelievable and completely insane. I should be freaking out right now . . . but I'm not." She gave a bitter laugh. "Which is bothering me."

"Why?"

"Why is it bothering me?"

"No, why aren't you freaking out?"

She held her hands out to the fire, turning them one way and then the other. "You know, my whole life I've had this crazy draw to everything paranormal. I tried to write it off—told myself that lots of kids were into that kind of thing and that I wasn't weird. But I was different. I had this . . . It was like an itch, one I couldn't scratch, an irritation that was always there no matter what I did. Nobody understood. The only time I didn't feel like I was going to shimmy out of my own skin was when . . ." She bit her lip. "When I was talking to you."

Grey's chest constricted. *Shimmy out of my own skin.* That was exactly how he'd felt. His fascination with all things paranormal and fantasy had been like a bad addiction, one that made him feel whole only when he was immersed in it.

His first experience with Tate had been terrifying, but his fear had soon been overshadowed by validation. He wasn't crazy. Between the hell of his home life and the fact that he felt uncomfortable pretty much anywhere, the only peace he'd found was in studying the supernatural. Hell, it didn't even have to be something as real as translating Latin documents—cheesy vampire movies would scratch the itch. He swallowed. "You're trying to tell me that you felt the same way I did?"

"I tried to talk to you about it so many times, but I didn't know how to explain. I didn't want you to think I was a freak."

"You didn't want *me* to think *you* were a freak." He snorted. "There's irony for you."

"Grey, I'm serious!"

So was he.

"That's why you asked me what I felt—in the library."

"Yes. You know, we're a lot alike. I was just better at hiding it than you."

There were too many things he hid. He couldn't find the need to disguise the one thing that made him feel whole. He uttered the most honest declaration he'd ever shared with her: "I didn't want to hide it." But it was so far under his breath, it went unnoticed.

Rune stared at the fire, her jaw chewing on her next words before she spat them out. "I think Ryker felt it too."

Grey was not prepared for that. It sucker punched him in the gut, and his hands curled into fists. His throat constricted so hard it burned. He honestly thought he couldn't hate Ryker any more than he already did. But if this was true—if Ryker and Rune had truly felt as he did . . .

Rune must have known exactly what he was thinking—it couldn't have been that hard to decipher the look on his face.

"I think that's why he was so horrible to you," she whispered, not meeting his eye. "That scream you heard all those years ago, I'm positive it was Ryker. We were playing hide-and-seek, and I heard him scream. I'll never forget that sound—no kid should ever have to scream like that. So much terror." She stared into the flames. "I was in our backyard. I tried to get to him, but the gate was stuck. I couldn't get it open. I pulled and yanked and . . . he just kept screaming over and over again.

"By the time I finally found him, he was . . . I don't know. Something had changed. Ryker was never the same after that. I asked him a hundred times what had happened, but he wouldn't say. It was the next day that he started acting so strangely toward you. You showed up in that trench coat, and he looked at you . . . like he wanted to kill you. I'd never seen so much hatred in his eyes before." She looked up, sadness now dripping from her features, pulling everything down. "I couldn't understand why he despised you so much, but now I think I do. Tate was at my house that night, and you and your trench coat were a constant reminder."

Grey's blood pressure had been building since she'd started her story, and he bit off a snide response. "You think?"

Tate melted silently from the shadows, holding three more of the miniature green pigs by the tails, and Rune jumped halfway off the log. "You scared me!"

"It's a lesson you could learn. I could hear you both a hundred feet out." He plopped down the fresh kill and shrugged out of his weapon-laden, dripping-wet trench. The mud was gone, but it looked like he'd chosen to leap into a pool of water fully dressed. "Planning on eating these before they're burnt?" He pulled the cooked pigs off the fire and handed one skewer to each of them.

Grey was salivating. He ignored the pig's appearance and carefully blew on the outside, trying to be patient and not burn himself. The meat was amazing, and he sighed with delight as the juices ran down his chin. It was even better than ham, which he hadn't thought possible—richer and with a perfect balance of salty and sweet.

He was halfway through before he noticed that Rune had lain her dinner to the side without taking a bite.

Tate finished gutting the rest and carefully placed them over the fire.

Once he was done, Rune cleared her throat. "I've waited. Can we talk now?"

"Yes." Tate wiped the blade off on his pants and leaned back to slip it into a belt sheath. "Did you have specific questions, or should I just explain?"

Grey licked the grease from his fingers. "Just explain." He couldn't think of a single thing he *didn't* have a question about.

"All of it," Rune added.

"All of it would take a month." Tate unlaced his boots and peeled off wet socks.

The markings on Grey's arm changed again. Somewhere on the return trip from the pools, they'd gone solid black, but now they were flickering the same pinks and purples they'd been while bathing. He paused with food halfway to his mouth. "Why does this keep happening?"

Tate glanced up from the blade he was cleaning. "Because," he drawled, visually sweeping every tree and bush that surrounded them with narrowed eyes, "those are a warning system. Are they the same colors you noticed at the hot springs?"

"Yes."

"Then I would guess your current colors indicate that something of the fae species is getting very close."

"You *guess*?" Rune said.

Tate was only half listening, still scanning their surroundings. "It's been a long time since we've had Venators."

Grey looked at his arms with increased interest. He'd been so busy trying not to die, he hadn't noticed that the color changing was anything other than random.

Tate reached into his pocket and pulled out another vial.

Rune leaned forward. "Is that what you used to get us through the gate?"

"No. And it didn't get us through the gate. The gate opened because we belong on this side. That particular potion redirected anyone behind us to exit through a different gate. It probably saved our lives. This," he raised the vial and shook the light pink potion inside, "is easier to brew, I'm told." He threw it on the ground near the fire, and a misty cloud rose up.

It stopped a foot above their heads and then spread out like a mushroom, raining down around the edges until it surrounded them in a clear dome. Once the mist met the ground, it hardened into a glass-like substance.

Rune gently touched it. "What is this?"

"In this world, you never know where eyes and ears might be hiding. You think we're alone, but there are creatures of every shape and size, some with abilities you've never even thought of. Judging by your markings, we definitely aren't alone. And you both, of all people, must be extraordinarily careful with what you say and where." He motioned around. "This will offer us a limited time in which we can have the privacy necessary to have this conversation.

"To answer the most basic question, there have always been two separate planes in this world. We've existed side by side, with time passing nearly identically from the beginning. But our two planes are vastly different in makeup and species, and as we go, you will discover many inconsistencies. Some things will appear similar to what you're used to, but they aren't. Just as werewolves and other creatures exist only here, in the beginning the Venator bloodlines existed only on earth."

"You keep using that word, 'Venator.' What is it?" Rune asked.

"You. We discovered your kind a few hundred years ago. This world was on the brink of a war. Many tribes fled through the portals to the other side, seeking sanctuary. Others went in search of new territories and people to conquer. It went well at first. They all found what they were looking for: escape or prey. As a result, more from this side made the exodus. And—"

"These tribes came to our side?" Rune interrupted. "Why haven't I ever seen them?"

"There are very few left, and they operate with an attitude of discretion. But I'm sure you've heard of them."

"All the stories are true, then," Grey said. "Dracula, Van Helsing, the old fairy tales . . ."

"Most are true, yes. But eventually word began to trickle back that a group of humans had begun to hunt us successfully—the Venators. Van Helsing was one, actually. Up to that point, humans had been viewed as a weak species. The fact that they were able to not only fight us but win was remarkable.

"Those fighting for peace on my side realized the potential of such a species and went searching. They hoped these new skills would prove strong enough to provide order, and the Venators did. They had a weakness, however, that was easy to exploit. A Venator changing to a vampire, for example, was not something anyone— besides the vampires—wanted. So their genetic makeup was altered, enhancing the abilities they already had and providing immunity to many dangers this world posed to humans."

"You modified their genes!" Rune burst out.

"Yes. And as you are direct descendants, the traits were passed down to you.

Rune frowned. "Then why weren't we born on this side?"

Tate raised one eyebrow. "Patience. If you want the whole story, we go in order." He took a moment to turn the roasting pigs. "The Venators were paid handsomely for their services, and they became the law, the equivalent of your justice system. They were the reigning judges, juries, and executioners for a very long portion of our history. At that time, the door between worlds stood open, and the Venators could pass back and forth with ease, performing their services like any other job. Many of their families had no idea what they actually did."

Grey struggled to get a mental picture of that. Mother packing a lunch in a pail with a cloth over the top as the husband went into the woods for a day of hunting . . . Only, he crossed to an alternate dimension and hunted werewolves, returning in the evening to kiss the kids good night.

Tate leaned forward, resting his arms on his knees as if the weight of the world pressed down on him. "But then it went horribly wrong. One of the Venators decided this world was too corrupt and contained too much danger for your side. The system we'd worked so hard to create crumbled. He decided there was only one way to grant your side the safety they deserved—the extermination of our kind. He gathered an elite group of generals, who rallied troops and converted many to the cause."

"They just started killing people?" Grey asked. "For no reason?"

"Millions. It was the greatest slaughter in our history." His eyes were haunted. "This world has seen horrors your side can only dream of. They all pale in comparison to the actions of the Venators."

There was silence, broken only by the crackling of the fire.

"How were they stopped?" Rune asked.

"The council concocted an elaborate ruse, years in the making. Suffice it to say, we managed to get most of the Venators on the other side, and then a witch sealed the doors between our two worlds."

"Most, but not all," Grey said.

Tate's face seemed to tighten, but it was hard to tell in the dark, especially with the shadows that moved over his face like water. Grey wasn't sure if he'd imagined it.

"No, not all of them. The remaining Venators were hunted with a vengeance. Some went into hiding, but Venators age at nearly the same rate as humans. All are long dead."

The glass dome cracked, and a large fracture snaked its way from one side to the other. Tate eyed it. "Running out of time."

Grey didn't understand. "If it was so bad last time, why would you bring us back?"

"That is the question, isn't it?" Tate pulled a pig from the fire and blew on it for a bit before biting down on it. He talked around the mouthful. "I'm willing to give you as much information tonight as I deem safe. But if either of you choose to repeat it, not only will I explicitly deny it, but I will be forced to make sure you both disappear—permanently." Tate calmly swallowed as if he had not just issued a death threat and then scanned them both, evaluating their reactions. "Agreed?"

"Do we have a choice?" Grey asked.

"Not if you want answers."

"Fine." Grey said.

Rune was shaking, but she nodded her agreement.

"Very good. To answer your question . . . The council gave a few valid—or at least believable—reasons as to why they are risking your reintroduction into our world. The council has been unable to defeat Zio as she continues to push us toward war—the loss of life will be catastrophic. The council is hoping you will both offer something new to the battle in order to tip the scales out of Zio's favor. They are also saying that in this state of unease, they need more assistance in enforcing laws and keeping the peace for the safety of the realm."

"But you don't believe that," Rune said.

"Well," Tate answered, chewing, "I believe they will use you in those capacities, yes. But they have other goals in mind."

"Such as?" Grey prodded.

Tate leveled a very serious gaze, implying that the information worth threatening them over was about to come out. "The council is corrupt to its very core. That you must understand. No matter what is said or what implications are made, the council has been constructed with betrayals, lies, underground connections, criminal activity, and more sins than I could possibly list. The land is losing faith in them. There have been several plays for power, only one of which is their main concern—Zio."

Tate pulled a second pig from the fire. "The council has been forced to take steps that it desperately resents in order to maintain a sliver of loyalty—visiting the villages, giving handouts to the poor. And, most recently, opening the council house doors to those whose grievances involve the highest crimes in the land: murder and kidnapping. These personal audiences are nothing more than show, feigning concern for those citizens affected most heavily by creatures stronger than them. The council abhors lowering themselves to the level of the peasants and those they deem 'helpless.' In the past, actions such as these would never have been considered. That's where you come in."

Tate used the skewered pig to point at Rune and then Grey before ripping a chunk off with his teeth. "I believe the council, with a show of power, hopes to regain the unquestioned loyalty they once had. Nothing else will strike as much fear into the hearts of their enemies as the return of the Venators—the greatest blight this land has ever seen. The council will bribe you with wealth and eventually blind you with it, turning you away from any moral compass you ever possessed until they transform you into the tools they so desperately hope to wield. They will then use you to squash those who challenge their position."

"And you brought us here to hand us over to that?" Grey exclaimed.

"No. That cannot be allowed to happen under any circumstances."

More cracks snapped across the surface overhead.

Rune peered suspiciously at Tate. "Wouldn't it have been better to just leave us on our side, then? Far away from all of this?"

"Yes. But the council is nearly untouchable, and if they wanted Venators, they would've found a way to get them, with or without my help."

"That doesn't make any sense," she challenged. "You don't agree, but you jump in to help?"

"I'm not helping them. Let me be very clear—the council's goals are not mine. I crossed through that portal the first time to search, not retrieve. I found a dozen Venators on several different continents, but I was looking for someone I hoped would be able to resist the corruption of the council. The Venators would be coming regardless. I was searching for two who had the potential to actually be what this world needs. I chose you."

"You 'chose' me? Am I supposed to feel special? Because I don't!" Rune raised her chin. "What if I want to go home?"

Tate shrugged, tossing the cleaned carcass over his shoulder. "You can't."

"Why not?"

"First of all, the council would never allow it. They would rather see you dead." He leaned forward, eyebrows furrowed. "If the council senses that you aren't what they're looking for or that you've betrayed them, it is entirely possible they will execute you and simply wait until they retrieve someone more suitable to their needs." Relaxing back, he continued. "Secondly, when the witch's original sealing spell faded, the wizard Arwin attempted to close the door permanently to prevent Zio from crossing over to your world. He was unable, so he cursed it instead. The door opens at random. You never know where or when it will open or for how long."

"So we wait until it opens," Rune said.

"You can't."

"I'm a very patient person. Don't tell me what I can and can't do."

Grey hid a smile, but Tate openly snorted. "Yes, clearly very patient."

Rune opened her mouth, ready to lay into Tate, when he slyly added, "Besides, what about Ryker?"

She deflated like a balloon. Not the kind that's released to whizz around the house, but the kind that slowly sinks to the floor as the helium escapes its Mylar prison.

"You don't understand," Tate said. "The door could open anywhere. You have to find it and get through before it snaps shut again. After my first visit, I intended to return within three years—once you'd aged a little more. The gate didn't open for six."

"Six years?" she whispered.

"Yes. The council was . . . angry."

A boom ripped through the air, and the dome shattered into thousands of pieces that rained around them. Grey ducked, and Rune squeaked, throwing her arms over her head.

Tate acted as if nothing had happened. "I'm surprised you're upset, Rune."

She slowly unfolded, shaking the shattered glass from her arms. "You're surprised? You take me away from my family, my friends, and my *brother*! You throw me into a world that's crawling with who knows what, act like I'm a piece of property to this . . . council, and you're surprised I'm upset?"

Grey was listening but fascinated with the bit of magic he'd just witnessed. He reached down and picked up a piece of the dome to examine it. As soon as his fingers closed, it altered to a gel that squished between his thumb and pointer. When he relaxed his grip, the gooey magic started steaming, quickly evaporating into nothing.

"The old Venators always said they felt calmer on this side," Tate told Rune. "They said time at home caused them anxiety."

Rune jerked ramrod straight, the color fading from her cheeks.

Grey sighed. "So what now? The council wants us to step in where the old Venators left off?"

Tate chuckled. "You'll need training. And some adjustments in procedure will have to be made. There used to be hundreds of Venators—now we only have two."

A strange howl went up, joined by more and more until it morphed from one lonely call to a multitude of frenzied barks and yips. Tate's hand moved to his belt of weapons. "Werewolves."

Grey looked to his arms. They were still shining pink and purple. "Do our markings alert us to werewolves?"

Tate nodded in the affirmative.

"How close do they have to get?"

"I'm not entirely sure."

"Of course not." Rune bolted to her feet and began to pace, three steps in one direction, three steps in the other. After several passes, she took a deep breath and planted her feet, her game face on. "OK, if you're telling the truth about us being stuck here, I want to know what to expect. So far we've encountered faeries, werewolves, and goblins. What else?"

The howls slowly went quiet, and Tate relaxed. He leaned back on his elbows with a lopsided grin. "Anything and everything you've ever read about probably exists here. It's all real."

Grey found a place to sleep that was just below a break in the canopy but near enough the fire to enjoy the warmth. He lay with his arms behind his head, staring up at the mess of glinting stars. An abstract masterpiece.

Rune's voice broke the magic. "What do you think is going to happen when someone finds those bodies in your room?"

"After they get done freaking out? I don't know. Some government agency will probably swoop in and shut down the entire campus."

Rune shook her head. "No, that's not what I meant. Before we left, Tate started to say that we needed to dispose of the bodies, but there wasn't time. Why would Tate care if our government is confused? What are they going to do? Decide to find a portal to an alternate dimension? Invade? No way. Tate knew that none of us were coming back to that room. Which makes *me* wonder why he was so concerned about eliminating the evidence?"

The way she asked it was less of a question and more of a push—hoping Grey would vocalize the answer she'd already arrived at. "You obviously have it all figured out. Why don't you just tell me what you think?"

"Tate said being a Venator is genetic."

"So?"

"Sooo." She propped up on her elbow. "Contact with the supernatural was what turned these markings on, Grey. What if one of our parents is shown the bodies, or something else crazy, and suddenly they have glowing tattoos? Or—" She waved one hand in a small circle, searching for a new scenario. "What if someone at the police station just happens to have Venator blood? What then?"

He hadn't thought about that. "I . . . I don't know."

Rune huffed and dropped back flat, staring up.

"Maybe if they're dead, it won't—"

"It doesn't matter. Good night, Grey."

"Uh . . . good night." Suffering from emotional whiplash, he found himself just staring at her in confusion. He'd known Rune forever, and she'd never been as short with him as she'd been since crossing. He couldn't help feeling like a puppy who'd just been kicked. Nursing his hurt feelings, he closed his eyes and tried to empty his mind. He was almost asleep when Rune's voice broke the silence again.

"Grey?"

"Yeah?"

"I can't stop thinking. About Ryker and my parents and the fact that I'm in an alternate dimension. My mind knows I'm worried on an intellectual level, but . . ."

He opened his eyes. She was lying on her side again, staring into the glistening embers and blinking back tears.

"Tate's right," she finished. "All I feel is calm."

"Why is that such a bad thing?"

"Because I shouldn't be!" Her jaw clenched as if she could stem the tide of worries from flowing out. "Calm is the *last* thing I should be. I felt calm before we left, too—when I chose to go with you instead of checking on Ryker. I've always trusted my gut, but . . ." She slowly shook her head. The firelight reflected back the haunted look in her eyes. "I don't know what I'm feeling anymore."

"Rune," he said gently, wanting to reach out to her. "It wasn't your fault."

She scoffed. "It doesn't really matter, does it? We'll never know what would've happened if I'd made different choices. My brother is here, my parents are devastated, and instead of looking for Ryker or trying to get home, we're headed to meet . . ." She shivered. "The council."

She'd heeded Tate's warning about listening ears and did not expound. But her vocal intonation relayed what she couldn't say— fear, resentment, and uncertainty.

"But we'll stick together, you and me. It'll be OK. We're strong, Rune."

"Strong." She repeated the word, then exhaled with a scoff of disbelief. "You don't even know me."

KIT

Grey woke to someone shaking him. Grunting, he opened his eyes. Tate's dark face filled his vision.

"Where's Rune?"

It took a moment to process what Tate was asking, but when it registered, Grey sat straight up, slamming his head into Tate's. "Ow!" Grey scrambled to his feet, his palm against his throbbing forehead. "She's gone?"

"Didn't she tell you where she was going?"

"No, no—nothing. You don't think . . ." He spun in a circle, looking through the trees. "Rune!" he shouted.

Tate hissed and grabbed him from behind, wrapping a massive hand across his mouth. "I could've done that, you idiot!"

A rustling came from somewhere in front of them, followed by a snapping branch. Tate released Grey and slowly pulled a sword from the sheath at his hip. His eyes were intent on the source of the sound, and he bent his knees slightly, ready for battle. The sun glinted off the raised white markings on his neck.

Rune stepped into the clearing and then stumbled back at the sight of the sword in her face. She raised her hands. "Whoa! It's just me."

Tate huffed in aggravation. "Where were you?" He slammed the blade back into its sheath.

"Washing my face." Her hair, braided last night, now hung in neat waves.

"At the hot springs?"

She looked at him as if he'd lost his mind somewhere in the night. "You said it was safe."

Tate gripped his bald blue head as if it might explode. "No, I said it was safe last night. That does *not* mean it's safe this morning." Kicking dirt over the ring that had been their fire, he jerked his head. "Come on, let's go." And just like yesterday, he strode ahead without waiting to see if they would follow. Which . . . really, where else would they go?

Rune looked to Grey, her mouth partway open. "What was that all about?"

"You scared him, and me. Next time you feel like wandering off, how about telling me where you're going?"

"I didn't want to wake you. I was trying to be nice."

"Well, wake me. OK?" He was snapping at her. But he didn't care—his heart was still pounding.

"OK." Hurt edged her words. "Sorry."

"It's fine," he mumbled. Ducking under a branch, he followed after Tate.

The sun lit the forest, and for a moment Grey forgot they weren't at home. Everything looked nearly the same. Then he spotted some glowing blue mushrooms with iridescent spots growing up the side of a trunk, and the illusion was shattered.

They hadn't walked long before they crested a hill that over-looked a town. Grey squinted and resisted the urge to rub his eyes. It was like they'd traveled back in time and come upon a village somewhere in medieval Germany. The buildings were one to four stories high and covered in white-cream stucco with brown timber framing.

Tate turned to face them. His eyes rested on their flickering tattoos. "We can't go any farther until I make you both presentable."

Rune's hands went to her hips. "I don't look *that* bad."

"The Venators have a reputation to uphold. Right now you both look weak and young. Not to mention strangely dressed. Stay here. I'll be back." Tate sprinted down the hill, looking far too graceful for a man his size.

"Dressed strangely." Rune rolled her eyes and dropped onto the tall grass with a huff. "He should look in a mirror sometime."

With nothing to add, Grey stood awkwardly. He crossed his arms, then shoved his hands in his pockets. He should apologize. He shouldn't have snapped at her like that. But why did she—?

"So, Grey. Looks like we have some time. When are we going to talk about you?"

He flinched. "Uh, what about me?"

"Are you going to pretend I didn't see anything last night?"

"Huh?"

"Yeah, you know—the fact that you probably could've kicked my brother's ass, and instead you always just sat there and took his crap. Oh, and you don't play a single sport, I've never seen you at the gym, and somehow you look like," she motioned to him, "*that*."

"You're not letting this go, are you?"

"No way."

Resigning himself to the conversation, he sat down a couple feet away. She pursed her lips in annoyance. The intentional distance hadn't gone unnoticed.

"You're right. I could've taught Ryker a lesson."

With his strength, speed, and martial arts training, he could've kicked his ass eight ways to Sunday.

"So why didn't you?"

"And bring the wrath of the whole school down on me?" He raised his arms in the air. "All hail Ryker Jenkins, lord of football." He snorted. "Yeah, I could've, and I would've paid for it in spades."

No way he could've fought off an attack from Ryker's football posse without revealing some of his gifts. However, that hadn't been the only thing holding him back. He couldn't have stood the look on Rune's face if he'd done to her brother what he'd wanted to.

"Hmm," she grunted. "Maybe."

"Not maybe. The football team would've made sure I ended up in the hospital."

"And what about the other question? When did you start looking like that?"

Grey scrubbed his fingers through his hair. "I used my step-dad's gym in our garage, all right? I also run a few miles a day and train at a local martial arts school after hours."

"That kind of physique doesn't come easily. We're talking a lot of time."

"So?"

"So! You work hard, and you hide it under baggy clothes like you're ashamed of the way you look."

Mercifully, Tate was coming back up the hill with someone who was obviously not human, saving Grey from any more questions.

The woman was fewer than five feet tall, with green skin and bright-red hair. Her dress was minimal at best: a tiny blue thing that was cut out in multiple spots and covered only the basics.

Rune and Grey got to their feet as the woman's eyes ran over them both with curiosity. "So, these are your little Venators?"

Tate pointed. "This is Rune and Grey."

"Kit." She inclined her head in greeting. "I gotta give it to you, Tate. I was convinced they were just a myth."

"Can you help us or not? We're on a schedule."

"Don't ask stupid questions. Anything can be done for a price." She held out her hand, and Tate plopped in a gold coin. She peered at it as if it were an insect, seemingly unhappy with what she saw. Finally, she clenched her fist, and the coin disappeared. "I see my work is highly valued amongst the council."

The sarcasm could've been sliced and served for lunch. Tate seemed oblivious to it.

"Very well," Kit said, a dangerous glint in her eye. "Let's get on with it."

"How is she going to help us?" Rune asked.

One red eyebrow shot to the sky. "She's annoying me, Tate. That's going to cost you."

Tate growled under his breath and put another gold coin in Kit's outstretched hand.

"Annoying you! I didn't do anything."

Kit leveled her gaze at Rune, lips pulled into a tight smirk. She held out her green hand a third time.

Tate shot Rune a clear *shut up* look before slapping down one more coin. "I am not paying you another. Either help us or give me my money back."

"I've been ready to help from the beginning." She batted her eyes up at Tate. "Now then, how far are we going?"

"The inn."

Kit extended her hands and began weaving green magic from her fingertips. Once she held a substantial ball of magic in front of her, she whispered to it. The orb changed from shimmering green to teal. She blew, and the magic burst out, fluttering around them like the stems of a dandelion puff.

"There." Kit dusted her palms off on her legs.

Grey held out his arms, trying to figure out what she'd done, but he could see no difference.

"We look the same," Rune said.

Kit's eyebrows went up again, but Tate cut her off. "I said not one more coin." He shook his head. "Kit enchanted the pair of you to allow you to walk around unnoticed."

"Completely unnoticed, as if you were invisible . . . for the next ten minutes." Kit winked. "I'd run if I were you."

"Kit!"

"Tate, darling, you know the game. If I work for cheap," Kit smirked and shrugged her shoulders, "the work is cheap."

Tate growled something about fae as he nudged both Rune and Grey toward the village. "Go."

Kit's high-pitched laughter danced behind them as they ran. By the time they reached the village, Grey's blood was just starting to pound, and his body ached with the desire to keep going. Man, he loved that feeling.

Tate cut in front of them and slowed to a walk. "Don't touch *anyone*," he whispered over his shoulder. "They can't see you, but they'll be able to feel you."

Easier said than done.

Luckily the dirt beneath their feet had been packed so hard and flat from years of use that there wasn't any dust as they walked. Grey and Rune stayed tight behind Tate as they threaded through the village, allowing Tate's hulking figure and sullen demeanor to clear the path. Even still, a strange-looking man with vines for hair crossed right behind Tate, and Rune had to practically jump on Grey's back to avoid running into the man.

None of the villagers seemed relaxed. Regardless of age or species, everyone looked both alert and on guard. Weapons bulged beneath several tunics, but most wore them outwardly—swords and daggers strapped to backs, arms, and legs. The few who didn't appear to have any weapons walked in a way that suggested they held powers that didn't require the use of them.

The overall vibe of this place made Grey nervous.

A little boy ran in front of Tate, chasing a goat. Rune snickered quietly. The animal had three horns and two pointed little beards on the tip of its chin.

Finally, Tate pushed opened a door to a three-story home that was twice as large as the small buildings on either side. The inside matched the rustic outside. They'd stepped into a pub. Rough, hand-hewn wood tables were spread across the room, anchoring the patrons who sat there with tin mugs. A barmaid bustled about, delivering drinks and plates of food.

"You've got to be kidding me," Rune whispered. "Do they even have electricity?"

Judging by the candlesticks that dripped wax on the tables and the oil lamps that flickered on the bar, *no*.

Tate gave a subtle jerk with his head, indicating they should follow. He walked to the bar and leaned over, whispering something in the bartender's ear. The man nodded and pointed up a set of stairs.

The stairs were coated with a thick layer of dust that puffed out with each step. Anyone watching would've seen Tate's feet throwing up dirt, followed by two unexplained dusty clouds right behind him. Luckily, everyone in the room seemed to be intent on the food and drinks and nothing more.

When they reached the top, a long hallway stretched out, lined with knot-filled planks. Simple wooden doors stood on either side like old, gnarly sentinels.

Tate swung open two doors and stood back. "These are your rooms," he muttered under his breath. "I'll be sending some things up for you. Until then, don't go anywhere."

❦❦❦

Rune slowly closed the door behind her, looking over the plain room—a single bed with a handmade quilt, a dresser with a washbasin, a candleholder, and a simple wooden chair.

She moved to the window and rested her fingers on the frame, looking out at the strange world they'd stumbled into. Another three-horned, two-bearded goat meandered through the village while people in a variety of different styles of clothing and skin colors moved around. Some looked very human, others not at all. One lady carried water in two buckets set across her shoulders with a stick. Behind her, a little boy hopped along, waving his finger like a wand to direct his water bucket as it floated through the air. The boy's facial features reminded her of the woman, but his skin was light blue.

She tried not to smile, but she couldn't help it. As much as she wasn't ready to relax into this realization, it felt like she'd come home. It was hard to accept a place when she was technically a prisoner, stripped of the ability to leave. But around the bitterness seeped the comfort of being exactly where she was supposed to be. She suspected Grey felt the same—he'd never looked so happy.

The only thing still nagging her was Ryker. Was he here? Was he safe?

Suddenly, the concern morphed, shifting into an angry beast that had broken free of its containment. She'd been dumping all her authentic thoughts and feelings into a personal Pandora's box for years, depositing everything while holding tightly to the "should dos" or "should feels." But her decision to walk away that night had cracked open the box, and those emotions had spilled out in a swirling mess that she had no idea how to deal with.

Her hands balled into fists, and she clenched her teeth, squeezing her eyes shut. The craziest sequence of events had just occurred—a sequence that *could have* set her free. But no; the unknown status of her brother forced her back into the old role of protective sister—sacrificing her desires for his needs, again.

Why did they have to take him? Why couldn't she have come on her own and simply *missed* him—instead of being angry?

Her face flushed in shame.

Ryker could be dead, and all she could think about was herself.

Should've, would've, should not. She should not be angry, she should not be selfish, she should not feel good or comfortable or like she'd come home. Should not!

She pulled out the necklace from under the collar of her shirt—the white half of a yin-and-yang symbol. It had been her gift to Ryker on their fifteenth birthday. They'd both worn them ever since.

She missed him . . . the old him.

A thought tickled at her consciousness, and it was beautiful. Once she'd stepped through the gate, the itch had vanished. If Ryker were here, surely this side would offer him the same peace she'd found. What if it brought him back? The old Ryker could still be in there somewhere, and now that Rune knew what had caused the change in him all those years ago, she could think of no better place to fix it than here.

That line of thinking was comfortable and warm, and Rune gratefully allowed it to wash away all the shameful and selfish anger. She would find her brother, and when she did, she would *truly* get her twin back. Things could be like they used to be.

Below the window, a familiar green-skinned woman strutted through the square. Kit. She moved with her eyes focused on a target—a very large man with broad shoulders wearing a long black cloak, the hood pulled up to obscure his face. She walked straight to him and pushed up on her tiptoes to whisper something. The figure beneath the cloak went rigid, and his head swung to look down at the faery. Kit lowered with a smirk, one hand on her hip.

The man reached beneath his cloak, his head not moving away from her, and pulled a brown leather pouch from his waist. She hefted the bag, weighing to judge what was inside, and smiled. The pouch disappeared a moment later, the same way the coins had vanished when Tate had paid her. Kit leaned back in, whispering more.

Rune found herself with palms and nose pressed against the window, trying to decipher what was going on. Something told her it was bad. Call it a gut instinct, but—

A knock at the door pulled her attention from the window. The markings on her arm flared up again—red.

What the hell did red belong too?

With poorly veiled hesitancy, Rune called, "Come in," unsure if she actually wanted whoever it was to come in or not.

A petite girl who looked to be about her age nudged the door open with her shoulder, arms piled with clothes. She had blonde hair, red lips, and huge blue eyes. She wore snug black pants with a low-cut blue top that laced in the front to show off her figure.

"I'm Verida." She set the clothes on the chair in the room and smiled, exposing a delicate but deadly looking pair of white fangs.

Rune stared and then blurted, "You're a vampire!"

Matching the shock in Rune's voice but adding a thick layer of mockery, Verida responded, "You're a Venator!"

Unconsciously, Rune took a step back and hitched against the wall. Feeling like a fool, she cleared her throat and tried to think of something intelligent to say.

"Well, you don't look very surprised to see me." *Damn it*! That did not qualify as *intelligent*.

"That's because I knew you were coming. I work with Tate."

Rune nodded but didn't move.

Verida rolled her eyes. "You don't have to stand against the wall like that. I'm not going to bite." She leaned forward and put her hand to the side of her mouth as if revealing a great secret. "And even if I did, you're immune to vampire venom." Grinning, she straightened.

"Oh."

The vampire tilted her head, looking at Rune like a bug on a slide. "You really don't know anything, do you?"

Realizing how ridiculous she must've looked pressed up against the wall as if death were coming for her at any moment, she forced a laugh. "Not even a little."

"Honestly, I should probably be more afraid of you than you are of me. Let's try this again." She stuck her hand out. "I'm Verida."

Her arm hung in the space between them until Rune finally peeled herself away from the wall and stepped forward to shake. "Rune."

She expected Verida's hand to feel cold . . . dead, maybe? But her skin felt normal.

"Nice to meet you." She jerked her head over to the pile she'd brought in. "Tate sent up some clothes for you."

"What's wrong with what I have on?"

Verida smirked and dropped onto the edge of the bed. "Let's just say—it's not the look Venators usually go for."

"I thought we were extinct," Rune quipped, feeling more relaxed by the second. "How do you know what look we go for?"

"Vampires are extinct on your side, but you still recognized these." She pointed to her fangs.

"Valid point." Rune picked through the stack, crinkling her nose. "They're all black."

"Of course they are. Nobody's maid wants to be cleaning blood off your clothes."

Rune dropped the shirt. "Blood? Whose blood?"

"Oh, honey. Tate told you what your job was, right?"

"He did, I just . . ."

"Never equated that with blood?"

"Yeah."

Verida laughed. "Well, try them on. I'll even look the other way. Tate tells me humans can be a little shy about their bodies."

Rune had to try on three pairs of pants before she found a pair she was comfortable in.

"No," Verida said when she turned around. "Absolutely not. Too loose. Try the size down . . . maybe two."

Rune could barely button them. They hugged her legs from hip to ankle. The shirt was black as well, tight, with sleeves that barely capped the shoulder. A wide black belt with loops running around it was added, per Verida's instructions, as well as a pair of boots that laced up to mid calf. She looked down at herself. "I look like I belong in a comic book."

"A what?"

"Never mind." She looked around for a mirror but found none. "How do I look?"

"Like a Venator. A new Venator, but one nonetheless."

"What? Why do I look new?"

"Your markings. You haven't learned how to shut them off."

Rune's head snapped up. "I can make them go away?"

"No, but you can make them stop changing colors. Have Tate teach you."

"Thanks."

"For what?"

Rune looked down at her shoes. "For not biting my face off."

Verida burst out laughing. "Come on. I'm supposed to take you downstairs when you're ready."

There weren't many patrons left in the bar, but the ones there fell silent as Rune marched through behind Verida. Her markings were going berserk, rolling through colors like a kaleidoscope. Red, green, orange, blue, and every color in between.

All eyes followed Rune. Some with a nervous fascination, others with excitement, most with distaste. After hearing their past experiences with Venators, she couldn't blame them.

A burly figure in the back of the room looked out from beneath the hood of a dark cloak. His mouth was set in a thin line, and his eyes blazed. Rune met his gaze—the hatred behind the stare seemed to crawl across the room like a living thing, sending a chill through her and freezing her to the spot. Although she hadn't seen his face earlier, Rune was sure it was the same man Kit had talked to outside her window. Same cloak, same size.

He lurched to standing, towering well over six feet, and issued a low growl.

Verida vaulted over a table in an instant, landing between Rune and the man. "There's only one of you," she hissed, lowering her stance.

The man hesitated.

Verida tilted her head, eyes fierce. "You want to go a round?"

It looked ridiculous: a waif of a girl egging on a beast of a man. But apparently he didn't "want to go a round." He turned, cloak swinging. A gust of air that smelled like the back end of a horse wafted over them as the man stomped to the door and flung it open.

Verida took a few steps, as if to chase him, but then stopped, staring as the door banged shut. The room was deathly silent. "What are you looking at?" she shouted. "Drink."

Hushed mutterings buzzed over the awkward clink of forced refreshment.

Rune came up along Verida's side, feeling more comfortable next to her.

"This isn't good," Verida muttered. "Not good at all."

"I've seen him before. Kit was talking to that man right before you came up."

"What?" Verida whirled on Rune. "Are you sure?"

Rune gave a small nod. "Positive." She lowered her voice, not wanting to be overheard by the straining ears around them. "He gave her a leather sack. I don't know what was in it." But she had a pretty good idea.

Verida clenched her teeth as if holding back a lengthy stream of curse words. "Come on," she growled.

Stomping to the corner of the room with her shoulders pulled up to her ears, she led Rune to an arched doorway sparsely covered with a tattered piece of burlap. Verida pushed it to the side, but then her head snapped up and she stopped midstep, the burlap still over her palm. "Whoa."

Rune peeked over Verida's shoulder. Another "whoa" would've been in order.

Grey stood hunched in the corner of the room, his hands shoved in his pockets. His hair had been cut—short on the sides, a little longer on top. The black hair emphasized the brightness of his blue eyes. The length no longer hid his facial features but complimented a strong jawline and high cheekbones. His clothes were as tight as hers, and the thin material of his shirt put everything on display.

Heaven have mercy.

Verida ran her tongue over the tip of a fang before pursing her lips in obvious appreciation. A flare of jealously rose up, and Rune mentally berated herself. This was Grey. She wasn't jealous because Verida was looking at Grey. She couldn't be.

Tate walked in behind them. He scooted around their obstruction of the doorway, oblivious to Verida's blatant staring. Rune was beginning to notice that he was oblivious to a lot, though she was unsure whether it was intentional or not. He sat down at the table and looked Grey and Rune over. "Perfect. You both look like Venators. Grey, stop slouching. You're supposed to look intimidating. Not terrified."

Grey wearily pulled his hands from his pockets and straightened, but his eyes remained on the floor.

"Come," Tate said. "Sit."

They sat around the table just as the innkeeper slid in. Rune tried not to stare at the one large eye in the middle of his forehead. He had three bowls balanced up one arm and held a single bowl in the other hand. He dropped the first unceremoniously in front of Rune, then Grey. Tate's was no gentler of a delivery, and the bowl clunked against the wood of the table. The contents should've sloshed over the side, but the stew that had been served was so thick and gelatinous that it merely jiggled.

"Thank you," Tate said, pulling his bowl closer to him.

The innkeeper looked at the meal he still held and then at Verida, unsure of what to do.

Verida smiled, exposing her fangs. "Give it to Tate. He's a big boy, he might need it."

The innkeeper shrugged and handed it over. "My mistake. That one's on the house."

Tate grunted his gratitude and waited until the innkeeper had left the room before taking his first bite.

"Did you secure the room?" Verida asked.

Tate nodded and shoveled more food in. "Had the magic woven by a half-rate wizard Arwin recommended while they were getting changed."

Verida drummed her fingers against the table, watching Tate eat through half-slit eyes. "So, how much did you pay Kit?"

"Why?" he asked around a mouthful of food.

"Just tell me how much."

"I can't remember if we left it at three or four gold dakems."

"Mmm, I see. And what did you start with?"

"One."

Verida's lips thinned, and her nostrils flared. "Is this the first time you've dealt with her?"

"Yes," he mumbled, shoveling another bite of stew in. "And hopefully it's the last."

Verida took several deep breaths through her nose before she continued in a tightly clipped cadence. "Kit has a minimum price to keep your business *your* business. And you didn't even come close to hitting it. She found another way to get the money she felt was due—paid by a werewolf who just marched into the inn to check if the information he paid for was good. He saw Rune and is on the way to tell the pack."

Rune's head snapped up. Werewolf!

"What!" Tate shouted. His spoon clattered against the table. "How could you let that happen? Couldn't you smell him before you brought her downstairs?"

"Don't blame this on me!" She launched to standing and slapped her palms on the table. "He was wearing a heavy wool cloak that smelled like it had been rolled in a barn! This one's on you."

"Me!" Tate rose to his feet.

"You should've let me come like we'd originally planned, and this never would've happened."

"Stop it!" Rune shouted over them. "How about you both stop bickering with each other and tell us what's going on?"

Tate looked at Rune and then Grey. His body sagged in defeat. "I knew I couldn't get you to the council unseen, but there's a large list of people from whom I wanted to keep your existence a secret until after you were safe within the confines of the council house." He paused and then grudgingly added, "It's not going as planned."

"OK," Grey said. "So what do we do?"

Tate shook his head in disbelief. "You two are handling this well."

"It's called naivety." Verida dropped back to her chair. "They have no idea what just happened."

"I'd hoped to spend a day here to prepare you both before introducing you to the council," Tate said, ignoring Verida. "But we'll have to shorten our stay and leave in the morning."

"Are you sure that's best?" Verida glanced toward the arched doorway. "We could smuggle them out tonight."

"No. The pack knows they're here. If we get caught in the woods after dark, I can't guarantee their survival. And neither can you."

At the word *survival*, Rune thought she'd be sick. Grey looked like he'd been punched in the gut. So much for naivety.

"They're Venators," Verida objected.

"Rune doesn't know anything. Grey can run, but that's all I know for sure."

Rune wanted to object, because that's what she did when told she couldn't do something, but she really didn't know anything. So she kept her mouth shut.

"We'll cover as much information as we can tonight and leave first thing in the morning. At least then daylight will be on our side."

"Very well," Verida said, leaning back in her chair and folding her arms. "They're your Venators."

Ownership . . . *again.* And *snap* went her hair trigger. "I am not anyone's Venator!"

"She didn't mean it like that," Tate said distractedly. "I'm responsible for you. That's all." He motioned at the untouched bowls. "Well, eat. We have a lot to discuss, and I can't have you hungry."

INTRODUCTIONS

Grey was in no mood to eat but took a bite anyway, trying to pretend he didn't see Verida staring.

"First," Tate began, "you'll need to learn names. The council won't take kindly to you not knowing who they are."

"We've never even met them," Rune said. "How can we be expected to know their names?"

Verida chuckled. "Trust me, darling. They don't care."

"First rule of politics—always know who you're dealing with. It shows respect and a grasp of the situation." Tate pulled a small globe from his pocket and set it on the table. It looked a bit like the one he'd given Grey all those years ago, but Tate tapped it, and a holographic image popped up. A severe-looking man with dark, slicked-back hair, a thin nose, and high cheekbones shimmered above the orb. "This is Dimitri. Head of the council and a vampire. He has no tolerance for imperfections, mistakes, or any type of emotion. He has little patience for anything or anyone."

"Especially if the person or topic runs contrary to what he wants," Verida added.

"Exactly. Retrieving the Venators was his idea, I'm told, and in regards to what we discussed earlier, watch your backs." Tate hit the orb again. The next picture was of an enormous man, shoulders wider than any Grey had ever seen, with bright-red hair that hung just past his chin in waves. "This is Silen, a werewolf. He won't say much, which is what makes him dangerous. You won't know you've offended him until retaliation arrives."

"This is like the mob," Rune said.

"Worse." Tate calmly tapped the orb. A tall, thin woman of exquisite beauty appeared. Her skin was pale green, but around her eyes and cheekbones were tiny spots of an emerald green that framed her face like a masquerade mask. Pointed ears poked out from beneath a waterfall of black hair that framed violet eyes.

"An elf, right?" Grey said, trying to talk around the stew that was threatening to glue his jaw together.

Verida snorted. "You were right, Tate, this was a good idea." She looked at Grey. "Call her an elf, and you'll likely spend the rest of your days in a very different form than your current one. Probably one with a nice curly tail."

"Her name is Ambrose. She's a faery, and a powerful one at that. Do not make a deal with her. Ever. Am I understood?"

Grey and Rune both nodded.

"This is the elf, Omri." A new pictured appeared of a man. His skin was black, but not like the pigmentation they were used to. This was a cool black, like fireplace cinders. His hair was white and so lustrous you could see light reflecting around the crown of his head. The strands fell sleekly around his pointed ears.

"Are all fae green skinned and all elves black skinned?" Grey asked.

"No. It depends on the tribe."

"Then how are we supposed to tell the fae and elves apart?" Grey studied the picture. "Aside from skin color, they look the same."

"In this image, maybe," Verida said. "When you meet them in person, you'll understand. They feel different."

Rune set her spoon down and raised an eyebrow. "They *feel* different?"

"It's hard to explain," Tate said. "But you'll understand soon enough." He pointed to the image of the elf. "Omri is a helpful ally to have, unless you cross his people. Then you have an enemy for life."

The next image was so stereotypical it was almost comical.

"It's Merlin!" Rune said.

"Merlin's son, actually," Verida said.

Rune's jaw fell open. "I was kidding."

She shrugged. "I wasn't."

"This is Arwin," Tate said. The man was short and stooped with a host of wrinkles that folded his face. He also had long white hair, but it looked coarse and poorly managed.

Rune peered closer. "There aren't stars and moons on that robe, are there?"

Tate stared at her over the glowing orb. "What?"

Grey smiled.

"Never mind," Rune said.

"The next council member is an incubus." An image of a handsome man with black, curly, perfectly coifed hair, richly tan skin, and bright-blue eyes popped up.

"What's an incubus?" Rune asked.

"Maybe Grey can answer that."

Grey jolted in surprise. He hadn't expected to be called on, and his mind had been otherwise occupied—repeating the names in his head and trying to memorize them all. "Uh, an incubus is rumored to be a demon. They prey on women."

"Shax will use charm, magic . . . whatever it takes to bed his victims. You need to be careful, Rune. Your genetics afford you more resistance than most, but you're not immune to his power."

The picture changed to one of the most beautiful creatures Grey had ever seen. She was a throwback to movie stars of old, when women had curves in all the right places—an hourglass proportion so perfect it shouldn't be possible. Her blonde hair was thick and shiny and fell down her back in soft waves. Her eyes were a pale green.

"This is Tashara, a succubus."

"She's like an incubus, only she preys on men," Grey finished for Tate.

"Worse." Tate clicked the ball again, and it went black. "Unlike Shax, who will leave you somewhat close to the way he found you—"

"Although possibly with child," Verida interjected.

"—Tashara feeds off your sexual energy. She can literally suck the life from you. All of it."

Grey swallowed. "Great."

"She's dangerous, but I need you to get close to her."

A hole opened up somewhere within Grey, and he thought he might vomit. He tried to keep his voice from shaking. "Why?"

"Verida suspects she has information she's not sharing. Information we need."

"What information?"

"I'd rather not say. If she gets you in a compromising position, well—that could be bad for all of us."

Grey gritted his teeth, truly wishing he could go back through the gate for the first time since they'd arrived. Yes, the horrible fae forest was bad, and the idea of going against a pack of werewolves was terrifying. But the mere thought of befriending a sexual predator sent the floor spiraling out from under him while the remnants of dinner in his stomach went rancid. Memories, tangled emotions, and repeatedly buried horrors rushed back with an intimate familiarity he despised.

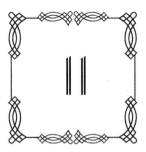

WOLVES

Grey had fallen asleep out of sheer exhaustion, but his mind had been unable to remain silent for more than a few hours, and he'd woken long before dawn. It was a pained wakefulness, one where sleep had fled but every limb felt like it had ballooned overnight. And now his body, weighing hundreds of pounds, pressed into the mattress in silent protest—*you're not going anywhere.*

Not one to fight against himself when the prospect of more sleep was involved, Grey stayed in bed, lying there with his eyes closed and fruitlessly hoping the exercise in feigned sleep would somehow result in a bit of rejuvenation.

Something rasped against the wood floor. He turned his head to the side, peeking through slit lids, half expecting to see some otherworldly tarantula scuttling across the floor. But there was nothing dangerous, just a piece of paper that had been slid under the door.

He rolled out of bed and grabbed it, struck with how thick it was. The handwriting was small, calligraphic, and impossible to read in the dark, but across the room the early light of dawn spilled in through the double-pane glass. He moved to the window, holding up the message.

Your party is waiting.

It was time. A strange feeling hung in the air. It wasn't dread, but it wasn't excitement either. A curiosity, maybe, although a dark one, laced with foreboding that added weight to his heart and created a small lump in his throat.

Dropping the paper on the crumbled quilt, he sat down and pulled on his boots. There was no need to change—he'd slept in the same clothes Tate had given him yesterday. They were all he had. Standing, he absently turned to look for his trench coat before remembering it was gone. He scowled and cursed the thief who'd stolen it.

These clothes stuck to him in ways nothing had in years. The fabric hugged every part of his body, and as he walked down the stairs, he had the urge to cross his arms around his middle.

The front room held fewer patrons than yesterday. He looked at the floor, the ceiling, the edges of the tables, anywhere and everywhere to avoid their curious glances, all while trying not to slouch—which was difficult, as it had been his posture of choice for the last few years. He pulled back the cloth that blocked the room they'd eaten in yesterday to find Tate and three bowls waiting.

"Good morning," Tate said.

"Morning."

Breakfast may have been oatmeal, maybe, but it had been cooked to the point of gruel. It coated every surface of his mouth in an unpleasant manner. He smacked, trying to force it down.

"What?" Tate eyed Grey's sick expression, scraping his bowl. "Didn't your mother know how to cook good food?"

"No," Grey answered. "I had to fend for myself." He tipped the spoon upside down and watched as the gray, glue-like oatmeal slid off and landed with a loud *plop* back in the bowl. "And I never made . . . this."

Verida sauntered in and gave Grey a coy smile. Her lips were bright red, and her checks were flushed with a glow that hadn't been there yesterday. Rune came in right behind her.

"Verida, you look *rosy* this morning," Rune said, a hint of acid in her voice. She plopped down and shoveled in a spoonful of gruel. Grey didn't miss her gag reflex.

"Yes, I fed," Verida said. "Thanks." She peered into Rune's bowl. "And I venture it tasted better than that."

Rune mumbled something, but her mouth was full, and it was unintelligible.

"Oh, please. A girl has to eat."

"There are many different ways of life on this side, and different nutritional needs," Tate said. "You'd better get used to it."

"Besides, you assume I harmed my meal. Unlike the meat you slaughter to consume, I'm sure he found it as enjoyable as I did." Verida gave Grey a pointed look, dressed with a smirk.

Grey blushed at the implication. "When are we leaving?"

"Right after breakfast," Tate said. "The council is expecting us."

The front door banged loudly, and the sound of footsteps cracking across the wooden floor planks brought the conversation to a halt.

"Tate!" the innkeeper bellowed. "They're coming!"

Tate jerked to standing. In his haste, his knees caught under the table, and it lifted up before it slammed back down, rattling the bowls straight off the edge and onto the floor.

Verida was already to the door. "How long?"

"A minute, maybe two," the innkeeper replied.

Chair legs grated against the floor, followed by the sounds of jostling and shouting as the entirety of the bar rushed for an exit.

Verida spun on Tate. "They can't see you. They know you work for the council, and Silen can't be connected with this right now. The pack will revolt, and all the work he's done will unravel."

"Kit probably already told them."

"We don't know that for sure, do we? I haven't been connected to the council, so I'll get Grey and Rune out."

"How?"

"I have a plan. Don't worry." She shrugged. "I always have a plan."

Tate stared at her for what was probably only a few seconds, but it felt like forever. He finally gave a tight nod. "I'll meet up with you at the road. Don't let anything happen to them." He darted out of the room, heading to the right instead of going for the front.

The bartender slid the bolt closed on the door and leaned against it. The knob rattled, and then someone started pounding.

"We're closed," he yelled.

"My ass you are," growled a voice on the other side. "I know they're in there."

"Come on!" Verida said. She leapt over the bar and cracked open the back door, shutting it just as fast. "Mother of Rana! They just came around the corner—we need to move fast. That way." She turned and dashed up the stairs.

Grey had to take them two at a time to keep up. "Mother of who?"

"Rana. The first vampire." Verida shouldered a door open and charged across one of the rooms. "We need to get to the next building without being seen." She yanked open a window and climbed out onto the roof.

"You can go out in the sun?" Rune blurted.

Verida poked her head back in. "Are you *serious* right now? You two are killing me. Perhaps you don't understand the seriousness of the situation. You are the *lost Venators*. There are hordes who will do everything in their power to make sure you never reach the council. Some of those happen to be surrounding the building. Now, if you would like to live, stop asking stupid questions. Shut up, and get your asses out on this roof, *now!*"

Grey clamped his mouth shut and slid through the open window. The roof was cut at a sharp angle, and the shingles were fashioned from thick pieces of wood, splintered and rough with age. Verida walked surely, which looked completely unnatural given the pitch of the roof. Grey had to redistribute his weight to one side to keep from sliding off.

Within the tavern, the sound of furniture slamming into walls and floors echoed upward.

"Stop it!" came a voice that Grey was pretty sure belonged to the innkeeper. "I'll report you to the council!"

Carefully stretching his neck, Grey peeked over the edge of the roof. Below them and just within view, two very large men leaned against a tree, their eyes fixed on the back door. Grey jerked straight. If any of them moved farther down the roof, they would be in plain sight to the guards below.

Verida motioned, suggesting they should move higher to keep their backs against the wall of the second story. They walked carefully, checking each room for movement before dashing across the window. They finally reached the end and cut around the side, now safely out of view. No sooner had Rune joined them than Grey heard voices reach the second level, then a crash as someone kicked a door in.

"Go," Verida whispered, motioning to the next obstacle, a good fifteen-foot gap between the tavern and the building next door.

"Are you insane?" Rune hissed. "I can't jump that!"

"You already did it once," Grey reminded her. "At the arch."

But fear clamped down, squeezing Rune in its grasp. Grey could almost see its fingers wrapping around her as she stared wordlessly at the empty expanse.

Verida rolled her eyes. "I do *not* have time for this." She grabbed Rune by the back of the shirt and tossed her across the divide like a rag doll.

Rune landed hard on her stomach. She got to her feet, glaring at Verida.

The vampire turned with a huff to Grey. "So, which way are we doing this? Am I tossing you, or will you trust me that you can make it?"

"I don't need to trust you." Grey took three steps and leapt.

He landed cleanly, but his overconfidence prevented him from taking into account the pitch of the roof and the unevenness of the wooden shingles. One foot wobbled, then slipped. Horribly off balance, he fell flat on the steep surface. He clawed desperately at the weathered wood—but it did nothing to slow him. A host of slivers embedded themselves in his forearms, wrists, and hands as he slid.

Rune dropped to her knees and grabbed his wrists. Gravity and their combined weight pulled her off balance and jerked her forward. They were both headed over the edge. Grey picked up both feet and brought them down hard, shoving the tips of his boots between two shingles. Mercifully, they stopped. But it hadn't been a quiet rescue.

They both froze, waiting. Scared to move—scared to breathe. Time ticked by painfully slow, but the sounds coming from the inn didn't change, and no feet came pounding between the two buildings.

Rune's face was inches from his. He could've counted the beautifully unique freckles that splashed across the bridge of her nose if there'd been time. "Thanks," he whispered.

She gave a quick nod. She pulled her knees forward and then leaned back, using the leverage to help pull him to his feet.

Verida landed above them with catlike grace. "Let's go." Without a drop of concern for their near fall, she marched her petite self over the peak and disappeared down the other side.

Rune looked like she wanted to slug her.

Leaning against the back of the house was a roughly made ladder that let them down into the darkness of a small alley next to what must've been a butcher shop. The smell was overwhelming—excrement, rotting meat from discarded bones and fat, and several other notes he couldn't identify. Not wanting to take a second whiff, Grey pressed his forearm to his nose. Rune gagged and then mashed both hands to her face.

In the dark, their tattoos should've shone like nightlights, but they had rapidly dimmed, almost as if they knew the light was dangerous. It seemed to be an internal response, like blinking or holding your breath when afraid. Whatever the biological force, Grey was grateful for it.

Movement caught his attention as two men—Grey assumed they were werewolves, though he didn't know what drove the assumption—walked past the alley without looking in. He understood in that moment why the ladder had been propped against this wall—why Verida had landed them here.

Nothing could pick out a human smell through this stench.

Verida stood more motionless than Grey thought a living thing could be. It was like she'd turned to stone, watching and waiting. When nothing else presented itself, she relaxed slightly. "I'll be right back. Keep to the shadows, and don't move."

Alone now, Grey became aware of Rune's strange breathing. It was heavy and hitching oddly, as if she were struggling to control the speed of it.

Grey touched her shoulder. "Are you all right?"

"No." She shook her head, ponytail whipping violently from one side to the other. "I'm not ready to die."

"You're not going to d—"

"She's getting ready to lead us through a pack of *werewolves*, Grey! You heard what Tate said last night—we stayed because he couldn't guarantee our *survival*."

There was nothing to say to that. His mouth opened and closed several times, searching for a response that would be both honest and comforting. But the two in conjunction was too tall an order for the current situation.

Verida slipped back around the corner holding two cloaks. "Put these on, and keep your heads down." She glanced surreptitiously over her shoulder. "I want one of you on either side of me at all times, and"—she held up a finger—"this is very important: no matter what, do not act shocked, surprised, or disgusted. Understood?"

"Yes." Grey took the cloak, knowing better than to ask what Verida was planning, and swung it over his shoulders, pulling up the hood.

Rune stared at the cloak in her hand. "Verida—"

"Pull yourself together!" she snapped before Rune could finish the sentence. "I could hear your heart pounding halfway down the street. You're a Venator, whether you like it or not. And your life is in danger no matter where you go from here. Put. It. On."

Rune's hands trembled as she pulled the cloak around her shoulders.

Verida tugged at the edges, wrapping it tighter around Rune. "And whatever you do, keep your arms covered. One look at those markings, and it'll all be over."

⋙⋘

Rune's heartbeat thudded in her ear—*ka-thunk, ka-thunk, ka-thunk.* Verida was leading her to the enemy, and she couldn't even lift her head. All she could see was the side of Verida's boots tapping against the hardened dirt, leading the way.

Yesterday there had been sounds everywhere—talking, laughing, the bleats and clucks of goats and chickens. But today the village was silent, with the exception of male voices ringing through the air. She heard the word *Venator* several times.

Venator. Genetically modified humans. The law.

A target.

As she walked, keeping an eye on Verida's boot, the word *target* tumbled over and over again in her mind like a rock in a polisher. It rubbed away the sound and construction of the word, leaving only feelings. Raw and unbridled. Her mind raced through a dozen horrible scenarios, each rapidly ending in death.

Target acquired. Target accessed. Target eliminated.

Verida leaned over and pressed her lips against the hood at Rune's ear. "Slow. Your. Heartbeat."

How was she supposed to do that? She'd done it a million times for games, but that was different . . . although the technique might work. She forced several deep breaths, pulling air in through her nose for several counts and then releasing it in a steady, even stream. Focusing on her shoes, the only things she could really see, she picked out details to occupy her brain and derail the runaway terror train.

Leather, handmade by the looks of it. The stitching was wide and thick, slightly uneven by the machined standards she was used to at home. The soles were thick leather as well. The laces were soft, like suede.

"What have we here? Verida, isn't it?" The stranger's voice was deep and gravelly.

Target acquired. Thoughts of shoes blasted away, and Rune's heart resumed its breakneck speed. *Ka-thunk, ka-thunk, ka-thunk.*

"No. And I'd thank you to not confuse me for that traitorous little witch. She's betrayed my father one too many times."

The softened thud of shoes against packed dirt came as whomever they were talking to moved closer. Next, a question, slow and suspicious. "We're looking for two Venators. I don't suppose you've seen them?"

"Venators?" Verida laughed. "You wolves have really lost your minds this time. No one has seen any of those in decades."

"It's funny you say that," the male said, "because one of my pack described seeing a vampire with a female Venator last night. Oddly enough, the description he gave matched you. And now here you are, with two cloaked figures who won't look up. Strange coincidence, don't you think?"

"Don't!" Verida's word cut like a knife, and Rune jumped. "Those belong to me. Touch them, and you might start a fight you can't finish."

Rune trembled, feeling the imagined brush of fingers that had just reached for her.

"I assure you, *wolf*, I can tear your heart out before anyone else arrives to help. Now listen closely. This member of your pack—big man, right? Thick beard, blue eyes." She chuckled. "Yes, he saw me, and I saw him. I don't suppose he told you what he was actually doing here last night?" Before the man could answer, she continued, "He was looking for a little action. Something new. But as he smelled like a horse's ass, I turned his smelly hide down."

The male sputtered. "He would—"

"Never go after a vampire? That's what they all say. But trust me, when you have a reputation like mine, classification makes no difference." Rune could hear seduction winding through Verida's voice. "I'm really, very, *very* good."

There was a low chuckle—much deeper than the male who'd been speaking. Which meant there were at least two of them out there. What Rune wouldn't give to be able to see! How was she supposed to interpret dead silence without any visual clues? It was maddening.

"You really don't know who I am, do you? If I were to say the name 'Vega,' would you recognize . . . Ah, see?"

There was a slight break in conversation and a sharp kissing sound—Rune could almost see Verida's bright-red lips pursing to shoot off the sarcastic gesture through the air.

"Your pack mate knows me. Good. I'm going to break down what happened to make sure you both understand. Your friend came to me and then, too embarrassed to admit what tail he'd sniffed, took a story home to his pack. Hoping, I'm sure, that the ever-faithful followers could serve up a healthy dose of revenge on his bruised ego."

Someone growled. "He would never—"

"He would, and he did. Listen to me. He's making fools out of your entire pack. Can you imagine how this will look when the innkeeper reports your little raid to the council? Werewolves going rogue and ransacking his inn while claiming to be looking for Venators? It's laughable."

"If what you say is true, why not just show me their faces?"

Rune had no idea how Verida thought she would talk her way out of this. But still, there was a waver of uncertainty in the werewolf's voice.

"My breakfast dates are human, as you can smell . . . or at least they are for now. I expect their classification will change very shortly."

"I don't want to smell them. I want to see them. And you know why."

Verida started to giggle. It quickly escalated into the cruel laugh of someone who knows something the other doesn't. "Were you not listening? I am *Vega*. The breaker of customs, the unbiased giver of pleasure. Do you think this reputation was gained easily? I am renowned, above all, for the privacy of my clients."

"Privacy of your clients!" The man scoffed.

Verida moved away, and Rune felt the absence of her presence like the void of a black hole.

"It's a bond I hold sacred." Verida's voice went low and throaty. "Until, that is, a client or a prospective client decides to bring down a pack of werewolves on me with false accusations. There are lines that are not crossed, and your friend just crossed one."

Rune heard a set of footsteps heading back for them. She tensed, but Verida's boots came into view. She roughly grabbed Rune's face and turned it toward her, making sure the corners of the hood hid her features. Verida rolled her eyes coyly to the side, looking at the werewolf. "Now, unless *you're* interested in what your pack member was, I'm hungry."

There was a snort of disgust.

"No? Are you sure? Too bad; you're much nicer to look at, and I've always been a sucker for attractive meals." Verida shrugged and grabbed Rune's wrist, keeping it carefully wrapped in the cloak and exposing only the bare underside. She sank her teeth deep.

Two barbs rammed through Rune's skin, and it was anything but the pleasant experience Verida had bragged about at breakfast. Pain radiated up her arm, and it was everything she could do not to cry out.

Verida's lips pressed against her skin, creating a suction, and she pulled blood from the vein, drinking deeply. The feel of lips, teeth, mouth, tongue—all acting without Rune's permission—left her feeling violated. Anger swam through her vision, tinting it red. But she couldn't pull away, not without blowing the ruse.

Verida's eyes shifted again to the male that blocked their path. She smiled with her teeth still embedded in Rune's wrist. When she pulled her head up, blood dribbled down her chin. "Do you honestly think a Venator would let me do this?" She lifted Rune's bleeding arm like an offering. "Care to join?"

"Not if my life depended on it."

Verida gave Rune's wrist a lick before dropping it. "It might."

"Are you threatening me?"

Verida took a step forward, closing the gap between the wolf and herself. "No, darling. My threats look like this—get out of my way, or I will splash the name of your pack member from here to the Blue Mountains. No matter where you go, no matter how hard you try to distance yourself from the truth, your pack will be known as the pack that lies with vampires. And, if I'm correct—and I know I am—your territory is awfully close to Cashel's. I've heard he has no patience for trysts with vampires." She leaned forward and whispered. "I've also heard Cashel has his eye on *your* territory. Were you looking for a new alpha?"

Both werewolves growled.

"Now who's threatening who?" Verida said.

"Get out of here," one of the males said. "Now."

Verida returned and placed a firm hand on the small of Rune's back, steering her and Grey around the male. Behind them, the shouts grew closer as the wolves found nothing in the inn and widened their search.

Rune's anger simmered with every step until it rose to a boil that spattered against her eardrums. Her logical mind said the action had been necessary, even genius, but that voice was quiet and quickly overwhelmed by something completely illogical.

The feeling of Verida's lips on her skin, the suction as she had pulled the blood from her arm . . . It was a complete violation, and something Rune didn't think she could ever forget. Even the replay sent bile rising up her throat. And then the other issue—what if she turned into a bloodsucking monster?

How could Verida do this to her?

Not paying attention, Rune tripped on a stick as Verida steered them through the trees that edged the small village.

Verida grabbed under her arm. "Careful," she murmured.

The touch of her fingers triggered a dark feeling that bloomed in Rune's chest, and she was seized with the desire to rip Verida's head off. Literally.

Somehow she knew she was completely capable of doing just that. Which should've frightened her, but she'd never felt this kind of anger. It instantly overwhelmed any sense of right and wrong, killing all moral thought processes. Rune struggled to control it, but it didn't want to be contained. The horror mixed with angst and fury until she was a powder keg waiting to explode.

Verida finally stopped. "We're clear."

"That was amazing," Grey said. "I didn't think—"

Rune ripped her hood back and shoved Verida as hard as she could. "You bit me!"

Verida stumbled backward before righting herself. "Don't. Push. A vampire. Especially this one."

"You *bit* me!"

"I warned you something like that might happen."

"No, you didn't warn me of anything!" She stepped toward Verida, her hands balling into fists.

Grey hovered nervously in her peripheral vision. "Rune, what are you doing?"

"You need to calm down." Verida's eyes glittered like flint. "Tate promised me he'd chosen carefully, but you're reacting exactly the way this world feared you would."

"I'm supposed to be OK with you biting me?" She took two more steps forward, driven by a rage she had no idea how to control.

"Rune!" Grey stepped between her and Verida, grabbing her by the shoulders. "Stop. What's wrong with you?"

"She's a Venator—that's what's wrong." Verida crossed her arms. "This is exactly what happened to the last ones. It's her breed."

"My *breed?*"

"Yes! I drink blood, the werewolves turn into beasts, and *you* hate anything that's not human."

Rune jerked back like she'd been slapped. In an instant of perfect clarity, she understood exactly why Tate hadn't wanted Ryker here. The hate oozed from her brother like a festering sore, apparent to all. And she could feel it oozing from her right now, like thick black tar squeezing from her pores, letting everyone know that more was hiding just beneath the surface.

"No," Grey said. "Rune's not like that. She's just overwhelmed and scared. That's all."

Verida stepped around Grey, her eyes locked on Rune. "We all have something inside us that we're not proud of—a base instinct that goes against what we believe. This, what you're feeling right now, is part of you—like it or not. But it's up to you how you deal with it. You can fight who you are or give in to it. But I promise you this, little girl: neither Tate nor I will allow a repeat of history. If you can't control this, you will be *controlled.*"

The way she emphasized the word *controlled*, along with the look in Verida's eyes, gave the word a whole new meaning.

Controlled: to be silenced, eliminated, put down.

The threat fed her fury like gasoline on a fire, but in the intensity of her feelings, she saw her twin brother reflected back to her. Because she'd been the one on the outside, watching his actions with the clarity of a third party, the truth of what she'd just become was undeniable.

Rune dropped her gaze and stared at the rich black soil under their feet. She took stuttering breaths, pulling air slowly through her nose while blinking back angry tears.

Grey reached out and took her hand, gently, hesitantly, kneading his fingers into the center of her fist until she relaxed her grip. "Hey," he murmured. "Look at me."

She didn't want to, scared he would see all the feelings roaring inside as easily as she saw them in Ryker. She didn't want him to think she was like him. Not after what he'd done to Grey; not after—

"Look at me," he repeated.

The softness and kindness in his voice made it impossible to refuse. It was like trying to say no to a kitten. She slowly looked over.

His eyes swept over her face, taking everything in. Worry crept across his brow. He'd seen.

She shrank away.

"Listen." He applied gentle pressure to her hand, trying to pull her back to him. "Verida's right. You get to choose how you react to this. I've been through . . ." He glanced away as if ashamed. "A lot. But no matter what happens, you can pick who you're going to be and how you're going to act. You were fine with Verida before she bit you because you saw her as a person. She's still a person, just different than you. She saved your life, both our lives—that's what the bite was, an escape from danger. Nothing more. You have to focus on that."

She tried to turn away, wanting to disappear. He lifted her chin with one finger—not a demand, but a gentle request that she not shut down.

"Verida saved our lives, Rune."

She closed her eyes, remembering the stories Tate had told their first night here. The old Venators had come to this side, feeling completely at ease. But they soon developed a hatred for those they were supposed to be protecting, overtaken with a desire to eliminate every species not their own, triggering a holocaust of even larger proportions than the one on earth. Is that what she wanted—genocide?

No. She could not, *would not*, allow herself to become that kind of person.

Ryker's face flashed behind her dark lids, and she saw the hatred—the remote clenched in his hand, knuckles white, as he'd watched the man dressed as a werewolf. The tightness of his jaw, the obsession, the loathing. She used to think he'd felt the itch as she did, that it had fueled his descent. But it wasn't the same at all. He'd already surpassed that itch and had been living in the immense cascade of dark feelings currently drowning her.

"No," she murmured, more to herself than anyone. "I won't be Ryker."

Letting out a long breath, she released everything she could, focusing on the feel of Grey's palm against hers. But the shrouding darkness fought back, clinging at her soul. It took several minutes of all-out war for her heart rate to slow and the blackness to fade. When she finally opened her eyes, she looked to Verida. "I'm so sorry."

Grey turned her hands over, exposing her wrists. "Where's the bite?"

"Right th . . ." There was nothing. Not the slightest mark or discoloration. She turned her wrist from one side to the other. "I don't understand."

Verida crossed her arms. "I told you already—you're immune to vampire bites. I couldn't turn you if I wanted to."

Feeling even more foolish for her earlier reaction, she flushed a bright red. "I . . . I forgot."

"OK, but self-healing and immunity are completely different." Grey ran his finger over where the mark had been. "There's nothing here. Is that normal?"

Verida frowned, and she looked nervously behind them as if she'd heard something they hadn't. "Yes, it's normal. Come on, let's walk. The wolves are widening their search." She slid farther into the trees. "Just don't touch anything, all right? Our scent trail will be strong enough as it is."

Rune stood there for a moment, continuing to look down in awe at the unbroken skin. Now that she thought about it, since coming to this side, every small injury and bruise had healed on its own. "Hey!" She ran to catch up. "Am I going to heal like this all the time?"

"Mostly. But you have weaknesses that can impede your body's natural abilities."

"Such as?" Grey asked.

"Gold. Weapons made of gold or tipped in gold will do the same amount of damage as a regular blade would do on your side."

A sizable black bird interrupted them with a strident *caw*. The crow spread its wings and puffed out its chest, flapping slowly in a distinctly unbirdlike fashion.

Verida glared up at the bird. "Beltran."

The crow gave another *caw*, followed by a throaty sound that remarkably resembled a chuckle, and then flew away.

"Who's Beltran?" Grey asked.

Verida stared unseeing at the branch where the bird had last been. "I ask myself the same thing all the time."

EBONY

Arwin was deep in the outer forest, huddled down in the roots of an ancient tree. Long ago, the roots had surfaced, only to dive back under again like a sea serpent. Their exposed wood made a superb place to sit and watch the mountain for movement. He'd spent so much time here, it almost felt like home, albeit one where guilt lay heavily and the *would've, could've, should've*s danced like dainty performers, always hitting their mark.

This particular spot pointed him toward a sparse section of forest that framed a clear view of the twisted mountain Zio had stolen from the sorcerer who had once occupied it. The rock rose up from the ground like a towering cloud formation that had been grabbed at the summit and twirled.

But while the view from a distance revealed its elegance, up close it was rough and jagged. This beast of a mountain was formed from hard volcanic residue. Huge, flat slabs sloughed off in strange rectangular shapes so precise it was hard to believe they hadn't been carved. In all his travels, Arwin had never seen a more . . . *unnatural* natural formation.

Halfway up the mountain face, an ebony castle nestled comfortably between two sheer rock faces. It was rumored that the castle halls ran several levels deep and were nearly impossible to navigate without getting hopelessly lost—but he'd never been personally invited for a tour to verify that fact.

The council had wanted the castle for itself but due to its location had been unable to breach it. In order to reach the front door with an army, you would need to spend hours walking up the winding path, leaving you in plain sight the entire trek. This would allow the castle occupants to pick off every member of your force with magic, arrows, and—if you got close enough—great iron kettles of boiling oil that would wash you off the mountain while simultaneously boiling you to death.

If you did manage to reach the castle on foot, you would find yourself at the edge of the eastern cliff, facing a drop of thousands of feet and an empty expanse of nearly a hundred from cliff edge to castle doors. With the drawbridge up, the way was impassable.

And then there were the magical wards to worry about.

It was rumored that Zio had succeeded in her assault after being invited into the castle by the wizard Naturian, who was the previous occupant, and launching her takeover from the inside. But it was also rumored that she'd grown wings and flown to the front door before they could destroy her. And, of course, she'd supposedly grown to the size of a mountain and, in a fiery ball of magic, blown the doors off their pins. The latter two stories Arwin found highly suspect, which made the first one harder to place credence in despite its simple appeal to logic.

Regardless of how she'd succeeded, in the time since, she'd managed to fortify it even further—coming up with a way to get her minions in and out of the castle and away from those who might attempt a siege at the base. A passage would appear out of nowhere and allow her minions, or even Zio herself, to step from the castle into a predetermined location.

Magic was Arwin's specialty, and he'd never seen anything that matched the enormity of what Zio had accomplished—with the exception of the gates to the other world. But the magic that had formed those was ancient and had been lost for thousands of years. That was why it had been so difficult to seal the gates when the Venators had threatened his world—you can't counteract a spell you don't know.

Though many had tried, no one had been able to reproduce the magic of the gates. Until now. By mastering this method of transportation, it was clear that Zio was growing uncomfortably close to the correct spell work, and Arwin could not figure out how she was doing it!

When the gates to the other dimensions were about to open, they sent out a magical frequency. Zio's did not. The only warning was the light preceding the opening. He had no idea what the limitations to her spell were—size, distance, length of time. But once he realized what she'd done, it was a race against time to fortify the council house before Zio and her army appeared in the dining room.

Arwin had been forced to construct the spell from scratch. But new magic was dangerous, and the creation of spells was a practice long since dead due to the mortality rate. Magic was not something you played with. You learned, and you practiced. You did not invent. The fact that Zio seemed to be not only dabbling in spell creation but mastering it was cause for immense concern.

In the end he did manage to fortify the council house, but he stumbled upon the winning combination out of sheer, dumb luck. And *luck* never instilled confidence in his ability to repeat the trick. Arwin grimaced. His back was beginning to ache, more from age than the position, and he shifted. Finally, the blinding flash of light he'd been waiting for burst forth. Between the front doors and the east cliff, a pinpoint of light grew rapidly, announcing the return of the last party Zio had sent out.

The drawbridge to the fortress began to lower, and Arwin got to his feet. His knees popped, kindly announcing to the entire forest that he was older than he appeared—which was saying something.

Even if he'd had the vision of his youth, the castle was too far away for him to get a proper look at without a spell—so he whipped one up, running his fingers over his eyes. The drawbridge became infinitely larger, and he watched the events unfold as if he were standing just on the side of the road.

The light hovered high in the air and expanded steadily into a perfect circle. Once it reached approximately seven feet tall and seven feet wide, it snapped into place. The drawbridge groaned as the chains unwound. It leaned away from the main doors, stretched out across empty air, and smashed into the east cliff—bridging the two. The boom of metal and wood against stone echoed around the mountain.

Zio's ugly little goblins stepped out from the brilliant, glowing portal onto the drawbridge. They marched in military formation—two by two. But something was wrong. Arwin had seen the force leave, chasing the same magical frequency he'd sent Tate after. At that time, the werewolves had led the assault, and they should've been leading the group back—a wolf would never follow something with as low a rank as a goblin—but they weren't here.

The fact that the wolves had not returned was interesting. Either they'd been separated from the group on the other side, which was unlikely, or they hadn't survived Tate, which was good news.

His spirits lifted. Perhaps the Venshii had finally accomplished their goal and managed to return with a Venator or two.

But his joy was short lived. Two tusked goblins emerged, pulling what appeared to be a human boy between them. His clothes were strange and clearly marked that he wasn't from here. Their captive was trussed in chains and wore a ratty burlap sack over his head. But Arwin didn't need to see his face—beneath the boy's short sleeves flared the markings of a Venator.

"Blast," he whispered. "She got one."

His amplified vision was suddenly filled with black feathers and flapping wings. Arwin yelled and jumped back, waving his arms. He took off the magnification spell to see a single large black crow.

"Beltran!" He spat out the name like a curse word of the vilest variety. "Blasted shape-shifter, one of these days I'll turn you into a toad!"

The crow landed on the ground and began to morph. Wings extended, feathers shrunk, legs grew, and beak vanished. A moment later, a man with black hair and bright-green eyes stood smirking in front of him. "I can turn into a toad any day I want."

"Yes, but I am capable of keeping you that way!"

"Now, how am I supposed to do the council's bidding as a toad?"

Arwin smoothed out his beard, grumbling. "Tell me, what did you see?"

"Same thing you did. They've got themselves a Venator." He held out a necklace. "The boy dropped this. It missed the draw-bridge and fell—lucky for us."

Arwin examined the piece. "It's not magical." He handed it back. "We need to get a message to the council and let them know Zio got one through the gate."

"Tate also made it through. Looks like we've got two Venators of our own."

"Good, good." He peered up at the castle, worry creasing his brow. "But are they the right ones?"

RACE TO THE COUNCIL

Giant ferns squatted around the bases of trees. They reached out with tall, arching fronds and brushed Grey's arms as he passed. Their thin leaves were strange, dotted on the underside with tiny black nubs that stuck to his skin like the feet of a cockroach.

Verida had been moving with a sense of urgency, subtly sniffing and listening as they went. Their speed had gradually increased as they zigzagged deeper into the forest. Having spent years honing his abilities, Grey found it relatively easy to keep up. Rune, however, struggled.

After she tripped for the third time, Verida whirled in frustration. "This is ridiculous!"

Rune huffed and shoved her ponytail over her shoulder as if it had somehow offended her. "I don't know what you expect from me. Cut me some slack!"

Grey cringed and tried to interrupt before the exchange could deteriorate into the one they'd just finished, but Verida plunged forward before he could say anything.

"I expect you to stop stumbling around like a baby, holding on to your human side because it makes you more comfortable. I'm not here to keep you comfortable—I'm here to keep you alive."

"I don't know what to do!"

Grey didn't have a lot of experience with women, but he wasn't dumb. Jumping into that firestorm was ill advised. He leaned back against the trunk of a tree and crossed his arms to watch.

"Yes, you do," Verida snapped, closing the distance between them in two combative steps. "It's all in there, inside"—she roughly jabbed a finger at Rune's chest—"begging to come out. All you have to do is let loose."

"Let *what* loose?"

"Stop. Being. Afraid. Your fear is locking down your abilities, paralyzing you while it feeds your anger."

Grey worried as soon as Verida poked Rune that it would trigger the hate he'd seen earlier, but the only things in her eyes now were tears.

"I don't know how."

Verida sighed. "Look, I'm not a Venator. I can't teach you what you need to know. But if you can't figure it out, you're going to die."

Rune rolled her eyes. The motion pushed a tear out, and it trickled down her cheek. She quickly swiped it away. "Oddly enough, the death threats aren't really helping."

"Why not? I'm trying to help you out, and I can't think of anything more motivating than *death*!"

Rune's lips trembled, and the truth burst out as her walls collapsed. "Because I'm so scared I can hardly think straight, that's why!"

"Maybe," Grey interjected over the top of the argument, "you could start by just enjoying it."

Both turned to look at him—Verida with a soft smile, Rune in confusion.

"Think about it." He shoved off the tree. "Remember when we were running for the arch? I want you to forget the fear and forget the things chasing us. Just think about what you did. How amazing was it to run like that, to have that speed? You weren't winded. It wasn't hard. It just happened."

Rune shrugged. "It was pretty incredible."

"Pretty incredible? It was *way* more than that. It was like all your childhood dreams of being a superhero came true overnight."

Rune's lips pulled up in the start of a smile.

"Just let it happen," he said. "Trust me."

Verida's head snapped up. "Shh!" She rotated slowly, listening. "They've found us." Her voice was so low it barely registered above the hum of insect wings. "Don't move." Walking in a careful circle, she sniffed the air, her feet not making a sound. "They've nearly formed a perimeter—we have to run. If you can't keep up, I don't know if I can save you. Understand?"

They both nodded.

"There will be no talking, only running, and you will follow me no matter what." Verida locked eyes with Rune. *"No matter what."* She pointed to the west. "That way."

❈❈❈

Rune broke into a sprint, pushing her legs as hard as they would go, jumping over branches and dodging trees. But despite her efforts, she wasn't moving any faster than she had back home. Verida and Grey rapidly pulled away.

As she pumped her arms, her markings flickered—not only the red of Verida but a deep maroon. The wolves were closing in.

A man-made howl rose up, alerting the others their prey was within reach.

Grey's head snapped back, looking for Rune. The distraction cost him, and he almost went down.

The knowledge that she was being hunted wrapped around her heart, ripped it out, and dropped the still-beating organ somewhere around her little toe. Her vision tunneled; her breath came in short, rapid gasps. Up until this moment, she couldn't have comprehended this level of fear if she'd tried.

Grey slowed, looking back with worry and uncertainty.

Damn it! His concern would be the death of him, and it would be entirely her fault. She wanted to call out, to tell him to leave her, to save himself. But Verida had specified no talking, and Rune wasn't about to be the one who led the wolves straight to them.

She mentally pleaded for more—more energy, more faith . . . more *speed*. She dug deeper, but her muscles burned in a way that warned of their impending crash into the performance wall. A fallen branch caught on her pant leg, scratching from knee to ankle as she flew by. She gritted her teeth, determined not to cry out. And then, like a merciful answer to a prayer, something sparked inside her—the same feeling she'd experienced on the way to the arch.

A little ball of energy ping-ponged around her chest, begging to be released. She loosened her resistance—a struggle while running full speed in utter panic—but it didn't take much. The ball of energy ignited, flooding her body with energy. A pins and needles sensation erupted in every muscle group, and she surged forward.

Her strides increased, and the wind whistled past as she gained on Grey. Her vision sharpened—showing her every fallen branch and fine details in the bark as she flew past. Colors were crisper, sounds clearer. Her body was functioning in a way that defied logic—the faster she went, the better she felt. Not a hint of the fatigue from mere moments before remained.

The sound of branches cracking behind her broke the euphoria.

Rune turned her head just as a large man burst though a line of short trees and undergrowth, running straight for her. She opened up further, pumping her arms and focusing only on Grey and Verida. No time for doubt now. A second glance over her shoulder confirmed she was losing him.

Ahead, Verida ripped around trees, turning ninety-degree angles without slowing. Grey was right behind her, equally impressive. It was obvious he'd worked with these abilities before.

But she hadn't, and at this speed her feet nearly slid out twice. Rune prayed there was more to Verida's plan than outrunning the wolves—it was only a matter of time before she took a nosedive on a corner.

The roar of water somewhere ahead registered over the whistle of wind in her ears. Another large man leapt in from the side. His fingers brushed Grey's arm, but he missed and slammed into the ground, rolling. Rune leapt over him. He reached up and wrapped a massive hand around her calf, but her black pants were too slippery for him to grip. Rune stumbled, pinwheeling her arms. She lost valuable seconds before pulling back up to speed.

A wave of nausea rolled over her—too close.

The water grew louder, and so did the shouts of new werewolves joining the hunt behind her. Where had they all come from? Had there been that many at the village?

Verida shouted back. "Trust yourself!" She leapt off a cliff Rune hadn't even seen coming.

Mist from a waterfall filled the air. Its pounding drowned everything out. No more howls or shouts or even the slapping of her feet. Just a welcome blanket of white sound.

Eyes on the ground in front of her, she trusted her body.

Grey leapt.

A moment later it was her turn, and she catapulted off the edge. Cutting through the air, she experienced the rush of flight, the excitement of weightlessness . . . She smashed into the ground on the other side, completely off balance with her weight on her heels. First her knees buckled. Then both feet slid out. She sat down hard, skidding across dirt and rock.

In a cloud of dust, Rune turned at the waist to see if any of their pursuers had followed.

The same werewolf that had stopped them on their way out of town slid to a stop at the edge. "You want to have a good time now, you little vampire wench?" he shouted across the divide. "How about I show you how very good *I* am?"

Rune let out a sigh of relief and got to her feet, brushing off her backside. Eight werewolves lined up on the opposite rim, all breathing hard.

Verida put one hand on her hip and cocked it to the side. "Absolutely. Why don't you just come on over, and we'll make it happen?"

"Oh, we'll make it happen, Vega, trust me." He bared his teeth and snarled. Then he turned and melted back into the trees, followed by the rest.

"Who's Vega?" Grey asked.

Verida grinned. "My sister. And she's got this coming."

Rune walked up to the edge to get a good look at what she'd just jumped. She didn't know how long the stretch was, but it made the gap between houses she'd worried about earlier seem laughable. "Whoa."

"See, I knew you had it in you." Verida patted her on the shoulder. "Now we just have to get back across and find Tate."

Rune's mouth fell open. "Say what?"

Grey crossed his arms and stared out over the canyon. "They'll be waiting for us."

"I know. We'll stay on this side as long as we can, moving upriver, and cross closer to where Tate's waiting. The less distance we leave for them to corner us, the better." She glanced up at the sun. "And we don't want to be out here when the sun sets. Let's go."

Tate repeatedly ran his palm over the hilt of the sword that hung at his waist. He'd been waiting next to the carriage he'd secured for several hours—watching, listening, scanning the tree line for any sign of movement.

For a moment he thought he saw something. But whatever it had been, the fleeting shadow was gone before he could take a second look. He was desperate, and this was not the first sighting that had been merely imagination fueled by frenzied need.

Seven curses! They should've been here by now.

The sun had set, and a large full moon hung above. There had been a time when his only freedom was the slim view of the night sky through a barred window. Better than the stars or the occasional shooting star were the nights when the moon was at its fullest. It would swallow up his entire window and chase away the shadows from the darkest corners. It made him feel, for a few hours, that he'd fled his cage and was lying out beneath the wide-open sky.

But tonight was different. Tonight the moon hung low and heavy. Of all the nights to lose two Venators, this was possibly the worst. The werewolves would be at their strongest—something even Verida had enough sense to be worried about.

Tate growled in frustration. It was his responsibility to get Grey and Rune to the council. To bring them this close and fail—it would be unforgivable. Everything he'd put together, all his plans, would crumble. They would be back to square one—except fighting against, instead of with, two new Venators who would be hand chosen by the corrupt council members.

He paced back and forth, the gravel crunching beneath his feet. The horses became agitated, which Tate attributed to his own distress. But the animals grew worse, snorting and stamping. Tate took a step forward. Their eyes were wide with fear, and they tossed their manes, flinging chunks of the froth that coated their bits.

Tate turned, leapt onto the back ledge of the carriage, clambered onto the roof, and began scanning the area.

He was completely surrounded by trees. Even the path the carriage would take to the council house was lined with thick pines for the next fifty feet before the ground gave way to sheer cliffs. Nothing looked out of the ordinary, but he hadn't inherited the sight of the Venators, and he could make out very little in the dark.

The horses were now in a full panic, whinnying and throwing their heads while fighting against the harnesses. The carriage lurched forward and knocked him off balance. He grabbed the edge to stay atop, yelling the halt command to the frightened beasts.

Something was coming, no doubt. He strained his ears, trying to hear past the chirp of insects and slight hiss of the breeze. Finally, the sound of bodies crashing through the thick forest came from his right. He pulled both blades from the sheaths on either side of his hips and crouched lower, ready to leap.

Verida burst out with Rune and Grey at her sides. "They're right behind us!" she shouted. "Get ready."

Tate jumped off the roof and resheathed one of his swords, leaving his left hand free. He grabbed the carriage door and wrenched it open. The others were halfway to him when three large wolves surged out from the shadowy trees and into the wash of moonlight.

Tate swore. "Come on!" he shouted. "Faster!"

Grey leapt inside, followed by Rune.

Verida slid to a stop. "Get in," she demanded. "You'll need help from the outside."

Tate jumped in, shouting to the horses. "Sum-*ha*!" The horses were anxious to comply, and the carriage jolted. The inner compartment was large enough to sit four across on either side, and the open space left Tate without anything to brace against for balance. He stumbled and fell forward, landing on Grey.

Verida hung on the outside of the carriage, one arm wrapped through the window. A wolf jumped. She swung up and kicked, catching him square in the chest—terminating all forward momentum. It yelped and dropped.

"Who's driving this thing?" Rune shouted.

"No one." Tate scrambled to the other side of the carriage. "The horses won't stop until they reach the council house."

A wolf crashed into the door. Its claws gripped the rim of the open windows, sinking into the trim, and a large muzzle entered the carriage.

Rune screamed. Tate deftly sliced his blade across the top of the wolf's feet. Blood bloomed through fur, and it cried out, retracting its claws and vanishing from view. Tate leaned his head out to make sure the werewolf hadn't managed to grab onto the back as it fell.

A thump came from the roof as the third beast landed, the thin wood sagging beneath the weight. Tate's head was still out the window, and before he could pull himself inside, Grey ripped the second sword from his sheath and shoved it up through the ceiling. The wolf screamed, a ghastly mix of human and beast.

Finally the trees dropped away, leaving nothing but cliffs on either side of the path and no avenue for the remainder of the pack to flank them. Verida slipped inside the carriage feetfirst.

Tate turned, huffing as he wiped the blood from his face with the back of his arm. "A little close, don't you think?"

"Oh, I'm sorry. Maybe you didn't notice the full moon." She plopped down next to Rune. "I'll have you know—we were just fine, had a nice lead, actually, until the sun set."

Grey handed Tate back his sword, coated with blood.

"Nice move," Tate said.

"Thanks."

Howls rose from the forest, and Verida glanced outside. "Those wolves will be angry tonight."

Tate's expression darkened. "I know, and I worry who will feel the heat of it."

BLOODLINES

Grey let out a long, slow breath and leaned his back against the silk cushion. They'd just been hunted.

Flat-out hunted.

It had been the longest day of his life. After they'd evaded the wolves by jumping the canyon, they'd spent until late afternoon moving down the valley and looking for a spot to cross back over to meet Tate. By the time they'd finally found a place where Verida couldn't smell any wolves, the sun had been dangerously low in the sky.

They hadn't made it very far into the forest when the wolves found their trail. Shortly after that, the sun had set. He would never forget the sounds. How a howl coming from a man could change midcry as his face shifted into that of a wolf. It morphed from something flat and one dimensional to a rich, resonant sound as the vibrations of the cry moved up the length of the snout. He hadn't been able to see the werewolves, but he'd literally heard the change happening. Once in animal form, they'd been a close match for speed to Verida and two Venators.

They'd run for longer than Grey had ever run before, and nearing the end, he'd finally felt fatigue. That had terrified him. A waving red flag that he was, in fact, not invincible. Nor did he have unlimited energy, as he had previously suspected. It was possible that his speed and endurance could fail him, and failing in this world meant death. Tonight it could've come as claws ripped out his throat. He shuddered and pulled himself from that abyss of thought—it would do nothing but harm.

Rune stared out the window. Her face was drawn, and her shoulders hunched. Grey knew exactly where her mind was—the same place his had been. But she didn't seem to be pulling out of it, and that worried him.

"Hey, you did well today." Grey leaned forward, elbows on knees. "You about outran me a couple of times."

"Thanks."

"It was like watching you at the state tournament."

Rune half-smiled. "Yeah, just like it. Except I don't remember the other team trying to bite my face off."

"See? Biting is motivational—you moved much faster than you did at state."

Verida chuckled, and Rune finally laughed. "Yeah, I did."

Tate had been wiping the blood from the swords using the bottom edge of his trench coat. He carefully maneuvered around the carriage occupants to sheath the blades. "Were there any other problems besides the wolves?"

Verida glanced to Rune, who tensed, eyes pleading for discretion.

"No, no other problems. A pack of wolves on a full moon is sufficient."

"Good."

Rune mouthed a small *thank you* to Verida. Tate didn't seem to notice.

"I'm sorry I had to leave you. The council didn't want confirmation of their involvement until the announcement—political reasons. Plausible deniability. Verida's work with the council was suspected but not verified—"

"It's verified now," Verida muttered.

Rune's nose crinkled as her eyebrows pulled down in puzzlement. "But you said word already got out that we were coming."

"Rumor got out." Verida gave a sly smile. "Since only about fifty percent of rumors are actually true, the council can deny until things are verified. Deniability is the situation of choice, and as annoying as it is, it's a thought process you would do well to learn."

Tate leaned to the side, peering out the carriage window. "We're almost there. Now listen. Verida will introduce you to the council. Don't say anything stupid. Listen, observe, and figure out what you're dealing with." He gave a stern look. "And remember their names."

"You're not coming in with us?" Rune asked.

"No. I have a few things to do first, and then I'll be waiting for you outside the dining hall." He saw their disappointment and added, "There are a lot of things about this world you don't understand yet. I apologize, but I can't introduce you."

Something about the way he said it didn't sit well with Grey, like Tate was trying to carefully cover a hole with grass mats—one step, and you would tumble into spike-laden truth. "Why not?"

The muscle in Tate's jaw jumped.

"They'll find out soon enough," Verida said. "We might as well tell them now."

Tate's eyes slid over to her through half slits, but he didn't object.

"Tate can't introduce you because his status isn't high enough."

"His *status?*" Grey sat up straight, disgusted. "What does that even mean?"

"It means they trust me enough to train you, teach you, and die for you, but I don't have the right bloodlines to present you."

"Bloodlines!" Rune burst out.

"Tell me you're joking." Grey looked from Tate to Verida— neither seemed amused. "That isn't right."

"I know."

In a land filled with vampires, werewolves, humans, fae, and elves—creatures of every different size, shape, and color—where outer appearance didn't seem to matter, Tate was discriminated against for his bloodlines. Grey looked at him, wordless, because there was nothing adequate to say. But there should've been words—something—and he searched for anything besides a simple, *I'm sorry.*

Tate must've seen what Grey couldn't articulate, because a glimmer of hope flickered in his dark eyes. He reached out and gripped Grey's knee. "Maybe someday things will change, but today is not that day. You'll go with Verida."

The carriage slowed as the horses came to a stop. Tate popped the door open and leapt to the ground, all emotions dropped. "Welcome to the council house."

Grey let Verida and Rune out first, then stepped down and looked around.

A black stone castle stretched into the night sky, all walls and spires and paned windows. Its dark walls were washed in moonlight that was unable to dispel the dismal gloom that wrapped around it. Stone gargoyles trimmed the higher ledges and were broken up with stained-glass windows that told stories he was too far away to make out. Large torches hung on both sides of the tall black double doors, crisscrossed with thick iron braces. The torches blazed, but instead of adding an air of warmth, they solidified the overall feel of doom. On either side of the door, draped in thick shadows the torches failed to penetrate, two statues stood well over fifteen feet high, each holding a battle-ax.

"When you said *house*, I expected something . . ."

"Smaller," Rune interjected.

". . . and less like Dracula's castle."

Tate chuckled as he unhitched the horses from the carriage. "Dracula's castle looks quite a bit different, but if you'd ever like to visit, Verida could probably get you in."

"Thank you *so* much." Verida managed to glare and roll her eyes at the same time. "Would you like to add anything else, *Tate?*"

He clicked his tongue at the horses and turned to lead them away. "Not really. If you don't want to give them a tour, just say so."

"Somehow I don't think a tour of the dungeons would be their idea of a good time," she called after him. "But maybe *you'd* like to see them!"

"Quite familiar with those already," Tate tossed back over his shoulder.

Grey was both confused and intrigued. "Dracula?"

"Don't ask. And I mean that in all seriousness. Just don't." She marched toward the front entrance.

They were nearly there when the statues moved. They stepped into the light, their battle-axes swinging down to cross in front of the door. The towering men wore kilts that came to the tops of their knobby knees and white button-down shirts they seemed to have outgrown—the buttons bulged, ready to yield to their terrible task at any moment. The sleeves had been ripped off at the shoulders, and fraying threads hung down their arms like strands of wet seaweed.

"Who goes there?" said one of the things Grey had mistaken for a statue. The giant peered down at them through beady eyes.

"Stan!" Verida snapped. "No one says 'who goes there' anymore, and you *know* who it is!"

"You didn't answer his question," the other giant said.

Changing tactics, Verida batted her eyes and cooed, "These are the new Venators. You don't want to make them angry, do you, Bob?"

Stan and Bob both jolted up straighter, raising their battle-axes. "Sorry, Verida," they muttered simultaneously. Bob, who had blond hair matted to his head and small black eyes, reached over and pushed one of the doors open with an enormous hand.

Rune and Grey stared up at the two hulking figures as they passed. Stan's face was so flat it looked like he'd been sat on shortly after birth, and Grey wondered how he breathed through that nose.

Stan glanced down and winked.

Rune hurried forward. "Are those giants?" she hissed.

"Yes," Verida said.

"And their names are *Stan* and *Bob*?"

"Is there something wrong with that?"

Grey walked backward to watch the towering figures swing the outer doors closed. He chuckled. "Stan and Bob. I like it."

Verida just shook her head. "Good. Because that's probably the last thing you're going to like for a while."

The long, rectangular foyer was immense but somehow still seemed to close in on Grey at the same time. The walls were covered with portraits of myriad different creatures. Each wore a robe with a red-jeweled brooch on the shoulder in the shape of a four-pointed star. Their eyes seemed to track them as they walked. Normally he would've told himself he was being paranoid, but tonight, in this place, he wasn't so sure.

The floor was tiled in one-inch pieces that had been used to create mosaic landscapes. Bright-pink swirls twisted through the tree branches. It was hard to fully see the art while walking over it. He would need to look at it from the second level.

The castle was deathly silent, and their footsteps echoed loudly. Grey thought he saw another set of eyes hidden in the shadows above, but when he looked again, they were gone.

They headed toward a set of double doors at the back of the foyer, where two guards stood watch. One looked very human; the other . . . Grey had no idea. The man had skin with a faint orange tint to it, four arms instead of two, and horns that curled around his ears like a ram's. Grey tried not to stare, but it wasn't working very well. All his years of studying, and he still only recognized half the things they'd seen so far.

Verida lifted her hand to knock, but the doors swung open. Standing just inside, with her hip cocked to the side and a coy smile, was Tashara, the succubus. It had to be. She stood nearly at Grey's height, with thick blonde hair that fell down her back. Her dress was red and cut very low, hugging every curve and leaving little to the imagination.

Her eyes glittered the same eerie green Grey had noticed in the images, but they were even more striking in person. He imagined falling into them and never coming out.

The accuracy of that thought jolted him, and he looked away.

Tashara leaned in and sniffed him. "Well, hello," she purred. "You do not disappoint. Welcome to the party."

"Thank you." Verida stepped deftly between Grey and Tashara. She extended an arm in introduction. "This is Rune and Grey."

"Grey," Tashara mused, completely ignoring Rune. "What an interesting name. Pleased to meet you."

Verida put her hand on Grey's shoulder and steered him into the room, motioning for Rune to follow. "Keep your eyes off her and your thoughts out of your pants," she murmured in his ear, "or she'll suck you dry."

"I thought . . ." What had he thought? That a succubus stole life from a kiss? "She . . . she can do that?"

"Not kill, at least not from a distance, but she'll feed off the sexual energy you emanate, leaving you so exhausted you'll wish you were dead."

Grey pulled away from those sea-green eyes to focus on the task at hand. But his mind rebelled, turning again to Tashara against his will.

Magic. He was fighting succubus magic.

He glanced over to Tashara, who watched him with a playful smirk.

Grey jerked harder to be free of her, reaching into his mind with determined fingers and nudging the temptations out of their hiding places. His thoughts responded, but slowly, resisting every move away from the succubus.

The room was the size of a ballroom and extravagant. A crystal chandelier, heavily laden with sparkling gems, hung over a long table. Against the back wall was a cavernous stone fireplace that Grey could've walked straight into. And around the perimeter, chairs and loveseats had been arranged into several vignettes, placed carefully to encourage conversation.

At first glance, it appeared all council members were in attendance. Although some looked human, there was raw power coiled just beneath their skin that Grey could sense. He began identifying faces. In an overstuffed armchair sat Dimitri. The vampire had a lithe figure that, in and of itself, wasn't intimidating, but his face was all angles and razor-sharp cheekbones framing harsh, glittering eyes. The danger was in those eyes. He watched the room as a cat watches a mouse—evaluating, calculating, planning. When his gaze settled on the three of them, Grey once again felt like prey. He swallowed.

Silen was easily recognizable thanks to his mane of shoulder-length red hair. He leaned against the fireplace, a looming presence in the room, due to not just his height but his girth—those shoulders would put bodybuilders to shame.

As their Venator presence was recognized, the council members either stood or turned to face them. The old man with the long white beard, Arwin, was nowhere to be seen.

With the attention of the room, Verida held out her arms, motioning to her right and her left. "I would like to present your two new Venators. Grey and Rune."

Omri dipped his head in the most subtle of greetings. His posture was impeccable. He stood tall in a long silver robe that set off his inhumanly black skin and white hair. When he looked up, his eyes shone like glittering blue gems against ash.

Ambrose was the last to stand, and she did so with a certain lazy reluctance. She cocked her hip and rested her hand at the waist, making it quite clear that she didn't feel their presence warranted a formal greeting. The fae's skin was pale green, her hair raven black, and emerald-green dots formed a mask around her eyes like a spray of freckles.

Seeing Omri and Ambrose in contrast, Grey now understood what Tate meant when he'd said they would be able to tell elf from faery in person. Omri, the elf, had a dignity about him that practically rolled across the room, whereas Ambrose reeked of mischief.

From behind Grey, Tashara spoke. "Shax, darling, I know you're distracted, but you might want to pay attention."

Shax looked up from the serving girl he'd pinned in the corner. His gaze roved over Rune and froze, desire heavy in his eyes.

Shax wore a skintight pair of dark pants, a bright-blue vest, and a white shirt rolled neatly to the elbows. The crisp look complimented his naturally wavy black hair, which had been cut to just above the collar. His copper skin was flawless. But as his eyes roamed hungrily over her, Rune felt undressed and unexposed. She wrapped her arms around her waist.

"I expected more, Verida." Silen crossed his arms. "These two can't even control their markings. What good are they to us?"

Rune was lit up like a Christmas tree. Grey was no better.

"There hasn't been time for training," Verida said. "We were attacked by a clan of wolves and barely made it here alive."

Ambrose plopped back down on the loveseat. "A werewolf attack. Isn't that interesting." She crossed her leg, and the slit on her purple dress rose up her thigh.

"Ambrose." Silen said in warning.

"What?" She smiled over her shoulder at him, twirling a piece of black hair around her green finger. "With rumors of the wolves looking to separate themselves from the council, this *is* interesting."

"Enough!" Dimitri wasn't overly loud, but the command cut through the room like a knife, resonating deep. "Our guests have just arrived, Ambrose. A little decorum?"

She smirked. "Of course. As you know, decorum is of the utmost importance to the fae."

Silen growled but returned his attention to Dimitri. "I heard no news of any plans to attack."

Dimitri took in a deep breath, releasing it slowly through his nostrils. "No," he said coolly. "I don't imagine you did."

In the tiny space between one moment and the next, the vampire wiped away his expression of disgust and became a textbook image entitled *The Picture of Sophistication*. The change was so rapid and yet so smooth that Rune blinked, wanting to rub her eyes. This new image of Dimitri would've had subtitles and side texts explaining how to be the perfect host for any occasion.

"Welcome," he said. "It's been a long time since Venators have walked this side of the gate. We're pleased to have you. Come, sit. You must be hungry."

Verida's fingers pressed into the small of Rune's back, urging compliance with Dimitri's request.

Rune's weight was on her heels, not wanting to step further into the room, but under Verida's encouragement her legs numbly carried her forward anyway. This was madness—she shouldn't be here. The light grew too bright, her breathing too loud. The council members moved in from every direction like otherworldly birds with carefully placed footfalls and an alertness that surpassed their immediate surroundings. Each one evaluated, noting Grey and herself but also each other.

Tate had warned them, and he'd been right. They'd just walked into a pit of vipers masquerading as party hosts. Rune sat, feeling like a rat in a cage, looking up while giant faces peered down, calculating her usefulness in some twisted lab experiment. Every sense she had was screaming, *Danger!*

And that was all it took.

The Venator fury she'd unleashed earlier on Verida began thrashing its ugly head, beating against her ribs and pummeling the base of her esophagus, demanding release. But release was the one thing it couldn't have. She could see the predators beneath the masks, see the darkness and power that lurked under their skin, and she knew that if anyone besides Verida realized the battle raging inside, they would put her down like a rabid dog.

Mercifully, Grey settled next to her, offering the calming influence she desperately needed. She twisted her hands together in her lap to keep from grabbing his.

Tashara sashayed behind them, suggestively running a finger down Grey's ribs. He jerked ramrod straight, the color fading from his face.

"Tashara, *darling*." Shax straightened his vest before he sat. "Perhaps you could stop trying to tempt the boy. I don't think he's replaceable."

"*Everyone's* replaceable," Dimitri said, his words dripping with meaning.

Tashara breezed right over it. "I don't know what you mean, Shax."

"I didn't come here to watch this." Omri's white hair hung behind him like a sleek pelt. He raised his chin. "Do what you must in your own chambers, not at the dinner table."

"Not at the dinner table?" Shax gave Rune a sly smile. "What a titillating existence you elves must live."

The downward spiral of sexual innuendoes and growing tension was interrupted as a stream of creatures entered from several doors, all carrying steaming platters.

"Thank Rana," Verida muttered under her breath.

The food was served and taken away shortly after. It was followed by another course and then another. There were crisp vegetables that reminded Rune of several she'd had at home, only all wrong. Carrots that were a deep maroon, peas that were orange . . . green potatoes. They all tasted right, if she didn't look at them. Then came meats swimming in rich, bright sauces, breads and rolls, butter and jam, tarts filled with berries.

The food was probably amazing, but she was too busy to notice—watching the small, tense exchanges between council members, ignoring Shax, and trying to memorize names and faces, all while fighting her inner demons. By the time they reached the main course, her appetite was gone, and everything tasted like sand.

As dessert arrived, the members talked with one another about clans and boundaries, payments and promises, future plans and past problems. Overwhelmed and overloaded, she tuned out.

Grey was still attentive, grasping every piece of information.

While he was busy focusing, she stared, taking in the newly exposed Grey. How could this boy have been right in front of her for years, yet she'd never truly seen him? What she noticed now went beyond the shocking reveal of his face and physique. Grey was smart and sweet and had stepped in to put her at ease every time she thought she would fall apart. Even in the carriage, she'd seen the look on his face when he'd closed his eyes. He'd been scared but had put it aside to reach out and make her feel better.

His shoulders were no longer hunched, and he'd stopped dipping his head to hide beneath his hair like he had before. He grew more confident by the second, which made him that much more attractive.

Shax breathed in deeply, as if inhaling a delectable aroma. It was so loud that it caught the attention of everyone at the table. Rune startled—Shax was staring straight at her, and his blue eyes blazed with hunger. A smirk tugged at his lips, and he sniffed again in her direction.

Tashara twirled her fork in the center of the dessert plate. "Do control yourself."

Shax winked.

Verida reached beneath the table and gripped the top of Rune's thigh in warning.

It took Rune a second to catch on, but then her stomach lurched. Shax had picked up on her attraction toward Grey.

A serving girl leaned over Shax's shoulder to take his plate, and his attention shifted to her, smiling broadly.

Verida leaned over to Rune, whispering in her ear. "Stay focused. Shax will bed every female within a mile radius and use whatever magic it takes to make that happen. And *you* would be his magnum opus. Keep your thoughts under control, and give him a wide berth."

After all the plates had been cleared, Dimitri turned his chair slightly to the side so he could easily look down the table to Rune and Grey. "I speak for the council when I say we're thrilled to have two Venators back on our side. We have high hopes for this new arrangement and are pleased you agreed to the position."

She held back a bitter laugh. The way Dimitri made it sound, they'd approached her with a job offer, laid out all the perks, and then thanked her for choosing them. The only choice she'd made was to go after her brother.

"If I may," Grey began, the perfect picture of decorum.

The council members relaxed under Grey's manners. She even saw the hint of a smile from Omri. Rune could learn a thing or two.

Dimitri motioned. "Of course."

"What is expected from this position?"

Dimitri's eyebrows began a calm and controlled ascent skyward. "Verida? I was under the impression you'd explained."

Verida's flinch was subtle but there. "Just to reiterate, we *were* interrupted by a pack of very angry werewolves. Details were missed."

Ambrose loudly scoffed at the end of the table. "I thought you more than capable of handling a few wolves, Verida. Perhaps we've misjudged your value." Her violet eyes glittered with mischief.

Verida leaned her head around Rune, meeting the faery head on. "I am quite capable. I apologize that, while being chased down with no weapons and two untrained Venators, I didn't get all the details in. I chose instead to *not* let the wolves chew on the two of them while I handled the rest of the pack." She gave a painted smile. "But perhaps next time you can show me how it's done, so I can get it right."

Ambrose's expression soured. Omri leaned back, looking delighted.

"To understand what we need from you," Dimitri said in answer to Grey's question, "you need to understand that our domain is very different from yours. I know little of your world, but I do know that your power structure is constructed of humans alone."

The way he said *humans* sounded like he wished to replace the word with *vermin*. Rune bristled.

"Those seated at this table offer a representation of the strongest species. As council members, we speak for our kind in order to prevent this world from being in a constant state of war. Unfortunately, with strength comes independence and power. Species such as ours never do well living under constraints for long."

"Silen." Ambrose interrupted. "Perhaps you can attest to this?"

"Or maybe Ambrose can help illustrate the point." Tashara leaned back, resting her elbow on the arm of her chair. The movement was simple, but in the hands of a succubus, it played out as subtle seduction. "Last I heard, the fae had been straying from their borders despite orders to the contrary."

Ambrose's eyes flashed, and what Rune could only assume was magic rolled across the table like fury made tangible. The magic was visible in that subtle place between seeing and sensing. There was a ripple in the air, like a breeze . . . or the soft tendrils of barely there fog. Goose bumps erupted up and down her arms as the temperature in the room plummeted.

Omri's head twisted sharply toward Ambrose. "We are on neutral territory, and you will keep your magic in check."

Tension crackled between the elf and fae.

"As you can see," Verida said. "We are in need of some mediation from a third party."

They needed a hell of a lot more than that!

"Mediation?" Grey repeated.

"Dimitri, may I?" Verida received a quick gesture of assent and continued. "Your species is genetically strong enough that, with training, you should be able to withstand ours. But as you have no history here, neither of you are involved in the power struggle that has this land in a stranglehold. The hope is not only that you, as Venators, will be able to speak for the council but that you will also enforce the rules and laws of the land without ulterior motives."

Grey nodded. "You're looking for a neutral party."

"Indeed." Dimitri said.

Rune didn't care about the drama or the politics. She was here for one reason. "And what about Zio?" she asked. "Where does she play into all of this?"

Dimitri's eyebrows rose. "Where did you hear about Zio?"

"There was a small amount of time on their first night through the gate," Verida said. "I was able to share a few pieces of our history."

The deletion of Tate from the story was obvious. Out of the corner of her eye, Rune saw Grey frown.

"What an interesting choice on the order of details."

Verida and Dimitri looked to be having a silent argument as they stared at each other down the table. Finally, Dimitri leaned back and tented his fingers. "In time, it's our hope that you will be assets in our fight against Zio, yes. But this goal is long term. First we must pull together our people under the direction of the council. Present a united front. This is where you come in."

"You want us to scare people into following you." The words were out of Rune's mouth before she could stop herself.

Ambrose laughed darkly. "Look how quickly the little monkey learns, and how freely she speaks."

Rune's inner demon started crawling up her throat. She ached to wrap her hands around the fae's throat.

Omri sighed with irritation. "It has grown late. Perhaps our Venators would like to retire?"

"I just have one other question," Grey said.

Verida rolled her eyes and flopped back in her seat.

"When do our responsibilities begin?"

"You'll both need to be trained extensively before we let you out of the castle," Dimitri said. "You'll need to understand your roles as the law in this land and how you will act under the direction of the council. You will need training on weapons and history—"

There was a loud crash outside, followed by shouts. One of the doors opened, and the guard with ram horns curled around the sides of his head hesitantly stepped in. "I beg your pardon, sir, but there's a request for an audience with the council."

"I gave you strict instructions that we were not to be interrupted." Dimitri bit off each word like one would cut the head from a snake. "They can come back in the morning."

"I know, sir, and I would, sir"—he dipped his head low—"but this man won't make it until morning. I give it no more than ten minutes before he bleeds out in the entry, and . . ." He looked over his shoulder to the foyer.

Silen slapped a hand down on the table. "Spit it out."

The guard jumped. "He came under the decree that grievances of death and kidnapping would be given an audience. To deny him now would end in his death, which would break the agreement offered to the people."

Tate had informed them how much the council despised having to take such action, and Rune could see it all over their faces—like they were looking at a cockroach.

Silen growled. "Oh, let him in, Dimitri. The Venators should get a taste of what they're agreeing too. Where is our dying friend?"

"Just outside. Tate is trying to calm him so he doesn't bleed out faster."

Dimitri's nostrils flared, but he gave a curt nod.

The guard bowed and exited. A moment later, the man stumbled in. Rune gasped. Two long gashes had ripped his cheek open from eye to chin. Another had peeled back the skin across his forehead—white skull peeked through the skin and blood. His shirt and pants were soaked in so much blood that it was impossible to tell how many more wounds there were.

Tate walked in behind the man, his expression neutral, and stopped a respectable distance away.

⋘⋙

"Please, help me." The victim weaved as he attempted to cross the room. His feet barely remained beneath him. "They must save them. The Venators—I saw them in the forest." He gasped, wrapping a hand around one side. "The Venators, please."

Now that the man was closer, Grey could differentiate between the fabric of his shirt and the flaps of blood-coated skin. Whatever claws had shredded his chest and sides had been incredibly sharp and as thick around as Grey's pointer finger.

"They have my wife and my son." He groaned, stumbling the rest of the way forward. He gripped the end of the table, smearing bloody handprints over the white cloth, and focused only on Grey. "You have to help me . . . They took them." A cough racked his body, and blood sprayed all over Shax's crisp white shirt.

Shax crinkled his nose.

Reality tunneled in around Grey, blackening his vision on all sides and leaving only this dying man, featured and framed. This was what he was signing up for. Most of him rose through the horror, propelled by righteous anger. But a small part cowered in the corner, feeling like a child playing at superhero when danger came calling.

"Please," the man muttered, crimson dripping over his bottom lip. "Ple . . ." His eyes rolled back, and he collapsed to the floor.

"Tate, don't just stand there." Shax distastefully dabbed blood from his face with a cloth napkin. "His pleas are useless without information."

Tate took several quick steps and picked up the man, yanking him into an empty chair and kneeling in front of him. "Tell us what we need to know." The man's head flopped forward, and Tate shook him.

"Stop!" Rune jerked to her feet, her chair screeching backward. "He needs medical attention!"

"Those are werewolf marks," Shax said. "If he doesn't die, he'll turn at the next moon. There's nothing to be done." The man's eyes fluttered. "Considering the pack that lives in the area, I'm sure he's hoping for death."

Tate shook the man again. "Tell us what we need to know before you bleed to death."

It was too late—he was gone. But then the man's eyes flickered open, and he slowly pulled his head up as if it weighed a hundred pounds.

"We were traveling home along the outer edge of the pack's territory. We saw them." His eyes fluttered to Rune. "Venators." The words were slow and pained, spoken through ragged breaths. "But . . . then the wolves came. We waited, but we . . . we were too far out when the sun went down. The howls." He groaned, the memory raw enough to cause pain. "They came—I tried to stop them. They took my wife, and then . . ." He leaned to the side, spitting out the mass of blood and drool that had accumulated in his mouth. "They took my son . . . my only—" A violent fit of coughing cut him off. "They took them, they'll sell them. Please, save—" He opened his mouth as if to say more, but his eyes rolled back, and he slumped forward.

Grey slowly stood, icy horror seeping through him. "They'll *what?*"

Tate's expression was dark, and he wouldn't look at Grey as he spoke. "Werewolves that go bad are both bloodthirsty killers and sexual predators. If they let this man's family live, they will . . . *enjoy* their prey. Then they'll keep them until they turn into new wolves. Once that happens, the pack will sell them."

Enjoy. The word stabbed at Grey's heart. "We have to save them."

"No." Dimitri calmly laced his fingers together on the table.

"The night of a full moon is not the time to go after a pack of werewolves if you want to live," Silen said. "Especially this pack."

The decorum he'd worked so hard to wear shattered. Grey shouted down the table, "I won't just leave them out there!"

The silence was deafening.

All eyes, down to the servant girl in the back, stared at him the same way Verida had stared at Rune when she'd lost her temper in the forest—veiled fear, recognition of a possible danger, and thin patience held back by a hair trigger.

He swallowed and lowered his voice. "My apologies. I do not understand why we aren't helping. Isn't that why you brought us here?"

"Perhaps the Venator should take his seat," Omri said tightly.

"Of course," Grey managed to say without betraying his inner turmoil. "Again, I apologize."

In his peripheral vision, he saw Tate pick up the body and carry the dead man out. But worse than the act itself was the council's reaction—impassive—as if someone carrying dead bodies from the room was an everyday occurrence.

Tate said he'd waited to bring them over until they were old enough to recognize the council for what they were. Grey couldn't fathom ever being blind enough to overlook the evil sitting at this table.

"Silen is right," Tashara said. "This pack is dangerous anytime, but tonight they are nearly unstoppable."

"Unless it's your death you are seeking," Ambrose added, "you will abide by the will of the council."

Thankfully, they were interrupted again. The door cracked open, and Dimitri's head snapped toward it, fury simmering. But instead of a guard, an enormous black crow flew into the room. Dimitri relaxed and sat back as the bird dropped a scroll into his lap and then flew out.

He unrolled it and carefully read. "Arwin reports that Zio's minions have returned through the gate."

Rune practically leapt forward, leaning against the table. "Do they have my brother?"

"Your brother?" Dimitri cocked an eyebrow. "Isn't that interesting?"

The way the council members looked at each other suggested it was not interesting but concerning. Which Grey found . . . interesting.

Dimitri scanned the scroll again, then released it, letting the message snap shut and roll down the table until it hit a serving platter of tiny cakes. "It doesn't say."

"His name is Ryker. If they're back through the gate with a Venator, it has to be him. Please, I have to help." She withered, looking childlike.

Ambrose giggled behind slim green fingers. "First they want to go after a wolf pack, and now the little beast thinks she can stumble into Zio's stronghold and ask for her brother back." Her laughter grew until it bounced off the crystals of the chandelier above them.

Rune's face flushed, and she gripped the table with white-knuckled hands.

Verida stood abruptly, her palms flat on the table. "This has been a lovely dinner," she said over Ambrose's hysterics, "but our new Venators are in desperate need of sleep."

Dimitri nodded his consent. "I think that would be best. We can reconvene in a week, after they've had some lessons." He looked down his nose at Grey's fluctuating tattoos. "Start with those dreadful markings."

Verida gave a respectful nod and turned her back to the table, glaring daggers that only Rune and Grey could see. "Come on then, *Venators*, I'll show you to your rooms."

TASHARA

Verida stormed ahead, the heels of her boots clacking on the stone floors. She led them up a set of stairs padded with a luxurious carpet runner. The thick mahogany banister was shiny enough from years of wax to throw back distorted reflections. Once at the top, they turned to the left and headed down a long hall lit by sconces of opaque glass.

Verida casually glanced over her shoulder and gave the air a little sniff. She must've deemed them alone, because she stopped abruptly and spun. "What is the matter with you two? Didn't we warn you about the council? Weren't we *explicitly* clear about not making enemies? All you had to do was sit there and shut up, but noooo, you both went mouthing off. And you—" She shoved her finger into Grey's chest. "Standing up like that? Practically facing down the council. What were you thinking?"

Instead of stepping away, Grey leaned into Verida's finger. He was not going to back down. Not on this. "That man died right in front of us, *begging* us to save his family. What was I supposed to do?"

"You were *supposed* to talk to me about it later!"

"Why?" Grey snapped. "What are you going to do? Save them yourself?"

Verida's arm fell back to her side, and she took several deep breaths, nostrils flaring. "First of all, you have no idea what I'm capable of or what I would do. Second, you don't understand what you're dealing with. Without the council's help, the odds of you rescuing that woman and boy are slim to none. The odds of you surviving are only slightly better. This clan we're talking about is the most powerful in the land, and the most ruthless. Besides, you don't even have a weapon. What are you going to do? Go in and fight them with your bare hands?"

Grey stepped in again, closing the distance Verida had just created. He looked down at her, refusing to waver. "Then. Give. Me. A. Weapon."

"Grey—" Rune started.

"No." Verida held up her hand. "He's right. You need weapons. But there's nothing to be done tonight. I'm sorry. First thing in the morning, we'll start weapons training. You'll be ready next time."

"That's not good enough! What do you think those werewolves will do before they sell those poor people? Rape them? Torture them?"

"Yes."

Grey ran his hands over his head. "This is insane! You know what they'll do, and you want me to forget about it. To pretend there isn't a pack of wolves abusing two people right now. That a man didn't beg me with his dying breath to help them. And what is wrong with you? All of you? Aren't there any laws, rules of any sort, that prevent werewolves from murdering people just because they want to?"

Verida snapped, "The wolves attacked because they couldn't get their hands on *you*!"

Rune gasped.

"So it's our fault!" Grey's voice reverberated off the glass sconces.

"Keep your voice down!" Verida lunged forward, pressing a finger to his lips. "You're in a castle full of beings whose hearing far exceeds your own."

He leaned back, shoving her hand away. His ears were burning with shame.

"You just told us that a man died because we outran a pack of wolves. How did you expect him to react?" Rune said.

Verida looked genuinely regretful, parting her lips and then closing them again, struggling with what to say. "Look, this is my world, and now it's yours. I wish I could tell you this is the worst thing you'll see, but it's not. This is why you're here—why we need you. Of course there are rules and laws. That's what keeps the more powerful species from wiping out entire villages. But this is an entire planet—not everything can be watched."

"There has to be something—"

"Grey! There is nothing. Travelers who are foolish enough to be on the roads past dark become targets. Sure, they might be missed, but with woods as full as ours, no one will know exactly who or what took them. Punishments are difficult to dole out when there's no proof."

Her intensity grew, begging them to understand. "You are in a position to help, but it'll be wasted if you're *dead*. Who'll save the next one, or the one after that? You'll have to make some choices from here on out, some really ugly choices about who lives and who dies. And it never, ever gets any easier." Her lips pushed into a thin line, pressing against the fangs beneath. "Trust me."

Her passion was met with stony silence, and she looked from Rune to Grey, searching for understanding. "I'm trying to help you both."

"And what about my brother?" Rune asked. "Who's helping him?"

"No." Verida turned to Rune, shaking her head. "*No.* You have to put him out of your mind. Right now."

"How?"

"Tate told me about your brother after he returned the first time. I know you love him, but—"

"Look." Rune's head drooped. "I know who he is. I know why Tate left him." Grey jolted in surprise, and she gave him a withering look. "I'm not blind, Grey. But regardless of what stupid choices he's made, or . . ." Her voice faded. "None of it matters. He's my brother, my *twin.* He will never be out of my mind, no matter what happens. If this . . . Zio has him, then I have to save him."

"Listen to me." Verida reached out to grab Rune's shoulders, but she thought better of it and dropped her arms back to her side. "Zio's fortress is impenetrable, the defenses so advanced not even the council has seen the likes of them before. Arwin hasn't the slightest clue how to get around them. She has connections everywhere, and you will never know if you're talking to a spy. If Zio were anything less, the council would've eliminated her years ago. If she has your brother"—Verida held up both hands, emphasizing her words—"and we don't even know that she does—there's nothing we can do."

"If there's nothing we can do about *anything*, then Grey's right— why are we here?"

"You have a great purpose, but you have to be patient."

Grey chuckled a single mirthless laugh. "Patience. Maybe that's what you should tell everyone who comes to your door for help. Patience. And if they're lucky, they won't bleed out on the floor while they're waiting."

Helplessness wound through him, the absolute worst feeling he knew. Because he despised it so thoroughly, it fed upon itself—growing larger as he struggled to control it.

Verida touched the back of his arm, but he flinched away. He couldn't stand here a minute longer. "Where's my room?"

Verida's eyes widened, but she covered it, stepping to the side and pushing open a large oak door. "Right here."

Grey shouldered past.

Verida growled at the wooden door that had just been slammed in her face. She closed her eyes and looked to be counting before she turned. "Your room is this way."

Rune followed a few paces behind in stony silence. Too many conflicting feelings swirled inside her, and she couldn't process them. To resolve the intensity of the situation, her brain resorted to a self-preservation technique—the reboot. She grew frigidly numb, surrounded by a heaviness, as if a blanket had dropped and smothered any thought which might cause her pain.

Despite that, Verida's words prickled, begging to be let back in. Her brother was likely in the possession of the most dangerous person this world had ever seen. When Verida had tried to persuade Rune to put Ryker from her mind, the fear had been palpable.

Verida was scared of Zio.

They moved four doors down from where Grey was sleeping, and then Verida stopped. "You have nothing to say?"

Rune blinked through the haze. "No."

"Fine. Don't leave your room. Period."

The demand pushed down like four walls of a prison, pinching off her air supply. "What? Why?"

"Shax."

Grey rested his head against the door. The heavy oak was cool against his face. Out of all the feelings he'd ever experienced—and there'd been some doozies—helplessness was the one he despised the most.

To control your own body and thoughts was a right, not a privilege. Everyone should have power over themselves.

A little voice nagged that Verida was right. If he'd run out into the woods like he'd wanted, he'd probably be dead. But that voice was so hard to hear when a man's dying pleas jangled through his ears. He growled and punched the door, grateful for the distraction of pain.

There was nothing he could do. As much as he hated it, the situation was the same, and no amount of kicking and screaming would change it.

He stood straight and squared his shoulders, then turned to face his new life. The room was enormous. He could've fit half the rooms in his house in here.

A dark wood bed sat against one wall. Pillars rose from all four corners, so wide that surely each had been fashioned from a single tree. Deep burgundy covered the bed and draped from the posters. Thick tapestry fabric hung from ceiling to floor, covering the windows. A decorative screen stood in one corner, an enormous wood desk near the other. In addition to a large dresser, two chaises and three chairs dotted the room. It felt spacious, empty, and lonely. He walked over and peeked behind the screen to see a large washing tub and a chamber pot.

A chamber pot—a lovely surprise on an already lovely evening. He scowled.

There was a knock at the door, and it creaked open. Verida stuck her head in.

"What?" he snapped.

She gave him a stiff smile, the one you offer when you say hello a little too early in the morning. "I forgot to tell you—don't leave your room for any reason. I'll come get you in the morning."

"Anything else I'm not allowed to do, besides leave my room or speak?"

"Good night, Grey." Verida closed the door.

A little ashamed of himself, but not enough to apologize, he shook his head and pulled the draperies open, exposing a set of doors that opened to a balcony. Without the thick fabric covering them, the outside air seeped through the bubbled glass, skimming over his exposed skin. Brass knobs, dulled with age, were engraved with delicate filigree. He grabbed them, startled by how icy they were, and stepped outside.

The moon hung low in the sky, larger than any he'd ever seen. His room was so high above the forest floor he stood even with the moon, easily making out the light and dark variations across its surface.

Howls went up, filling the air with a deeper darkness than the one he stared into. The treetops of the forest reached high, yet they were so far below him they looked like nothing more than a faint texture on a mural backdrop. He heard a scream . . . and then another.

Horrors rushed into his mind, old but not forgotten. Unwanted touches, hot, disgusting breath, and the smells.

He vomited over the rail.

Grey wiped his mouth with the back of a sleeve. The rancid combination of stomach acid and the chocolaty dessert from dinner coated his tongue. He coughed, then gagged again. Turning, he frantically searched for water. A ceramic pitcher sat inside a matching bowl on a table next to one of the chairs, and he ran for it. He snatched it by the handle, peering inside, but the pitcher was bone dry.

Hearing some rustling outside the room, he moved to the door. In the hall, one of the servants from dinner quickly bustled past, holding an armful of bed linens. "Hey," he called, "can you tell me—?"

The servant whimpered and hurried down the stairs.

Grey jogged after her. "Please, I just need some water—"

A figure stepped out from one of the doorframes. Grey skidded to a stop, coming nose to nose with Tashara, the succubus.

"Well, well, well," she purred. "Surely you were told to stay in your room?"

He was hit with a wave of desire so heavy he could barely think, almost forgetting why he was in the hall in the first place. "Y-yes," he stuttered, trying to keep his eyes on her face and away from the tantalizing neckline of her dress. "I . . . I was looking for some water."

"Water?" Tashara smiled and stepped forward, pressing against him. "I can offer something much better than that."

Grey's brain screamed at him to run, but his body had a mind of its own, bypassing logic, and he melted. Tashara sighed. Her eyes glowed brighter, and then she kissed him.

With the touch of those lips, a heavy, pulling sensation encompassed him, seeping through the pores of his skin. Deeper it moved, rooting out his center and yanking until he thought his very soul would escape though his mouth.

His head was fuzzy; thoughts would no longer formulate. She ran fingers up his arm and over his chest. Unwanted touch.

Or was it?

Realization snapped through him like a bolt of lightning, bright and fast, leaving behind a seared warning. She was *feeding* on him.

"No!" Grey jerked away.

So weak.

He bent over, taking heaving breaths, but stumbled forward on weighted limbs. Propping himself up with hands against his knees, he tried desperately to formulate any mental picture besides the one there now. But the voraciousness of the craving that accosted him was stronger than any narcotic, and he floundered.

She moved for him again, but Grey refused to look up, staring instead at the succubus's feet. It was the only safe place he could think of to put his eyes. But then the dress she'd been wearing slid over her legs like liquid silk and pooled around her ankles. He averted his eyes as quickly as he could and stared dry mouthed at the glittering puddle of red on the floor, his hormones racing. A groan resonated from deep within, animalistic in its need.

Tashara gave a small giggle and stepped closer.

He closed his eyes.

She placed her hands on his upper biceps and pushed him up straight. But the moment her fingers touched him, his life force began flowing out, and he understood how a man could stand here and die . . . with pleasure pulsating through him.

It was a predator of the most dangerous kind that made you *want* to die.

"You *are* strong," she murmured.

She was so close. He waited, blind, his breath wheezing out in terrified bursts.

Velvety soft fingers ran up the back of his neck, and more of his energy willingly leapt to her.

"Please," he whimpered. "Stop."

She reached his hair and flattened her fingers, putting pressure on the back of his head and sliding up over his skull.

Maybe death wouldn't be so bad.

What!

His eyes flew open. She smiled wickedly. He had to get control of himself, but a single thought now occupied his mind, placed there by Tashara. It worked like a parasite to push all other thoughts away. Because of it, his traitorous body remained, willing to die. But there was one thing, one group of memories, that not even her powers could twist into something beautiful.

The last working part of his mind settled on the one image that killed all desire instantly. His darkest moment. It was buried in the furthest recesses of his mind for the damage it did any time he brought it into the light. The desire fled like rats from a sinking ship, and he shakily stumbled away from Tashara.

Her eyes rapidly dimmed, and she tilted her head to the side, examining him. "You've been hurt. Badly."

Grey flinched. "I don't know what you're talking about."

"Don't lie. It doesn't suit you."

"You don't know anything about me."

Tashara smirked before breaking into a grin that tumbled into delicate laughter. "On the contrary. You resisted me after I had already begun sucking the life from you. That tells me more than you can imagine." She leaned back into him, lips parted.

With a start, Grey jerked his head to the side, and the kiss landed on his cheek. He dug his nails into the palms of his hands. The ugly memory was still playing in 3-D, full color, and optimum resolution. Nausea washed over him. "You're trying to kill me."

"If I was, you'd be dead." She licked the edge of his ear before whispering, "I can make it all go away, you know. The pain, the betrayal, all the memories. I can give you such fantastic feelings, ones you can't even imagine, and everything else will just . . . wash away."

"I don't want it to go away," he ground out. That might be a lie. He wasn't sure. He'd given it hours and hours of thought, and though he wasn't grateful for the excruciating pain, he wasn't naive to the strength and compassion it had built within him. To eliminate *it* was to eliminate part of who he was.

"Are you sure?"

"I want to keep it from happening to someone else."

"Ah, this is about the man and his family, isn't it?" She stepped back and stared at him with a look he couldn't decipher, but it was softer, more human. "I must admit . . . I have a touch of empathy for souls such as yourself."

Grey looked at her incredulously. Souls such as her were why souls like him existed!

She sighed. "To use your own words, you don't know anything about me, Grey."

He retreated several steps. "I'm going back to my room."

"If that's what you wish. But I was going to offer a bit of help, if you'd like to stay just a moment longer."

His suspicion was so intense the hairs on the back of his neck prickled. "Help? Why?"

"You may call it an apology." She smiled. "There are two reasons why the council would never sanction a mission of mercy such as this. One, the man didn't have any money. In light of the decree, they've become very particular about who receives help. And two, the head of that clan is named Cashel. He's been threatening to take on the council for years, and now he has enough strength to do it. Dimitri is terrified. One wrong move, and he could have the strongest werewolf clan in the land scaling the walls. Sure, most will die, but when the survivors of that pack get their hands on him . . . Well, Dimitri will be wishing they'd just torn his head off and mounted it on a spike." She stalked forward and pressed her lips slowly against his cheek.

"Enough!" Grey pushed her off, careful to only touch the tops of her shoulders. "Why should I believe anything you say?"

"Very good." She nodded with approval. "You have a mind of your own. That's more than I'd hoped for."

He was *not* going to continue the conversation like this. He put his hands on his hips, simply because they needed somewhere to go, and twisted partially to the side. "Tashara, could you put your dress back on?"

She raised an eyebrow.

"Please."

She exhaled, then sashayed past him, taking the long way to her clothes. Grey settled his gaze on the thick mahogany beams that ran the length of the ceiling as a workable distraction.

"I'm sure you were warned about the council," Tashara said. "Tate is much smarter than my comrades give him credit for. The corruption runs deep, and loyalties run shallow. Don't trust anyone."

"Including you?"

"I'm dressed now. You can stop staring at the ceiling."

Grey looked down with hesitancy. He'd been instructed to become friends with her—she might have information they needed. He'd anticipated it would be hard, but having her this close was more difficult than he could've possibly imagined.

"You've passed the first test, but where trust is concerned, that depends on you."

His mouth fell open with indignation. "This was a *test*?"

"And not your first."

"You could've killed me."

"As we've already discussed, if I wanted you dead, you would be. You're strong, but you needed a minute to find your resistance, and I offered that minute. Had I come on full force, you wouldn't have survived."

They stared at each other, but while his glare was all anger, hers danced with amusement.

"Tashara?"

"Yes, Grey?"

"If you want to be 'friends' . . ." He shook his head, trying to clear it. Her influence was still making him groggy. "Don't ever do this again."

There was silence for a moment. Her smile dropped but was quickly replaced with calm satisfaction. "You're different than I expected. I have hope for us."

"Is that a yes?"

"Conditionally, yes." She ran a finger down his cheek. Having pulled back whatever magic she'd flexed earlier, it felt no different than a touch from any other inhumanly gorgeous woman. "Betray me, Grey, and all promises are void."

"Understood."

"Good." She turned to go.

"Tashara, I have to help them." He was desperate. "What can I do?"

She turned slowly. "The woman and her son?"

"Yes."

"Why?" she asked, honestly curious.

Because he would have done *anything* for someone to have saved him. "Because it's the right thing to do."

She evaluated him carefully. The predator was gone, her demeanor softer, stance passive. She folded her hands demurely in front of her. "I believe you mean that. But be warned: not everyone on the council will be pleased with your feelings. You will need to learn some performance skills, darling, for your safety. Right now you wear your heart on your sleeve. The weapons room is located past the kitchens. Within you will find silver-tipped battle gear. Without training, I don't believe you stand much of a chance, but I have a suspicion that help may be waiting for you there as well."

"Thank—"

"One more thing. My room is on the third level, last door on the right. To offer a sincere and proper apology for forcing you to relive what you just did, I'll leave something outside to help. It'll be in a red bag. Don't let anyone see you."

"Thank you."

"Don't thank me now—you've yet to survive the night." She stepped forward and put her hand on his chest. "And I truly hope you do."

"Grey!" Verida's shrill voice came from behind him.

Tashara's smirk returned, and she offered a playful little wave before sauntering off. Grey watched her go until Verida stepped up next to him.

"Are you all right?"

"Um, yes," Grey said, but his voice shook from exhaustion. "Yes, I'm all right."

Verida rubbed at the lipstick on his cheek and then grabbed him by the shoulders, shaking him. "What is wrong with you? I explicitly told you to stay in your room. You could be dead right now!" She pulled back and looked at her hand, slowly rubbing the fingers together that were coated with red lipstick. "I . . . But . . . You resisted her. How?"

"It doesn't matter. I have to find the weapons room."

She scoffed, placing her hands on her hips like a mother staring down a three-year-old. "I don't think so!"

Grey proceeded to tell her everything Tashara had said, including the offer of a little red bag. Verida leaned in, listening intently, eyes lit with curiosity.

THE GIFT

Rune balanced on the very edge of the bed, toying with the rich satin overlay. It was late, and she'd had an incomprehensibly long day, yet sleep was as far away as home. She'd never seen a man die before.

Silen's voice was in her head, stuck on repeat. *"Let them see what they're agreeing to."*

She did *not* agree. But what choice did she have? It's not like she could politely decline the offer and request they send her home. They would have no use for her. One way or another, she'd end up dead.

Dead, like the man in the dining hall. Carried out of the council house by Tate. Dead.

Bolting off the bed, she crossed to the window without a purpose, just an undeniable need to move. Fight or flight, with nowhere to fly.

Rune yanked back the bulky drapes, looking for an escape from these four walls. But the candles that flickered around the room denied her, transforming the window into a mirror. A reflection stared back, wide eyed, haunted, and barely recogniz-able. She was struck with the fact that she had never been in a situation bad enough to cause this particular expression to cross her features.

The fear so plainly splashed across her face only frightened her further.

Anxious to be rid of the reflection, she nudged a hip against the drapes and leaned forward, pressing her nose to the glass and cup-ping her fingers around her face. The outside air burrowed through. It iced the sides of her fingers while the heat of her breath fogged up the pane. She pulled back, shifted to the right, and tried again, holding her breath this time.

The world came into view. This land was so different from home. There, they always had artificial lights, whether from the neighbor's porch bulb or a glare from the convenience store at the end of the street. Frankly, she'd always liked it. Yes, it dulled the stars, but it also pushed back the terror of the unknown. Here, there was noth-ing. Only the inky paint of an all-natural night, brushed over by the haloed touch of the moon—its dimmer light would never penetrate all the corners and alleys and dark places of this world.

The absence of sound buzzed strangely in her ears. No hum of car engines or that distinctive noise tires made as they rolled over wet pavement. No doors slammed outside, and gone was the jingle of dog tags.

This silence was a beast unto itself.

A giant black shape swooshed toward her, barely discernible against night's camouflage. She recognized it only a moment before it crashed into the window with a loud *thunk*. Rune jumped back with a shriek.

The black bird's wings slapped against the pane as it fought to get its claws around the small ledge. Once secure, it deliberately moved in, close enough that the tops of its head feathers brushed against the window. Rune couldn't shake the feeling that it somehow knew the glass was reflecting back the inside light. Its beady eyes found her; then it cawed and shoved one foot against the glass. Something hard and metallic clanged.

Wrapped around three scaled, avian claws was a silver chain holding a familiar-looking pendant.

She gasped. "Ryker?"

The bird leaned closer, looking straight into her eyes, its own bright with intelligence. Her hands trembled as she slowly reached out for the latch. It watched her movements carefully, twisting its head to the side in evaluation. She was almost there when it cawed again and flew off.

"No!" She pressed her palms against the window, fumbling with the small gold latch. It finally yielded, and the thick pane pushed outward. There, coiled carefully on the ledge, was the necklace—the other half of her yin and yang. She brought it inside, examining it as she absently pulled the window closed with the other hand. On the top of the black swirl was the nick from when Ryker had dropped it down the disposal on accident. On the bottom was a smear of dried blood.

It wasn't speculation anymore. Ryker was here. She clenched her fist around the necklace. The metal of the chain was freezing, and it bit into her skin. Finding the pain appropriate, she clenched harder, seeking a twisted sort of penance. "I'll find you. I don't care how long it takes." Pressing her fist to her lips, she murmured, "I swear."

But to keep that promise, she needed help. Verida had to see this.

Striding across the room with Ryker's pendant clutched in her fist, she pulled open the door and peeked around the corner, wary of running into Shax. A whispered argument floated toward her. Verida and Grey were standing in the hall.

Rune slipped out and headed straight for them.

"You don't even know what's in the bag!" Verida snapped. "It could be a trick."

"You don't know either," Grey argued. "Maybe it's exactly what we need."

They stood nose to nose, yelling at each other in the loudest tones Verida deemed safe.

"What bag?" Rune interrupted, joining them.

Verida sputtered in exasperation. "And what are *you* doing out here? I gave you both strict instructions not to leave your rooms!" She looked to the ceiling, muttering to herself. "It's like I'm not even speaking."

Grey focused in on the silver chain in Rune's fist. The metal gleamed in the lamplight. "What's that?"

She opened her fingers. "It's Ryker's. A large black bird just dropped it off on my windowsill."

"A bird." Verida reached over and picked it up, holding it high to examine the spinning pendant. She gave it a quick sniff and wrinkled her nose. "Goblins. Are you sure this is his?"

"Yes." Tears welled in Rune's eyes, and she rubbed at them with the back of her arm. She didn't like crying. "They have him." Watching the pendant twist in Verida's fingers irritated her. She snatched it back, closing her fingers protectively around it. "I can't just stand here and do nothing."

Verida pressed her lips together so tight it looked like she was trying to keep back Niagara Falls. "Both of you in here—now."

Pushing open the door to Rune's room, Verida shooed them both in with agitated waves. Once the door was shut safely behind them, Verida turned, nose crinkling as she opened her mouth with what was sure to be a tremendous lecture. Rune braced for it, flinching in advance. But nothing came. Verida's nose stayed crinkled because she was looking around the room in utter distaste.

"You can't be serious." Verida walked over to the bed and picked up the corner of the velvet-and-satin coverlet like it was a dead rat, holding it at arm's length. "We need to talk to the council about your accommodations."

"You're worried about the *room*?" Rune held up the pendant, shaking it. "Verida! My brother!"

"Look, Rune, I'm sorry." Dropping the coverlet, she absently rubbed her fingers off on her pants. "I wish things hadn't happened this way. But I already told you—if Zio has him, it's impossible."

"No. I don't believe that." Rune pointed, then thought better of it and put her hand down. "You said that Zio was part of the reason the council came looking for us. She's the reason we're on this side of the gate. Why would they do that if it were really impossible?"

"Fine, it's *nearly* impossible—"

"Exactly! And—"

Verida's voice rose over Rune's interruption. "But it is absolutely impossible right now! You have to be trained. You don't have the slightest clue about your abilities, and you need the council."

Grey snorted. "Why?"

"To avoid being murdered, for one thing! Oh, come on," she said in response to their faces. "Don't you get it? You have to see how scared people are of you. Wrong moves equal death. I can't make it any clearer. Now, let's say the council does agree to help you get your brother back. We'll need information, time to ascertain Zio's weaknesses, plant spies—this kind of thing takes years!"

"But Ryker doesn't have years. He might not have days!"

"Zio won't kill him," she said flippantly, wandering over to the basin on the nightstand. She peeked inside, shaking her head.

Rune rooted her feet to the floor and pulled her hands into fists to keep from grabbing Verida and shaking the answers out. "How do you know?"

"He's too valuable. If Zio had wanted him dead, she would've had her minions do it on your side instead of going through the trouble of hauling him over here." Verida ran a finger over the thick oak bedpost and checked it for dust.

"Stop it!" Rune yelled. "The room is fine!"

More than a yell—it was a roar. Verida stiffened and turned her head slowly. The stare Rune received came from beneath cold and furrowed brows, like a scientist observing the subject of a dangerous behavioral experiment.

Rune knew exactly what she was thinking. "Don't look at me like that. Yes, I'm angry. But it's different from before. My brother has been kidnapped by the same person you brought us over here to help destroy. I have emotions. If you wanted someone who didn't have feelings, you should've found yourself a robot."

It took a few more seconds of scientific examination, but eventually the right side of Verida's perfect red lips twitched into a partial smile. "I don't know what a robot is, but I get the point." She dipped her head. "Fair enough."

"OK," Grey said. "If Zio isn't going to kill Ryker, then what does she want with him?"

"I suspect she wants to use him like the council wants to use you, but I really don't know. It's not like we've sat down for tea and discussed it."

Grey huffed in aggravation. "You never wanted to help us in the first place."

The blue of Verida's eyes drained, replaced with a soft red. Her lips pulled back to expose fangs. She took a quick step forward, her heeled boot cracking against the wooden floor like a gunshot.

Even though she'd already been bitten, Rune had never seen Verida in the form she'd always equated with *vampire*. But she saw the dark predator now, and her mouth went dry.

"You have no idea what I've done to be in a position to help you. What I've lost, *who* I've sacrificed. And I will not stand here and have my loyalty questioned. I have come too far to turn back now, and I will do whatever necessary to help you. But out of all the things I will do . . ." Her shoulders sank with a deep weariness, and her eyes fluttered, slowly changing from red to blue again. "I will not allow you two to kill yourselves. Nor will I allow you to make decisions that put you on the council's bad side. You need them, just as much as they need you. If you want to get anything on this side, you have to befriend the council."

"Befriend! How can you expect us to—?"

"Rune, friendship can be faked, it can be manipulated, but it cannot be skipped. You have to—"

"But what if . . . ?" Grey stopped, frowning, then turned to pace, his face twisted in contemplation. He walked back and forth until he finally spun to face them, a mischievous smile lighting his eyes.

"What?" Rune and Verida blurted at the same time.

"Tashara told me the council is terrified of Cashel because he's threatening a coup and has the power to do it."

"Who's Cashel?" Rune asked.

Verida waved a hand over the question. "That's true. What of it?"

"Cashel's the one who took that man's wife and son, right?"

"I would bet on it."

Grey nodded. "The council wants to control us, just like they control everything else. They want to be in charge of what we do and who we serve. But what if we brought Cashel to the council? Would that be enough of a bargaining chip to allow us to do what needs to be done, including taking steps to get Ryker back?"

Rune's chest constricted in gratitude. After everything her brother had done to Grey, he was still willing to try to save him.

"Maybe," Verida said slowly. "If nothing else, it would be a step in the right direction." Her toes tapped out an irritated rhythm on the rug. "All right. I'll go and get the bag. If—and I do mean *if*—whatever's in the bag is something I deem useful enough to make this something besides a suicide mission . . . then fine. But—"

"Deal," Grey said.

"Hold on there, little Venator. You haven't heard the other part. If it's a trick or the bag turns out to be nothing, you will both return to your rooms without further argument." She pointed a reprimanding finger. "And so help me, you will remain there unless the council house is engulfed in flames and you're forced to jump out the window."

"Well," Rune muttered, "that was specific."

Grey's face fell, but he agreed.

"Rune?"

"Deal. What bag?"

"I'll explain on the way." Grey headed for the door. "Let's go."

Verida pursed her lips, watching him as he went. "You know, Grey, you're all sorts of sexy with this new confidence."

His face immediately turned red, and he ducked his head.

It was a gesture Grey had done as long as Rune could remember. At home he would use his mass of black hair to cover his embarrassment, tipping his hair forward and hiding behind that and the collar of his trench. Then, if possible, he would dash toward an escape route.

Rune almost felt bad that he'd lost both his security blankets, but his blushing cheeks were just so cute! "Verida, leave him . . ." She couldn't get it out before she started to giggle.

Grey glared.

"I'm sorry." Rune put her hand over her mouth, trying to stop. "It's just . . ." Another giggle popped out. "You're blushing."

His cheeks flared brighter.

"Yes, he is, and it's adorable." Verida brushed her fingers down Grey's arm as she moved past. "Stay here. I'll be right back."

"But—"

"Nope. Red bag first—our deal hinges on that."

※━◆※◆━※

After the door closed, Rune turned to Grey in exasperation. "What red bag?"

He told the story of Tashara again, leaving out parts that might lead to questions about his past. When he finished, there was a silence so awkward that Grey couldn't help but imagine little crickets chirping around the room while Rune stared. He couldn't decipher what was behind her gaze, but it was uncomfortable. Desperate to break the moment, he shifted his weight to the side. It worked.

"I'm glad you're all right," she said quietly. She turned and laid her brother's necklace on a wooden chest of drawers. The movement was slow and fluid, the way one would set a rose on top of a casket. She reached behind her neck to unclasp her own necklace. "Grey . . . Thank you."

"For what?"

"Caring about Ryker."

Her thanks were unwarranted. He didn't care about Ryker. Not even a little.

Maybe his lack of concern for a fellow human made him a bad person, but their history was dark and made of the stuff that smothered sympathies. Grey took a bit of pride in his self-control— after all, he hadn't taken Ryker into some alleyway and beaten him within an inch of his life. Although he'd had dreams that were extremely satisfactory.

The only reason he cared about Ryker's predicament was because it hurt Rune. But now was not the time to repeat his utter distaste or confess the driving force behind his motivation. The only thing to do was shrug, as if to say, *It was nothing.*

Rune carefully slid Ryker's pendant off his chain and added it to hers. The two white-and-black yin-yang halves nestled one over the top of the other. The thick enamel coating muted the clinking sound they otherwise would've made.

"I bought these for Ryker and me on our fifteenth birthday." Rune reached back and clasped the necklace, setting it gently around her neck. "It was two years after everything went bad . . . after the night Tate showed up."

She turned around and leaned against the dresser, smiling bitterly. "Of course, I didn't know that then. I just knew that, overnight, my brother completely changed. That suddenly there was this distance between us that, no matter what I did, I couldn't bridge."

She ran her finger across the two halves. "I got these thinking it would remind him of how much we'd always meant to each other. How we were better together."

"Did it help?" Grey asked gently, not wanting to break the spell of revelation.

"Not really. But he wore it. I never saw him take it off, and that meant something." She shrugged. "At least to me."

"You two are so . . ."

"So what?"

He searched for a word that was nonoffensive. "Different."

She smiled, but it was weak, and her eyes were sad. "We didn't use to be."

Grey couldn't remember Ryker being anything other than a total asshat. But then again, his memories of Ryker didn't really begin until after that night. His first memory was actually of that day he showed up to school in the trench coat that he'd stolen from a thrift shop—it was the only thing he ever stole. Somehow the coat made him feel safe in a world that was anything but, and once he saw it hanging there on the rack with all the other unwanted things, his thirteen-year-old self couldn't fathom living without it.

"We liked the same games," Rune said. "The same movies, the same people, even the same foods." She laughed. "Except broccoli. He loved the stuff, and I would gag. We were so close, I knew what he was going to say before he said it." Her smile faded. "Not anymore."

Grey knew how desperate Rune was to find her brother, but he worried. Especially with the council in play, watching their every move, and the burst of Rykeresque anger he'd seen from her in times of stress.

"Rune, I . . ." He dipped his head, trying to think what words to use to make her understand.

She sighed. "Just say it."

"I know you love him, but . . . but what if, when you find him, he's worse?" He looked up. "I mean, if one exposure to this world changed him that much—"

"No." She shook her head violently from side to side, as if the very action could shoo away the thoughts Grey had just released. "No. He was just a kid. He didn't understand what was going on. He was confused and angry. But he's here now."

"Why does that make it better?"

"Because! We're calmer on this side, you and me. Ryker's got to be calmer too. And to know that this is all real, that he's not crazy—" She grew more animated, talking with her hands and leaning forward. "Because that's what he had to be feeling, right? Totally nuts. And he couldn't let it go because you were this con-stant reminder—"

"*What?*" Grey reeled, taking a step back.

"I'm not saying it's your fault. I'm not. I'm just saying that he couldn't let it go, which had to have made him feel even more insane. And I didn't know what to say because I didn't know what happened. But now . . ." She gestured over to the window. "Being here will change everything. I know it will."

She stared at the darkened pane, her expression a million miles away. "It has to."

Grey didn't realize he'd been holding his breath, but when she was done, it came out in one skeptical burst. "Rune—"

"Grey, *it will.*"

He swallowed. Then slowly nodded. "All right."

She gripped the pendants in her fist. Tears rimmed her bottom lashes. "I just want my brother back."

Damn it. "I know." And then, because there was nothing else to say, "I know."

The door opened, shattering the moment. Grey and Rune both jumped.

Verida strolled in, kicked the door shut with her foot, leaned back against it, and crossed one ankle over the other. "I don't know whether I'm impressed or irritated." She tossed a red silk bag into the air and caught it.

Grey sighed in relief. "You found it."

"Oh, I found it." She tossed it again and then snatched it out of the air. The silver cord it was tied with wrapped around her wrist like a snake. "What exactly happened with Tashara?"

"Nothing more than what I told you."

She shook her head in disbelief. "Grey, I don't know what you did or how you made her like you." She rolled her eyes skyward. "It's not like I've tried to make nice for the last ten years or anything. But whatever you did . . . it just earned you passage out. This"—she held up the bag, shaking it like a treat for a dog—"is exactly what you needed. Take a look, lover boy."

Verida tossed it, and Grey caught the bag, scowling. "Don't call me that."

"Hey, you earned it. Whatever kind of romantic voodoo you pulled, it paid off."

The silk was fine, and the calloused skin of his fingers caught on the delicate fabric, snagging it in several places. He worked at the silver cord to loosen the drawstring, teasing open the pleated top of the bag.

"What is it?" Rune grabbed his forearm, leaning over to peek.

Inside the bag were three glittering spheres. He glanced up. "I have no idea what I'm looking at."

"That is your ticket to survival. And a deal's a deal. I honor my contracts . . . even those I made under the supreme confidence that both of you would be spending the evening in your rooms. So much for vampire intuition." Verida held the door open and motioned them through. "Let's go. And seriously, no talking until we get to the weapons room. We really, *really* don't want to get caught. I'm not giving you the gory details as to why, so you'll have to trust me."

The three moved through the council house like ghosts—silent footfalls and sealed lips. Verida led them through a maze of halls and doors and winding staircases. Grey tried to make mental notes of their path but quickly lost track. His memory was good, but not this good.

The thick carpeting gave way to wood, then marble, granite, and back to wood again. The first spiral staircase they descended was made from a white marble with gray veining that swirled delicately through it. The banister was made of the same material and had been carved into the likeness of a host of different creatures— fae and werewolves among them. Every mouth was shaped into a pain-filled O, as if crying for freedom from the stone.

Several times, Verida froze, holding her arm out to indicate they should stop. She listened and then hurried them in the opposite direction and down another hallway.

They tiptoed past an arched stone opening large enough that an eighteen-wheeler could've driven through. Grey stared as they passed. It was the kitchen. Wood-burning fireplaces lined the back wall, six of them, with over a dozen black iron pots hanging in each. Suspended above those were smaller cast-iron kettles. Across the room stretched tables, still covered in flour from bread making. Enormous bowls were stacked, and slabs of meat hung from hooks. Somehow he'd come to the conclusion that food preparations for a palace this size would be assisted with magic. Obviously he'd been mistaken.

They kept moving, past the kitchen and deeper into the castle, until they finally came to the end of the small hallway and found it blocked by slim iron doors. Verida placed a palm on each and pushed them open, striding in. Rune and Grey hesitated on the threshold. Rune seemed frozen by nerves. Grey was in awe.

The sconces were already ablaze, and firelight glittered off weaponry that hung on every inch of wall space and lay in stacks around the edges of the room. In the center was a long oak table scattered with stray weapons and helmets. There were swords and daggers, crossbows and scythes, throwing stars and nunchucks. Every weapons era from home was accounted for, every culture.

Grey wondered where these designs had actually originated— at home, carried to this side by the old Venators, or the other way around. In addition to all he was familiar with, there were some items he didn't recognize.

As he stepped inside, the smell became stronger. It was interesting, metal and leather and something else that had a distinctive bite on the end. Grey suspected it was whatever they used to oil the leather.

At the end of the room sat Tate, legs kicked up on the table and hands behind his head. Once Grey and Rune were inside, he dropped his feet heavily to the ground, simultaneously pulling one arm forward. Rune jumped, and Tate loosed a dagger he'd held between two fingers. It flew end over end straight at Grey.

He spun to the side as the blade flew past with a whistling sound, a soft wave of displaced air tickling his nose where the blade had nearly shortened it. It thudded into the wall, quivering. His Venator reflexes served him well, thankfully, or he would've been the human representation of a butterfly on a board.

He should've been terrified, or at least angry, but he was only amazed. In that moment, his eyesight had sharpened, and he'd been able to make out the design etched into the handle as it twisted past. That should've been impossible, but a glance at the blade in the wall confirmed what he'd seen.

"What the hell!" Rune shouted.

"Good, you can dodge a blade. We might survive."

"And if he couldn't?" Rune's voice rose. "You aimed for his face!"

"I knew he could. I just needed him to know he could." Tate stood, looking pleased. He tucked another blade somewhere inside his trench coat. It already looked heavily weighed down with who knew what kind of weaponry. "I wondered how long it would take you to find your way here. Although I wasn't expecting her." He motioned to Rune.

She crossed her arms. "I know Zio has my brother."

"Ah," Tate said. "That explains it."

"Would you like to know *how* she knows?" Verida snatched the dagger from the wall, looked it over, and tucked it into her belt. "A large black bird delivered proof."

"How very . . . thoughtful." He held out a hand. "I believe that's mine."

Verida huffed and handed it back, hilt first. "I like that one."

"Find your own." Tate slipped the dagger up his sleeve like a magician might vanish a deck of cards. "There's a nice selection."

Rune wasn't paying attention. She stood, absently rubbing at the two yin-and-yang pendants, eyes glazed over. Body in the room, mind gone. "I've never seen an animal act like that before," she muttered. "It watched my reaction and then just sat there looking at me, like it was thinking it over."

"The thinking is questionable." Verida chuckled at her own joke, which made no sense to Rune or Grey but received a rare grin from Tate. "And trust me, stay clear of the . . . *bird*."

Rune scowled. "Why did you say it like that? '*Bird*.'" She made little quotation marks in the air. "I know what I saw."

"You know what you *think* you saw. Trusting your eyes on Eon is a dangerous habit." Verida grinned and gave a little wink.

Grey wandered over to a wall that had a large variety of throwing stars displayed. He was still thinking about what Tate had said as he ran his fingers over the surface of one, careful to avoid the razor-sharp tips. "How'd you know I'd come?"

"From what little I've seen, I didn't think you'd let this stand. Glad to see I didn't misjudge you."

"Whoa!" Verida stepped between Grey and Tate, blonde hair whipping to the side. "Are you serious? You had every intention of taking him out behind my back without any training?"

Tate looked down at her, one eyebrow cocked. "I don't know what you're so upset about. You're the one who escorted them down here."

"Against my will!"

"Then why did you?"

"Because I made a damn promise I was sure I wouldn't have to keep." She rolled her eyes while stepping out from between them and giving her head a sharp jerk to the side. "We're here because of that."

Grey held out the gift that had made the rescue mission possible.

Tate took the bag, untying the silk cord. He looked in and inhaled sharply. "Where did you get this?"

Verida answered. "Tashara."

Tate's eyebrows slowly rose, and he cocked his head as if to say, *Really?* Verida gave a smirk in return, finishing the silent conversation.

"Interesting." Tate pulled one shiny crystal ball free of its velvet container and held it high between two fingers, twisting it back and forth.

It was faceted like a diamond, the size of a baby's fist, and reflected bright reds and blues in the firelight just as brilliantly as if it'd been displayed with professional lighting in a fine jewelry case.

"These," he said, "are nixie drops. Bubbles that are trapped by magic and solidified. Hard, stable, and very difficult to come by. They're sold on the black market for a price that limits the possession to a small group of elite."

Rune reached to touch the crystal, but Tate slipped it into the bag. "Nixies live in lakes or something, right?" she asked. "Their bubbles can't be that rare?"

"Nixies are little demons wrapped in a pretty package." Verida crossed her arms and shuddered. "I *hate* nixies. They're smart, cunning, and fast. Most poachers don't survive the collection."

"But if most die, then how . . ."

Grey stopped listening. Under normal circumstances he would've found this information fascinating, grabbing every bit he could and storing it in the supernatural data bank he'd amassed. But now was not the time for information—now was the time to act. They had to get out there before it was too late, and instead they were all standing around chatting about nixie bubbles as if it were a soirée.

"What do they do?" he said loudly, interrupting Rune and Verida's conversation.

"They render you invisible for a limited amount of time," Tate said. "As long as you stay within the bubble-like shape, you'll remain hidden. But reach out for a strike, like this," he pulled his arm up, "and your arm will be seen. These offer *no* protection other than invisibility. An arrow will still kill you, invisible or not."

Grey would've preferred actual protection, but beggars can't be choosers. It was something, and it was the something that had persuaded Verida to help.

"I'd like to know why Tashara just happens to have a bag of nixie drops lying around," Verida said.

"That's a question for another day, isn't it?" Tate tossed the bag to Grey. "And one for our favored friend here to ask."

"Me?" Grey shrunk a little inside.

"Well." Verida snorted. "She isn't going to tell *me*."

Tate moved to the wall, perusing the options that were mounted from ceiling to floor. They had been carefully placed for ultimate space maximization, only a few slivers of plaster showing between the weapons. He pulled a crossbow from the wall. It had a stained wood stock and a dark leather strap attached. "This would be a great option for both of you. There's little experience needed, and your natural abilities should take care of aim and difficulty of pullback." He grabbed a sheath of bolts. "These are silver tipped and have the potential to be quite deadly to werewolves."

Grey took the crossbow, hefting its weight. Without modern technologies, the bow lacked the lightweight carbon fiber he was accustomed to. This one had been carved and forged of wood and metal.

Tate handed Rune a second, slightly smaller bow. "You transport it like this." He put his arm through the leather strap on his own bow and spun the weapon around so that it lay flat against this back. The leather crossed his chest at the same angle as a rifle strap. "If you need to fire, you're going to pull here." He gripped the strap with his left hand and dragged it across his chest. The bow rose, and Tate grabbed the stock with his right, pulled it the rest of the way over his shoulder, and placed it in firing position.

Grey imitated the move.

Tate nodded. "Exactly."

Rune looked at the bow with reservation. "I've never used a weapon before."

"I would suspect tonight is the last time you'll be able to say that." He motioned for her to try.

Verida shoved several of the helmets that littered the top of the table out of the way and hopped up, spinning around to face them before leaning casually back on her palms. "You're not letting them go alone, are you?"

"What kind of fool do you take me for? I'm not trying to kill them."

Grey had assumed Verida was coming with them. "You're staying?"

"Ooh, yes. First of all, there are only three nixie bubbles. One of us has to stay. And I was charged with ensuring the two 'unpredictable and possibly dangerous Venators' stayed in their rooms." She snorted. "Dangerous as a pile of kittens."

"A pile of kittens? Really?" Rune pulled the bow around with the strap and held it up, peering through the sights. "That's not what you said earlier."

Verida smirked and inclined her head toward Rune. "Well played. But see, the trouble is, I can't claim ignorance if I go with you. I'll be in enough trouble when you get back without joining in on the fun. And as far as Tate is concerned . . ." She leaned forward, her red lips overexaggerating every word. "He. Was. *Never.* There. Understood?"

READY FOR BATTLE

Grey and Rune both slung crossbows over their backs and secured pouches of throwing stars and silver powder to their belts. Daggers snuggled into the sheaths that had been constructed into their pant legs, Grey felt heavy but ready for battle.

Tate jerked an ax off the wall. It had a blade around four feet long and seemed to have been made for Stan and Bob, the friendly guard giants.

"There's no way I can swing that," Grey said. "Venator or not."

"This isn't for you." He tossed the ax to the side, grunting from the effort.

It smashed down hard, tipping from the end of the handle to the top of the blade and back again, clattering like the lid of a pan.

Verida jumped. "Why don't you just sound the alarm, Tate?"

He ignored her and pushed at the wall where the ax had hung. It clicked, and a panel popped out just far enough for Tate to wrap his fingers around the edge and swing it the rest of the way open, revealing a hidden tunnel. A gust of musty air welcomed them.

"Servant passageways. It's imperative that we're quiet. We'll be passing multiple doors that allow servants to emerge in different halls throughout the council house. The last thing we need is for someone to realize their two new Venators are sneaking out of the castle." Tate reached over Grey's head and grabbed a torch from the wall.

The flames were too bright for a normal fire. They burned almost white at the center and put off very little heat. Grey suspected they were fueled with magic.

Tate swung the torch inside the tunnel entrance. Rats scurried from the light, squealing displeasure at the interruption.

Rune groaned. "I hate rats."

"Tate." There was an unmistakable edge of fear in Verida's voice. "Bring them back alive, all right? For all our sakes."

"Of course."

Grey and Rune looked back and forth between the two, trying to decipher the unnamed punishment Verida had alluded to. But neither seemed willing to elaborate.

Tate gave a subtle jerk of his chin. "I thought we were in a hurry." He placed one hand on Rune's shoulder and pushed her into the tunnel, then reached over and gave Grey a shove. Once inside, Tate squeezed past, holding the torch high and heading out with a quick gait. His footfalls were remarkably silent given his size and heavy footwear.

Rune jogged forward on the balls of her feet, softening her steps. "Hey! What will they do to Verida?"

Tate grunted something indiscernible.

"What?"

"You don't want to know."

"But we can't—"

"It's her choice," Tate interrupted sharply. "Leave it alone."

Grey looked over his shoulder. Verida hopped off the table and pushed the door shut behind them. The light from the weapons room vanished, and they were swathed in thick darkness— penetrated only by the probing fingers of the torch's firelight.

Grey's diminished sense of sight increased his already acute awareness of the smell—damp and musty, mixed with the pungent aroma of a ripe latrine. Rusty water dripped slowly down the wall, depositing gleaming orange along old brick that was briefly illuminated as Tate passed.

The shape of the tunnel created an acoustic hot spot. The slopping stone amplified every sound. It picked up the nuances between a trickle of water and the occasional drip and bounced them around until the drops sounded like buckets of water being dashed against the stone and the trickle a river.

Tate expected them to be quiet? Everything was loud. Breathing, walking . . . even Grey's thoughts seemed deafening.

The floor had been worn smooth and was slick with a coating of slime. His feet slid, and he nearly landed on his back end several times before finding a comfortable, solid gait.

They walked, taking right turns, then left, then right again until Grey knew he'd never be able to trace his way back. Tate kept a good pace, slowing only when they came upon the doors that led to the council house halls.

They didn't look like doors at all. They were covered in the same stone as the tunnels, aged and worn. A line of horizontally laid bricks ran around the frame in a perfect rectangle. Grey looked closer in passing, trying to peer through the gloom in order to figure out how it would open. There were no handles, no finger holds, just a line of missing mortar on either side that could allow a hinged door to open.

They turned yet another corner, and in the middle of the passageway stood a rat.

It pushed up onto its hind legs and fearlessly stared them down, its pink nose twitching. Rune yelped and jumped backward, then slapped her hands over her mouth. Tate hissed at the rodent and waved the torch. The rat ignored the first pass of flame, which was strange, but scampered off on the second, offering an indignant little squeak as a parting gesture.

Rune shuddered. "I *really* hate rats."

Tate hung the torch low, sweeping it back and forth in search of the rodent. "The feeling is probably mutual."

"You said these passageways were used by servants." Rune wrapped her arms around herself. "Why haven't we run into anyone yet?"

"I ensured that wouldn't happen. Let's go."

"You cleared the tunnels because you somehow 'knew' we would end up in the weapons room," Rune said, walking nearly on Tate's heels. "That's a lot of work for a hunch."

"Have you always been this suspicious of everything?"

"No," Rune snapped. "It's been a fairly recent development, actually."

Grey chuckled and was reprimanded with a sidelong glance from Tate, half hidden in shadow.

"Your suspicions will serve you well here, but keep them pointed in the right direction."

"Meaning?"

Tate whirled around on her, the flame of the torch painting his movement in an arch. "Away from me. You'll have to trust me with your life tonight. If you're not ready to do that, you're putting all of us in danger. It's not too late to head back."

"I'm not going to—"

"Think about it." Tate straightened. He held one hand out—a silent instruction to stay put—and moved cautiously toward the next bend.

They had to be very near an exit. A soft light spilled in from around the corner, and a gentle breeze slipped through crevices, whistling a haunting tune. Water dripped somewhere ahead of them in an odd syncopation, and the bleating of goats punctuated it all like drumbeats.

Once Tate reached the bend, he set the torch down on the stone floor—out of sight to whoever might be around the corner while still offering a hint of light for Rune and Grey. He pressed his back to the wall and moved around the curve with small, controlled steps.

After he was out of sight, they waited.

Rune ran her fingers aimlessly over the horizontal bricks that outlined the last doorway. She watched with interest as her fingers jumped from the higher brick material to the lower divots of the mortar.

Grey wondered what she was thinking. Was she contemplating opening that door and heading back? Part of him wished she would—wished she would stay here and out of immediate danger. But no, it probably wasn't that. He'd heard the conviction in her voice when she talked about finding Ryker.

She was all in, whether she wanted to be or not.

Rune breathed deeply and leaned against the tunnel wall. She pressed the bases of her palms into her eyes.

"You OK?" Grey whispered.

Wearily, she turned her head. The hair from her ponytail caught against the rough brick. "You keep asking me that, but I don't think it matters."

"It matters. We're about to—"

He was interrupted as their Venator marks flickered a dark red. Rune slowly looked down at her arms and then back to him, her mouth partially open in a soft *O*.

Grey twisted to look toward the torch. Nothing. He turned back the way they'd come. Dread slowed his movements in a way he knew was counterintuitive but couldn't override. There, the darkness stretched out before him, seeming to transform into a living, breathing thing—malicious in its intent to hide their enemies from them.

His Venator side rose under the threat, and his vision enhanced, allowing him to see a little deeper into the gloom. But there was still a line he couldn't push past where darkened depths blocked him, refusing to reveal their secrets.

Something banged violently against the wall behind Rune. She jumped forward, spinning to look at the spot where she'd just been standing. Tiny pieces of mortar clattered to the floor. The door cracked open, and a stream of light slashed into the tunnel.

Rune froze, fixated on the light. The only discernable movements were the slight changes in her face as terror spread over her features.

"What's going on out there?" came a voice through the crack.

Grey would've recognized it anyway, but the maroon on his arms solidified the speaker as Silen.

Rune was out of view for now, but if that door cracked one more inch, she'd be visible. Grey reached out and grabbed her by the wrist. Her head whipped in his direction, looking like a deer caught in headlights.

"I don't know what you mean—no, no!" a second male begged. "I'm sorr—"

There was a grunt, then the sound of someone being forcibly dragged and slammed back against the wall.

Grey used the noise to cover his movement. He jerked Rune toward him. The sudden jolt frightened her further, and she started to squeak. Grey clapped a hand around her mouth and pulled her against his chest, dragging her backward to the hinging side of the door—the last place they'd be seen if it opened further. He pressed as flat to the wall as possible.

Rune reached up and peeled his hand away.

"Tonight," Silen began, "I was informed by a *vampire* that the new Venators were attacked on their way here. I was forced to admit in front of the entire council that not only was I unaware of any intent but that I hadn't even heard that the event had occurred. Do you have *any* idea how that makes me look?"

"That only happened hours ago," the second voice said. "The Venators were practically at the gates when the attack—"

The words were cut off by a gagging sound. The door creaked open a little bit more. "Please—" the second male croaked. "Silen!"

"Should I squeeze harder? There's no excuse for mistakes, so stop making them." Silen's voice was low and dangerous. Grey felt a shiver run up Rune's spine. "Did you know your pack kidnapped a family this evening? Yes, I thought so. You knew, but I, acting council member for the werewolves, did not. Do you see my problem, Amar?"

Amar wheezed. Then came the sound of something, or someone, being dragged *up* the wall. The door inched further open. The heels of Amar's boots beat against the wall twelve inches up. More mortar dust pitter-pattered against the floor.

Grey leaned his head against the bricks and squeezed his eyes shut. Werewolves had enhanced senses too, and that door kept inching wider. How long before Silen caught their scent? A minute? Five?

It was only a matter of time.

"Can you imagine," Silen asked, "how it must've looked to the rest of the council when a man stumbled in tonight, bleeding all over the floor and begging for help to save his family from Cashel's pack? Can you?"

There was a thud as Amar's body crashed to the floor.

"It looks like I don't have control over my own wolves—that's how it looks," Silen barked. "Now talk!"

"Cashel heard the news . . ." Amar fell into a fit of coughing. ". . . of the Venators. The pack is getting ready to move."

"This isn't news."

"It's different this time."

"Different? Oh, for hell's sake, get on your feet. *I said*, on your feet!"

There was rustling as Amar pulled himself up from the floor. He coughed, then gagged. "What is that smell?"

Grey and Rune tensed.

Silen ignored the question. "Does Cashel's pack have the needed support?"

"They do now."

There was a long, low growl. "Who joined?"

"Ransan's pack. They've already lost wolves." Amar snarled. "Did the council's little Venshii tell you that?"

"How many?"

"Two dead, one severely injured."

Tate reappeared around the bend. Grey shook his head frantically, trying to get his attention before he took one step too close and alerted the wolves. Tate didn't see Grey, but he immediately noticed the slice of light coming in from the council house halls and froze.

"Where is Cashel's pack headed first?"

"I don't know." There was the sound of a single, heavy footfall. Amar's voice rose in panic. "I tried to ask. I did. But the pack was getting suspicious. You know what they do to spies!"

"So instead of facing the wrath of your pack, you decided to come to me? Risking your cover—and thereby your value—with *nothing?*"

"It's not nothing. I know the pack has entertainment for the evening . . ." Realizing what he'd said, he cleared his throat. "As you found out. But it sounds like Cashel will wait until the next moon, using the time to finalize alliances before moving on your pack."

Silence. Excruciating, blind silence.

"*What did you say?*"

"It's true. That much I did hear. Cashel is betting the attack will force you out into the open. He plans to take control of your pack . . . and then your seat."

"He wants my spot on the council?"

"What better way to gain access to Dimitri? The plan is cleaner than trying to storm the walls with Omri and Ambrose here."

"Cleaner." He spat. "What honor is there in that?"

Amar gagged again. "Bloody bones, what *is* that smell?"

"Servants' tunnels."

"It's burning my nostrils."

Grey closed his eyes in relief, sagging back. The stench of the tunnels had covered their scent.

"Burning your nostrils, is it?"

The door inched open just a little more, and the heel of a black boot stepped into view as Amar retreated.

"I don't give a rat's ass about your nostrils." Silen was so close now, his voice had started to echo through the tunnel. "Get me information. I need to know exactly when Cashel plans to move. My pack will be ready and waiting. Fail me again, Amar, and I will gut you while you still breathe and wave your large intestine under your nose so you can get a whiff of *that*. Understand? Good."

Amar stepped forward, vanishing back into the council halls. The door creaked a little further open and then yanked shut.

Tate, Grey, and Rune waited, motionless. Seconds ticked past until finally the color in their markings faded to black. Tate relaxed and waved them forward.

As they moved, his eyes stayed glued to the door. When Grey and Rune came up next to him, he asked, "Silen?"

"Yeah."

"Hear anything important?"

"Cashel is planning to go after Silen's pack and then take his council seat," Grey said.

234

"At this rate, Zio won't have to destroy the council. They're going do it for her."

"You know . . ." Rune rolled her neck and shook the tension out of her arms. "Maybe we should just let them."

Tate looked down at Rune, a deep frown cutting lines down his face.

"What?" she asked. "Why not?"

"Why not? Because Zio only keeps those around she finds useful. If the council, although corrupt, were to suddenly be eliminated, it would create such an upheaval, there wouldn't be anything or anyone standing in Zio's way. And much like the Venators of old, she would destroy everything." He cocked an eyebrow. "Is that what you want?"

Rune pulled in a breath to answer but held it there. Finally, her features softened, and she exhaled. "No."

"Good. Because if that ever changes . . ."

She held up a hand. "Elimination, death. Yeah, I know. Please, stop reminding me."

"Some things need remembering." Tate jerked his head for them to follow and headed for the exit.

As they stepped free of the tunnel, the sharp ammonia of barnyard excrement assaulted Grey's nose. They were surrounded by stables full of horses, cows, sheep, and goats. The stable with the lowest roof sat nearest the servant exit, and inside stood so many of the unique goats he'd seen when they first arrived that he couldn't count them. Little double-bearded chins poked over the top of gates as the animals watched the three intruders with curious black eyes.

"We have to move," Tate said. "Quickly."

Horses whinnied in their stalls as they ran past. Grey worried the universal agitation amongst the animals would be cause for alarm, but Tate had been thorough—there didn't seem to be anyone here.

Tate's hulking frame slipped behind the furthest stable, using it as a blind between them and the council house. He put a finger to his lips and motioned them lower. Together, the three of them moved forward in a crouch.

It took longer than it should've for Grey to realize where they were heading, but as the ground dropped away in front of him to show open sky, he knew. The cliffs.

Standing half-bent at the waist, he looked over the edge. The walls were completely vertical, descending hundreds of feet to the valley floor. The wind raced up the cliff face and slapped at him. Grey got the distinct impression it was speaking to him: *Stay away, you fool!*

The placement of the mansion had been strategically chosen. On their way up, it had been the cliffs that offered protection from the wolves. Now that security had become his obstacle.

Tate turned and slid over the edge, keeping his weapon-laden belt from scraping against the ground while using the grooves in the rock to lower himself until only his head was visible. Neither Rune nor Grey moved to follow. "Don't know what you're waiting for. This is the only way down."

"Are you crazy?" Rune hissed through clenched teeth. "We don't have any safety equipment."

"Nor will you ever. Now get down here, or go back before you get us all caught."

Grey had avoided heights because, though he'd never said it aloud, he was terrified of them. Admitting the truth now seemed both terrible timing and a pointless act, as he was not willing to let two people die. So he kept his mouth shut, laid on his belly, wiggled out over the edge, and tried not to vomit.

Tate disappeared, but his words floated up. "This is what you both wanted, right? Just call it your first day of training."

"Yeah," Rune said. "This is exactly what I had in mind." She mumbled a few choice names for Tate.

Grey honestly expected her to turn back, but instead she was on her stomach next to him, preparing to begin the descent. He locked one toe into a groove and placed weight on it, only to have his foot slip.

"Grey!" Rune gasped.

"I'm OK."

He did not feel the slightest bit OK. His hands were dripping sweat, his muscles were taut to the point of pain, and his stomach had turned to a thick, pulsating mass that was now lodged in his esophagus.

"We don't have to do this, you know."

He looked over at her, wanting so badly to succumb to fear and walk away. "I have to do this. But you can stay—it's not too late."

She closed her eyes tightly, shaking her head. "Grey, if I don't make it . . ."

"Rune, stop."

"Find Ryker. Promise me."

The height was forgotten for a moment. All he really wanted was for Ryker to disappear with the rest of the world they'd known. But Ryker was here, and Rune was looking at him with wide, brown, desperate eyes, and the words *Request denied* withered to a pile of dust and blew away with the breeze. "Yeah," he promised. "I'll find him."

"Thank you." Rune peeked over her shoulder at the drop below. "Ready?"

"Nope." Grey forced a smile that hopefully looked less demented than it felt and began the descent.

It was pathetic at best; he paused two times to wipe the sweat from his palms before his head even vanished from view. Once completely over the edge, he pressed his body as flat to the rock as possible, checking and double-checking each hand and toehold. He made tediously slow progress.

There was nothing between him and certain death. No ropes, no harness. All it would take was one slip, one mistake, and then . . . No! He had to control his thoughts. Maybe if he didn't look down, his palms would stop sweating.

No such luck.

The next thing Grey knew, Rune was moving past him with the ease of a seasoned professional. He sputtered.

"This is amazing!" Rune grinned, looking more alive than ever. Grey's terror must've been painted across his face, because she tossed back the words he'd fed her earlier. "Don't let your fear get in the way. Just *feel* it."

Rune continued easily, and he craned his neck out as far as he dared to watch her descend like a rock monkey, mocking him with every sure hold. She quickly caught up to Tate and passed him. Grey shook his head. Unbelievable.

Halfway down, he pushed three fingers into a slick crevice, testing it. Deciding it was secure, he shifted, preparing to move to the next toehold. In that moment, one hand slipped free. The jolt knocked his feet out, and he dangled by one arm, twisting in the air. Time slowed to a crawl. Tiny details became overwhelming—the feel of the rock under his fingers, the way the world spun out below, how his body tensed as it hit and then bounced off the wall.

A bird swooped inches from his face and screeched, restarting the clock. Time rushed to catch up. Grey gasped and spun back to the rock, swearing. He slammed against the cliff and scrambled to secure all four points of contact, sucking in air like a fish out of water.

Desperate to get off this wall before it killed him, Grey ignored everything—pounding knee, thudding heart, sweating palms, dry mouth—and moved faster than before. Still, it felt like an eternity before he reached the bottom.

With feet on solid ground, Grey leaned over his knees. "Never again. Never, ever again."

Tate gave him a side eye. "Get used to it."

Rune's blood sang. Earlier, she thought she'd understood when Grey had tried to explain—there *had* been a rush when the Venator side was finally unlocked and they'd run. But that had been nothing compared to this.

Climbing was effortless, wonderful, a high unlike anything else. She wanted to turn around and climb back up just for the fun of it. The thought of needing safety equipment made her laugh now—as if she could fall. She felt . . . well, she felt invincible. And she *liked* it.

"We all survived," Tate said. "Off to a good start."

"Any more climbing?" Grey looked ill.

"Not until we come back." Tate pointed. "This way."

Grey gave a loathing gaze back up the cliff before falling in behind Tate. They trudged into the thick forest that surrounded the castle.

The moon illuminated the night. It had been extremely helpful coming down the cliff, but now the rays were broken by the wash of branches above. Inexplicably, and despite the interruption, the forest floor was bejeweled with strange patches of light. She searched for the source and discovered globs of glowing blue mushrooms that danced up the south sides of trunks, the heads of the fungi fanning out like ball gowns on sprites. Adding to the magic were the night flowers winding down branches on delicate, curling stems, their petals spread and luminescing in an array of reds and pinks. Strange clicks and chirps filled the air, made by animals and insects she couldn't see.

A glowing pink-and-blue butterfly fluttered in front of her face, and Rune smiled, watching until it flitted away.

They'd been walking for nearly an hour when some bushes rustled near Grey's foot, followed by a sneeze. He quickly pulled a dagger, advancing on the threat with more confidence than Rune would've.

"Wait." Tate pushed Grey's wrist down, stepping between him and the offending plant. "Either you can come out, or this bolt is coming in."

No response. Tate pulled the crossbow from his back. A *snick* announced the bolt was loaded.

A squeak burst out. "Stop!"

Tate frowned over the sights of the bow as if the squeak were somehow familiar. "Show yourself. I'm not telling you again."

There was rustling, and then a small creature crawled out from beneath the leafy plant. Rune jerked back involuntarily. It was unlike anything she'd ever seen. The animal had short, squatty legs and long, thin arms, similar to an ape or orangutan. It didn't have fur but instead was covered in gray, wrinkly skin and looked exactly like a hairless cat's. Its perfectly round face held two enormous, bat-like ears, bright-blue eyes the size of small plates, and a tiny button nose. Its appearance was so strange, she couldn't decide if it landed in the "ugly-cute" zone or solidly in "completely hideous."

Tate growled in irritated recognition. "Danchee." He seized the thing by the ears and picked it up, ignoring the squeals as it kicked with scrawny legs. "Who hired you?"

Danchee stilled, his lower lip trembling. "I's not working, sir."

"Really. Then why are you spying on us?"

"I's here for me own curiosity. I's heard rumors, stories, and wanted to sees if the stories were true."

"Stories?" Tate snapped, giving the creature a couple rough shakes. "What stories?"

Danchee squeezed his eyes shut as he rattled around. "You's didn't exactly come through the gate quietly."

"Who did *you* hear it from?"

"Feena." He cringed to the side as if expecting a blow. "But Danchee didn't say nuthin', nuthin' about you and the council. Nuthin'. I's just there, that's all. I swears it!"

Tate glared, taking several deep breaths through his nose. Rune was sure he was mentally counting to ten . . . or maybe fifty. Arms and shoulders corded in tight control, he slowly lowered Danchee.

Rune glanced at Grey's markings, which had gone black. Hers were the same. Why didn't Danchee's presence trigger a reaction? Now that she thought about it, this was the first time her markings had been solid black since they'd arrived.

Back on the ground, Danchee rubbed his ears indignantly. "I's didn't do nuthin'. Tate should learn to ask nicely," he muttered.

Tate growled and took a step forward.

Danchee squealed again. He ran behind Grey and peeked through his legs. "You's make me not want to tell you what I's be hearing at Feena's."

Based on the murderous look on Tate's face, the middle was not a good place to be. Grey quickly high-stepped to the side over Danchee's head.

Tate crouched down so the two were on eye level. "I don't have time for this right now, you traitorous little mutt."

"You's have time. Trust me. But if I's tell you what I know, we's even. You's not be telling Dimitri you's saw me."

Several howls broke the night, and then came the faint sound of a human scream. "Tate," Grey pleaded. "We have to go."

Ignoring him, Tate levered back to his feet. "Deal."

"Feena said that . . ." Danchee's voice changed. It lost the strange vocal patterns he used and took on the sound of a distinguished female diplomat. "'Tate needs to be taught a lesson. He's forgotten his place. I've arranged a spectacle. The next games will be just like old times.'" Whoever Danchee was imitating tittered with laughter. "'A family affair.'"

The words brought an immediate transformation. Tate's spine jerked as if struck by lightning. The scene played out in slow motion. Tate took a step toward Danchee while one hand flipped his trench coat to the side. His fingers wrapped around the handle of a dagger. Danchee squealed and fell to the ground.

The creature was even more stupid than he first appeared if he'd decided playing dead would help against Tate. Dirt flew back as Danchee tunneled down like a mole. His progress was fast, but Tate bent over, hand outstretched. There was no way he'd escape. Danchee's bottom disappeared beneath the soil, and he shot off like a rocket, leaving a crescent-shaped path of slightly heaped earth behind him. Dirt and rock spattered the tree trunks like shrapnel.

Tate kicked at the mound of dirt, letting loose a string of obscenities. When the words dried up, he stood there, hunched, staring at the hole and taking deep, hissing breaths.

"What games?" Grey ventured.

Tate deflated, stumbling to the side. "No games . . . not now. I don't . . . I can't—" And then, as if it were a switch that he had the luxury of flipping on and off at will, all the rage and sorrow disappeared. He lifted his head. "We have werewolves to deal with."

A sinking feeling overtook Rune. She didn't understand anything about this land or the people. Those she was supposed to trust had pasts she knew nothing about. It would take trust and time to unravel what she'd walked into. But with danger appearing out of every nook, cranny, and squeaking bush, ignorance could be fatal.

NIXIE BUBBLES

The forest was beautiful and otherworldly, but Grey wasn't in a mental state to appreciate it.

He and Rune trailed behind Tate, who was purposefully staying far enough ahead to avoid the possibility of conversation. Rune had slowly lost that Venator high she'd been running on after the cliffs and was now jittery, startling at every noise.

Grey's anxiousness was a bitter taste lodged in the back of his throat. What if they were too late?

Tate skirted them widely around a blue bush whose leaves were edged with razor-thin lines of glowing red. He grunted something that sounded like, "Don't touch that."

"How much farther?" Grey asked.

"It's hard to know," Tate said. "The howling stopped."

Grey wanted to punch something. He settled for kicking a bush, but the soft give of the foliage wasn't satisfactory. "The moon is full, and they're in wolf form, so why aren't they howling?"

Tate stopped for a moment, orienting himself, and then turned abruptly to the west. "Werewolves can only change when the moon's full—though they retain their strength and healing the rest of the month. But during a full moon, they aren't limited to their wolf form alone—they can turn at will. Those who choose the pack life change when convenient or when hunting. If they're at camp, it's likely they're in human form. Wait—" He pulled up short, fingering a broken branch in front of a trampled patch of night flowers.

Grey came up next to him. "Wolves?"

"I don't know. Possibly. Something came through here in a hurry."

Rune absently ran her fingers over a patch of shiny green leaves while gazing at a particularly bright grouping of blue mushrooms. A slick substance coated the tips of her fingers, and she yelped, jerking her hand away.

Grey jumped. "What is it?"

"There was something on the leaves. I'm sorry, it just surprised me." She frowned, rubbing her fingers together. "What is this?"

Tate grabbed her hand and held it up to the cerulean light. "Blood."

Rune yanked away, frantically wiping her hand on her pants. "Does werewolf blood carry the . . . virus?"

"No. Just the saliva. But you don't need to worry about it. Venators are immune to most threats in this world." Tate crouched to look at the leaves. He pushed one up with the tip of his finger and examined underneath.

"*Most* threats?" Rune asked.

"Most." Tate rose slowly and rotated in a careful circle, scanning the ground. "You can still be killed in most of the usual ways—drowning, stabbing, fire, falling from a great height, dismemberment—"

"I got it! Man, remind me never to come to you for a pep talk."

Grey squatted down on the opposite side of the bloody plant, next to fresh impressions in the soft forest floor. "Here—footprints."

"Man or wolf?"

"Both."

Tate swore. "I could tell from the howls they were hunting. I had hoped it was deer."

"What . . ." Rune swallowed. "What *were* they hunting?"

"The son."

"But . . . that means he escaped, right?" At Grey's grief-filled stare, she added weakly, "Maybe he made it."

"That would be a much better story." Tate moved around in a widening circle, checking for footprints and broken branches. "But no. They let him go on purpose. This was a game—a hunt."

That visual was too much for Grey. Darkness crept around him, pressing down like a physical presence. He'd wanted to be in a position to help, to offer security to others—the security that was never offered to him—not stand here while an innocent boy was hunted down like an animal. Not to work for a council who couldn't care less about what was going on right outside their gilded walls. He leaned one arm against the rough bark and rested his head. He'd romanticized living in this world, or at least amongst these things, from the day Tate had rescued him. The flaw in his thought process was glaring.

"Do you think he's . . . dead?" Rune asked.

"He has to be." Grey's voice cracked. "It's too quiet. The game is over."

A scream rose and fell. Tate looked in the direction of the cry. "But the next game has just begun."

Grey lifted his head, a dark hope blooming in his chest. It was hollow and beaten down by defeat, but it was there.

Tate pulled open the drawstrings to the bag and handed them each a nixie bubble.

"Already?" Grey asked. "I thought we were saving them for when we found the camp."

"You need to pay better attention."

"The bubbles only protect our shape," Rune said, repeating Tate's instructions from the weapons room. "Any extended movement"—she pulled a dagger and swiped it outward—"will be seen."

The corner of Tate's mouth twitched in what looked like the start of a smile. "Exactly. I'm glad one of you was listening. Even the crossbows are long enough to break through the spell and become visible. So unless you intend on fighting with your arms by your sides, we use the bubbles to get through this forest and past the hunting parties unseen." Tate held up the solidified bubble between two fingers. "We use these to put us in position to strike, nothing more. Put your lips against the side, and breathe in."

"But how are we supposed to see each other?" Rune asked. "I don't know where to go."

"You'll be able to see me and Grey." Addressing Rune's confused look, he added, "Trust me."

Grey put the bubble to his lips—it was cool to the touch—and pulled a breath in. The shimmering orb shrank in his fingers. What felt like liquid trickled down his throat.

Tate and Rune vanished.

Grey panicked. He couldn't see them at all!

"Tate?" Rune's frightened voice came from the same spot she'd been standing in before she vanished.

A short moment of silence . . . and then Rune and Tate reappeared, surrounded by a white film that muted their silhouettes. Grey assumed it was the nixie magic he was looking at—whatever it was that made them all invisible to the naked eye.

They ran in the direction of the last scream. It wasn't long before Tate pressed himself flat against a tree trunk. With his arm tucked tightly at his side, he flicked his fingers, motioning for them to do the same while remaining within the confines of their bubbles.

Grey stepped back, imitating Tate's stance, and pushed against the trunk nearest him. In the distance came the sound of breaking branches. The sounds grew closer until the rumble sounded like an oncoming freight train. He held his breath.

A small pack of wolves tore by twenty feet to the left.

The monstrously large bodies flew past in a blur. Grey's heart slammed against his ribs, and he tried to press himself even flatter to the tree. He'd known logically that the wolves were fast. After all, he'd known how fast he could run on earth, and the wolves had almost matched their speed. But standing at a dead stop and watching them go by put things into a terrifyingly new perspective.

And they were *so close.*

The only thing saving the three of them now was that the wolves were both running and distracted, because the nixie bubbles did nothing to hide their scent—that much he'd remembered from their talk in the weapons room just fine.

When the last wolf had streaked past, Tate waited to move until the forest became quiet once again. Finally, he held a finger up to his lip—reminding them they could still be heard—and continued on.

The howls of the pack guided them further into the forest. But it wasn't long after that the wolf cries intermixed with two screams—one male, one female.

"They took more than we knew about," Tate said under his breath as they rushed toward the sounds. "They probably found a traveler."

"How do people not know to stay out of the woods on a full moon?" Rune leapt over a fallen log, and the bottom halves of her legs extended past the bubble's protection.

"Careful!" Grey warned. "Smaller steps."

"They do know, but the traveler was probably captured earlier and held for entertainment. The others were just trying to get home," Tate said.

But didn't make it because of us.

Tate slowed. "Hush. We're getting closer."

Grey's Venator abilities took over, and his senses amplified. The lines around him became sharper, and small details like the tiny ridges in the hard bark of the pines became as clear as if he were holding a magnifying glass over them. The smell of slow rot tickled his nostrils, mingled with pine sap and a sickly sweet floral aroma.

As they crept closer, the sounds of laughter and music danced, putting a joyous spin on the morbid situation.

Rune was also tapping into what she was capable of. Her eyes were narrowed and focused, and she set her feet down like a tiger stalking prey—silently and efficiently.

Following Tate's lead, they slowed to stop. "The nixie magic will be gone soon," he whispered so softly Grey had to strain to hear him. "Move as quickly as you can." He crouched, then moved forward using the palms of his hands and balls of his feet. Grey and Rune followed, copying the position.

The trees grew thinner, giving them fewer places to hide. The film around Tate and Rune was growing significantly lighter, and without the trees, Grey understood the urgency. They moved toward a section where the undergrowth thickened, and he had to look carefully before he put a foot or a hand down in fear he might break a branch and alert the wolves. The laughter grew louder, and Tate flattened to his belly and waved them up next to him. Once they were all in a line, he reached out and pulled a large, leafy branch to the side.

They were situated at the top of a small incline, about twenty-five feet above the werewolf camp. The pack had settled inside a natural bowl in the earth, surrounded by trees on all sides. Tents were scattered around the area, and multiple campfires burned. Somehow, Grey had not expected tents. Even less expected—clotheslines ran between tents. Pants, shirts, and dresses twisted in the gentle night breeze. Men and women sat around the fires, talking and laughing. Children ran freely—some in human form, others in wolf, tiny pups bouncing and rolling. One of the were-wolves stood near a larger fire, playing a fiddle.

Where were the barbarians? The human hunters? All he saw were families and happiness.

"We're visible again," Tate whispered. "Be careful."

A group of wolves burst over the rim on the opposite side, their muzzles and paws covered in blood. They padded toward the fires and, one by one, morphed back into men. Legs elongated, spines snapped straight, muzzles shrunk into human noses and jaws.

"The boy screamed like a little girl," one announced, and the camp erupted with laughter.

And then Grey saw what he'd been looking for originally—barbarians, truly.

"Who got to rip his throat out?" one of the males asked, his arm wrapped around the woman next to him.

A large man with bronze hair and green eyes strolled forward. Muscles rippled beneath his skin. "I did."

The group laughed and clapped again. Rage kindled in Grey's gut.

"Cashel," Tate muttered.

"How are we going to do this?" Rune whispered. "There are too many of them."

As Cashel walked away from the group and toward the tents, Grey saw what they'd come for. A post no more than five feet tall was hammered into the ground, and strapped to it was a woman, her dress torn to shreds and hanging in tattered pieces. They'd bound her in a standing position with straps across her chest and stomach, her arms secured behind. She appeared to be unconscious, her head lolling forward.

Cashel picked up a bucket of water as he walked and threw it on the woman. She sputtered back to consciousness.

"It's a good thing I didn't save the boy for the games," he mocked. "I wouldn't have gotten much. Easiest hunt we've ever had."

The woman lunged, screaming. Her shoulders rotated so far while straining against the bonds that Grey thought she'd dislocate them.

Cashel laughed and ran a finger down his own blood-smeared cheek. He looked at it, then traced a line of her son's blood down the woman's face. She jerked her head sharply to the side, meeting his insult, and bit down. Cashel yelped and backhanded her with the opposite hand. "Now you . . ." He shook out his fingers. "You should fetch a fine price."

Another wolf sauntered over, a younger version of Cashel in every way. "She's a pretty one."

"Cashel's son, Beorn," Tate narrated quietly. "Heir to the alpha if anything were to happen."

"I'd keep it in your pants until she's a little more worn out." Cashel chuckled. "Or she might bite it off."

"This is insane. We're not ready for this. Grey?" Rune looked at him, pleading. "Verida was right. There's no way we're getting out of this alive."

Below, Beorn's eyes ran over the woman, desire pouring out like fingers, groping—exploring.

"Rune," Grey groaned, willing her to understand. "I *have* to."

"Listen," Tate whispered. "Part of the pack is out on another hunt. This group is smaller than it should be, and the man we heard scream earlier isn't here. That's good for us." Tate slowly let the branch down. "But Rune's right—we won't survive this the way the cards are stacked. We need to get the majority of the pack out of camp."

"How?" Grey asked.

"They need something new to hunt."

"The only way we're getting back into the council house is if we take out Cashel," Grey said. "If his pack leaves, he leaves."

Tate shook his head. "I don't think so. He wants his turn with that woman just as much as Beorn does."

"His *turn*?" Rune looked disgusted. "She's not property."

"No, she's not, but they think she is. And they won't let her go willingly. If we can get Beorn to join the hunt and you take out Cashel, the pack will be without leadership, and it will fall apart."

"But how are we supposed to kill Cashel?" Rune asked. "Look at him!"

Tate shook his head. "No, I'm not giving you a plan. You're Venators—by breed alone you're strong enough to overcome Cashel. But you're at a disadvantage. Without proper training to lean on, you'll have to trust your instincts—act without thinking. And you'll need to move fast. There's a reason Cashel is alpha—he's cunning. If you stop to question if you can or can't do something, you're dead. And I'd rather you not be dead."

"Don't be dead. Sounds simple enough. Not sure why I didn't think if it." Rune's sarcasm bit. "Why aren't you coming with us?"

"One, I can't be seen. Two—"

"They're going to be hunting you," Grey finished, sighing. "Aren't they?"

"Me and someone else." Tate's mouth turned up into a bit of a smirk. "Beltran," he whispered. "Come out. I know you're there."

Grey and Rune looked at each other in confusion.

"Come on, Beltran," he whispered again. "First the rat in the tunnels, then the bird at the cliffs. What really gave it away was the ridiculously bright butterfly—that was a poor choice. Since you're not known for your poor choices, I'd say that means you want to play. So let's go."

A faint chuckle came from behind. Rune twisted as a boy stepped out into the open. He was of average height with spiky black hair and bright-green eyes. "And you made no effort to lose me, Tate. Except for the little nixie bubble trick, which, let's be honest, wasn't that hard to follow when watching for footfalls from the air. This tells me you're hoping for a game."

"I thought you might be of use."

Beltran looked over to Rune, grinning. He rocked back on his heels, eyes full of mirth.

Rune crinkled her nose. "What are you? Twelve?"

"You don't like it? I thought a child would be less intimidating." He winked. "No worries, sweetheart, I can be whatever age you need me to be." At that, his face began to morph, aging him at least ten years.

"*What* are you?"

"A shape-shifter. You know—rat, bird, butterfly . . ." He put one hand to the side of his mouth as if whispering only to Grey. "She's not very bright, is she?"

Grey rolled his eyes. Beltran was *that* guy. The one he usually wanted to punch in the face.

"Enough, Beltran," Tate said. "We need to get most of the wolves out of camp."

"I know—I heard you." The shape-shifter pushed between Rune and Grey and peered through the bushes. "That's a large pack, and we both know what they're capable of. You sure you want to come with me? These little Venators might need some help." He looked over at Rune. "I mean, she looks nice enough, but does she know where to put a dagger?"

Rune snatched the knife from her boot and brought it up under his chin. She raised an eyebrow. "Would right there do it?"

Beltran chuckled, pushing down the knife. "A little high, but you've got spunk. I like it."

"It's unfortunate the sentiment isn't reciprocated."

Grey peered back through the leaves. "We need to decide what we're doing . . . *now*."

"Relax. I've got it covered." Beltran morphed into a bird and flapped away.

Rune stared at the spot he had just been, mouth hanging open. "Did you . . . ? Did you . . . ?"

"Yes, we saw it." Tate moved back into position to watch the camp, this time resting on the balls of his feet with a dagger in his hand. "Don't trust Beltran," he said. "Ever."

"What? We're trusting him *now*!"

"Not really. We're simply trusting him to have a good time, and he can always be counted on for that."

Grey stepped away and gently nocked a bolt on the crossbow. It clicked into place. He looked up, hoping the sound hadn't carried. When nothing responded, he slid down next to Rune. She was shaking. He reached out and placed a hand over hers. "Hey, relax. You weren't scared to take on Beltran."

"He pissed me off."

Grey grinned and jerked his head toward the pack. "These guys are pissing *me* off. How about you?"

She almost smiled and nodded.

"Think you can handle it?"

It took a moment, but the shaking stopped, and her grip relaxed. "I don't know why, but, yeah, I think I can."

There was a commotion to the east of camp, and the conversations below quieted as the pack turned their attention.

"Here he goes," Tate said. "Sit tight until I give the word."

They all inched closer to the edge, watching.

Silen stepped out from the tree line.

Rune gasped and then clamped her hand over her mouth.

As much as Grey disliked the shifter, his skills were impressive. Not only was he an exact replica of the real Silen, but his posture was identical, the chin cocked up with the same superiority.

His appearance had the desired effect—numerous members of the pack slipped into their wolf forms. The change in the wolves happened faster than Grey had thought possible. Instead of the bone-cracking transformation he'd always imagined, this was more like watching Beltran change forms.

"The council has decided your pack is no longer welcome here," Beltran announced with Silen's voice. "You will move tonight, or the price will be steep."

Beorn stepped casually to the front of the pack with an arrogance that could be read from any distance. "You think you can just march into camp and tell us to move, Silen?" Beorn laughed. "I hope you brought help."

Silen's likeness just stared at him, emotionless. "You have until morning. It's a generous time frame."

Beorn threw back his head and laughed harder. He turned with his arms out. "You hear that, my brothers? We have until the morning." The pack broke into a strange chorus of howls and giggles, the snapping of jaws and the stamping of feet. "Maybe we should grovel in thanks for their generous offer." Beorn turned back to Silen, and the smile dropped from his face. "I think we'll send our answer back to the council in the morning . . . in the form of your head." He raised his hand and crooked two fingers. "Now."

At least fifteen wolves leapt forward, snarling.

Beltran shifted into wolf form—just as Silen would've done—and disappeared into the trees, a small hunting pack on his heels.

"That's not enough!" Rune hissed, scanning the nearly full camp. "There are still too many of them."

"He's not done yet." Tate pointed to the black crow flying low around the tree line.

"Black bird." Rune grasped at the necklace beneath her shirt. "That's why Verida laughed. It wasn't a bird. It was Beltran . . . *He's* the crow."

Tate shot her a side glance. "That took you entirely too long to put together."

Rune glared back. "Oh, I'm sorry. In my world, I don't usually wonder if everything I meet is a shape-shifter in disguise. Forgive me if it wasn't my first thought."

Tate almost smiled at her sarcasm. Grey did.

Beltran dove into the trees on the west side. A moment later, Dimitri's likeness slid from the branches, silent as death. The faux Dimitri grabbed a werewolf from behind and pressed a silver knife against the man's neck.

Shouts of warning went up around the camp, but the sounds quickly changed from human voices to barks and snarls as the remaining pack members morphed to wolves.

Across the clearing, Cashel remained in his human form. He postured, facing down Beltran. "Vampire."

Beorn stepped next to his father, baring his still-human teeth at the enemy. Around them, the rest of the pack moved into a defensive formation, flanking the alpha with hackles raised.

"The council has grown weary of your threats," Dimitri said, raising his voice over the noise. "And now we've spoken. You're no longer welcome in this territory."

"You think we abide by your laws?" Cashel's lip curled. "Not anymore. You claim you speak for all of us, and then you bring Venators through the gate." When there was no response, he threw back his head in a full-bodied laugh. "Not even a denial."

The wolves snarled and snapped their teeth. Their paws punched up and down, antsy to attack the vampire in their midst. The hostage tried to twist away, but Beltran yanked him back against his body, pressing the knife harder into his neck.

"Bringing those demons here was foolish, Dimitri. The other packs have been too fearful of retribution to join me. But with that move . . ." Cashel swept his arms wide, grinning. "You've handed me all the power I needed."

"The packs will have to find someone new to follow," Beltran said in Dimitri's cool, dismissive tone. "You and your pack have been banned to the other side of the Blues."

"How _dare_—"

"Father, let me handle this." Beorn cracked his neck from one side to the other, staring Dimitri down with a look of gleeful anticipation. "I've been waiting years to rip out a vamp heart." His arms transformed—claws jutted out in place of fingernails, and thick fur sprouted along the backs of his hands.

Beltran tilted his head in a perfect imitation of Dimitri's cool and haughty demeanor, looking down at Beorn's show of power as if it were the vilest and most base demonstration he'd ever seen. "You'd send your son after a head vampire? Cashel." He clicked his tongue. "As I recall, _you_ barely survived our last encounter."

Beorn lunged forward, his lips pulled into a snarl, but Cashel flung his arm across his son's chest, barring the way.

"I'm ready, Father. Let me go. Let me prove my loyalty to you and this pack."

An unspoken conversation passed from father to son. Cashel's brows furrowed. Beorn stared back, wide eyed and insistent.

"Very well." Cashel lowered his arm. "Let the council know our opinion on their rules and their judgments."

"Gladly."

Grey saw something that looked like glee wind through Beorn. It lifted his posture and the corners of his lips.

Beorn stalked through the rest of the pack, pulling out time in a dramatic show of prowess. "We'll have Silen torn to pieces by the end of the night," he said, puffing out his chest and flexing his claw-tipped fingers. "You'll soon follow."

The expression on Dimitri's face was simply . . . bored. "Doubtful."

The breeze shifted, and the hostage stilled in Beltran's arms. He twisted carefully, trying to look at his captor from the corner of his eye.

Oh no.

Grey didn't know how the wolf suddenly figured out that Beltran wasn't Dimitri . . . but it was written all over his face. Grey leaned forward, wrapping his fist around the grasses that lined the rim, willing Beltran to sense what had just happened.

The man tried to pull away, shouting, "Cashel, this isn't—"

Beltran pushed the blade against his throat hard enough that a thin line of blood trickled down his neck, cutting off the warning.

"Wandering in here alone was very stupid . . ." Beorn trailed off, his eyes narrowing. "And very unlike you." He raised his chin and sniffed the air.

Tate tensed. "Beltran's upwind."

The shifter finally realized his mistake. Before the alert could be sounded, he slid the knife across the hostage's exposed throat. A wave of red gushed, painting his hand and bubbling down the dying man's neck. Dimitri's likeness grinned, shrugging with a silent *oops*.

Beorn lunged for him, but Beltran pushed the body at him and disappeared into the trees as gracefully as he'd appeared.

The camp exploded with movement. Beorn joined the others in wolf from and bolted after him.

Finally, only a few of the pack members remained—mostly women and children, with a handful of men around the perimeter acting as guards.

"All right, *now* he's done. Don't think—just act. I'll give them one more thing to chase." Tate wiggled away from the ledge and took off in the direction Beltran had headed.

Grey stood and leapt off the ledge without a second thought. Rune jumped because she couldn't let him go down there alone. The second the decision had been made, panic clutched at her, screaming in her ear the entire way down: *What are you doing?*

The ground rushed up too quickly. Grey hit and rolled, coming gracefully to his feet. Rune tried to imitate the movement, but during the roll, one shoulder jammed into a rock, throwing everything off balance. She stumbled forward like a baby giraffe trying out its legs for the first time.

Grey went to steady her, but something caught his attention. He stepped smoothly to the side and wrapped his fingers around her upper arm, pulling until they stood back to back. She looked over Grey's shoulder. A werewolf was running at them, shifting midstride. His face elongated into a warped mix of human and canine. His back arched higher, claws bursting from his fingertips. Before Rune could register what to do, Grey swung his crossbow and pulled the trigger. The bolt flew and caught the werewolf in the chest. It fell to the ground, dead.

Rune turned away a moment before a charging she-wolf was on top of her. Pulling up the dagger on instinct, she shoved it forward. That seemingly small action was followed by a series of gruesome firsts—the feel of the knife in her hand as it slid through flesh, the warmth of blood as it spilled over her fingers, the look in the woman's eyes as her momentum slowed.

There was no scream. Rune expected it, but the woman's mouth only gaped as her hand went to the knife, helplessly feeling the blade with jerky, disjointed fingers. A low whine escaped, and the wolf dropped to her knees, the bloody knife sliding free of her belly.

Rune vaguely heard yelling, but everything faded as she stared in horror at a single drop of red-black blood that had collected at the tip of her blade. It dangled there, reflecting the flicker of campfire light, then stretched and fell, rotating through the air and splashing onto the forehead of the woman who knelt at her feet.

Grey leapt in front of Rune, shoving the woman to the ground unceremoniously. Rune's mind slowly twisted back to reality just as he flipped his crossbow around and used the back end as a club, slamming it into the side of another wolf's head. She heard its skull crack—distinctly different from a thud, an actual cracking of bone—and it collapsed.

"Rune, I need help!" Grey loaded another bolt and pulled the trigger, taking out the last wolf that stood between him and his goal. He sprang away, heading toward the woman they'd come for.

Rune went to follow, but another wolf jumped in from the right, barring the path and cutting her off from Grey.

❖══✾✾══❖

A fist came from the side, and Grey ducked, barely dodging it. The attacker was too close—he couldn't fire. Swinging around fluidly, he brought the crossbow up and smashed it into the man's stomach. The werewolf grunted in pain, his chest popping forward as his abdomen was forced in the opposite direction. Grey shifted his weight, ready to move on, but the wolf wrapped his partially formed paws around the bow and pulled down as he collapsed, disarming Grey. Before he could retrieve it, he heard the thud of feet and a low growl behind him.

Grey spun, pulling the silver-veined dagger from its sheath. Cashel stood between him and the unconscious woman. The man was a behemoth, over six feet tall with biceps that looked capable of crushing a man's skull.

The alpha's eyes flickered over the glowing tattoos on Grey's forearms, and he spat. "The council sends its newest pets to remove me. How did I find myself so honored?"

"I'm not here for you. I'm here for the woman you kidnapped."

Cashel looked confused for a second. "The council would never—" He broke off and grinned, cocking his head to the side. "You're not here at the council's bidding, are you?"

Grey realized he'd made a terrible mistake. Cashel was right, and everyone who was anyone would've known the second he revealed the true mission.

The alpha took a predatory step forward, and Grey moved back instinctively.

Cashel laughed. "You two are all on your own." He waved off the guard that was coming up behind. "Two Venators coming to the rescue of a poor human lost in the woods. The council doesn't even know you're here. I wonder how long before someone discovers you're out of bed."

"No. The council is with us—you saw them yourself."

He took another step forward, enjoying the game. "If the council were truly behind this, you'd have a little magical help from Ambrose. My guess is the council's pet shifter was here."

There were cries and shouts as Rune battled behind them. He'd left her without thinking through the ramifications of separating—his second mistake since jumping off the ledge. So much for acting on instinct . . . He'd most likely just signed their death warrants.

At his silence, Cashel laughed. "You're a fool." He pulled his chin up and stretched his mouth wide as massive canine teeth descended.

Lowering his stance, Grey brandished a dagger. But the alpha whirled away from him, took four steps, and grabbed the woman's shoulder, sinking his teeth deep.

Her head snapped up with a scream, and her feet flailed beneath her.

Grey surged forward. "No!"

Cashel released the bite and pushed off the ground, rapidly closing the distance between them and slamming into Grey's chest.

❦❧

The wolves moved in an ever-tightening circle. Rune stepped and turned, twisting her neck, trying to watch for an attack from every angle. The pack stalked closer, each paw placed ever so carefully, muscles tense and ready to pounce. She'd meant to follow Grey, but that male had stepped between, separating them. Smart. And now she was surrounded.

Rune was an exceptional athlete, but she had no experience in any type of fighting or weaponry. She didn't fully trust her Venator side, but depending on her human abilities was out of the question. Seeing no other option, she followed Tate's advice, accessing the Venator within. It was easier now that she knew what to look for, and the warrior roared to life. It was darker here, alone with her inner beast.

One of the guards shifted into wolf form and started to howl. A call for help—Rune knew it instantly. The pack could not be allowed to return. Leaping forward, she slashed a blade across the guard's throat, cutting off the warning.

Something landed on her back, and sharp claws pierced her skin. Rune screamed, swinging the dagger over her shoulder. The blade met flesh. Reaching up with her other arm, she grabbed a fistful of fur and yanked the wolf off.

Its body crashed limply to the ground, and she realized it was a pup. Nothing more than a baby. Rune recoiled, and her human side shoved back into play with all its culpability and sick regret.

A female wolf shrieked in a way only a mother could, with loss wrenched from a place so deep it actually colored the sound. She charged.

Instinct said to prepare for the attack. But Rune's flight response said to run. She looked to the side, hoping for an escape . . . but there was none. And help wasn't coming. Grey was pinned to the ground, Cashel on top of him.

That glance, that consideration of trusting her human side, was a mistake.

The enraged mother leapt over the bleeding pup and smashed into Rune. As they fell, the human face shifted into beast; fur erupted down her neck while her nose and mouth merged to become a snout. Rune wrapped her fingers around the wolf's neck, barely managing to keep the snapping jaws at arm's length. Hot breath washed over her face. The crossbow was still strapped to her back, and it dug painfully against vertebrae as she twisted, trying to protect her throat and keep the animal restrained at the same time.

Then the weight was gone.

Tate grabbed the she-wolf by the scruff of the neck and threw her against one of the trees.

Rune had never been so glad to see anyone. "You came back!"

Tate spun, pulling a sword from its sheath. "The rest of the pack will figure out Beltran's trick any second now. We're almost out of time!"

Grey struggled desperately to get out from under Cashel, thrashing and bucking. But he was outweighed substantially. Cashel reset his grip, wrapped fur-covered fingers tightly around Grey's neck, lifted his head, and slammed it back down.

Grey saw stars.

He fumbled with the alpha's wrists, trying to pry them back, but they might as well have been made of stone.

"Goodbye, Venator. I hope she was worth your life." Cashel leaned his weight forward and squeezed.

Pain exploded up and down Grey's neck, and the stars previously dancing in his field of vision grew into brilliant pinpoints of light. He let go of Cashel's wrists, gasping for air, and frantically swept at the dirt, trying to find a stick or rock or *something*!

Cashel released the pressure just slightly, and Grey's eyesight focused. Cashel could've already finished him, but as the alpha's looming face filled his vision, the gleam in Cashel's eyes said he was enjoying watching the light go out of Grey's.

He squeezed tighter, and the lack of oxygen spread like a fog over Grey's mind . . . Consciousness was fleeing.

But then, like the last bubble of air that gurgles up from a drowning man, a burst of survival-triggered inspiration rose to the top, and Grey remembered the leather pouch on his belt. He reached over the top of Cashel's leg, fumbling for the throwing stars. His fingers were thick and heavy, and he struggled to maneuver the drawstrings on the pouch. The tip of a razor-sharp blade sliced open his palm. Grey barely recognized it. Finally, he got two fingers around the star, yanked it from the bag, and sliced it down Cashel's face.

Cashel roared and swung away, his hands flying to his wound. With the wolf's weight off balance, Grey bucked again and threw him. Free, he rolled over, coughing and gagging while struggling to get back to his feet. But his head swam with the sudden return of oxygen, and he staggered one way and then the other.

Two snarling beasts had clamped down on Tate's forearms, one on each side. They hung there with locked jaws. Tate spun, wrapping one around the trunk of a tree. There was no yelp, just the sound of a spine snapping before it fell limp.

Another wolf leapt. Rune lifted the crossbow and braced it against her shoulder, shooting the wolf in midair. The animal dropped to the ground, sliding a few feet and not moving again.

The body count climbed higher, and the pack grew wary, their advances ceasing. Rune and Tate were still surrounded, but now the wolves growled and snapped their jaws from a distance.

Rune took that moment to locate Grey. He was on his feet again, but something was wrong. He was hunched over, arms hanging limply, and struggling to walk—zigzagging from one side to the other.

Cashel slowly got up, blood pouring down the side of his face from a long gash. His eyes landed on Grey, and he stalked forward with sure steps, murderous intent oozing.

"Tate!" Rune yelled.

The wolf on Tate's other arm released its hold just long enough to spring for his face. The two fell to the ground, rolling.

Rune was on her own. Surrendering totally to the inner roar of the Venator, she loaded another bolt and aimed it over the heads of the wolves that were, once again, advancing. This could go horribly wrong, but she knew no other options. Praying that aim was driven by some undiscovered instinct, she released the bolt.

⟨⟨⟨⟨⟩⟩⟩⟩

Mostly incoherent, Grey hadn't realized Cashel was so close. The werewolf seized Grey by the shoulder, twisting him around. No time to react. In horrific déjà vu, those thick fingers closed around his neck again. Cashel's lips pulled back in a snarl as he lifted Grey off the ground. Grey grasped the alpha's forearms, trying to alleviate the pressure of his own weight cutting off his air supply. Cashel squeezed—not the slow game he'd played earlier but each finger digging in with extraordinary pressure. Black crept in around the edges of Grey's vision. His fingers started to slip, rushing him closer to death.

Cashel grunted and released his hold.

Grey smashed into the ground, his knees folding and jamming into his stomach. Crumpling, his head cracked on the ground. Right in front of him lay Cashel, eyes staring ahead—wide but not seeing. A bolt from a crossbow had punched straight through his neck. Blood streamed around the shaft and pooled on the ground.

"Are you OK?" Rune called.

Grey tried to speak but couldn't. Wheezing, he got to his feet. His legs were leaden, and he staggered to the side, flashing Rune a thumbs-up.

Crossbow still raised, Rune turned in a slow circle, facing down the pack. The few werewolves remaining backed away with their ears pinned to their heads, whimpering for their fallen leader.

Tate stepped free of the circle. "Let's go. Grey, grab the woman."

Howls went up from the surrounding forest, first one and then many.

"We're out of time." Tate reached down and grabbed Cashel by the hair. He swung his sword, cutting the head off in one movement. That sound, both slick and bone crushing at the same time—Grey would never forget it.

"What are you doing?" Rune shouted.

"You're going to need this." Tate snatched a blanket that was draped across a log by a campfire and wrapped the head in it, tying the ends together in a knot. "Grey, don't just stand there. Get that woman now, or we're leaving without her!"

Phantom fingers were still around his throat, but the oxygen was restoring mental and physical functions. He ran to the post where the hostage hung, bending to scoop up his knife along the way. Grey sliced through the ropes and caught her as she fell forward.

"We have to get you out of here," he rasped, gently helping the woman to stand. "The rest of the pack will be back any second."

"Let them come," she whispered. Her fingers fluttered like a ghostly white butterfly around the bite mark Cashel had left. "It doesn't matter now."

The howls came again, closer.

"Grey!" Rune and Tate stood at the edge of camp, tense and dying to run.

"Leave me, Venator. Please."

He could not honor her request. When they'd started this journey, he'd expected the rescue to be received differently. Everything was all wrong. Bending at the waist, Grey levered the woman over his shoulder. She resigned silently and lay against him like a sack of potatoes. Grey sheathed his dagger and hurried to grab his crossbow.

Before they could clear the ridge at the edge of camp, a snarl came from behind.

Grey looked over his other shoulder. It had to be Cashel's son, Beorn. The wolf was too large to be anyone else. Off balance and running through terrain thick with vegetation, Grey stumbled. If he stopped to lower the woman to the ground and load a bolt, they were dead.

"Rune!" he shouted.

She turned, raising her crossbow as she went, and pulled the trigger. It *twanged,* and the wolf behind them went down with a yelp.

They leapt up the ridge. When they landed, the extra weight sent Grey to his knees. Tate hooked an arm under his elbow and pulled him up. Together they bolted through the trees. Behind them, the sounds of bodies crashing through the woods grew closer.

Grey pushed harder. "We're never going to make it!"

The forest had lost all its beauty as they ran for their lives. Rune was, for the first time, frustrated by not being able to go as fast as she knew she could. Tate's speed was impressive, but he wasn't a Venator, and she had to rein herself in. She felt like a horse with a bit. They would never outrun the wolves at this pace, and with Cashel missing a head, the wolves were out for blood.

A figure burst out of nowhere, appearing from behind a tree and placing himself right in their path. Rune slid to a stop, nearly falling over backward as she tried to bring her crossbow up.

"Whoa, pretty lady." Beltran held out his hands. "Easy there."

Rune was sorely tempted to show him how a bolt through the kneecap felt when fired by a pretty lady.

Tate skidded, breathing hard. "We need a way out."

Beltran scratched his chin with a heavy dose of drama, as if there were not a pack of angry werewolves on their heels. "I could probably help with that," he drawled. "It wouldn't be too difficult. But first, I would need to hear you say 'please.'"

"Please," Tate ground out between clenched teeth.

Beltran put his hand behind his ear. "What was that?"

"Please!"

"That'll do." Two enormous wings burst from his back. He stepped forward, wrapping one arm around Tate and the other around Grey and the woman, then flew into the branches above.

Rune's heart dropped to her feet. He'd left her. "Beltran!" she hissed as loudly as she dared. "Beltran!"

A large white wolf crashed through the trees behind her. Its lips pulled back in what looked like a twisted grin as it lowered its center of gravity, ready to pounce.

Rune raised the bow as smoothly as if it were an extension of herself and pulled the trigger. The bolt slammed home. Another wolf leapt over the dead one. A gaping wound on its shoulder bled freely—Beorn. No time to reload the crossbow.

She ran, unleashing everything. Although she'd expected to lose him easily, between the battle, the lack of sleep, and the fact that this was her second time being hunted in fewer than twenty-four hours, fatigue nipped at her heels. Her speed lagged just enough that Beorn kept even pace. His long wolf legs ate up the ground easily. The shoulder wound didn't seem to be bothering him, probably numbed by adrenaline and hatred.

Another wolf, brown this time, exploded out of a bush, nearly catching her arm with its teeth.

They were surrounding her.

No. She pumped her arms faster, determined not to lose the grip on her crossbow.

"Beltran!" she shouted.

A third wolf burst from the trees on her left, its body stretched out in a giant leap. This one wouldn't miss. She swerved to the side and brought an elbow up hard, smashing it in the top of the wolf's rib cage. The wolf yelped and went down.

"Beltran!"

Arms slipped beneath hers, and she screamed.

"Relax, little Venator, I've got you."

Beltran pulled her into the air. Beorn leapt for them, his jaws snapping inches below her feet. Then he fell, twisting back to the ground.

"Ha!" she yelled down.

"Let's not goad the angry werewolf—bad form."

He held her tight, spiraling around outstretched branches. Multiple times, Beltran cut in a little too close, and the boughs swiped across her exposed arms, cutting with hundreds of needles. She didn't complain. Then they shot free of the canopy into a clear night sky. Rune sucked in mouthfuls of air, grateful to be alive.

Beltran's giant, down-covered wings flapped evenly behind them. He turned her around, pressing her against his chest. He looked so smug that, grateful or not, she wanted to smack him over the head with the butt of her crossbow.

"You left me to die," she said tightly.

"I certainly did not. Out of the three of you, you would be the last one I'd abandon."

"Where are the others?"

"In a tree. We'll go back for them in a little while, after the wolves disperse."

There was something intense in his gaze, and Rune couldn't hold it. She looked away. "Why are you helping us?"

Beltran smiled. "I like to play games. I believe Tate mentioned that."

The calm, cocky attitude didn't set well with her. Never had and never would. It was always hiding something. "That's not the whole reason."

"Why do you say that?"

She met his eyes again, wanting to gauge his reaction. "Because you just put a target on your back. Every single one of those wolves knows you helped us. That's not a game—that's life and death, and no one plays *that* game without a reason."

His face had grown still, the amusement gone. "Very good, little Venator. You see more than most. More than Tate."

STAND UP AND FIGHT

Tate straddled a branch, watching as the wolves howled and pounded by below. Normally he'd be worried about Rune, but he'd seen the way Beltran had looked at her. Though he didn't like it, he felt sure the shifter would get to her on time.

Just across from him, Grey eased the woman off his shoulder. Using one hand to support her neck and with the other on the back of her shoulder, he gingerly reclined her against the trunk. When she was situated, Grey leaned back, and Tate got his first clear look at the one they'd risked so much to save. The angry red puncture wounds of a werewolf bite shone on her shoulder.

His heart sank. "You didn't tell me she was bitten."

"What does it matter?"

The boy had so much to learn. But after watching how tender he'd been, Tate didn't have the heart to spell it out. "Think. I'm sure you know."

A flurry of emotions flashed across Grey's face. The realizations were obvious but faded fast, as if he knew the truth but was forcing the knowledge away with a comfortable friend—denial.

It was the woman who spoke. "My life is over."

"No." Grey whirled to face her. "Don't think that."

"My son is dead. My husband is dead too . . . isn't he?" When Grey didn't argue, she nodded. "And I will turn on the next moon."

"That doesn't mean your life is over." Grey reached out and then pulled back, not sure if his touch would be welcomed. "Surely there are ways to be a werewolf without being . . ." He gestured. "Like them."

A few beats of awkward silence passed. Grey stared in desperation, the woman looked at her hands in quiet defeat, and Tate watched the scene unfold with a sadness he couldn't fully quantify.

Finally, she sighed. "You're a kind soul—I can hear it in your voice." Her lips pressed thin, and she looked past him. "You have no idea what you're talking about."

How right she was. Grey had no comprehension of what this woman had been sentenced to . . . but Tate did. Regardless of the path, claimed by a pack or sold to the games, death and horror awaited. Horrors he'd experienced firsthand. Tate could not, would not, force anyone down such a path. "What would you like us to do?"

"I knew you'd understand." She gave him a soft smile, meeting his eyes. "I know what you are. Please, just let me die."

Tate's heart constricted, more for Grey than for the woman who'd made her choice. She wished to avoid the otherwise unavoidable. How could he deny her that?

"What? No!" Grey looked between the two of them, horrified. "How will your death change anything? Your son and husband will still be gone, and this pack will go on doing what they did to you. How . . . ?" Grey seemed to struggle for the right words. "How can you slide into oblivion so *easily*?"

Tate flinched. The boy may have been searching for the right thing to say, but that wasn't it.

The woman's head snapped up, all gentleness gone from her demeanor. "You think this is easy?"

"No, I don't. But you're making it easy for *them*."

Howls now came from all around as the werewolves tried in vain to pick up their scent. Grey glanced down. The woman took advantage of the distraction and made a play for his dagger. Grey grabbed her hands before she could pull the blade.

She broke into hysterics. "Please, please, let me die. You're sentencing me to a life of hell. I'll die anyway. *Please*."

Grey's eyebrows pulled together as he watched her, emotions rippling across his features. "What's your name?"

"Val—" Her chest jerked with a hard sob. "Valerian."

"Valerian." He gingerly peeled her reluctant fingers from the hilt of the dagger. "My name is Grey."

She collapsed back against the trunk of the tree. "The stories of your kind's cruelty are true."

Tate jackknifed up at the waist. That boy had just risked his own life to save her. "Valer—"

Grey held up a hand. "No. Please. Let her finish."

"You sentence me to a fate worse than death, Venator." She glared at Grey, fingering the wound at her neck. "Do you know that?"

He looked down, swallowing. The seconds ticked by, and Tate wasn't sure if Grey would respond at all. But then his voice came, thick but confident. "I know very little of this place, and you're right, I don't fully understand what I'm asking of you. But I do know this: without someone to stop them, this pack will continue to prey on people. To abuse people. To destroy lives. Tate brought us back to help, but there are only two of us. Two Venators. We can't possibly right every wrong in this world."

Valerian gave a weary shrug. "Then we are doomed."

"But what if you lived?" Grey said on a breath laced with conviction. "What if you transitioned into a werewolf far away from this pack. Somewhere you could choose your own destiny. What if you gained allies? What if, because you lived, you and others like you were able to stand between these wolves and those they seek to destroy? *What if* all you need to do to save the lives of others is refuse to give up your own?"

Grey's words were powerful, little drops of his own faith fluttering down around them. It was like watching a glorious flower of hope and love bloom in the branches of a pine—a flower long gone from the world Tate inhabited. It touched his heart, and he couldn't deny the boy was right. He'd only been here two days, yet he saw and understood . . . though only to a point.

The power Grey had infused into those words hung heavy, and they seemed to touch Valerian as well. Her shoulders relaxed, and she slowly brought her eyes up. There, Tate saw the thing he'd been working for and dreaming to see.

Burning in her was hope . . . Hope born of a Venator.

Tate had known he'd chosen well when he'd found the boy, but he'd had no idea how well. Watching this scene unfold left a burning lump in his throat. Grey was truly a diamond in the rough. Although he still didn't know Rune well enough to predict what her outcome would be, Tate was confident Grey would not allow himself to be played by the council.

It was a long endgame, what he aimed for, but he saw the means in this young Venator who'd obviously been through far more than most in his few years. Tate had seen that immediately, the maturity far and above what one should've gained. It was easy to recognize a kindred spirit. He too had been through more than most in his years. However, unlike Grey, Tate's anger had stunted his wisdom. The acquisition of that important skill had not begun until the day he met his beautiful wife.

Thinking about Ayla brought a soft smile to his lips.

That woman had saved him, had taught him how to think. And now it was his turn to save her. His wife's face floated through his mind's eye, framed by his son's laughter, and then the image was rapidly tainted by Danchee's words. *The games will be a family affair.*

His mood darkened.

If that faery queen laid one hand on his family, he'd kill her. Even if it meant the possibility of spending a thousand years as a weed in her twisted little garden.

❖❖❖❖

The position in which Beltran held Rune was intimate, and she didn't like it. His arms kept her from death but smashed their bodies together, giving them a clear mental picture of the other's physique.

Trying to readjust, Rune wiggled.

"Do you want me to drop you?"

She huffed.

"Your gratitude is overwhelming."

"I already said thank you."

"Yes, you did. Although the words had a nice bite at the end."

Rune peered at him. "You're the crow, aren't you?" If they were stuck together, she might as well get some answers.

Bemused, Beltran smirked. "I don't know about *the* crow. There are thousands of crows, and you sound rather accusatory. What did this particular crow do?"

"It left my brother's necklace on my windowsill."

"Ah, yes." He nodded, laughter dancing in his eyes. "That crow. Yes, that was me."

"Why?"

"I thought you might want it."

"So you've seen my brother?"

"Of course. How else did you think I found your lost trinket?"

Excitement burst through her. "Is he all right? Where is he? Take me there. We have to go—"

"Whoa, little Venator. Whoa. I have no idea if he's all right. He's alive, and that's the best you're going to get. No, I won't take you there, because he's in the heart of Zio's stronghold. If I could break in, I would've done it ages ago. It's impossible." He leaned his head forward slightly and lowered his voice. "You have to let him go."

"Why does everyone keep telling me that? He's my brother—I can't just forget he's here!"

He evaluated her, eyes flicking back and forth in tiny movements as he searched hers. "No, you can't, can you?"

Rune blinked back watery guilt. "It's my fault he's here."

"Though I highly doubt that . . . I understand. More than you know. What are you willing to do to get him back?"

"I'll do anything."

"That's easy to say, harder to do. If you truly want to get your brother back . . . you'll need one thing." Beltran stared at her, not finishing the sentence.

"What?" she blurted out.

"Patience."

Of all the ridiculous . . . Rune opened her mouth to speak, but Beltran rushed ahead, silencing her before she could start. "And when you've used it all up and think you can't possibly live another day with the burden . . . find just a little more."

He spoke sincerely—she could hear it—but the answer seemed to mock her nonetheless.

"Patience," she spat. "That's your advice."

Beltran's giant wings flapped slowly, backlit by the full moon. He stared her down, silent, those green eyes boring a hole through her. It wasn't until she finally relaxed again in his arms that he continued. "Lots and lots of patience. Think, Rune. Patience bides its time; patience tempers the mood; patience allows tiny pieces to move forward in your game of chess until the game board is set as you wish. Patience is the only answer."

He had wisdom there—she could see it now. And it fit so well into the world she'd seen thus far. Caution was prudent given the situation, and what went hand in hand with caution better than patience?

Unfortunately, that had never been among her redeeming characteristics. Strong willed, stubborn, persistent . . . but never, ever patient. Rune swallowed and looked over Beltran's shoulder into the endless night. In order to win back what she wanted, she would need to change herself. The tasks ahead seemed even more monumental than if she needed to cross a sea or scale the tallest mountain. The impossibility of it was drowning her. She abruptly changed the subject. "We should go for the others—make sure they're OK."

"No, not yet. I've answered your questions honestly. You'll have to trust me when I say I don't make common practice of that. Which means you owe me. You ignored the council's orders and went out hunting Cashel. Why?"

"Why do you want to know?"

"Because I wasn't expecting that, and I hate misjudging people," he answered frankly. "Staying ahead of the game is what keeps me alive."

She bit her lip, weighing what damage a truthful response could do. The deciding factor was his blown cover, which meant Beltran stood neck deep in this mission with her. "To show the council they can't control us."

"Interesting . . . bold . . . a little stupid."

"Stupid! You came trailing behind us looking for a 'good time'!"

"Unlike you, my absence hasn't been noticed."

"Why would *your* absence have been noticed at all?"

He smiled and waited for her to come to it on her own.

She wilted. "You live in the council house, don't you?"

"Certainly."

"Are you on the council?"

Beltran laughed. "Certainly not."

Considering everyone she'd met since entering the council house, this bit of information did not put her at ease. New suspicion sent questions tumbling out. "Whose side are you on? Did someone send you?

That smile of his was never ending, and he seemed to be enjoying her suspicion even more than her confusion. "'Sides' are such primitive concepts. Don't you agree?"

She pursed her lips. "Not really, no."

"I have a feeling that someday you're going to change your perspective on that. But for now, I'd *love* to know what's going to happen next. Think you can just walk back into the council house and all will be forgiven? Your Venator status will buy you privileges—I'll grant you that—but they won't turn a blind eye to blatant disobedience."

"We're hoping that by getting rid of Cashel, forgiveness won't be an issue."

"And whose plan was that? Yours?"

"Grey's." Her ribs were starting to throb from the pressure of his arms around her.

"Ah, I see. Luckily, Tate shoved Cashel's head into a bag to act as your . . . peace offering, if you will. But now comes the interesting part. If I've judged Grey correctly, he will quietly march into that hall and hand over Cashel's head before retreating to his room, pleased with the day and the life he saved." He raised one eyebrow, implying that something was amiss.

Rune could see where he was going, and the picture he aimed to paint leapt off the page. If Cashel was to be used as a bargaining chip, it had to be done carefully. Because once the council knew they'd killed Cashel, forgiveness was the best they could hope for.

But Rune needed more than that. She needed an ally in the fight to get her brother back.

What she needed was a favor.

Although Silen would be overjoyed to hear the news—given the conversation they'd overheard in the tunnels—it was clear Dimitri was the one in charge. And if she were going to risk her life to get a favor, Dimitri was who she wanted it from.

MAEGON'S PRISON

Zio stood on the ledge high above the dragon's pit, admiring her handiwork as she did every visit. Since her takeover, she'd initiated many improvements, but this was one of her more brilliant architectural designs.

The main room was spacious, the large, curved ceiling dotted with the tiny remnants of stalactite formations Maegon had broken on his indoor miniflights. Though nothing could transform the room from what it was—a cage—Maegon's prison was regal in its rugged beauty. Stalagmite pillars, so wide a giant's arms could not span them, sprouted from the floor and merged with the ceiling. Three of them stood clustered in a triangle. It was there, at the base of the majesties, that her dragon chose to sleep. He lay stretched out between them with his tail coiled around one and his head resting against another.

His emerald-green scales were magnificent. The power beneath his skin was awe inspiring. But the most beautiful thing to her eyes was his very nature, so much like her own—dangerous, deadly . . . hungry.

To the side of her sleeping giant was a fissure in the stone floor. It had spread over time to become a gaping mouth whose black throat dropped into the bowels of the mountain. Maegon's wings would normally have made this inconsequential, but while the center of the room was domed, the sides slanted sharply, leaving only ten feet of clearance at its tallest section. The ceiling was too low for Maegon to use his wings and the chasm too wide for him to jump.

The only passage to freedom was if Zio opened the castle's hidden front doors.

If Maegon were to escape into the castle, the destruction would be so thorough that Zio would be fighting the rest of her battles alone. The deaths of her minions would not cause the tiniest bit of sorrow, but they were useful.

A commotion of hushed arguing approached, and the loud shuffle of reluctant feet woke her emerald beast. Maegon lifted his scaled head to watch the activity on the opposite side of the canyon. Her goblins moved into view as they took their places at the winch, which was positioned precariously close to the edge. And although her followers were out of range from Maegon's teeth, the winch stood well within reach of his fire. And they knew it. She could see the nervousness in the way they jockeyed for position. The front spots stayed open until the weakest of the group were shoved out of line and forced to take them. They would most likely die. Maegon had been cooped up for too long—he would spit fire for the sheer enjoyment.

She could relate. Like her winged pet, she was not meant to be caged.

What were the odds that, on their first night here, the Venators would wander out of the council house, untrained and barely protected? The sweetest part of the situation was that she'd never have known if it weren't for her many eyes and ears. Spies were a beautiful thing, especially thick droves of them infiltrated so far into every society and every species that the council had no idea where to start looking.

Preparation was tedious but so thrilling when it paid off in such a handsome dividend.

Not that long ago, her response to the council's move of bringing home two Venators would *not* have come in the form of dragon fire, which was too passive, too weak. No, her own two hands would've delivered punishment. These hands, these fingers, were the authors of her destiny.

Her nails dug into the palms of her hands as a familiar ache of desire pooled in the pit of her stomach. How she craved those days, the ones spent with swords and daggers, slicing out the impurity of foul lives without mercy, unleashing torrents of blood. Some blood was better spent watering the fields than coursing through veins.

But the more power she'd gained, the more careful she'd had to become to hold on to it. The rashness of her youth no longer worked, and years had passed while she waited behind these walls, biding her time. It grated on her nerves every hour of every day.

Breathing tightly through her nose, she raised her head and gave the command. "Now."

Arwin peered at the castle through his magnification spell. His eyes watered from the hours spent watching and waiting. His brain ached in his skull like a bad tooth, overworked by the size of the images he was forcing it to process.

The guards were gone. Normally Zio's beastly little goblins sat inside barred windows at the top of the turrets, scanning for anyone foolish enough to attempt to approach the fortress. Years past, there had been many attacks. Recently, no. Still, their absence was strange. At first he'd thought perhaps they were changing the guard, but as time rolled on, their stations remained empty.

He groaned and stretched his back, wishing for the umpteenth time since he'd arrived at this cursed tree for the body of his youth. Removing the magnification spell from his eyes, Arwin turned, trying to decide on a method of transportation. Nothing more would be learned by staring at an empty room. It was time to go home. Water jumping was the fastest, but—he shuddered—that was to be avoided out of sheer discomfort. If Beltran were still there, he would've utilized the shifter's gifts. But he wasn't, and such thoughts were "wasters of headspace," as his father used to say. There were enough thoughts bouncing around his mind without the unnecessary ones.

If he'd remembered to bring the portal orb, it would've at least gotten him close to the council house. But as it were, his memory had been a little fuzzy of late. Messaging the council for retrieval was always an option, but they would ask why their assistance was needed, and he'd have to admit the lapse in mental facility.

"Mortality," he grumbled under his breath and spat.

A great cracking sound rent the air, and Arwin froze, turning slowly to look at the castle with dread and the overwhelming feeling that he'd missed something. The crack was followed by the grinding of stone against stone, harsh and unending.

Why couldn't he see where it was coming from?

Then, like a beacon, red fire billowed out from the base of the castle where it melded with the mountain. It was only then, illuminated as it was, that he saw the ever-widening crack in the stone. A giant door was being winched open. Another burst of flame and smoke escaped. Only one thing would cause plumes like that.

Thoughts, memories, history, and connections—years deep in their layers—raced through Arwin's head. His brain fired rapidly, at the speed it once had—adrenaline was the drug his aging mind craved. The answer came clearly. Zio was releasing her most prized possession, and he could think of only one reason why that would be happening tonight.

The Venators were out of bed.

He had to go. Now. Water jumping would be his transportation after all. The tips of his fingers began to glow, and he searched the ground and trees, looking for the nearest entry to his exit.

Behind him, the mountain rumbled with the roar of the beast and the scraping of rock.

A reflection sparkled, and he turned, scrambling to locate the water.

He glanced over his shoulder—the head and neck of Zio's pet were now out and stretching for freedom.

Arwin swept his hand back and forth, shining light on sticks and rocks and leaves and a disturbingly large spider, but no wat . . . *there*! The water gleamed like a beacon, but his joy was short lived. It was a pitifully small amount. The leaf held a tiny pool from the last storm, but it was small, no bigger than the palm of his hand. The forest would grow wetter the deeper in he traveled, but there wasn't time.

This was going to hurt.

He whispered a string of words made powerful by his gift at birth. The liquid glowed yellow, then silver. This molten portal was far less convenient than Zio's, a great deal more unpredictable, and—judging by how calmly her minions walked into hers—drastically less comfortable.

Arwin touched his pinkie to the silver puddle.

The moment his skin made contact, he was sucked into the leaf. Pain ripped through him—shrinking, stretching, yanking. Pins and needles exploded in every extremity, and his heart stuttered in his chest. The cry of agony lodged in his throat, now too thin to carry sound.

The goblins took hold of steel bars and pulled. Their tusks swung from side to side, their heads wagging as they grunted and groaned beneath the weight. The chain snapped taut and squealed. At first, nothing but anticipation rang through the air, and then the stone door inched to the side. Fresh air spilled in.

Maegon shifted and rolled to his feet, his reptilian eyebrows arched upward, framing large, golden eyes. His tongue flicked out first to taste the world. Then he sniffed and took a step closer.

The stone had been cut and then reset in its original home so that it rested seamlessly against the mountain. No tracks or grooves could be visible—nothing that would be considered a weakness.

Zio had no patience for weakness. Not in her slaves, not in her guests, and certainly not in her stronghold.

Maegon hadn't seen the world outside in years, and his chest glowed with burning embers waiting to be spewed. The temperature in the belly of the castle soared exponentially. The dragon roared and stomped, thrashing his tail back and forth. It struck the wall, and chunks of rock fell and clattered across the floor.

He whipped his head and glared at the winch, displeased with the slow process. The goblins whined as they leaned hard against the handles, sweat dripping off their noses. Maegon's jaw opened wide as he released his fiery inferno, wrapped in a thundering roar.

The first line of goblins burst into flames. They ran, flailing and screaming, while new ones hurried to take their place before the work was undone and the door slid closed, forcing them to start again.

Zio watched as they burned. Their pain was pleasant, soothing, their screams a balm. But the more she killed, the fewer she had. Bitter at her predicament, she growled, waving her hand to extinguish the flames. Despite the burns, two goblins moved to their knees, praising her kindness. The third didn't get up.

She moved closer to the edge, skirts rustling. Tonight it was Maegon who would hunt, but she would be there. There would be no smells, no tastes. She would not experience the euphoria as warm blood spilled over her knuckles. But she would see. That was something. Grabbing the pendant that hung nearly to her waist, she ran the pad of her finger over the blue stone again and again until it began to warm.

The initial connection felt like an electric jolt that crossed through her eyes and into her mind. Maegon's head snapped back, and their eyes met. The pain was gone as quickly as it'd come, and the dragon returned to pawing and pressing himself against the door. His sides expanded and then contracted sharply as he shoved his snout through the opening to let loose flame and smoke.

Zio looked down at the pendant. Reflected in the sapphire were the night sky and the shadows of the dark forest as seen through Maegon's eyes. She would now be able to watch her plan unfold, thwarting the council once again.

Ironically, the return of the Venators was exactly what she'd wanted. But not in *their* hands. Had they been chosen by *any* member of the council, she would've opted to abduct the Venators instead of sending out Maegon to destroy them, but these two had been handpicked by Tate. A moralistic half breed who, despite his status, had managed to become a thorn in her side.

It was almost amusing that the council was so blind concerning Tate. Then she thought of all the times he'd advanced despite her, and her expression soured. Of course, there was the slightest bright spot. Without Tate, she wouldn't have found exactly what she'd been looking for—the handsome, angry Venator he'd left behind.

Maegon thrust his head through the opening, wiggling and twisting his body to force the stone door, his claws scraping against the outside edge. The leverage helped, and the next pull of the winch resulted in a much larger slide.

"Maegon!" she yelled.

The dragon pulled back in and turned slowly to look at her. What a magnificent sight he was. Black smoke twisted from his nostrils, entwining his neck like a string of onyx pearls born of hell itself.

"The Venators are in the forest that surrounds the council house. Fly low. We don't need to rouse Dimitri's attention until it's too late for them to meddle. When you find the Venators . . . kill them both." She fingered her necklace, gazing down at her toy. "Once you've completed your mission, you will come home, but you may do as you wish on the way. Kill whomever catches your eye."

Dragons were rare indeed, and controlling one took years and powerful magic. It had been a chore, and several times she'd questioned her sanity. But Maegon now did as he was told and appreciated her little offerings, such as the limited freedom she'd just extended for his flight home.

The door screeched again, and it was finally wide enough. Maegon slipped through as elegantly as an eel and was gone.

Zio held the pendant out, smiling as she watched the ground rush below.

HELL'S JAWS

Valerian had fallen asleep in the crevice, straddling the branch where it dipped down to meet the trunk, her head leaned back. Grey had moved closer to make sure he could grab her if she slipped. Tate had just laughed and said if there was one thing humans on this side knew how to do, it was sleep in trees. Still, Grey stayed, watching the rise and fall of her chest and trying not to stare at the gaping wound on her shoulder.

They had been in the tree for at least an hour. The increasingly uncomfortable aches in his back and buttocks counted off every passing minute. The people here might be used to sleeping in trees, but he was not. He leaned over the branch, trying to look up through the canopy. "Is Beltran coming back?"

"I don't know." Tate was stretched out across a branch with his back and head resting against the trunk, eyes closed. "It depends how interesting he found you."

"He's been gone a long time. He wouldn't just leave us here . . . right?"

Tate chuckled. "I never make any guesses as to what Beltran will or won't do."

A series of mourning howls broke to the west of them, rising and blending together in a vocal eulogy.

"The pack has returned to lament Cashel," Tate said. "It should be safe to go soon."

Although he couldn't get out of this tree fast enough, something had been nagging at Grey since they first arrived at the council gates. "Tate," he blurted. "What *are* you?"

Tate slowly rolled his head to the side, looking at Grey from under thick black brows. "Why?"

"Valerian said she knew what you were. People react differently to you, and you couldn't introduce us to the council. Since we'll be working together, I'd like to know."

Tate scowled for a moment longer before his eyebrows relaxed and his shoulders slumped. "I guess you'll figure it out soon enough anyway. I'm part Venator."

Since he and Rune had been brought through the gate *because* they were Venators, Grey couldn't see the significance. "And what else?"

"It doesn't matter what else. I could have the purest vampire blood in the land flowing through my veins, and it wouldn't change a thing."

"I . . . I don't understand."

"Look." Tate sat up, letting his legs fall to either side of the branch. "When Venator blood mixes with *any* species besides human, it creates a half breed—a creature who holds a small portion of the abilities gifted a full-blooded Venator and none of the traits of the other parent. The Venator gene blocks all aspects of the other bloodline. Half vampires are not immortal, half werewolves can't change, and half wizards are incapable of magic. We're half breeds, useless and hated by most of the planet as vehemently as they hated the Venators before us. Your kind—" Tate paused to correct himself. "*Our* kind tried to exterminate the planet. That leaves deep wounds. When the gate was closed, the hatred didn't just go away. Most of the full-blooded Venators were gone, and without a physical representation to take out their anger on, the people turned it all toward their descendants.

"We're used and tortured, killed or maimed. We're without rights and without privilege. I inherited more of the Venator abilities than any they'd ever seen, which was remarkable considering how diluted the blood lines had become. It was because of my unique abilities that I was able to pull myself from the depths of hell to find you and Rune, but few of my people are so lucky. They call me a Venshii."

"And Venshii is the nice word," Beltran said as he landed on a branch, feathered wings framing him. "I've heard much worse."

"Oh good," Tate said dryly, "you decided to return. Where's Rune?"

"Just over there. Don't worry," he said with a wink, "I took good care of her."

Grey peered in the direction he'd pointed. Rune's shape was silhouetted on a branch two trees over.

"So." Beltran crossed his arms and grinned like it was his birthday. "Are we heading back to the council house, or are there any more suicidal stops you had in mind?"

"Actually," Grey said, "I was hoping you could do me a favor before we go back."

"Mmm, unfortunately, favors are not usually the coin I play in. But . . ." He turned and walked out to the tip of the branch, one foot in front of the other with perfect balance, his wings drooping low to prevent catching on a limb overhead. "Since the word *favor* would imply a return on my investment from a Venator, I'm listening."

Grey glanced to Tate, looking for guidance on the wisdom of making a deal with Beltran.

Tate shrugged. "If you want to get her out of here, you haven't got much of a choice."

Not the answer he'd been hoping for. Grey explained their plan to move Valerian somewhere where she could turn without the possibility of being found by the pack, allowing her to become strong enough to resist the other wolves when the time came.

After some discussion, they finally settled on a place Tate referred to as the Blue Mountains.

"All right, we have a deal," Beltran said.

Grey preferred the term "favor" to "deal," but a deal was exactly what it had become. He moved to wake Valerian, gently shaking her. She smiled weakly but then frowned, looking over his shoulder at Beltran. "I've never seen anything like you before."

The wings on his back changed from white to black in an instant, and the shape morphed until feathers were replaced by the smooth, leathery wings of a bat.

Her eyes grew wide. "You're the shifter."

"Pleasure to meet you." Beltran dipped his head.

"We're going to take you into the Blue Mountains," Grey said. "It'll be safe for you there. You can change—"

"Shh!" Tate jackknifed up and leapt into a crouch, placing his hand against the wood for balance.

Everyone froze, listening. Grey heard a cacophony of sounds—bugs, animals, the rustle of tree branches in a slight breeze—but nothing that would cause alarm.

He was about to question whether Tate was just hearing things when the layers of sounds began to drop off one by one. Eventually, nothing remained but the whistling of the wind. Then he heard a repeated *whoosh*, like the flapping of wings. Really large wings. Following that was a sound similar to the grumblings of an agitated volcano.

Valerian's eyes grew to saucers, and she covered her mouth with her hands.

Beltran's face went slack. "She wouldn't. Not this close to the council house."

"Go check." Tate jerked his chin toward the canopy.

"Are you insane? Or do you *want* me dead?"

A bellow ripped through the forest. It vibrated at such a low register that the fibers of the tree, along with Grey's insides, buzzed like they'd entered a bass speaker. The sound increased, and a sudden pain snapped in his eardrum. He ducked, covering his ears with his hands.

"Time to go!" Beltran shouted.

The shifter moved for Tate, but the Venshii shook his head. "Not me, them!"

Beltran snatched up Valerian in one arm and Grey in the other. He kicked off and shot out of the branches, tipping straight down. The ground rushed up. Too close. They were too close! Grey flinched, turning his head away and squeezing his eyes shut. Beltran pulled up mere seconds before impact. Grey's shins scrapped dirt, the toe of his shoe gouged into the ground, and then he was yanked up and roughly dropped on his feet.

"Run!" Beltran yelled. *"Run!"* He pushed up, heading back into the trees.

The bellow came again, and Grey didn't need to see what it was to know he should be afraid. But Valerian was human and not capable of the kind of speed they needed.

"I need you to hold on." Grey scooped her up, one arm sliding behind her knees and the other around her back.

Valerian wrapped her arms around his neck and shoved her face into his shoulder as they ran. Hot breath washed down his neck as she mumbled something over and over again. He couldn't make it out. He went to leap over a fallen log and pressed their heads together to prevent them from slamming against each other, and then he understood the words.

Whispered like a resigned prayer to fate, Valerian was repeating, *"We're dead, we're dead, we're dead."*

The balcony doors in Verida's room stood open, the moon back-lighting Dimitri as the points of his nails dug into her neck.

It hurt. A lot. She would not give him the satisfaction of crying out.

Vampire faculties were both a blessing and a curse. Her skin could sense the slightest change in wind direction or feel the breath of an attacker. It added to her pleasure but also increased pain.

Dimitri leaned in, his movements slow and controlled, as they always were. Her eyes picked up every quiver of his lashes, the way his jaw muscles twitched—so slight it was imperceptible to the human eye. And then the movement of air as he opened his mouth to speak. "Tell me one more time how two untrained Venators managed to get past you?"

He was so close. She wanted nothing more than to rip his heart out. With his arm up and a hand around her throat, she could have a fist through his chest cavity before he could stop her. Her fingers twitched at her side, itching. But she couldn't—not yet. More pieces had to line up; more moves had to be made. To reveal herself now would mean failure in the larger scheme.

"I was distracted," she repeated for the third time. "And not where I was supposed to be. I didn't hear them leave their rooms." This time she added a little extra at the end to hurry things along. "I've failed you and will take my punishment."

"Yes, you will." Dimitri's pale-blue eyes glinted. "And if they're dead, your punishment will be worse than you can possibly imagine."

Verida thought she could.

A roar rumbled across the forest. It was a sound Verida had only heard a few times, but one didn't forget the bellow of a dragon. It did something to you—left a tiny piece of fear nestled in your heart. The mere possibility of its return stoked those remnants, causing a flare of immediate, heart-stopping dread.

Dimitri dropped his hold on Verida and strode onto the balcony. He wrapped his thin fingers around the iron railing.

In the distance, the moon fully illuminated the beast sliding through the sky. Verida stared, shocked and confused. The council house was protected by layers of magical wards. Zio knew this

. . . which meant they weren't the target. A sick feeling washed over her.

"Zio," Dimitri spat. "She knows the Venators are out."

Verida came up next to him, her legs leaden. "But I don't understand. How could she possibly know that?"

"We have a spy." Dimitri looked sideways at her. "One with better eyes and ears than you."

Grey and Rune would not survive a dragon attack, of that there was no doubt. Her chances were only slightly better, but she couldn't stand here and watch them be destroyed. Verida turned to go, but Dimitri reached out in a flash, grabbing her by the wrist. "Where do you think you're going?"

"To help."

"No."

All the calm decorum that had been beaten into her for the first two hundred years of her life crumbled, and she shouted, "You can't just leave them out there! We need them!"

Dimitri smiled thinly and turned to face her, taking a long, slow breath. "'Need.' I've always despised that word. It's so . . . *weak*. It's when we decide that we 'need' another person that we become less than we are. You of all people should know that."

Verida looked over his shoulder. The dragon grew closer.

She was trying to keep her heartbeat even, to hide her feelings from Dimitri, but it wasn't working. "It took years to get them here—years! Who knows how long it will take to find new ones. The gate might stay closed for ten years this time, or more."

Dimitri prided himself on his cool decorum regardless of circumstance. She'd only seen him lose control a handful of times. But now she saw the telltale snap in his eyes. His hand lashed out, grabbing her face, his thumb and forefinger pressing into her cheeks. "I don't care how long it takes. I despise the situation we find ourselves in—allowing commoners into the council house, disgusting shows of compassion to the people. But if you think I am so desperate to change those circumstances that I will run out to rescue two Venators who are oozing with palpable goodwill, who dared raise their voices to the council and then proceeded to disobey a direct order to rescue a *peasant*, you have clearly forgotten who I am."

"Then *why* did you care that they were gone in the first place?"

"Perhaps, Verida, my dear, my anger is simply at your failure."

The dragon released its first burst of flame—it had found a target. All her planning, all the years spent putting things right, planning revenge. Verida closed her eyes to prevent Dimitri from seeing more than he should.

He gave a small huff of disgust and dropped his hand from her face, heading for the door with even, controlled steps.

"Do I not get a chance to redeem myself?" She turned. "I am Dracula's daughter. I will train them into what you need."

He hesitated midstep, his back to her. "You cannot change the nature of a beast. And those two creatures Tate retrieved from the other side are weak."

"As I recall, some of your fellow council members expressed their concern about bringing Venators back to this side, worried their nature would be too much to control. But that's exactly what you were hoping for, wasn't it? A beast on your leash—you pull the strings, and it destroys everything but its master."

Dimitri turned, his profile to her—long, thin nose over tight lips. "As the daughter of Dracula, what did you *think* I wanted?"

He was right. She should've known better than to think Dimitri shared the council's fears. He wanted to direct the destruction, not avoid it.

She had one more card to play to hopefully procure at least a measure of help. "I saw Rune lose control," Verida blurted. "Her Venator side took over. She attacked me."

Dimitri finally turned far enough to look at her, a faint smile across his lips. "Did she? Now *that* is interesting."

"No, that is hope. What you're looking for, it's in there, but they've been raised human. It will take time and reprograming, that's all." Verida motioned toward the balcony and the orange fire that flickered in the distance. "Call for Ambrose. Help me save them before we lose them."

He seemed to mull this over. "If they are what you say they are . . . they can get back on their own."

"Dimitri! It's a dragon! I don't even know if *I* could get back."

He continued on as if she hadn't interrupted. "I will need a demonstration of this worth you speak of, because I've yet to see it. You'll have to forgive me if I don't take your word for it. Your timing of this confession is a bit convenient, don't you think?"

"And if they die?"

"Then we will bide our time until I find what I'm looking for. In this, I will not settle."

"When the council finds out you've sanctioned their deaths without consulting—"

Dimitri bared his fangs. "Then we will both be dead. Because at the first whisper of an accusation, I will personally separate your head from your body and place it on a spike for all to see what happens to those who attempt to cross Dimitri of Valehadden." He paused. "I expected more sense from you than issuing such a threat, but you always have had problems with letting your heart overrule logic."

⌘

The first bellow sent a foreboding chill through Rune's body, but it didn't overshadow her need to know what it was. She scrambled up the tree like a squirrel. Climbing was so easy now—she loved it. Hand over hand, sure feet. It was like a sixth sense had been born the moment she'd begun the cliff descent.

There were shouts below, but she ignored them, poking her head through the top of the tree and out into open sky. The source of the bellow flew toward them on wings the size of a jetliner. She recognized the shape immediately but then questioned herself. It wasn't possible.

"D-d-dragon?" she stammered.

The dragon's backbone and the tips of it wings were awash with a cool light from the night sky. It looked black, maybe green, and glowing smoke plumed from the nostrils and traveled down its length, wreathing the body in reddish-black. Its head swept from one side to the other in a methodical search pattern, looking for something—or someone. Probably dinner. And it wasn't going to be her.

Rune shifted one hand, preparing to lower herself below the camouflage of branches. But the slight movement caught its attention, and the dragon's head snapped toward her. The beast was so close now, she could see its eyes as they narrowed on her. Target acquired.

Go, Rune. Move!

The dragon's mouth opened wide, and she could see a glow down its gullet. The light got larger, closer. A plume of fire exploded, rapidly eating up the distance between them.

Fingers wrapped around her ankle. The surprise broke her daze, and she screamed. Then the hand jerked, and she dropped from the branch, her eyes to the sky as fire rolled overhead, vaporizing leaves and turning branches into thin arms of glowing embers. The heat seared her skin and lungs. She fell into Beltran's arms.

"Hold on!"

Rune scrambled to wrap her arms around his neck as they continued to fall backward.

They smashed into a branch. Beltran grunted, then twisted around so he could fly again, pulling Rune in with one arm around her waist and the other against her upper back. He tucked his wings in tight, and they shot across the forest at a downward angle, heading for the tree that Tate was rapidly descending, using one hand to lower himself while the other held the bloody bag.

The canopy was on fire. The dragon let loose another rumbling cry. Rune's cheek was pressed against Beltran's, and she peered through the smoke, her hair whipping against the raw skin of her forehead. The shadowy shape of the dragon was making a wide turn, returning for a second attack.

Beltran shifted her to the side, holding her with one arm. Her feet swung freely.

"I've got to get Tate," he said. "Be prepared for a rough ride."

Tate leapt out to a branch as they got closer, dangling from one hand. Beltran pulled into a tight turn, looping around to come at Tate from the front. Beltran's shoulder pummeled into Tate's chest, ripping him from the branch. Tate's arm smashed into Rune's face as he grappled for a hold. Beltran dipped into a dive. They skimmed just above the ground until they caught up with Grey, who was carrying the woman they'd rescued from the camp.

"All right," Beltran shouted. "I'll have to turn you around, then I want you to hit the ground running. Rune, let go of my neck."

That was the last thing she wanted to do. But she did as she was told. Beltran tossed her outward while wrapping his hand around her ribcage to pull her into a twist—similar to a move she'd seen in a figure-skating competition. It had looked graceful on TV. It did not feel that way in real life. She spun, arms flailing . . . and then she was falling. She screamed.

An arm wrapped around her waist, and Beltran pulled her back against his body one handed. Her shoulder rammed into Tate's elbow. She grunted in pain, but she was facing out now, held only by his arm while her feet skimmed the ground.

"OK," Beltran said in her ear. "On three. One, two—"

He let go of her, and she took off running.

Beltran flew over her head, twisting into a barrel roll to avoid a tree. Tate bellowed out a stream of swear words. Using both hands to control Tate's larger size, Beltran flipped Tate out, grabbed him, and lowered him to the ground as well. A moment later, Beltran touched down. His wings vanished into his back, and he ran.

Above them, the dragon hovered, taking aim. It sent down a pillar of fire through the trees. Behind them, the fire ignited the trees with a *whoosh*. Burning pine needles and pieces of fallen branches blew out in all directions. Rune swatted at her smoldering hair as she ran.

"Beltran!" she shouted. "Can't you turn into a dragon?"

"Not a good idea," he yelled back.

No time to ask for an explanation. She pumped her arms harder. Tate was starting to fall behind. "Grey! Hard left."

Grey obeyed immediately, turning a ninety-degree angle. The rest followed.

Beltran looked over his shoulder to see where the dragon was. "How much farther?"

"Too far," Tate grunted.

Behind them, the forest was awash in flame.

A wolf jumped out in front of Grey, who skidded to a stop. The woman screamed, clawing at Grey's back to stay in his arms. At the same time, a stream of fire, continually fueled by the flapping dragon above, exploded to Rune's right and billowed outward. She dove to the side, rolling away.

The wolf retreated, howling to the others.

Tate's trench coat was on fire, and he shrugged out of it as fast as he could. Then he dropped, rolling the bag with the head over the ground to extinguish it.

"We have to hide!" Rune scrambled to her feet.

"It's no good—dragons can see body heat." Beltran's eyes searched the sky.

"They have thermal imaging?" Rune couldn't believe it. "This day keeps getting better and better."

"We have to get to the river," Tate said. "Just keep moving."

The dragon had obviously figured out their destination, because it swooped in ahead of them, dropping a line of fire that blocked their way. With nowhere to go, Grey turned and ran next to the fire line. They were so close. The woman's feet brushed against the flames, and she cried out in pain, jerking her legs back.

The dragon screeched and swung its head from side to side, searching along the boundary it had just created. It looked right at them, and Rune cringed, sure death was imminent, but its eyes slid past once, then twice. Almost as if . . . *it couldn't see them at all!*

"That's it!" Rune yelled. "Run as close to the flames as you can. It can't sense our body heat through the fire."

Beltran hooted. "Tate, she's a genius!"

One by one, they all followed Grey, pulling in as close to the fire as they could tolerate and tearing down the line.

The dragon roared in fury overhead.

FREE FALL

Water transportation was tricky and limited to a certain distance. Arwin had emerged in several different places, each time finding another source to continue his journey. Finally, he exited the spell beneath the Sarahna River and burst to the surface, gasping for air. The water around him was a bubbling soup, slapping into waves that broke against each other.

He'd exited much closer to the falls than intended.

Before he had time to utter either spell or curse word, the current seized hold of his cloak and yanked him down like murderous hands. Beneath the surface, the water twisted and spun in every direction, flipping him upside down and sideways. His back smashed into a rock. Then he was jerked violently to the side, cracking his head on another. A new current swept in and twisted him free of the rocky deathtraps, only to send him hurtling toward the lip of the falls.

He uttered a spell that came out in bubbles. Luckily, magic had never been terribly particular about mode of delivery. He was buoyed up by summoned forces and lifted from the river until he hung above the swirling foam. Breathing hard, he pulled the strands of beard away from his eyes and mouth and smoothed it down. His head and back throbbed from the beating he'd just taken, but there was no time to worry about that now.

The falls pounded mercilessly, filling the air with mist and deafening Arwin to the outside world—he wouldn't hear a dragon if it were right on top of him. Ahead were three great arching stone monuments that had been placed at the head of the falls eons before. The water split and rushed around them before cascading down. He'd studied them extensively in his youth. The monuments were etched with magical runes so old no one knew the meaning of half of them. Youthful hubris said he would be the one to unlock their secrets . . .

He was not.

Arwin came down lightly on the center of the three arches, keeping the spell in place to prevent falling, and scanned the valley below. Under normal circumstances, such a tactic would yield him nothing. It was dark, and the trees stood like an elevated carpet, hiding whatever secrets might be unfolding beneath. But he was looking for a dragon, and *that* attack would shine like a beacon for miles in every direction.

He could see nothing to the north, west, or south. *Surely not.* Arwin turned, looking to the top of the cliffs in the east. The forest was lit in flaming destruction, pillars of smoke billowing skyward. Above it all, the dragon twisted in the sky, not yet returning home but coming around for another pass.

His eyes widened. Zio had never sent her dragon this close to the council house before. If there was one thing dragons were susceptible to, it was magic. And with himself and Ambrose in residence, Zio had never risked her most prized possession. If the beast was there, she wanted those two Venators dead—badly enough to take the gamble.

But the dragon was still hunting, which meant the Venators were likely alive.

Arwin floated back over the raging river, whispered his transportation spell, and dropped. His body was compressed, and he was sucked upstream in a crazy, desperate attempt to save the lives of two Venators he'd never met.

⊰⊱✤⊰⊱

Sweat poured down Rune's face and trickled between her shoulder blades as they ran alongside the fire line. The wall of flames on her right licked out without warning, singeing hair and blistering skin.

"Rune! Slow down!" Tate called.

The dragon swooped over again, laying down a blazing trail. It was now randomly placing attacks, hoping to hit what it couldn't see. This one landed a few feet behind them.

Against every survival instinct she had, Rune slowed to allow Tate to come up next to her. His face gleamed with sweat. "We have to split up. It's the only chance we've got. There's a mound of rocks coming up—I need you to get to the top."

"I'll be out of the fire," she protested as they ran. "The dragon will see me."

"I know. I need you to draw the attack."

"I'm bait!" The head in the bag Tate held slammed against Rune's leg, and she thought she'd be sick.

"I'd do it, but I'm not fast enough. Once he sees you, jump down. The rocks will protect you from the heat. I'll be waiting at the bottom. Got it?"

Her climbing gift suddenly seemed less appealing. "Yeah, I got it."

"Good. Now tell Beltran they're going off the edge."

She turned on the speed, catching up to Beltran. "Tate says . . . off the edge."

"Easy for him to say!" Beltran shouted. "Damn it! This is going to hurt."

Not seeing the rock formation, Rune fell back to Tate.

The fire line exploded between her and Beltran. A ball of heat rolled out, spitting embers and separating the groups prematurely.

"Through, through!" Tate called from behind.

Rune screamed and leapt, wrapping arms around her face and holding her breath. For a moment there was nothing but a roar of crackling sound. And then heat—clawing and biting. The two seconds within the inferno felt like minutes . . . She hit the ground on the other side, dropping immediately into a roll. Pain flared on her right arm and left shoulder. She was on fire. Rune slapped at one arm while rolling the shoulder into the ground.

A moment later Tate was there, pulling her up. "Almost there! Go! I'm right behind you."

The rocky outcropping rose through the smoke. She continued to run next to the fire line as long as possible, then veered left. Vulnerability washed over her. She was in the open, totally visible. No matter how hard she pumped her legs, it didn't seem fast enough. She could almost feel the heat of dragon's breath on her neck, but nothing nipped at her heels besides the galloping of her own fear.

Rune hit the formation and jumped the first two boulders, landing on a large, flat rock. She focused on the task: hand, foot, *don't worry about the dragon*, hand, foot, *faster*, hand, foot, *leap*. She pushed off, then slapped the next rock with flat palms, using momentum to push herself one handhold higher.

Landing on the highest rock, she straightened. But the dragon must've spotted her the moment she left the fire, because bearing down on her was the open mouth of death. Fire burst out of the dragon's gullet like a boiling geyser. No time to scream; Rune turned and leapt off the edge in a swan dive.

❖❖❖

The fire line was coming to an end. Ahead, the arms of flame shrank down to nothing, starved by a dirt expanse and the rocky edge of a cliff. The lack of heat left them nowhere to hide, and the approaching drop off left nowhere to run.

Valerian's hold on Grey was growing weaker. She was exhausted from her ordeal, and her shoulder had begun to ooze puss. Grey tried to think of a solution, but it was like rattling around an empty tin can . . . nothing.

He glanced back, trying to determine how much time they had left. The dragon was coming in for another pass, but this time it was focused on something in the distance. He followed its line of sight and found the prey. Rune was scrambling up a rocky outcropping, unaware the beast had her locked in its sights.

His feet stuttered. "Rune!"

Beltran pushed him hard. "Keep moving!"

Valerian lifted her head to see what the commotion was about just as Rune turned and leapt off the top of the rocks, disappearing beneath the wash of flame and brimstone.

"Rune!"

"She'll be fine," Beltran shouted. "Cut to the right. Here! Now, now, now!

Grey gritted his teeth and veered, leaping over charred earth that flickered red and orange with live embers. There was nowhere to go! He skidded to a stop at the edge of the cliff. Valerian squeezed his neck, whimpering for the first time. It was hundreds of feet to the ground, and along the bottom, a hopelessly narrow river snaked.

Dark, leathery wings sprouted from Beltran's back. They were almost twice his height, towering over him with fingerlike claws at the tips while the bottoms dragged behind like a gothic skirt, trimmed with the same thin claws. "Jump," he demanded.

"What?" Grey hissed, taking another look over the edge. "No, there has to be another way."

"Are you seeing what I'm seeing?" Beltran gestured backward, waving his arms wildly.

The trees that had offered sparse protection in the beginning had faded to rocks and tall grasses along the cliff's edge. The dragon took advantage of the new landscape and dropped in. Having forgotten Rune, it was now focused solely on them. It skimmed the ground, its curled feet brushing the grass blades.

"Hold on to her, Grey. Don't let go." Beltran's eyes were on the dragon. "I'll protect you. Just jump. *Now!*"

If he leapt, it was likely they wouldn't survive. But if he stood here, they would die without question.

"I'm sorry," he whispered to Valerian and stepped off the edge.

They clung to each other as the wind whistled past. Grey rolled onto his back, intending to offer the only thing he had left—protection upon impact. His eyes were now on the receding cliff instead of the approaching river, and with nothing above him but the starry sky, for the briefest moment, he felt peace.

Beltran leapt. Then came a roar that would forever be painted on Grey's memory as the sound preceding a dragon attack, followed by a rush of air and sharp crackling. Fire spewed harmlessly over the ridge above Beltran, turning his form to shadow.

The dragon followed, sliding out over the edge and looking for its prey. It tilted its head down and spat out another attack, this one perfectly on target. Inside Grey, the fear of death morphed into something new—a calm acceptance of their pending demise. They would die burning.

Beltran tucked his wings in, shooting toward them. He reached around Valerian, grabbing Grey by the shoulders and pulling the three together. He hooked Grey's legs with his feet, and then Beltran's large, leathery wings wrapped around them completely, encasing all three of them from head to feet in a cocoon.

Grey couldn't feel the fire engulf them, but he knew the second it did because Beltran threw his head back, screaming.

The swan dive ended much less elegantly than it started. Rune tumbled down the rocks, cracking her spine, elbow, knee, head, and every other possible place before coming to rest at the bottom. She groaned. Everything hurt, and the world was a little fuzzy from the crack to the skull . . . but she wasn't on fire.

Tate bent to help her up. "Come on, this way." He jerked his head toward the tree line a few hundred feet ahead.

She needed to check on Grey. "Just a second." Hurrying in the opposite direction, Rune peeked around a boulder just in time to watch him disappear over the cliff. "No!" Rune pushed off, surging out from behind their protection without a second thought, pumping her arms as fast as she could.

Tate yelled for her to stop. She ignored him.

Beltran went over the edge, followed by the dragon, its tail slapping the edge as it vanished. Rune slid to her knees and then flopped onto her belly, crawling the last foot to look over the ledge.

"Rune!" Tate shouted again.

All her senses diminished, replaced by a pounding in her ears and an overall feeling of dread. Grey was falling, holding Valerian, Beltran and the dragon in pursuit. Rune's fingers clenched, her nails digging into the edge.

"Grey!" The cry was quiet, tied down by a stranglehold of grief.

A thick arm wrapped around her waist and jerked her up.

"Stop it!" She struggled against Tate, kicking and punching. "Let me go!"

Rune's heart was breaking in two. After *everything*, Grey should not be the one to die. He was kinder, better, stronger. She didn't deserve to be the one at the top of this cliff.

Tate set her on her feet and grabbed her roughly by the shoulders. "Rune, there is no—"

"They're going to die! Grey is—" Her chest jerked in a hard sob. "This can't be happening. Verida told us not to go. We shouldn't have gone."

"*Rune, stop it!*" Tate roared, shaking her. "There is nothing we can do! Do you hear me? Nothing!" His brown eyes burrowed into her own. "Their fate is in Beltran's hands. There was only one shot to possibly get us out of here alive, and this was it. You distracted the dragon long enough to get them off the cliff."

"That was the plan?"

"Yes! And you'll ruin everything if you don't shut up and listen. If that dragon returns, we're dead. I know you're worried about Grey, but Beltran is with them—he's clever and a survivor. That's all I can offer. No more hesitations, no more questions. Just run."

23

STRATEGY AND SACRIFICE

Secured inside Beltran's wings, they hit the water at an angle and torpedoed to the bottom. Miraculously, the water did not penetrate, leaving them protected in a leather-clad pocket of air. The first impact knocked the breath from Grey's chest. The second whip-lashed his head forward, cracking it into Valerian's shoulder wound. She gasped, her body shuddering in pain.

They were alive.

Beltran pulled his wings around them tighter, wedging every-one in place so he could relax the grip he'd held on Grey and Valerian. But then they were moving, sliding along the bottom. The pod began to tip upward, preparing to return to the surface. The muscles of Beltran's wings tensed, and they jerked to a stop as if anchored. He suspected Beltran was using those claws on his wing tips to hold them in place. But the movement slightly opened the seal at the bottom.

The first drips of water entered the pod.

The darkness was absolute, and sounds had a strange, hol-low resonance—similar to the way a voice echoes inside a cave.

Beltran's breaths were shallow and coming out between his teeth in a hiss.

"Are you all right?" Grey asked.

He gave a mirthless chuckle. "Not. At. All. But I heal as quickly as you. I'll be back to my chipper self soon."

"Valerian?"

"I'm alive," came the weak reply.

Liquid trickled in faster, pooling around their feet and rising rapidly up their shins.

"Damn it," Beltran grunted. "I can't hold us here with the extra weight of the water." They started to slide again, dragging along the bottom.

"We don't have much time before we run out of air. Our heat signatures are gone for the moment, but the second we surface, he'll see us."

When he didn't elaborate, Grey asked, "What are we going to do?"

"I'm thinking. We're as trapped as we can be. Above us is a dragon, we're running out of air, and we're being pulled toward Sarahna Falls. The falls are only a little shorter than the drop we just took, but with a much rougher landing. I can survive it—I suspect a Venator could too—but . . ."

"I won't." Valerian filled in the blank.

"Not likely."

"Can't you fly us out?" Grey asked.

"One word. *Dragon.* I hit the air, I'm dead. It's why I didn't just fly us out to start with. Beltran tapped the weapon on Grey's back. "How good are you with this crossbow?"

"Good."

"For all our sakes, I hope so. A dragon has few weak spots, its eyes being the easiest to hit with a bolt. It's an option, but if you miss—we're dead."

The water was now up to their knees.

Valerian's breath grew more rapid, and she stretched, trying to push herself higher. "Can you keep the water from coming in?"

"At this point, that water is the only thing keeping us from bobbing to the surface."

The current's speed was increasing, bringing them closer to the falls with every second.

"How am I supposed to hit a dragon eye while floating down the river . . . underwater?"

"You have a better plan?"

Grey ground his jaw. "No."

"Me either, and I'm an excellent strategist. All right. I'm going to open my wings. Stay under until the dragon's been hit. The second it sees our heat signatures, it will be on top of us before we can get out of the way. One, two—" The pod filled with the sound of everyone taking deep breaths, and then they were tumbling through the river.

The cold was a shock. It pressed against Grey's chest and almost caused him to expel the little air he had left in his lungs. The surface of the water lit up as fire rolled above them. Grey reluctantly released Valerian and flipped to his back, grasping the bow. But the current fought back, twisting his limbs at every opportunity. He kicked and struggled, trying to remain in a position from which to shoot.

Beltran swam over, his wings gone, and positioned himself under Grey. He wrapped his legs around Grey's waist and used his arms to traverse the current and keep them level.

More secure, Grey looked up through the murky river water. No dragon in sight. Beltran leaned in, pointing. There, upriver, was its lurking shadow. His heart sank. The dragon was too far away, *nearly* impossible to hit from this distance but *completely* impossible while lying underwater, fighting both the current and surface distortion. The beast had to be closer for him to have a prayer of accomplishing the shot, but they couldn't lie in wait. His lungs were already starting to burn, and every second they delayed was a second closer to the impending doom of the falls.

This was a terrible plan.

Valerian grabbed his arm, her grasp gentle, tentative. Hair swirled around her face, and she looked at him like a sad water nymph, eyes full of emotion and trying to speak through the silence. She squeezed his forearm once and then turned, kicking away. Grey jerked, moving to follow, but Beltran held firm, grabbing his shoulders and twisting them back into position to fire the bow.

To the left, Valerian broke the surface, feet churning below. It was mere moments before the shadow of the dragon swooped in and fire enveloped her. Red and orange boiled around them. Valerian's legs kicked and jerked . . . and then went still. This time, the water would not act as refuge but as a grave. Her lifeless body glided beneath the surface, face blackened and completely unrecognizable.

Grey looked away. A sob broke free, releasing a single bubble that rose to the surface.

Having eliminated the first of its targets, the dragon now knew where to look. It dropped close to the river with slow wing beats, keeping level while sweeping its head in a search pattern.

Grey raised the bow, bolt nocked. Waiting. Its head was larger than he and Beltran together. Its nostrils sniffed at the water, eyes searching. For the size of its face, its eyes were quite small and protected from below by an arch of bone. The fact that it was this close and still couldn't see them suggested thermal imaging was its main source of vision. Beltran frantically tapped his arm—*now!*

The dragon flapped its wings, and an armored belly skimmed over them. He'd missed his chance, and his lungs were on fire, screaming for air. The current picked up again, and Grey twisted, looking over his shoulder to see the white bubbling mass that was surely the rapids preceding Sarahna Falls. But this time, the imminent danger acted as a delivering angel, jerking them forward and racing the two toward the dragon's head.

Grey raised the bow, but there was only one possible way this could happen. He motioned with one hand to Beltran, pointing. The shifter understood and began to push toward the surface. Grey stretched out prone and bent his neck up so the bow and his head would exit simultaneously. There could be no warning.

His face broke the surface, and he sucked in a mouthful of air. The dragon's eyes widened. Grey pulled the trigger.

The bolt flew true, embedding deep in its eye. The dragon threw back its head, emitting a high-pitched cry. Its wings crumbled, and it crashed into the river, pushing out a wave that picked up Grey and Beltran and tossed them into the rapids.

❦

Beltran kicked to the surface only to duck back under—the dragon was thrashing upstream, trying to claw the bolt from his eye and spitting fire in all directions. The water acted as a brilliant shield, protecting him from the heat . . . until the water sided with the enemy. Liquid hands slammed him against a boulder and pounded down, pinning him beneath the surface.

Beltran struggled but realized quickly his efforts were futile. He dislocated his shoulders—being a shifter had many benefits—and twisted his arms around to push flat with his palms against the rock, kicking free. He burst to the surface in a minefield of rocks, undercurrents, and branches, sucking in air and wishing he were a fish.

But no. Tonight he would stay in human form. He needed to communicate with the boy, and searing his face into the Venator's memory was a highly attractive bonus. He decided from the moment he'd joined the wolf fight that he wanted the Venators in his corner, and he would be damned if he was going to watch this one die.

A small wave washed over him. He spit out a mouthful of water, sputtering. The speed and violence of the water made evasive maneuvering almost impossible.

Beltran twisted, searching the river, and finally caught sight of Grey's black locks just as his head slipped underwater, caught in a swirling death eddy that had formed between two large boulders. He didn't come up.

A burst of flame spewed over Beltran's head, and he ducked, cursing the half-blind beast. Approaching the eddy, he dove with eyes open. Grey was caught, swirling head over feet in a mess of other captured debris. Beltran kicked hard and fast, barreling into him and knocking them both free of the whirlpool.

They popped to the surface and Grey gasped for air, choking and coughing.

"You're all right. Breathe," Beltran said.

A boulder loomed ahead, and Beltran shoved Grey to the side, swimming after him to avoid the rock himself.

"It's back in the—" A wave splashed Grey in the face, cutting off his words. "Air! It's back in the air!"

Beltran turned around, kicking hard to keep himself upright. Behind them, the dragon was rising to the sky again. A broken shaft protruded from its destroyed eye, but the other eye was focused on them. There had been a part of him that had hoped it wouldn't be necessary, but going over the falls was the only option left.

"Grey, listen! When you hit the bottom, kick with everything you've got for the surface. We'll get separated! Just keep swimming."

"Look out!"

Fire spewed toward them.

A pillar of water came from behind. It rushed over their heads and smashed into the flames, neutralizing them.

"What was tha—?" Grey was yanked down a dip in the rapids and shoved past the last line of obstacles before the falls.

Beltran's thigh scraped against a rock, and he swore as blood bloomed into the churning mass of white water. Wanting to locate their rescuer before he went over the edge, Beltran kicked and stroked, fighting the current to hold himself in place.

A figure floated above the rapids, the bottom of a robe trailing behind. Arwin.

"Get the Venator out of here, Beltran," the old wizard yelled without taking his eyes off the dragon. "Don't lose him!"

Arwin shouted several spells. The dragon opened its mouth. Arwin lifted his arms, and a pillar of water rose on command. Fire shot out, eating up the sky between the two just as Arwin pushed a liquid pillar forward, this one thicker than before. Fire and water met head on and exploded in a cloud of steam. Beltran couldn't see anything through the mist. The water pushed on, continually fed, and punched through the steam cloud, driving its way down the dragon's gullet. Steam poured from the beast's mouth and nostrils, thick and white.

Arwin had managed to extinguish the burning inferno within.

"Yes!" Beltran screamed, slapping the water.

"Beltran!"

Grey was swimming as hard as he could against the current, only a few feet from the lip of the falls. Beltran almost laughed. The boy was powerful, he'd grant him that, but not powerful enough to avoid the falls forever. Nor did they want to. An angry, fireless dragon still had wicked mean teeth.

Beltran stopped his own strokes, and the current sent him speeding toward Grey. "Hang on, Venator. This is going to be rough."

"No! Beltran, stop."

Beltran crashed into him, and they tumbled over the edge.

SOUL SCARS

Grey crawled onto the bank, coughing and spitting out water. The falls had almost done him in. He'd finally escaped the churning mass of undercurrents but had been afraid to leave the water. He'd floated down river, watching and waiting. It was long after the dragon had disappeared into the distance before he'd dared to move for the shore.

Plopping down, he threw one arm over his knee and stared at the calmly flowing river. The water gave no indication of the violence it had just endured—a bit like him, he supposed. Did he bear the marks? Probably not. After all, he'd walked through life with scars crisscrossing his soul, and nobody had ever noticed . . . except Tashara.

Beltran strolled over and sat down next to him. Grey waited for a snide comment or an off-color remark. When none came after several minutes, Grey spoke with a thick tongue. "This is not how it was supposed to go. We did everything for the right reasons. Valerian wasn't supposed to die." He dropped his head to his arm.

Water dripped from strands of hair and ran down his cheek. "The good guys should win."

Beltran snorted.

That was what he'd been expecting, and Grey swung to face him, ready to punch Beltran in his smug little shifter face. But Beltran's expression wasn't one of amusement but of bitterness. He was looking out into the distance, mouth screwed up in thought. "The righteous win in stories and tales, Grey. Not in this life. Right or wrong, makes no difference."

"Then why bother trying?"

Beltran seemed to really think about this. Grey waited, listening to the pounding of the falls in the distance.

"Sometimes," Beltran ventured, "sometimes you pick a side, and you think good has finally won, only to discover they've been pretending to be something they're not. Sometimes evil wins unopposed, and you watch hundreds of thousands die. Sometimes it all seems hopeless."

Hopeless was exactly what Grey was feeling. He scrubbed his hands over his face, trying to erase the tears that had formed in the corners of his eyes. "I have no idea what side I'm on."

"Why not?"

"How could I possibly know? Everyone has hidden agendas, and I don't think a single person has told me the whole truth since I walked though that gate."

"Very astute, young Venator, and I'm sure you're correct. But since when does that matter?"

"*What?*"

Beltran shrugged. "Truth, lies—they'll all pull you from your path if you let them."

Grey rolled his eyes and leaned back, resting his weight on the palms of his hands. "I prefer truth, thanks."

"People will tell you terrible lies, but they'll tell you even more terrible truths. If you take either and hold on to them as unchangeable—they will change you. You could come away deceived . . . or enlightened. I've found that lies tell so much more about the bearer than the truth ever would. Truth can cause you to give up or bend to another's will. The truth has a way of getting you to surrender to it, as if there were no way around what has been and no future beyond who you are right now. Sometimes truths are shared as a deliberate attempt to manipulate you."

"It sounds like you have experience in this area."

Beltran grinned, his green eyes twinkling. "I'm very good at a great deal of things. Manipulation is one of them."

"Thank you for so freely admitting it," Grey said dryly. "Is that what you're doing now?"

"You'll have to determine that for yourself—also an important lesson you'll need to learn. And quickly. *You* decide who you are. *You* decide what's right. And *you* decide where you stand. Stop trying to pick a side, because—speaking from one highly valued species to another—everyone you meet will try to get you on theirs. In this world, you are a tool to those in power. Nothing more. You must stand where you are, on your side, and decide just how exactly you're going to change this world. For better or for worse—the choice is yours. But it's a choice you need to make now."

Beltran took in a deep breath. It caught for a quick second, as if he weren't sure whether to say more or not, and it rushed out in a huff. "You're a fighter, Grey. A true Venator in the old sense of the word, back when they were the protectors. You lost this battle today, but your war is just beginning. You can decide to fight or quit." He glanced at Grey from the corner of his eye. "I understand wanting to quit."

"I don't want to quit."

Beltran chuckled. "Oh, I think you do."

Grey started to object.

"But I don't think you will. Hell, I've wanted to quit hundreds of times. But for me, from where I choose to stand, to stop trying is unacceptable." His lips pulled up on one side in a soft smile. "And I think you understand that."

Grey stared at Beltran. He'd assumed the worst of this man . . . this shifter, whatever he was . . . and heeded Tate's cautionary advice. Beltran, the man he would've deemed as untrustworthy, had done everything he could to keep both him and Valerian alive. He'd risked his own life.

Grey, despite being grateful, had written it off as a debt Beltran wished to rack up. Because, in the shifter's own words, a favor from a Venator was coin he wanted to play in. But then to sit here and listen to such wisdom coming from his mouth—it shook Grey's foundations. He had misjudged this man's character so severely. How could he traverse this world if he couldn't even trust his own instincts?

"How can I tell?" Grey asked, barely audible over the whispering river. "What is evil and what is good?"

"You can't. Not always."

"Just great." He breathed in, steeling his emotions. "OK, I decide where I stand. And after that? How do I know who to trust?"

Beltran stared out at the river. "You left the council house in the middle of the night, untrained, to face down a pack of werewolves that has been harassing the council for years. Rune had motiva-tion—her brother. But you did so without any thoughts of personal gain. Your only motivation was the injustice of the situation. Am I right?"

"Yes."

"Then I'd say that from here on out, you trust those who are invested in your cause—justice. I know Tate is—more so than he'll probably ever tell you."

"And Verida? How's she involved in all of this?"

"That's her business, but I can tell you she has her reasons."

"And you?"

"Am I invested?" He splayed a hand against his chest. "Obviously."

"Why?"

Beltran's old demeanor returned, and he grinned. "Nobody knows that. No offense, but we just met."

"Then how am I supposed to know if you're invested or not?"

"You don't know Tate's or Verida's reasons either. And if you're not convinced after I jumped off a cliff, chose not to swim away as a fish, and followed you over the falls, nothing I say or do will change your mind." He winked. "I stand where I stand, whether you see it or not."

Grey evaluated, trying to find some telltale sign of Beltran's motivation behind his eyes. But all he could see was the whimsical playboy Beltran loved to show everyone he met. The persona had been down, but it was back in play, and Grey would likely get noth-ing more. He looked away, fiddling with a pebble at his side. He picked it up and threw it. It made a small splash, the ripple barely noticeable.

"You're right. I'm sorry." The balance had tipped from impossible to possible the moment Beltran had joined their group. "Thank you for everything you did today. Without you . . . I wouldn't be going home alive."

THE UNEXPECTED ALLY

Rune stood at the edge of the cliff near the council house, hidden from view by the largest of the stables. She wrapped her arms around herself in a hug and stared out over the burning valley below, worrying herself sick that Grey had burned with it.

Behind her, Tate leaned against the back stable, silent except for the incessant tapping of his fingers against the hilt of the sword at his hip. Verida paced between the two of them.

The horizon grew pink. At first Rune thought it was haze from the fire, but the color gradually increased. Day was breaking. Extreme exhaustion knocked at the door, but she couldn't give in. Not yet. She turned. "It's almost daylight. What are we going to do?"

Verida blew. "I can't believe you left him out there!" She stopped her pacing just long enough to shoot a seething glare at Tate. "And with Beltran, no less!"

"For the third time, I had no other choice. And before you start yelling at me again, let's establish that there is nothing I want more than for Grey to be alive. *Nothing*."

"Then how can you just sit there?"

He stared at her intently. The pause itself stretched out like a silent accusation. "What do you want me to do? Wrestle a dragon? Run into a flaming forest? Tell me, Verida, what exactly would you have me do?"

"I don't know! Just bring him back!"

Bring him back. Rune's hands curled into fists at her sides. How dare she! When Rune and Tate had finished climbing back up the cliff, Verida had been waiting at the top, knowing full well a dragon was hunting them.

And she'd done nothing.

"Why didn't *you* come help?" Rune snarled.

Verida flinched as if she'd been waiting for the question . . . and dreading it.

When she didn't respond, Tate chimed in. "An answer I'd like to know as well."

"Dimitri knows I let you go. I denied it, but he knows." Verida crossed her arms and looked out over the forest. "He forbade me from leaving."

Rune felt like she'd been sucker punched in the gut. "I see."

"Do you?"

"I think I've got it, yeah." She bit off the words and spat them toward Verida. "You're here to help us. You're on our side . . . unless Dimitri forbids it, and then you'll let us die. Did I get it right?"

"You don't know what you're talking about."

"Then explain it to me, because I'm having a hard time seeing something different from where I am."

"You have no—"

"Verida," Tate broke in. "She's right."

Verida twisted back to face them, nostrils flaring, her fangs exposed. "She's *not* right! You have no idea what position I'm in. I'll pay for tonight dearly—I promise you that. If I'd stuck my neck out any further, my head wouldn't be attached to it."

Tate pushed off the stable wall. "I understand your dilemma. You know I do. But we might have lost one tonight. If Beltran hadn't followed us out there, we'd all be dead."

"I told you not to go!"

"And you were right!" Rune snapped. "We shouldn't have been out there tonight. There. Does that make you feel better? I hope so, because when Grey doesn't come back, at least you can console yourself with the fact that you were right."

"Beltran." A tired voice came from somewhere below them. "Enough. Get us up there."

Rune's breath caught in her throat, scared to hope. "Grey?"

A distinctive chuckle trickled up on the breeze. "Very well." Beltran rose silently from beneath the cliff's lip, wings flapping in a smooth, even fashion. He held Grey in his arms.

"Beltran!" Verida shrieked. She pointed at him and took several quick steps in his direction, stopping only when she came up against the cliff's edge. "I can't believe you were just lurking down there. I take it back—I can believe it. What were you hoping to hear, you twisted little bastard?"

"No need for name calling. And to be honest, I'd rather have *no* father than have yours, Verida darling." He smiled pleasantly and flew in, lowering Grey to the ground and landing beside him. "I wasn't hoping for anything, just acting out of habit. Listen first, act second."

Looking at them both standing there, safe, Rune's eyes welled with tears of gratitude. She ran to Grey, wrapping her arms around his neck. "You're OK!"

He stiffened. "Uh, yeah. I'm all right." When she didn't let go, he awkwardly reached around, gave her a halfhearted pat on the back, and pulled away.

Confused, she frowned.

He stuffed his hands in his pockets and rolled his shoulders forward—looking very much like the old Grey as he stared at his feet. "Valerian didn't make it."

She'd been so excited to see him alive that she'd missed the grief rolling off him in waves. No sentiment could express her sorrow besides the most basic, and she offered it, feeling woefully inadequate. "I'm so sorry."

He shrugged, not out of acceptance but to show that words had failed him.

"Thank you, Beltran," Rune said, "for bringing him back."

"Anything for the lady." He ducked his head in a bow.

Verida guffawed. "What were you doing out there anyway, Beltran? I made it clear you were to stay away from them!"

"Clear?" Beltran cocked an eyebrow. "Yes, you made yourself veeery clear. But you never asked if I agreed."

"I don't care if you agree!"

"Here we go," Tate muttered.

"You don't own me, Verida. Never have."

"Stop it." Grey was quiet but firm enough to stop the conversation. "Without Beltran, I'd be dead."

Verida's face puckered like she'd swallowed a lemon.

"How did you escape?" Rune asked. "I watched you go off that cliff, and . . ." Her voice cracked. "I didn't know if I'd ever see you again."

"Well," Beltran drawled, "after we dove off the cliff and plummeted a few hundred feet while on fire, Grey took out one of the dragon's eyes . . . with a bolt"—he winked—"while floating down the river."

Tate laughed out loud. "Disabled a dragon on his first day. I knew you were special, Grey."

Grey rolled his shoulders even further forward. He looked like he wanted to crawl out of his skin. "Arwin helped too."

"Yes, but *after* you took out that eye," Beltran corrected.

"Arwin was there?" Verida's eyes went blank, and she looked like the weight of the world was on her shoulders. "Dimitri will not be happy."

"I'm certain Arwin has no intention of announcing his involvement," Beltran said. "A bolt to the eye is a reasonable explanation for how they survived—nothing else needs to be mentioned. Neither Tate nor Arwin were there, and if rumor ever suggests I was there, well . . ." He held both arms out with a flourish, like a magician revealing a trick. "I was just having a little fun, that's all."

"This is ridiculous!" Rune burst out. "If the council wants us so badly, why leave us out there to die without offering any help?"

"Because nobody listens to me. That's why!" Verida snapped. "I tell you to keep your mouth shut at dinner, but do you? No. I told you this was a bad idea—does anyone care? No. Dimitri saw a little too much and is convinced his two Venators are weak, softhearted, and utterly useless. He'd rather procure another set from your side, even if it takes twenty years."

Beltran whistled. "Not good."

"And the rest of the council?" Tate asked. "Do you think they feel the same?"

"I don't think so—at least, not all of them. When I mentioned the council . . ." She gulped. "It didn't go well. Dimitri had a very specific idea of the type of Venator he was looking for when he proposed their return. What he wants is—"

"Ryker," Rune whispered.

"Exactly," Tate said grimly.

Verida continued. "I tried to tell you earlier that in order to survive this world, you need the council's help. And if you want their help, I need you to put on a show. Convince Dimitri you have darkness lurking inside. Especially you, Rune."

Grey looked daggers over the roof of the stable to the rising wall of the council house. "They need to know I won't stand here and let people die."

"No." Verida shook her head. "Bad. Very bad."

Grey turned to stare at her incredulously. "You really want me doing what the council asks?"

"We want you acting on your own," Tate clarified. "But you'll need to acquiesce to a few requests to prove you're worth keeping alive. It's a delicate balance, one of deception and careful word play. You both could do a lot of good, but not if you're dead or embroiled in a deadly cat-and-mouse game with Dimitri. For now, we need to repair the damage that's been done and get you both back in Dimitri's good graces."

"And how are we doing that?" At Tate's calm, impassive gaze, Verida rolled her eyes. "You already have a plan. Why didn't you tell me?"

"Because I've learned that you don't listen very well when you're angry," Tate said.

Beltran snorted with laughter, and Verida shot him a death glare. He shrugged. "It's true."

"You were so angry you didn't even ask me about that." Tate jerked his head in the direction of the bag he'd laid against the stable. "I know you can smell it. You don't think I brought home a random head, do you?"

"Cashel," Verida said. Her shoulders relaxed. "That might do it."

"Grey, are you ready to present this to Dimitri?"

"No." Rune squared her shoulders. "Let me do it."

Tate's eyebrows furrowed. "Why?"

"Because Grey isn't in a state to do that right now. Look at him—he's grieving. We need to show Dimitri we're strong, that we're the Venators for the job. Right now, I'm the one to do that."

Tate peered, looking at Rune, Grey, Beltran, and back again. It was obvious that Rune's speech had left him completely unconvinced of her motivation.

Verida sighed. "No, she's right. I already hinted that Rune has what he's looking for. Dimitri hasn't felt grief or remorse in so many years, I doubt he remembers what it feels like. The only view he has on such emotions is that they're signs of weakness. Grey is noticeably upset to the human eye, so imagine what I'm seeing."

"I don't know, Rune," Tate said. "You were a wreck in the dining room. Dimitri already thinks you're weak."

"All the more reason for me to go. I need to prove I'm not who he thinks I am."

"I could stand to have a little faith restored in me as well," Verida said. "If Rune can prove that what I said was right, Dimitri will be less suspicious of my reports."

Tate was still hesitant—Rune could tell by the set of his jaw—but he held out the bag, soaked black with Cashel's blood.

"No," Rune said. "Have Grey carry it. I don't want Dimitri to smell it until after we've talked."

Verida's eyes glanced at Beltran. "Good idea," she said dryly. "I wonder how you thought of it, Rune."

Beltran smirked. "She's a smart girl."

CAT AND MOUSE

They snuck back in the way they'd come, through the tunnels and the weapons room. As they passed the kitchen, Rune worried about the bloody bag Grey hauled. But the staff had been well coached on proper etiquette, as Verida put it, and no one stopped their work to stare at the Venators.

They headed into a new wing of the castle.

"Weren't there any doors coming off the servant tunnels we could've used to get here?" Grey asked.

"No. Dimitri had the one closest to his quarters walled up. And the rest of the doors only access the main hallways, not the residencies."

"What's the point in that?" Rune asked under her breath.

"They were built to allow the servants to move around during events without disrupting the guests." Verida slowed near a square oak pillar, putting a hand on Grey's arm. "This is as far as we go. Any closer, and we risk Dimitri picking up the scent."

Rune's breath caught in her throat as she stared down the long hallway. Dark wood panels ran from floor to ceiling. The wall sconces burned low, casting the hall in an eerie light. The shadows looked like fingers, shaking a warning, and she was half-tempted to listen.

"You're sure Dimitri's in the study?"

"That's where he always goes when he's angry, so yes."

"Just perfect." Rune tried to wipe her sweaty palms on her black pants, but they were covered in a thick layer of dirt and grit and blood.

"Hey," Grey said gently. "You've got this, Jenkins."

The name brought back years of competitions and reminded her what she was capable of. She grinned and nodded.

Game face.

"Leave your weapons here," Verida said. "All of them."

As she placed one foot in front of the other, it felt like the hall stretched out even farther in response, creating a never-ending journey. It was her own fear causing the illusion, but knowing that didn't seem to lessen the effect.

This is for Ryker. You can do anything for Ryker.

Grey and Verida were under the impression that she was going in to beg for forgiveness and then subsequently offer up Cashel's head as restitution for their wrongs. But she had another plan in mind. Beltran had given her a few bits of advice on how to get what she wanted, and at this point, it was all or nothing. She chose to roll the dice.

Stopping at the twelfth door on the left, Rune turned to face it, slowly exhaling a mouthful of jitters. Beltran's advice whispered in her mind. *Dimitri likes strength in his allies and his opponents. Don't knock when you reach the study—just go in.* This seemed like a good way to piss him off before they got started. But knowing nothing about this world or Dimitri, Rune heeded the advice and grabbed the iron knob, pushing the door open without knocking.

Upon meeting Dimitri earlier, he'd fulfilled her expectations of a vampire—cool, aloof, predatory. As such, she'd formed her own idea as to what his study would be like—dark, moody . . . maybe a velvet-lined coffin to relax in?

But the room was warm in temperature and color. Walls of books stretched around the room from floor to ceiling, broken up by tall windows covered with gold-embroidered red tapestries. Strips of gold wallpaper shone between the bookcases. Torches, each glowing brightly, hung from the walls. Several armchairs and coordinating small tables were placed around the room.

Dimitri sat in a deep-blue chair near the window, its wingback stretching far above his head. He held a book on his lap, and while his face remained passive, his eyes glittered with irritation. "If it isn't one of our disobedient Venators. I'm fairly surprised to see you alive."

Make him angry. He's a patient and thorough chess player, except when he's angry. Then he fails to think through possible future moves. That's what you want.

Rune took slow, easy breaths to control her heart rate and raised her chin. "Grey and I are not pawns in a game."

Dimitri carefully shut the book and laid it on the table next to him. "Is that so?"

"Yes."

He was out of the chair and standing toe to toe with her in a second—vampire speed was dizzying. He was taller by a head and used the height to threaten, leaning over her and baring the tips of his fangs. "And you thought you could come into my study unannounced, after disobeying the ruling of the council, and dictate to *me* the terms of your position?"

"No. I'm not stupid."

"Then why are you here?" He held up a finger. "Before you answer, I feel it proper to inform you that you're walking a very dangerous line." He smiled thinly, and his pale-blue eyes searched, reading every body signal she was putting out.

Vampires made her feel naked and exposed. The only thing that covered you from vampire senses was supreme self-control, the likes of which she hadn't mastered yet—as evidenced by the bead of sweat rolling between her shoulder blades.

"I'm here to make a bargain."

There was a beat when Rune thought Beltran had been wrong. Maybe Dimitri couldn't be pushed in this direction. Any second, there would be two fangs embedded in her throat. The danger made her inner Venator roar, and she became acutely aware of the lack of weapons on her belt. Her fingers itched to grab a vase from the table and smash it into his face.

Dimitri took a step back, looking like a lion who'd cornered a mouse, his smile so subtle it was barely discernible. "A bargain. What a rather amusing turn of events. What could you possibly have that would be of interest to me?"

Besides the fact that she was a Venator they'd spent years trying to kidnap and force to do their bidding? *Amusing* was one word for it.

But instead of laughing in his face, she lowered her head in contrition, repeating the line Beltran had suggested. "I would never presume to bargain in a world I know so little about and with a man I don't understand. I came to ask, what do *you* want?"

Dimitri turned and strolled to the window, his slim frame moving eloquently through the space. "Silen is quite agitated this evening. You went after the wolf pack without his permission. Does this concern you?"

"I would be foolish to say that it didn't."

Spinning crisply on one heel, he looked her up and down as if she were a specimen for purchase, judging her value against the price. "You've proven you can stay alive—that's something."

"Grey saved us. He shot the dragon in the eye."

Dimitri lifted his chin. "Unexpected . . . and impressive."

"Yes, but . . ." It was time to make her move, and though she knew it wouldn't be a surprise, dropping Cashel's name should still act as a subconscious suggestion—a nudge in the direction she wanted Dimitri to go. "Cashel saw us and recognized us as Venators. We barely escaped."

Dimitri skimmed a finger over a table on the way to his blue wingback chair. Settling in carefully, he leaned forward. "You want to bargain—very well. I want Cashel's head on a platter."

She offered a gasp of feigned surprise. "What?"

Dimitri leaned back, smug. "You asked what I wanted."

"If we bring you Cashel, then you'll give us . . ." She trailed off, allowing him to fill in the blanks.

"Your freedom. I'll allow you to pick your missions—in addition to those the council needs you for, of course."

"Of course." Rune nodded as if that were obvious. "But, Cashel . . . I'll have to convince Grey. That won't be easy." She met his gaze head on. "I'll need one more thing."

Dimitri repeated the request in a disgusted, clipped cadence. "One more thing?" The muscles around his eyes twitched, betraying his irritation. "The council will already be furious at the deal we've struck."

"I need a favor. A personal one. One that doesn't need to be mentioned to the council or to Grey."

Dimitri relaxed back in his chair, tenting his fingers. "You're entering the world of politics, little girl. I don't think you're ready for that."

Rune didn't blink.

"Name your favor."

"I don't know what it is yet, but when the time is right, I'll come calling, and you'll help me."

Dimitri's eyes darkened and flashed red. His lips pulled back as his face changed—the veins in his forehead popped to the surface, throbbing, and the skin stretched tighter against his razor-edged cheekbones. She'd pushed too far.

His fingers dug into the arms of the chair, snagging the delicate fabric. "You want an unnamed favor from *me*?"

There was nothing to say. This was the price, what she'd risked her neck for and why she'd deceived both Grey and Verida. She stared him down, still controlling her breaths.

"You'll never survive the attempt." Dimitri's eyes faded back to blue. "And after your little stunt tonight, followed by this brazen attempt to manipulate me, I'll be glad for it." He drummed his fingers across a knee. "Fine, we're in agreement."

She gave a bow and walked from the room. Crossing the threshold, she grinned and broke into a jog. Grey and Verida both waited, looking to her with silent questions.

"Well?" he asked.

Rune snatched the sack from him. "Grey, we have our freedom."

"What!" Verida bristled. "What did you do?"

"I'll tell you—right after I deliver this." She walked quickly back down the hall—it didn't seem nearly as long this time—and pushed open the door, tossing the bag to Dimitri. "It's not on a platter, but I think it's close enough to agree our bargain is fulfilled." She could not stuff away the look of triumph.

Dimitri took the bag in one hand, using the other to slowly push to standing. He stared at her, eyebrows furrowed, then opened the bag and gave a cursory glance inside—he already knew what it was. Reaching over, he dropped the bag on a small, round table. Cashel's head landed with a *thunk*. Dimitri pulled a handkerchief from his pocket and methodically wiped the blood from his fingers one at a time. "Well played, Venator."

"Our deal stands?"

"It seems I've underestimated you. You have your freedom and a favor."

"Thank you."

"Don't thank me just yet. I'll warn you now—make your request with caution. I'm not one to be trifled with." He squared to face her. "You were a worthy opponent today. I must respect that. You've proven there is more to you than I thought, but you used your previous show of weakness to blind me to your intentions. I won't be taken in so easily again."

"Understood."

His nostrils flared. "And I won't forget."

"Understood."

"Good." He leaned forward at the waist, eyes turning red. "Get. Out."

UNPREDICTABLE

Beltran shrank himself to the size of a pixie and sat on one of the rafters in Grey's room, his tiny legs hanging over the edge, eavesdropping as Rune retold what had transpired in Dimitri's study.

She'd taken the tips he'd offered and used them to accomplish what was needed, masterfully excluding in the retelling the real reason she'd been determined to approach Dimitri. He had to assume she'd succeeded at getting the favor—she was far too animated to have done anything but. She even showed a pinch of pride.

He leaned forward, softly chuckling at the way she bounced on her toes when excited.

The conversation turned into a buzz as he noticed how her eyes sparkled, the slight tilt of her head when she listened, the fluidity with which she moved through the room—not quite vampiresque, but beautiful. When she'd stuck that knife under his chin, it had been the last thing he'd expected. He'd been seized with a desire to lean over and kiss her.

Snapping out of the daze, Beltran jerked straight, breathing loudly enough he worried Verida would hear. What was this madness? Of course, he knew exactly what this was—he scrubbed his hands over his face—but this kind of thing didn't happen to him. Yes, there had been dalliances and a handful of relationships. He'd almost even fallen for a few. Loneliness was very . . . well, lonely.

But this girl . . . this girl was something new. They'd only just met, and these feelings twisting through him in a confused mass were terrifying. It was overwhelming and giving him a dangerous urge. For the first time in a very long time, Beltran wanted to be *seen*.

Pulled against his own accord, he looked back down at Rune. He was falling for her, as quickly as he'd plummeted off that cliff tonight.

No. Shaking his head and mentally berating the stupidity, he pushed up, pacing back and forth across the rafter. This was bad. Very, very bad. A Venator and a shifter. And not just any shifter—*him*. Hell, he didn't even know where his own loyalties lay half the time.

He'd destroy them both.

It didn't matter how strong the draw was. Over the years he'd denied himself more things than anyone would ever know, holding on to a path and a purpose—denying himself Rune was just one more thing on the journey. It could be done.

Another moment or two of continuing down that road of thought, and he might have been able to convince himself. But then, out of the corner of his eye, he saw her reach out and touch Grey's arm.

A jealous ache rose up inside, and he wanted her like he'd never wanted anyone before. "Damn it," he whispered. "Damn it all to hell."

Rune and Verida had said good night over an hour ago, but Grey hadn't moved from his balcony. He stared out at the valley. The smoke created a film over the sun, giving the edges a hazy look. He was bothered by many things, but one thought was currently at the forefront. Despite Dimitri leaving them out there to die, Rune had somehow managed to convince him to offer not only forgiveness but also a measure of freedom.

Although he was fairly certain Rune wasn't telling them the whole story—a few things had seemed too easy—it was obvious that Rune had done what Verida had instructed. She'd put on a show for Dimitri and revealed the dark, ruthless Venator he wanted to see.

Grey had faked a lot of things for a lot of years, but not cruelty, hate, and anger. They were traits he despised so thoroughly he could barely keep his lips from curling at the thought of taking them on as if they were his own. But the consequences of not being who the council wanted had been made quite clear tonight.

He thought he knew where he stood, but if he wanted to stay alive and protect the innocent, he would have to figure out how to portray that which he hated.

Making a decision, he turned and exited his room. Once on the third floor, he headed to the last door on the left. He hesitated outside.

This could be a terrible lapse in judgment. But then, what hadn't been lately?

He knocked.

The sound of soft footsteps came from inside, and the door swung open. Tashara smiled and leaned seductively against the frame, wearing a white silk robe that clung to her body. "Grey, what a surprise. I'm pleased to see you made it back alive."

He nodded, wringing his hands in front of him. Realizing how weak it looked, he forced his arms to his side. "Yes. I wanted to thank you for your gift. It saved our lives."

"You're very welcome." Her eyes scanned him. "You're filthy."

He looked down, startled. He was a mess. Covered in dirt and blood and still wearing clothes with singed holes in several places. "Oh, yes. Uh, almost dying gets a little messy, I guess." He nearly rolled his own eyes at how ridiculous he sounded.

But Tashara giggled, and a smile lit up her face. "Did you only come here to thank me?"

"No. I . . . wanted to ask you something. When we were talking, you said I wear my heart on my sleeve."

"And you do." She tilted her head, examining him. "It's breaking right now, although I'm not sure why."

Valerian. "You told me I needed to learn how to act, to put on a show, but . . ." He looked to the floor, unsure how to ask. "Maybe I shouldn't have come. I'm sorry. I don't even know—"

Tashara reached out and gently ran a finger under his jawline. No magic flexed, just as she'd promised him. "You don't know how, do you?"

He shook his head. "I need your help. Teach me. Please."

Tashara smiled and backed away, holding her arm out. "Come in."

Grey had made this choice, acting on his gut instinct, basing it on something he'd seen during their encounter in the hall. But as he walked willingly into the room, he couldn't help but wonder if he'd just walked into the viper's den.

Keep reading for chapter 1 in

VENATORS:

PROMISES FORGED

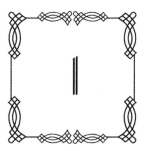

Ryker roused slowly, driven to wakefulness by an incessant pounding. Reluctantly, he peeled open his eyes. That motion alone was immensely uncomfortable—heavy lids felt like sandpaper, forcefully scraping away the sleep and booze.

He'd drunk a lot last night, but he'd never woken with a hangover quite like this.

The room slowly came into focus. The light was dim, and it took a while to make out his surroundings. He was in an empty room, a stone box. The walls and floor were made of individual blocks about twelve inches wide and six inches tall. They'd been mortared together with something that looked like tar, smooth and shiny. A foul smell—body odor, sweat, and barnyard, overwhelming in its potency—rammed up his nostrils. Barely turning to the side in time, he vomited, muscles contracting so hard that his spine contorted into a severe arch.

When it was finally over, Ryker hung limp. Spit and leftover bile drooled freely from his lips, drizzling into a vile puddle on the floor. It was then, because of the odd twist of his shoulders, that he finally realized his arms and legs were tied to the chair.

"What the hell?" Sitting up, Ryker wiped his mouth the best he could on the collar of his shirt and jerked against the bonds. "Chad? Luke?"

A torch was the only light in the room, flickering by the wide iron door. It was damn authentic for a prank.

"This isn't funny, guys!"

No response, only a dull thud as his words were swallowed by the room. He listened for something, anything, straining against the silence. But all he heard was a barely audible dripping. He squinted, making out lines on the stone walls where thin streams of water ran, so slight they made no sound except the occasional *ping* resonating from the furthermost corner where one splashed onto the floor.

He pulled and wiggled, trying to free his wrists, but made no progress. What happened last night? He couldn't remember anything. "All right, guys. I'm impressed," he called to the door. "Did Rune put you up to this?"

He loved his sister, but the nagging about his drinking was getting old. She'd lectured him so many times on all the things that could happen if he passed out and she wasn't there to save the day. He could repeat her speech verbatim. Leave it to Rune to try some stupid scare tactic.

Ryker twisted his neck, trying to get a look at the knot they'd used. Then he froze.

His arms were covered in tattoos, glowing red in the center. But around the edges, several other colors blinked on and off. The lines were bold, sweeping arcs paired with ninety-degree angles that knotted around each other, almost Celtic—but not quite. They were unique.

His previous conclusions suddenly became less plausible as his sluggish mind tried to determine how someone could prank this. These weren't stickers or rub ons. The colored light seemed to be coming from a deeper layer of skin, flickering like the glow of a jellyfish—from the inside out.

With a *click*, the iron door swung open. He whirled, looking at the middle of the doorframe. Movement pulled his gaze lower until he saw a short, squatty creature.

"No," he whispered. A wave of vertigo made the room spin, and bile once again burned up his throat.

The thing grinned. Its tiny black eyes grew even smaller as wrinkles of grayish skin pushed in around the edges. Its lips stretched around the tusks, growing so taut that the lip line faded into skin, leaving no definition where one started and the other began.

Instantly he was a little kid again, backing through bushes in the front yard, searching for protection. All the memories washed over him. The smells—dozens of irises had bloomed along the walkway, and he'd hated that scent ever since. The feelings—confusion, fear, and the pounding of his heart—all as raw as the day they were bred.

"Welcome, Venator."

It wouldn't have mattered what words the monster had uttered. The sight of it unleashed all the anger he'd bottled up for years. It burst from his mouth in a roar. He lunged against the bonds, wanting to wrap his hands around its thick neck.

The creature just grinned as two more of the monstrosities walked into the room, laughing with throaty croaks and grunts.

"Shut up!" Ryker snarled, struggling. "I'll kill you, all of you!"

"This Venator's tough," one mocked. "Too bad you's tied up."

The laughter burned through his ears, and he struggled harder for freedom. The ropes were tight, and the sticky wetness of blood flowed down the back of his hand from the effort.

There was a sharp click in Ryker's head, like a part of his mind had suddenly unlocked, and his thoughts raced. Multiple plans of how to fulfill his threat flowed through his head simultaneously . . . but only one was any good.

He started rocking, walking the chair back toward the wall. The smiles of his captors faded. He saw their uncertainty, and it felt good—like staring at ants through a magnifying glass. They had no idea what was coming.

He grinned. "What's the matter? You look nervous."

Their eyes shifted to each other, gauging. One stepped forward, squaring his shoulders. "You's tied up. You's can do nothing."

But an edge to his voice tickled Ryker's ears—a framing of fear.

One side of his mouth twisted up in a smirk. "Then I guess you can relax," he said, walking the chair the last few inches.

He'd turned himself so his shoulder and hip were against the wall. Tilting his weight to the opposite side, he used the toe of his shoe to balance the chair on two legs, and then threw his weight against the wall. The force was more than he'd anticipated—he hit like a battering ram. He had no time to wonder where the extra strength had come from. Over his own grunt of pain was the sound of the wooden chair cracking.

The three creatures yelped and scrambled for the door, shouting about weapons.

Ryker repeated the motion, leaning and slamming. The chair cracked again, and he repositioned, the square legs squealing as he spun to aim the force on the rounded top behind his neck. This time he felt the back buckle, and he leaned forward, wrenching the chair in two. He jerked his arms first one way and then the other, sliding free. The wooden back clattered to the floor.

With the extra slack in the rope, he was able to manipulate his hands so his fingers could loosen the knots. A moment later he was free and working on his ankles.

Shouts and feet echoed down the hall toward him. He swore and worked faster, stepping free of his bonds just as eight goblins flowed back into the room, swords and axes in hand.

The image was too familiar. A memory flashed of him peeing his pants as a kid, so raw and painful that it jolted loose the fear and replaced it with empowering anger. Ryker picked up the chair by the legs and swung it against the wall. The seat broke free, leaving him with two splintered bats for weapons. Not much against swords, but better than cowering in the corner. Or in a bush. He'd cowered once, and he vowed in that moment it would never happen again.

Ryker took a step toward his attackers.

"You's going to fight with *those?*"

Ryker noticed something he hadn't expected and nearly laughed out loud. "Ridiculous, right?" He waved the chair legs. "But you're *scared.*"

He took a second step forward, testing his theory, and all eight took a step back.

"Get out of my way," he said, trying to sell the bluff. Although lacking a proper amount of fear given the situation, Ryker's mind was functioning just fine. What the hell would he do with two sticks of wood against eight goblins with swords and axes?

"Stop!" A female voice rang from outside the door.

The goblins lurched as if they'd been shocked. Their weapons drooped to their sides as they shuffled back against the wall, heads bowed.

Ryker had only taken one step toward freedom when a woman walked into the room, the edge of her red silk gown skimming the floor. At first he thought she was floating. The moment he laid eyes on her, something washed over him like a bucket of water, leaving the rage simmering and steaming like a pile of dying coals.

"Who are you?" he stammered.

She demurely dipped her head. "My name is Zio. I apologize for your treatment. My servants sometimes forget themselves." She gave one absent hand wave, and the goblins hurried out of the room.

Her eyes were a deep purple and framed by hair so pale it had surpassed blonde and become platinum white. Dark brows offered a measure of severity to her heart-shaped face, and full lips were painted red to match the dress. A long silver chain slipped between a tease of cleavage at the top of her corseted gown and dropped toward her navel. Hanging at the end was a pendant, an almond-shaped eye, with a huge, blinking sapphire surrounded by diamond-crusted eyelashes. Another blue stone dangled from a tiny clasp, shaped like a tear about to fall.

"I'm very pleased to meet you . . ." She trailed off, one eyebrow rising in question.

"Ryker," he responded instantly, then frowned. He hadn't meant to tell her that.

Zio began speaking, but her words were a buzz as the memories of last night finally broke through the veil of too much alcohol. "Where's my sister?" he blurted, interrupting.

"Your sister?" Zio tilted her head, eyes wide like that of a doe.

"Yes, I heard her yell . . . I think." His confidence in his memories waned, but he pushed through. "Yes, before *they* appeared." He jerked his head toward the door.

"Ah." She crossed her hands demurely at her waist. "I'm sorry to tell you, but we had no hand in that. Your sister came to this side quite willingly. Or so I'm told."

"This side? Willingly?" Nothing was making sense. Although he had no idea where "this side" was or what that even meant, Ryker found himself sputtering, "She's here?"

"No, not here." Zio looked at him with pity. "I'm sorry, Ryker. This must be very confusing. You've crossed into an alternate dimension, one that runs parallel to the reality you know. Everything you've ever read about—magic, dragons, goblins, werewolves—they're all real, and they're all here. Your sister came to help a corrupt governing body take control . . . from me."

Time fled, and reality twisted. "What?"

"Don't you see? Your sister left you, Ryker. And we found you."

"She just came to this . . . this alternate dimension, alone? And then what? Sent those little servants of *yours* after me?"

"No. She didn't come alone. And the goblins were there on my order, to find you. The council wanted you destroyed. You weren't supposed to live, Ryker."

He wanted to call her a liar, to deny everything she'd said, but nothing else seemed to fit the current situation. *Down the rabbit hole.* The phrase rolled through his head like Alice had rolled into Wonderland, down a hole of the unexplainable. He stared at Zio, wordless. If it weren't for the splinter working its way into his clenched fist, the undeniable foul smell wafting through his nose, and the painfully fading cloud of beer, he might've convinced himself it was a dream.

He looked into Zio's hypnotic purple gaze. "But . . . who did she come here with?"

"I believe they call him Grey."

For a moment he wondered if he'd heard correctly. But then, of course he had. He'd always known Grey for what he was since *that* night, the one he'd tried to forget but couldn't. A blue man had saved Ryker and told him to look out for Grey—that they would need to lean on each other. When Grey had showed up at school the next week in a trench coat nearly identical to his rescuer, Ryker had known that Grey had seen the blue man too. And for a reason he couldn't understand, it had instantly birthed a firestorm of hatred for Grey.

But then it had gotten worse—the way Grey looked at his sister, the way he openly waved his flag of strangeness. The little freak was practically a walking announcement to the world of what had happened that night. Deep down, Ryker lived in constant fear that one day Grey would approach him about it, his secret would get out, and he would never be able to bottle it up again.

Ryker clenched his fists harder, imagining a new use for the chair legs. "Take me to them."

"Oh, I'm afraid that won't be possible."

ACKNOWLEDGMENTS

Acknowledgments are always filled with people gushing about how overwhelmed they are with how many people there are to thank.

I'm totally overwhelmed with how many people there are to thank.

First and foremost, my family. To my husband, who has never doubted me despite the fact that from the beginning this all sounded a little crazy, and who, no matter how difficult the sacrifices became, has stood by me and cheered me onward. He is a full-time hardworking father on his days on and has become mister mom on his days off to help free up my time. He never ceases to amaze me with his love, support, and sacrifice. And, of course, to my children, who put up with a lot of distracted-mother moments. I love you, little monsters. And don't forget, you two: life with normal parents would be terribly boring.

To all the people at Brown Books, who have been a delight to work with: thank you, thank you, thank you! You have all been kind and professional, and the results of your hard work have blown me away! I look forward to a long relationship.

To Tom Reale, who followed me out of the room at the Idaho Writers Conference to tell me that if I ever got sick of what I was doing, he'd love to look at my current project, and who from that day on has been my supporter and champion at Brown Books and beyond. Thank you for believing in me, my book, and my potential and for all the lectures on believing in myself.

And I can't forget to thank the Meridian Idaho Library District for running a small local competition that *Venators* won back when it was a (slightly smaller) self-published novel. That competition gifted me the tickets to the writing conference that put me in the room with Tom Reale in the first place. Without you guys, I can honestly say none of this would've happened. At least not at this point in time.

The biggest thank-you to Ellie Ann Lang, who has been my editor for five books now. Through her teaching and patience, she has made me into an infinitely better writer. To Erin Horn, who has been my technical editor for three books and who sends me the most adorable notes at the end. "OK, Devri, great job on last year's lesson. Now, on the next book, we're going to work on learning how to properly use an em dash." Erin, I'm now a better grammar wielder than I ever wanted to be. And to my newest addition to the team, Erynn Newman: thanks for the intensive editing pass that helped bump up the content and, overall, bring this novel up to a new level. You were a joy to work with, and I'm looking forward to book two. I couldn't do any of this without any of my editors. Thank you, all of you, for always making me look better than I am and taking me to higher levels.

To Victoria Faye, who has been through hell and back on this cover. From the first design concept, which we finished and then changed, to the four other mock-ups that I nixed entirely, to the new version, to the new-again version. Thank you for working with me and bringing this book to life in such a perfect visual form that grabs people across the room and says *READ ME!* Thank you for giving me something I'm pleased to have my book judged by.

To Allen Johnson, screenwriter extraordinaire and old and dear friend. He's been a sounding board and cheered me on. Thank you for tutoring me on the fine art of what a true sword should look like and what is an unholy abomination. For helping me to create some new weapons for Venators that were actually feasible to use. For chatting with me about how to create a sling for those darn crossbows that would function. For informing me that I cannot, in fact, have a character pull a sword from a back sheath. (What do you know? It *was* impossible. I tried.) For constant YouTube videos on fighting techniques, and for holding my hand through synopsis writing 101. And, of course, for believing in this story and seeing my vision.

My parents taught me to go after what I wanted and laid the groundwork for me to set foot in this direction in the first place. *Thank you* just doesn't seem adequate for a lifetime of love, support, and sacrifice. But Dad, thank you for reading that very first draft of *Wings of Arian* and telling me with a straight face that it was good. I'm impressed. I'm also equally impressed that you kept the truth to yourself and didn't tell me how bad it was until after I'd released four books. I'll never know just how much that straight face played into my continuing on this path.

And what kind of person would I be if I didn't thank the main contributing source? I'll call it God. But you can call it the universe or listening to your gut or whatever makes you go, *Ahhh, yes. I know that feeling.* I was pulled to this path, a path I never even considered, and am so grateful for the continuing whispers that it was going to be OK. For the calm assurances over the last seven years that even though I couldn't see how this was going to work out, it would. For the prompting to speak out in a writing conference and make myself seen despite being silent for the entire two days. And for the special experience that resulted in me signing the contract that lead to *Venators* being here now. I am humbled and blessed, and the credit is not mine.

To every person on this path who has been in the right place at the right time. To the gifts of encouragement, the kind words, the supporters, the readers, the artists. Thank you. For all the things that have been said in my darkest of times that lifted me up, thank you. For everyone who has in the smallest and largest of ways contributed to my personal miracles. Thank you.

DEVRI WALLS

Devri Walls is a US and international best-selling author. Having released five novels to date, she specializes in all things fantasy and paranormal. She's best known for her uncanny world-building skills, her intricate storylines, and the ability to present it all in an easy-to-digest voice. Devri loves to engage with her loyal following through online sessions organized for her readers and social media. Devri lives in Meridian, Idaho, with her husband and two kids. When not writing, she can be found teaching voice lessons, reading, cooking, or binge watching whatever show catches her fancy.

Teen/pb
Walls

6/18